I0549958

Shadow Angels

Richard R Hall

Shadow Angels Trilogy
Book One

Richard R Hall

Shadow Angels
By
Richard R Hall

© Copyright by Richard Hall, July 2014
TXu-1-870-137.v4
Cover Art by Elina Dudina 2016

All rights reserved. No part of this book may be reproduced or transmitted in any form or by any means whatsoever, including photocopying, recording or by any information storage and retrieval system, without written permission from the publisher and/or author.

True Look Publications

658 Central Ave.
Albany, NY
12206

ISBN-13: 978-0998780009
ISBN-10: 0998780006

For Debbie, Thank you for your encouragement and support.

Books by Richard Hall

Shadow Angels Trilogy:
Shadow Angels
Rise of the Queens
Brendel

Prologue

A lone man sat at the top of a tall, pyramid-shaped building at the base of a metal tower. The tower reached even higher into the night sky to give a home to a blinking red light, which took its place among a million other lights in the city. It was the Year of our Lord 2796, the city, New Chicago. He saw distant flames shooting into the night sky from the Enviro Stations burning off centuries of human waste. He watched as the hovering commercial drones floated by with advertisements flickering across their bright screens, the blare of their speakers calling people to a new life off-world, and he saw the airborne cars traveling their predetermined paths. He watched and listened to the city with absolute clarity, taking in the sights and sounds as a whole, or focusing his senses to a small, finite point. He watched and heard people in a window a mile away as if he were standing next to them.

A quarter-century had passed since his maker buried him to heal horrific wounds and emotional pain. The night was wet, soaked in a slow and steady rain. He saw the rain rinse years of dirt off his emaciated body. He watched as the dirt fell to the roof and washed away in various branching streams of water. His clothes, rotted and shredded, fell from his body to land in dark puddles. He had lost loved ones, vampires he had cared for over centuries. A terrible price he paid. He looked down at the skin on his withered arms and hands, which was the texture of leather and the color of porcelain. His wet, blond hair was long and stringy, and rain ran down his face and off the tip of his nose. The night sky would light up and then grow dark again as the quiet lightning snaked its way through the thick, heavy clouds above. The vampire had been trying to make it back to Washington but was too weak. He would have to find nourishment, which meant blood.

The battle had lasted for three days. The Archangel Michael had commanded him to fight evil, to fight the dark angels known as the Esmanaa. He turned his head to listen to what no human could possibly hear, to sense with psychic abilities what no human could imagine. These were the abilities of all Michael's warrior angels here on Earth, like all vampires with the blood of angels.

It is my beloved changeling, Katherine. The vampire had turned her centuries ago, and she was now a powerful vampire herself. He sensed her flying to him, to help him live again and give him blood. He sent his thoughts to Katherine. *I can feel you now. Can you feel me? Can you sense where I am?* He knew the sun would rise soon. He still had time, but he urged her to hurry.

Soon, he heard a thud behind him. He pulled himself up, turned, and leaned against the tower. His eyes were gazing on his beautiful Katherine again, her cheeks stained with blood tears.

"You are alive, after all," Katherine whispered, looking to the earth. "Thank you, Mother."

He watched her approach him in disbelief and felt her stroke his dried cheek. He heard her say, "You have returned to me. I will take you home, for you need blood, my love." He felt her powerful arms take hold of him as they rose into the night sky to begin their trip home.

As he lay in Katherine's arms, his thoughts drifted to his maker, Anne Bryce, the vampire that changed him eight hundred years earlier. Anne taught him how to survive as a vampire, to use his abilities according to the laws of the Archangel Michael. She was the head of their family and was loved by all. He thought of her beauty, their life together, and the love he would always feel for her.

Chapter One

S hawn was born in a time of plenty and lived a typical small-town life of the day. A boy that angels watched. He was born in the summer of the year 1951, in a small one-story hospital on Pearl Street. His town Dalton meandered along the banks of the Susquehanna River, seventy miles downstream from where the river left the clear mountain lake and started its long journey to the Chesapeake Bay, where it met the Unadilla River. He lived in a big, white Victorian house on Remsen Street, and from there, he could see the home of the girl he loved, the beautiful Marilyn Pomeroy.

The summer's day was hot and humid, and Shawn was mowing the backyard. The air stood still with a few long, thin, white clouds in the hazy blue sky. He heard the grind of the insects, the howls of children playing, and another far-off lawnmower. The smell of cut grass wafted through the air. He stopped his mower and reached for his sweaty Coke bottle. Looking toward Marilyn's house, he saw her walking across the field dressed in cut-off blue jeans and a yellow halter. Shawn found himself staring. He loved the way she walked and held herself—and what a pair of legs! *Where is she going?* Then she waved at him, and he realized she was coming toward him. He froze for a moment, trying to think of what to say.

"Hi," she shouted.

"Hello, I'm Shawn," he choked out.

"I know who you are. We do go to the same school."

He felt awkward standing there, his shirt off, sweaty, with Marilyn's eyes traveling up and down his body. Then she raised her eyes and gave him a mischievous grin. "I have a problem. My parents will give me five dollars if I have the lawn mowed by the time they come home."

"Sounds good," he gulped.

3

"But my lawnmower is broken, and I was hoping I could borrow yours. Maybe you could help me push it across the field. The grass is tall this time of year."

She was even more beautiful standing right in front of him than she was dancing in her backyard. Her hair was black and cut short. He loved the hint of freckles on her tan cheeks and her perky nose. Her lips were perfectly formed and moist, and he wondered what it would be like to kiss them.

"Sure, let me finish my lawn. Do you have gas for the lawnmower?" He stammered.

"My father has some in the shed."

He helped Marilyn mow her lawn that day, and from then on, he would always find ways to be with her. They spent their last year of high school together as boyfriend and girlfriend. They would talk for hours under the big oak tree in Shawn's backyard. Using the darkness of night, they first made love under that tree. At the end of Marilyn's last year, she became pregnant.

Marilyn's parents sent her to stay with her aunt in Syracuse and to abort the baby. The next year, she attended Syracuse University to become a schoolteacher. The following spring, just before he graduated, Shawn received his draft notice from the Army. Six months later, he found himself in the jungles of Vietnam. He saw Marilyn only one time before he shipped out. It was at a party that his friends threw the night before he left for the Army. Marilyn told him they should try to see other people, that they had been high school sweethearts, and maybe there was more to love.

They made love one more time, and in the end, she gave him a hug, a kiss, and said, "I love you, Shawnee, I always will." Marilyn left, and he never saw her again until that future, fateful night.

What Shawn remembered most about Vietnam was the heat and humidity, the nagging fear always in the back of his mind, and the death. He was eight months into his tour of duty in Vietnam. The day started hot and humid, like always. Sitting on his helmet, he felt the vibrations of the helicopter, making its way up his spine and into his teeth. He would concentrate on the whoop of the helicopter blades to keep his mind off the fear he always felt.

Shawn wrapped his drab, green towel tighter around his neck, trying to stop the flow of sweat from his head down to his chest and back. Two hundred fifty soldiers of Company C, 3rd Brigade, 1st Infantry Division headed to a landing area deep in the jungle. Their mission was to search a village for hidden weapons. He watched as his helicopter made a sharp turn, followed by twenty more helicopters, and descended toward a flare that marked their landing area. It was a small clearing thanks to the foliage killer, Agent Orange.

Shawn was the radioman and rode in the captain's helicopter. He saw the fear on Lieutenant Short's face. The man had recently arrived, and this was his first mission. The other men soon were calling him Lieutenant Shorty because he was a little guy. He watched him fiddle with his helmet and weapon and wipe his head constantly with his towel. This was doing nothing to help Shawn's own fear. One lesson he learned these last few months was how contagious fear could be.

"Settle down, Lieutenant! You'll be all right! Just follow me and do as I say," Captain Barney yelled over the pounding sound of the helicopter. "You don't want to scare the men any more than they are!"

Shawn knew the captain had little use for military pomp and protocol—he wanted soldiers that did exactly as he said. Captain Barney was a big, rough-looking man, with red hair, always in need of a shave and always chewing on a cigar. Shawn respected him because he felt he was a natural leader, and he gave him the best chance to make it home.

Shawn stuck his head outside to let the wind cool him and to scope out the landing area. Over the last month, he'd felt that maybe he would make it home. He had been on many patrols and nine firefights since coming to Vietnam and had killed — a detail that bothered him every day. He checked his weapon, and then checked the radio, adjusting the dials until he knew the needles were in the right spots. He pushed the button on the side of the headphone. "Victor Victor, this is Delta Charlie, do you read?" He waited and then repeated, "Victor Victor, this is Delta Charlie, over." Then he heard the harsh crackle of a voice on the other end. "Delta Charlie, this is Victor

Victor. Be advised that NVA have been seen in your area. I repeat, NVA are in your area."

Captain Barney grabbed the headphone from Shawn while spitting out some fine swear words and found out as much information as possible on the location of the enemy soldiers. The news only heightened the fear in the helicopter. They landed and disembarked quickly and formed two single-file lines, one on each side of the trail going to the village. The company reached the village around noon, crossed a large rice paddy, and entered a farming field in front of the village. The North Vietnamese sprung their trap, and the intensity of small arms fire was heavy.

Captain Barney yelled orders while pointing to cover, a hundred feet to the left. "Get your asses up! We can't stay here! If you want to live, follow me!"

Shawn thought his heart was going to beat out of his chest. The fear was so bad he could taste it in his mouth, and he saw men falling all around him. Never had he heard so many bullets screaming through the air along with the thump and explosions of the mortars hitting the ground. He caught his breath, ran toward the cover, and jumped into a crater left by a mortar round. The other half of the company, led by Lieutenant Short, fell back across the rice paddy and tried to move right to flank the enemy. The intensity of the enemy fire again halted the Americans.

"We stepped into some shit today, boys!" screamed Captain Barney. "Make every shot count! Watch your ammunition—there are more of them than us!"

Shawn was fighting for his life. An hour later, the firing stopped from across the rice paddy. This was not a good sign for Lieutenant Short and the other half of the company. He wiped the sweat from his eyes, looked around, and could see a few soldiers left from their half of the company. His eyes burned from the smoke of the gunfire, and he could taste the gunpowder. A short time later, Captain Barney took the headphones from Shawn and screamed into the radio, "Victor Victor splash Charlie Company! I repeat, splash Charlie Company! Bring all ordnance to bear!"

Then the crackle of the radio, "Delta Charlie, this is Victor Victor. Roger that. Good luck!"

Company C was no more. Captain Barney was letting the generals in the rear know this, and they could now blow the place to pieces. Shawn looked around and saw ten of them still firing at the enemy. Their backs were against the rice paddy, and he could see dead soldiers everywhere.

Captain Barney screamed, "Listen to me, you sons of bitches! Get across the rice paddy into the jungle and run! Don't look back! Go, or you will die here. That's our only chance!" Captain Barney destroyed the radio with the butt of his rifle. Two minutes later, he would lie dead with a bullet in his head.

Shawn ran crouching toward the rice paddy. He could hear the sounds of bullets all around him, kicking up dirt in front of him that peppered his face. Fear consumed him; his hearing would become muffled except for the pounding of his heart, and his world turned to slow motion. Then everything would speed up, and again he heard the clack-clack-clack of gunfire and the explosions.

Shawn made it to the rice paddy, turned left, and followed the edge toward a dirt crossing that ran toward the jungle. He had not gone far when he felt a force hit his thigh like a blow from a sledgehammer. The strike spun and flung him into the rice paddy. He tried to get up, but his left leg was not working, and then he realized he wasn't going home after all. The firing let up, and then there was none. Shawn wondered if he was the only one left.

He knew he wasn't going to run anywhere. He crawled further out into the rice paddy and tried to squirm himself in the muck and mud, between the tall blades of grass. He felt a pang of fear as he remembered he probably left a trail through the grass. He then waited for the bullets to hit him and watched his hands shake.

Shawn heard the chatter of North Vietnamese soldiers and the sporadic shooting mixed with screams. They were killing the wounded American soldiers. Deeper, he tried to squirm into the muck and water. He prayed to God not to let the enemy find him, and his thoughts went home and Marilyn. He thought how soft her skin was, her face, the times they made love, what it felt like, the taste of her lips, and knew he would never see her again. At least he had known love. He felt the heat on his back from the hot, Vietnamese sun, and he started to sob but quickly made himself stop.

Then came the noise of the jets, the deafening sounds of the explosions, the ground shaking underneath him. Intense heat, debris, and ash rained down on him. Everything became quiet, except for the ringing in his ears. Night came as he lay in the rice paddy with his pain and thoughts. He thought about how good his life had been until he came to this hell; the people back home and Marilyn; how humans became killers by order of their leaders, and how senseless it all really was. What caused people to behave this way, he wondered, to turn their lives into nightmares? Shawn thought of the people he had killed and promised himself he would never kill again.

He felt slugs crawling on his left leg, trying to feed on his blood, raised his head, and saw nothing, only sporadic fires burning in the darkness from the battle and smoke drifting across the ground. He could smell the acidic, sulfuric smell of explosives and the sweet smell of napalm. He saw large rodents chewing on a corpse and prayed they didn't come toward him and heard enemy soldiers screaming in pain from their burns. This is what hell is like. Lifting his head, he looked at the fires burning from the napalm and felt the evil all around him.

"There, I see it. No, that's just a shadow," Shawn whispered to himself. "My God, what is that?"

He saw a tall, dark figure of a man walking amongst the dead, a flash of yellow eyes, and saw the lone man pick up a corpse and bring his mouth down on the neck. The dark man then tossed the corpse aside, turned with a bloody face, looked at Shawn, and drifted back into the jungle. He shook his head in fear, felt lightheaded, dizzy, and the fear consumed him at times. He felt sick and relieved himself of bile in his stomach. His face fell back into it.

Suddenly, for the first time in his life, he felt that desire, that primordial instinct to survive. He felt anger at what had happened to him, and he knew he wasn't going home to his carefree life. He started to crawl toward the edge of the rice paddy and heard a woman's voice urging him on in his head, telling him he must live; it is not his time to die. *What a loving, caring voice,* he thought. The pain was terrible, but he made it out of the mud and water.

At the edge, he passed out and woke to the hot, morning sun. The buzzing of insects was loud, and they coated his wounded leg. He tried to lick his dried, chapped lips — his thirst was overwhelming. He heard two recon jets fly over to survey the situation and, soon after, saw helicopters land in the field. Shawn was found that morning, only one of six survivors of Company C. He was medically evacuated to a hospital in Japan, and later, to a VA hospital in Albany, New York. He would spend a year recovering from his shattered leg and spend the rest of his mortal life walking with a limp, carrying the nightmares of those horrible days.

Later, Shawn went on to attend the University of Virginia's School of Engineering and tried hard to forget about Vietnam. While attending school, he met Kristen. She found him drunk in a bar, picked him up and helped him outside for fresh air, walked with him, stayed with him, and helped him accept the things he had witnessed and done as a soldier. They married and had one daughter, lived in Richmond, and he found work at a large engineering firm.

Shawn loved Kristen; she was the first girl he met that could take the place of Marilyn. A car accident would kill Kristen and his daughter fifteen years later. He went back to Dalton, a broken man, and took a job as the town engineer. He lived with his parents again in the large, white, Victorian house and drank heavily.

Chapter Two

T he year was 1991, and Shawn had moved back to Dalton. He took a job for the town as their public works engineer. He had suffered a terrible loss; his feelings were numb, dead to him except sorrow and anger. Two years had passed since he lost Kristen and Chrissie. He had left work a couple hours earlier and was sitting at the local bar on Main Street, feeling the alcohol take hold. The owner, Gary Moreno, was behind the bar.

"Gary, one more before I go, my man," he demanded.

"Are you sure? Don't you think you should go home?" Gary replied.

"I'll be the judge of that. One more," he said. "I don't have far to go in this town. You should know that, my old buddy. One more, right here in front of me," he mumbled as he slapped the bar with his hand. He knew this was the last drink Gary was going to give him.

Then he remembered seeing Marilyn when he was walking into the bar. She was standing at the corner, staring at him, and when he stepped back out of the alcove, she was not there. *It couldn't be,* he thought, *she would look older now.* He knew Marilyn had gone missing some years back and remembered how heartsick he had been when he heard the news. The authorities had contacted him and asked if he knew anything about Marilyn, or if he knew of some secret place where she would go to hide. He told them no and started to contact their old friends to see if they knew anything, but nobody did.

This was when he became aware of her bad marriage. She had married a college jock that turned out to be a straw dog. The man was a drunk, had been abusive to her, and he learned that she had lost another baby. Before her disappearance, she had spent most of her time with a mysterious and beautiful woman. The police had never been able to find this woman. Kristen acted as though she were unaffected by Shawn's interest in the matter, but he could tell she was a little jealous of Marilyn. The years went by, and nobody heard from her. This also left a hole in his heart.

"Shawn, you should go home now and get some sleep," Gary urged.

"What are you, my mother? You should worry about yourself," Shawn mumbled as his head slumped down toward the bar.

A couple of seats down, he heard Tami Wilson: "I never thought I would see Shawn Nelson as a drunk."

"Be quiet," Shawn slurred, "or I'll tell everybody a secret I know about you."

"You need to go home before you get into trouble," Gary warned.

Shawn knew his anger was returning. It was probably a good idea to leave before he did start trouble. Staggering a little, he went outside and looked down at the corner where he thought he saw Marilyn earlier. Nothing — the street was just like it had been for eight years. She had vanished, and nobody has ever heard from her. Why did she disappear? What happened to her? He didn't want to think what he really thought — that woman had murdered her. Marilyn was special; she was fine wine. He remembered how beautiful she was. Tears came to his eyes, and he took a deep breath to clear his head.

The temperature was cold for an early autumn night in upstate New York. The streetlights cast their glare off the rain puddles on the street. He felt the bite of the cold and the dampness that went to the bone. Down the street, teenagers huddled in a group, planning their night's festivities. He smelled the moist air and heard the sound of tires traveling the wet road. Shawn crossed the street and got into his car to go home. *Funny,* he thought, *how even then, when he had been drinking, he felt the need to avoid his parents.*

He decided to go for a ride before he went home. Let the alcohol wear off a little, he reasoned. Instead of going left on to East Main, he went right onto West Main and out to the country roads. He punched the accelerator and gave the car a burst of speed. Hot anger built in him, flushing him red with the help of the alcohol. How could the world be so horrible? How could he lose his wife and child that soon? Maybe if he hadn't killed those men in the war... Hadn't he paid enough for Vietnam? He slammed his fist on the dashboard and mashed the accelerator. The force pushed him back in his seat, and the more he thought of this injustice, the faster he went.

"You fool!" he cried out, "A car wreck killed your family!"

He looked to his right and saw a bright light with the shape of a woman inside.

"What is that? You've finally pickled your brain," he whispered to himself. As he said this, he came to a curve in the road. He downshifted, which locked up the rear tires of the car. He felt the car spinning on the slick, wet pavement, and then it hit the gully. He heard stones and dirt striking the car around him, shattering the glass as the vehicle flipped through a wooden fence, followed by jerks that left him breathless, bangs, the crunching of metal, dirt, and glass pelting his face, and more jerks that he thought would never end.

His world went dark as the car came to rest against a tree. The twisted metal of the car held him tightly as he went in and out of consciousness. He could feel a warm liquid trickle down his face and fill his ears and mouth. Shawn could taste his own blood. *Strange,* he thought, *that he heard Marilyn's voice calling to him.*

"Focus, you're hallucinating," he sputtered as he tried to move. He turned his head and saw a young Marilyn looking at him as he lost consciousness.

*****

The vampire stood on a rooftop with her changeling next to her and watched the crippled, drunk man struggle across the street. She was an old and powerful vampire, and few creatures in this world were as powerful as her. Her name was Anne Bryce. She was born of Celtic origins around 400 AD at the end of the Roman occupation of Britannia. Her name when she was mortal was Anwen Eiren, and she had lived with her father Berwyn, her mother Crystyn, and twin brother Darryn in the Angelia area of Britannia. They had been farmers and raised livestock for the Roman Legions.

Sixteen hundred years ago, the vampire Bricius came to her and told her he had been sent by the Archangel Michael. The vampire told her that he had walked this earth for thousands of years, and the

Archangel charged him to turn her, to begin the destruction of the Esmanaa demons. Bricius was a solitary vampire, and the most powerful vampire Anne came across in her sixteen hundred years of life. His maker was Herit, one of the five original vampires given the blood of Michael. The angels of heaven had placed great power in Herit's blood, and she had given this power to Bricius. He had disappointed Michael, hid from the Esmanaa demons, and never used this power against them. Finally, Michael had commanded him to give this blood to Anne.

Anne turned and smiled at her changeling. How fearful Marilyn was for this mortal, and yes, Anne saw that she loved this man dearly. This was her first love, a strong love. She had found Marilyn in a bar in Syracuse. Being an old vampire, she quickly saw into her mind, her thoughts, and the turmoil of her life. She smelled her sweet blood, admired her beauty, and that drew her to the woman. Many nights she sat with Marilyn, listening to her troubles, and talking with her using her power to soothe the mortal's mind. Marilyn told her how she planned on leaving her husband, about her miscarriage, and told her how she had lost her true love, the man staggering across the street.

She stayed in Syracuse for her art show and spent most of her time with Marilyn and fell deeply in love with this fascinating, unique, and beautiful woman. Like she had done with Renee, she took pity on this mortal. The Roman soldiers, through there many rapes, had made Anne dislike men. Centuries had passed before she came to terms with them. When Bricius had changed her, she made the Roman soldiers pay dearly for what they had done to her. When she was a young vampire, Michael had sent Herit to her to quiet her raging soul.

Eventually, it was time to leave Syracuse. The night before, she sat with Marilyn and poured her a glass of wine, kissed her lips softly, and told her she was going to make her whole again, give her pride back so she could feel safe. That night, she allowed Marilyn for the first time to see her for what she was. She took Marilyn into her arms, drew her into her eyes, and forced her way into her mind. She took her blood and gave her supernatural blood in return. She made Marilyn a vampire that night, a warrior angel here on earth.

"There's Shawn! See him?" Marilyn whispered. Anne gave her a skeptical look.

"Yes, I see him. He looks drunk — just like a man. He's a sad man."

Anne had not wanted to bring Marilyn here, to see this man, but the angel Herit came to her and told her to come.

"You're right, he is sad—my dear Shawn!"

"Men love to get drunk, don't they?"

Marilyn sighed and said, "He was never a heavy drinker, I'm sure this has to do with his wife and child."

"He's a cripple," Anne said as she nodded toward him.

"The war damaged his leg."

Anne watched Marilyn's lost love stagger and sway across the street and get into his car.

"He shouldn't be driving in that condition. Can we follow him?" Marilyn asked.

Anne saw her desperation and said a little exasperated. "Fly next to me and let me know when you get tired. You have to give up human love. He will be dead soon, and you will be the same — you know that. I thought you said he was smart."

Anne, with Marilyn, followed behind Shawn as he drove his car recklessly on the country road.

"He's driving too fast for these road conditions. He shouldn't be driving like that!"

Anne sensed the terrible panic sweeping through Marilyn as she watched her lost love skid off the road.

"Try to stay calm. We will go see him," Anne said in a reassuring voice.

*****

The crash was bad, far worse than he knew. The car rolled over repeatedly, crushing the sides and the roof, all the glass was broken out.

"Shawn! Look at me! What have you done to yourself?" A frightened Marilyn cried. "Why did you drive like that, Shawnee?"

He was drifting in and out of consciousness when he heard Marilyn's voice calling him. How could that be?

"Focus your eyes, Shawn—look at me!" Marilyn pleaded.

Turning his head, he saw her, and she looked like a young woman. He must be hallucinating.

"Marilyn, is that you?" Shawn gurgled as blood came out of his mouth.

"Yes, it's me! Look at me, I'm real — look, Shawn!" Marilyn cried.

"Where have you been, and why do you look so young?" A dazed Shawn gasped. "Everybody has been looking for you. When I get out of this mess, I expect to see you in Dalton."

"I'm living in Washington," she said, the sadness in her voice evident. "Oh, God, Shawn! You aren't getting out of this! There is a big piece of wood from the fence through your stomach!"

Shawn looked down and saw that she was right.

"Please, Anne, save him! Please, Anne! I'm begging you to save him!" Marilyn pleaded.

A grim Anne answered, "Marilyn, I already have a changeling — I can't have two. That would be too difficult, and he is a man."

"I don't care about that! I'll do it myself if I have to! I'm not going to lose him!"

"You cannot do that. You will only make this man a rogue. Remember what you promised! Do you need a man? Am I not enough for you? You do! A woman is not enough for you!"

"Yes, Anne, I also need a man, and more than a woman, please!" Marilyn sobbed. "I need Shawn! I'm sorry, you have done so much for me, but I can't live without him."

The car jerked to the left, and Shawn turned to see a beautiful woman holding the driver's door in her hand. She tossed it into the field as if it were a Frisbee.

"Hello, Shawn, I'm Anne. It looks like you have yourself in quite a situation. Do you want to live, Shawn? Do you want to live with Marilyn and me? I can make that possible for you."

He had lost feeling in his legs and was fighting to stay conscious, but he thought this woman said she could save him.

"Yes, I want to live," Shawn said desperately.

"Are you sure? It will take half my blood to save you."

"Yes, I want to be with Marilyn."

"Please, change him, please save him for me!" Marilyn begged. "Please, hurry—I can't watch him die!"

"I will do this for you. I love you and can't bear to see you in this pain, but I will have to answer for this—to the Council."

Shawn heard Marilyn begging for his life. This woman must be a doctor, and then he felt pressure and sharp points penetrating his neck. He thought a wild animal was biting him, but he knew that couldn't be. The bite was strong, and then darkness came. He was floating in a gentle light, and soon, above a vivid, green field.

The day was sunny, but there was no sun in the sky. He found himself by a tree with big, shiny green leaves, and could taste blood in his mouth. *How sweet,* he thought. He loved the taste. Shawn looked, and standing in the field was a man with reddish hair, dressed in white pants, loafers, and silver chest armor. A white light surrounded him. The man waved at him, and Shawn waved back. The man's voice pushed its way into his being, *Greetings, I was once Erdin Kenmare.* Then he saw another bright light with a woman inside. The brightness made him want to turn away. It was the woman by the side of the road. He felt love coming from the woman, a sense of relief, and welcome.

Shawn woke lying on an old sofa. It smelled of mold, and he heard a rustling sound. His body was tingling, and he had pain in his stomach. It would rise in intensity, and then subside and repeat. He sat up and looked at the floor, his eyes drawn to a speck of dirt in the crack between the floorboards. He focused more and saw a transparent crab-like creature crawling on the bit of dirt. It was as if he saw it through a microscope, and then his sight went back to normal. He realized that this place was the old Vandenberg hunting lodge. While in high school, he'd come here many times with Marilyn and other friends. On occasion, they'd had sex there. He looked around and saw the familiar animal heads hanging on the walls and recognized his old friend the bear.

The voice he heard next was soft and reassuring: "Hello, Shawn, my name is Anne. Do you remember me from the crash? The noises you hear are mice rustling around in the walls. You will learn to use your new senses very quickly."

Across the room, he found the beautiful woman sitting in a chair, looking at him with a smile. Rarely had he seen such beauty, and he could tell there was something unnatural about her. She looked young, maybe thirty at the most, but her eyes had a look of someone much older. Long, wavy brown hair, a perfect face and form, beautiful lips, and a flawless complexion — she was stunning.

"Who are you, and how did I get here?" Shawn asked. He started to remember the car crash, the terrible pain, the blood, and his stomach wound. He looked down and raised his bloody shirt; there was no wound—it was gone. He felt a wave of panic wash over him, and then he remembered Marilyn was there. He clung to that idea. "Marilyn's with you, isn't she?" Shawn asked, hopefully.

"Yes, she is. You will see her soon. Now, I have to talk about what has happened to you. I want you to try to keep yourself calm. I know you are scared. I'm not a healer. You were in a terrible car crash and skewered yourself with a piece of a fence post. As you remember, Marilyn was there. We were following you. Marilyn could not let you die and die you would have…Shawn, listen to me. She begged me to save you, and that is what I did. I had no choice. I couldn't allow Marilyn to be in that much pain. Letting you die could have changed our relationship. I am her maker, and I love her very much. I am sorry your old life is over, but I had no choice. Now you must concentrate on surviving the next couple of months."

"You're not a doctor?" Shawn felt surreal, knew something strange had happened, and it unnerved him. "What is going on with my eyes and ears? Why are they so sensitive? And you don't feel right. There's something about you!"

"No, I'm not a healer, and I am not crazy. Prepare yourself for what I am going to say." The woman briefly stared at him. "I am a vampire. Marilyn is a vampire, and now I have made you one to keep you alive. Easy, Shawn. Focus and listen to me closely."

Shawn looked at the woman, her eyes did not blink naturally, not like a human's eyes, then as if a curtain had risen on a stage, he saw this woman for what she was, a supernatural creature. She disappeared and reappeared, sitting next to him, so close he could smell the scent of jasmine and feel her lips brush against his ear. He tried to draw away, but she took hold of his arm with an unbreakable grip. The strange woman smelled his neck; a vampire can tell much through their smell, whether someone is weak or strong if you're kind or cruel.

"Hear what I say. I have given you a life force you can't imagine yet, senses, strength, and psychic abilities. Someday you will come to appreciate the gift I have given you. I have given this gift to a man, something I thought I would never do. I am your maker, and you are my fledgling. You will be with me for a hundred years. I have not properly changed you. I know nothing about you, only what Marilyn has told me. I do not love you; as I have loved other humans, I have changed." She paused a moment and stare at him allowing her words to sink in. "I will teach you how to survive as a vampire. The blood I give you will make you powerful, and maybe we will grow to love each other. Now listen to me closely—you must do what I say when I say it. Never contradict me in front of other vampires. If you don't do as I say, I will turn you out, and the Vampire Council will have you killed. This is vampire law."

"This can't be. There are no vampires," Shawn muttered. "Take your hand off me." He felt the woman pull his arm more tightly.

"You must realize what I say is true. This is your reality now. There are creatures in this world mortals know nothing about."

Shawn looked around the room, searching for windows or doors through which to make his escape. He should try to get away from this beautiful mysterious woman, and find Marilyn so he could save her, too. If he made it to the woods, there was a quick way to the main road. Shawn tried to remove the woman's hand from his arm but couldn't even move one of her fingers.

A smile came over Anne's face as she said, "Beautiful. I have heard that a lot over my sixteen-hundred-year life. You cannot escape me, Shawn, that is impossible for you, as you can see, and you shouldn't want to, either. You would not survive. Like a newborn baby would not survive without his mother, you will need me for a while. Let's go for a walk. There is a lovely pond out back."

They went outside to the trail that traveled around the pond. The storm clouds from early in the day had passed, and the rain had washed the earth and cleansed the air. The night was clear, with a bright, full moon reflecting off the small pond, and a slight, cool breeze blew against his face. The wind rushing through the leaves sounded like a roar, and the croaking of the frogs echoed into the night. He could raise the sounds of the crickets to a deafening level. His senses were alive; he was receiving distinct signals from every cell in his body. These feelings frightened him, and at first, he shrunk from them.

If he concentrated, he heard a squirrel rustling in a tree from across the pond. Focusing his eyes, he saw the squirrel as if he were a couple feet from the animal. He could use his vision to see the tiniest microbe slither on the dirt between the blades of grass. His new sight could bring the stars so close he blanketed the night sky with them and thought they would crush him. He saw new shades of colors he never imagined existed.

"You'll get used to your new vampire senses," Anne told him.

He concentrated on Marilyn; it helped him with the shock. "Where is Marilyn? Is she here?"

"Yes, she is here. You will see her again. Soon, you will fall back to sleep. You are still in the process of transitioning into a vampire. Look at it this way—at least you will get one of your true loves back."

He would be with Marilyn again, kiss and make love to her again, and that gave him hope. That took away his panic—gave him purpose. They could escape this woman together...

"You will learn to block vampires from your mind in time," said Anne, cutting him off, "and Marilyn will not leave with you. We love each other. Her blood is my blood, a bond you know nothing about. She has been a vampire for eight years and would not want to be mortal. I am her maker, and she will not leave me, even for you. You will feel repulsed by me at first. My kind has hunted your kind for thousands of years. That will go away, and in time, you will accept me. Soon our blood will be the same."

The vampire was right. Even as he walked, he felt the need to distance himself from her, a feeling he was trying to control. They continued their walk around the pond. He had a million questions forming in his fear-soaked mind and wondered if there was any truth to what he heard of vampires in books and movies. He looked at this woman, how beautiful she was. She did not look pale and dead; on the contrary, she was vibrant and alive.

"My God, I'm not limping! How could that be?" he wondered aloud.

"The life force I have given you will heal your body much faster and better than your old life force," Anne explained.

"So, I'm not dead!"

A laugh came from this woman and a type of look given when you have heard an outrageous statement. "No, you are far more alive now than when you were human."

Shawn's head started to swim; he began to feel very tired. That damn pain in his gut was getting to him. He suddenly bent over, threw up, and watched foaming, dark blood splatter on the ground. "What is happening to me?" he choked. Then he had a strong urge to urinate and quickly went behind a tree. "You have poisoned me!" he cried.

"You will be all right." Anne laughed. "Your vampire body is getting rid of the last of your human fluids. That is why, during the change, you awaken."

When Shawn looked into this woman's eyes, they pulled at him; they beguiled him. Was it her beauty, or something else? Shawn wasn't sure.

"You are starting to tire. You will fall back to sleep soon. I am going to take you back to my home so you will have the time you need to adjust to your new life."

"Where do you live?"

"I live in northern Washington. The forest, lake, and mountains are beautiful, and the sunlight is low. You will find my home very comfortable. Marilyn and I were on our way to Boston, but our situation has changed. I have to feed. It took a lot of my blood to save you, and I got little back from you."

"Is Marilyn going back with us?"

"She will be with you for at least a hundred years. My limousine has just arrived. Let's go back to the lodge."

As they walked back to the lodge, he asked her, "You have been alive... for sixteen hundred years?"

"Yes," Anne replied. "I was a young girl when a vampire changed me. I have lived for a very long time."

"Are you immortal?" Shawn asked. "My mother would love to meet you. Well, maybe not."

"We are immortal, but few of us have the stamina to live forever. Remember this — if your heart or head leaves your body, you will die.

"Who made you?"

"He was an old and powerful vampire, a Roman. His name was Bricius. Herit, the angel that has taken an interest in you, was his maker. I'm afraid he had no desire for fighting demons, only flesh. We will talk more when we get home. There is much for you to learn."

They arrived back at the lodge. Shawn saw that the sun was starting to peek over the horizon. He looked at Anne to see what she would do. She lifted her foot, traveled five steps, not touching a one, and landed on the porch.

"Let's go inside Shawn. You could not take the sun now, you have not fed yet. That will be your next big hurdle."

They went inside, and he sat down on the large brown sofa. The dank old smell of the hunting lodge filled his new sense of smell. His head was swimming, and he wondered what his life as a vampire would bring. He felt exhausted, laid his head down, and promptly fell back to sleep.

Chapter Three

S hawn woke for the second time and found himself lying in a
big, comfortable bed, wearing dark blue pajamas. He sat up
and saw two windows and a set of large French doors, all with closed,
light blue draperies. Light filtered through and around the curtains. No
black-painted windows or taped cardboard. The bedroom was large,
with paintings on the walls, furniture throughout, and figurines on the
polished cherry wood tables. Ornate, white molding and light, pastel-
green decorative wallpaper covered the walls. Area rugs were in just
the right spots, laid over a polished oak floor.

He looked to his left and saw a large inverted, opened box with
curved edges and corners.

"What the hell!" he mumbled. He rubbed his hand through his hair
to feel his aching head and he still had a slight pain in his stomach.

The box was light blue with scenes of animals, humans, and clouds,
and with elaborate white molding around the edges. The strange box
attached to four poles at the corners. The poles attached to the floor
and ceiling. The box rose and lowered over another open box recessed
into the floor. The boxes were large: about ten feet by ten feet. He
would learn that vampires called this a couch, and this was where they
slept during the day.

He left the bed and crept toward the boxes, trying to calm the panic
he felt. Sensing no danger—and he definitely could sense better than
before, he looked into the one that was sunk in the floor. It had silk,
red quilts, and elegant, white linen sheets. Anne and Marilyn were
sleeping together in a spoon position, Marilyn's bare leg halfway over
Anne. They wore light green, silk nightgowns. He looked at these
beautiful women and realized he was looking at vampires, and then
he realized he was one, too. The thought startled him and sent a rush
of panic through him.

Across the room, he noticed a sword laid in a holder on a polished mahogany table. *How strange,* he thought, *the hilt is as long as the blade.* Engraved into the blade was the word "Deceida." A far wall held a door that led to a large bathroom. Shawn saw an entrance door to the bedroom and opened it quietly. On the other side was a long hallway, paintings hanging in plenty on the walls. He felt anxious and clammy and wiped his forehead with his hand. The site of red sweat only made him more frightened. He went left, pass more bedrooms, and then down a long flight of stairs and came to a large common room. Shawn marveled that he had no limp. There was no stiffness or pain, no deep scars from the many surgeries that helped repair his shattered femur after the war. He lifted his pajama shirt, checked his stomach, and saw no signs of a wound.

He walked to the far side of the living room and down a short hall. There was a large wooden door at the end with strange symbols carved into it. He concentrated and heard two humans in front of the house. Curiosity had taken hold; he went back to the living room and down another hallway, into a huge room that had many finished paintings, painting supplies, and easels holding half-finished paintings. On the far side of the room was a large, bronze door with a lion's head on the front.

The room was bright, and it made him want to withdraw, but he resisted. Again, large windows with curtains filtering the light. He walked and stood next to the light beams and watched the dust particles dance and swirl their way to the floor. The sun made him squint and slightly nauseous.

"Shawn, careful with the light," Anne warned softly. "You have to feed and grow a little older as a vampire, and then you can go out in the sunlight for a short time." She placed her hand in the ray of light. At first, the light bent strangely around her hand—nothing happened. Her hand didn't burst into flames.

"You see? I'm still here, not like Dracula." She smiled and then gave a soft laugh. He liked the way she laughed. It was a pleasant laugh; there was nothing forced about it. And he had to be honest with himself—he loved the sound of her voice almost from the first time he heard it.

23

"On an overcast day, I can swim in the lake all day. That is why I live in these beautiful woods," she went on. "The sun drains our life force, but it takes hours, and if the light level is low, older vampires can stay out all day. Remember this—if humans see you in the light, it's much easier for them to see you for what you are. Michael made us sensitive to the light… angels of the night. Michael wants us to hide from the mortals, so they think they are the only intelligent creatures in this world."

"Who is Michael?" Shawn asked.

"He is the Archangel," Anne replied. "He made our kind on this world, and our blood holds his power. He is the leader of our warrior choir of angels. I'm sure you have heard of him."

"I have. There is a woman in my dreams now. She seems so real, and I have heard her voice before. The first time was in Vietnam."

"Her name is Herit, and one of the five original vampires. She was Egyptian and lived along the Nile. She fought the Esmanaa demons, and they killed her. You must always be careful of these demons because of your Herit blood. They hate us because we're of the Herit covenant. Why she has an interest in you is not clear yet. The Archangel Michael came to this world seven thousand years ago and gave five humans the blood of the angels and five swords forged in light, to counter the five Esmanaa demons and their ever-growing evil. Michael told them to feed only on the depraved of this world. Only on Lucifer's children. These vampires formed the five vampire covenants."

Anne was still wearing a silky, light green nightgown. She looked stunning and was a woman any man would want. He raised his eyes quickly. She was smiling again; she knew what he was thinking.

"You are going to have to show me how to keep vampires out of my head," Shawn said with a sheepish look.

Anne laughed, and he was glad to see she had a sense of humor. "Your thoughts are very vivid to me now. We are vampires, and the blood that flows in your veins is mine—with your own special taste."

"Anne, you tell me I must feed. Do you mean I must take blood from people? Will I have to kill people?"

"Yes, it is crucial that you feed and take blood. You were near death when I changed you. You had a terrible wound in your stomach and lost most of your blood. I didn't have much to work with, and you needed more blood than I could give you. Now you look weak and pale." Anne laughed again. "What humans think vampires should look like." Then she turned serious, and he felt her in his head, searching his mind. "You will have to kill if you want to survive. You are a killer now. I see in your mind, you have killed before and survived death. I will take you to only the evil of the human race, those who spread Lucifer's darkness. That is the true purpose of vampires—to feed on evil and hold the dark forces back in this world. The Archangel Michael made us to protect the world from the dark angels. That is what Michael wants. Humans owe us their blood. It is a debt they must pay." Her voice became urgent. "Listen to me — blood is everything to a vampire. It is nourishment coming from mortals; it is power and strength coming from your maker. Vampires use blood to make a connection with each other. In sex, it is sensual for us, and it heightens our sexual feelings. Vampires need blood to survive, and so do you! I will teach you how to take blood. Soon you will have to take my blood, so you will be strong enough to hunt."

"I promised myself a long time ago that I would never kill people again," Shawn said as he tried to quiet the panic building in him. "The last time I killed, it turned my life into a horror I don't want to repeat." He knew Anne was now trying to calm him, to settle him for all she had to say. She started to walk toward him, past a window with light coming through the curtains. He could see the silhouette of her body through her silk nightclothes, The vampire disappeared and then was upon him; there was no escaping her. She smelled of Jasmine as her lips brushed his ear, sending electricity down his neck.

"Hear me," Anne whispered in his ear. He thought he felt some breath but wasn't sure. She ran her nose the length of his neck, smelling him. She was always in his mind, searching his life thoughts. "You have a week to take blood, or you will die. For you, there is little time to decide. If you reject the blood of the angels, the death you will experience will be agonizing! Your insides will be on fire, you will burn from the inside out, and you will wither and die, just like a grape left in the sun." Anne released him and backed up a couple of steps. "Shawn, take some blood from me — it will make you feel better. It will quiet your nerves."

This took him by surprise. Anne exposed her neck to him. A sensual desire for her came over him. She was pulling him toward her, forcing him to go next to her, the nape of her neck coming into microscopic focus, and he could see her capillaries, filled with dark blood, through her creamy skin. He could smell the sweetness of her blood, and it made his head swim. How strange this all was, had he slipped into some insane abyss? Had life finally become too much for him. He fell back from her and saw himself in a mirror. His eyes were a bright blue, and he had sharp, white fangs---shock traveled through him. There was viciousness in his look.

"My God, what have you done to me?"

"I have made you a vampire! It is up to you whether you live or die. I have done all I can. You must accept what you are, or you won't survive." Anne cut her wrist with her fingernail; the blood quickly filled his nose with a sweet smell. There was a longing for the blood— she was tempting him. Her eyes were drawing him to her. She was the cobra and he, the goose.

"Your blood will make me feel better?" Shawn gasped.

"Yes, it will. Taste it. You will see."

He brought her wrist to his mouth, licked, and tasted her blood. Never had he tasted such sweetness. He felt Anne take his hair, pull his head away, and within seconds, her wrist healed. Then she brought his head next to her neck.

"Sense my blood—you can feel where the artery is. Use your vampire senses to do what you feel. Always follow your vampire senses," Anne whispered.

"Puncture you and suck?" Shawn asked with a quivering voice.

"Yes, it's natural for us."

Shawn felt his teeth go into Anne's neck and find their target. He thought of how sharp they must be. The taste of her was intoxicating to him. Blood burst into his mouth while he stood and shook. He felt a surge of energy, elation in his being, and the sweet taste of her nectar.

"That is enough," Anne told him as she pushed him away. "I'm afraid I have little to spare. I will need to take two mortals tonight."

He heard the front door unlock, instantly smelled the mortal woman who entered, and quickly sensed her mission was to clean. Anne was also aware of the mortal. She disappeared, and Shawn heard her talking to the woman as if he was standing next to them.

Anne told her, "Not today, Linda. You will have to find something else to do."

"Yes, ma'am. Is there a new member to your family? Will I have to get extra supplies?"

"Yes, I have a new member, and he's male."

"A male!" Linda said.

"Yes, Linda, a male. Have I shocked you?"

There must not be many men in her life, Shawn surmised. His attention went to the bronze door with the lion's head cast in the front. The door looked to be heavy and had three large hinges, a bronze ring where the doorknob should have been. The door was old — he could see hammer marks left by its maker during an ancient forging. Soon, Anne returned to the room and offered a brief explanation for her abrupt disappearance.

"I have two Crimmian servants, and they live in front of the house."

"Where did that door come from? Whatever is on the other side must be valuable," Shawn said as he pointed toward the door.

"That door was at the first house I lived in after my changing. It guarded my maker's treasure and gave him a secret place to be alone and brood. He was very old and became tired of this world and a disappointment for the Archangel. You can see him in that painting over there…" She pointed to it. "His name was Bricius. He took me when I was seventeen years old, and I have spent sixteen hundred years, making myself look older."

"That's an amazing amount of time to be alive," Shawn said, still in disbelief of the fact.

"It is, and you have a very long time to hear about it. Would you like to see what is on the other side of that door?"

He thought and figured, why not? What else could happen?

"Sure," he said. "You can't turn me into a vampire again, anyway."

"Funny and charming. Marilyn was right about that. Come on, follow me."

He saw Anne take a large, metal key from a vase and unlock the door. She took the metal ring, turned it and pulled the door open, the hinges making a loud, grating sound. The lights came on automatically, but neither of them needed them. He went down stone stairs that curved in the middle and proceeded into a large room under the house.

The floors were of large, red, and light blue tiles laid in different patterns, with a mosaic depicting a golden lion's head in the middle. The walls were of brick and mortar. Four large rooms recessed into the walls. Light blue tiles covered their walls.

One of the cubicles had a strange-looking gold vase with a gold top sitting on a gold table. It was set apart from the other treasures. It must be important, Shawn thought. Gold vases and gold objects filled the rooms. There was a strong smell of cedar coming from the cedar boxes also stored in these rooms.

"That vase holds the blood of my maker," Anne said.

"Old blood--why?

"Demons!"

He stared in amazement at what he saw — the amount of gold was unbelievable. He turned and noticed a large, square opening in the floor. Two-foot high, red-tiled walls surrounded this large opening in the basement floor that led directly to the earth. The bottom was dirt, dark and rich, graded, and raked very neatly. Surrounding the top edge were white marble tiles. It looked like a small swimming pool filled with dirt. To the right of this opening, he saw a large, white marble table indented slightly with a drain. The table rested on a marble pedestal, and a water hose with a spray nozzle hung above the table.

"What is this all about?" he inquired, pointing nervously to the opening in the floor.

"We bring our family members here if their wounds are severe enough that it would take a long time for them to heal. We prepare them on the table, their wounds wrapped in linen, soaked with our blood, and then bury them so they may heal. The Mother cradles the vampire in her healing soil. After some time, they come out, we greet them and rinse the dirt from their bodies on the marble table. Vampires bury themselves to heal, to hide from their enemies, or get away from the sunlight. I will teach you when and how to bury yourself."

"Have you ever been hurt so badly that you had to be buried?" he asked hesitantly.

"Yes, an Esmanaa named Zepar hurt me. I sensed him coming, but he was traveling so fast I could not prepare for him. Two older vampires, Hegamar and Stephen, saved me. They took me to Amsterdam and buried me in the basement of the Council building. My first changeling, Renee, watched over me."

"What are Esmanaa?" Shawn asked in a shaky voice.

Anne's voice became grave. "Demons. We have enemies in this world. There is evil that would sweep us from this world if given a chance. Lucifer has great power in this world. When you get older, stronger, evil will challenge you, and you must be ready. That is the Archangel Michael's task for us. I can see in your mind that you have seen evil. Not all families have burial pits, but our family must. Our family is from Herit, and the five demons knew her quite well. They hate Herit blood. There are only four demons now—Erdin Kenmare killed the demon, Amon. If they recognize that you're from Herit's covenant, they will attack and kill you. You must remember Herit blood is what they hate most in this world. We were the covenant that fought them. That is why there are few Herit's. The Esmanaa demons were angels that plotted against Michael. He had these angels shunned in heaven, and he cast them from heaven, and this humiliated them. They turned to Lucifer, and through a trick, they came to earth. Now they will kill any guardians they can."

Shawn responded in a low, tired voice. "This is all too much. I'm going to need you. That is obvious to me now, but I don't know if I want to use you. I don't know if I want this life." How was he going to accept being a vampire, a guardian? Now, he realized that he was going to have to take blood to survive. And now he's told about demons! Anne reached out to touch his cheek, and he shrunk back from her, the anticipated contact making him feel worse.

"We are the same, and you are going to have to kill and drink blood," Anne told him, staring into his eyes. "If you want to be with Marilyn. Let's get you back to bed."

He went back to bed, pulled the covers over his head, and welcomed sleep. He was drifting again over the green field in the bright sunlight. Kristen was standing there, watching him. He didn't see her mouth move, but he heard her.

"I love you, Shawn. Christine and I are all right. There are angels here that want you to survive. They want you to accept your new life."

When Shawn woke, he felt somebody sitting at the foot of the bed, and he knew it was Marilyn. He pulled the covers from his head and sat up. She still wore her silk nightgown and was beautiful. The difference in his feelings was striking—he felt love and happiness to see her, but also felt that unnatural feeling. He knew immediately that she was a vampire, but she took his fear away. He had slept through the early part of the evening, and Marilyn was reading a magazine, waiting for him to awaken.

"Finally, after all these years, there you are," Shawn said. "You look beautiful, much younger than I would have thought."

"Surprise! Look what happened to me along the way. I would kiss you, but I know you wouldn't want that. You look terrible. This is going to be a hard time for you, but it passes. Why were you driving like that? I thought you were smarter than that," she scolded him. He could tell Marilyn was displeased with him and saw the flash of blue in her vampire eyes.

"Marilyn, when I lost my wife and daughter, I died inside. I have felt nothing for two years except anger, pain, and sorrow. I didn't care anything for myself, but I didn't mean to crash the car."

"I'm so sorry to hear about your wife and child. I know you loved them very much," Marilyn told him.

"This is beyond belief, Marilyn! You disappeared for eight years and come back into my life as a vampire! You talked that woman, Anne, into changing me into a vampire!"

"Shawn, you were the one who was driving crazy and crashed your car, not me. Either way, I couldn't let you die any more than you could have let me die. That is something I wasn't going to let happen. I could not let you die when I had the means to save you. So, Shawnee, it looks like you're a vampire now!"

"How did you end up as a vampire?" Shawn asked in amazement.

Marilyn looked at him, and sadness came over her face. "My marriage turned out to be a bad one. Jack was great when we were in college, but when we graduated and married, he was unable to get it together. He always seemed so overwhelmed, and he drank constantly. Then he would turn mean. My life was not going well, and I started to go to a tavern to meet friends at night. One evening, I met Anne there. She was easy to talk to, seemed understanding, and she took an interest in me. She was always where I went. We started to spend time together. I began to care for her... love her. One night, I found out she was a vampire, and that same night, she made me a vampire.

What she really did was save me. She made me something better, and eight years later, I can say to you I'm glad to be a vampire. I love Anne—I love her very much. I love her as I love you. As a vampire, you will learn you have the desire to be with more than one. To enjoy more than one person. We live too long to love just one. Anne told me it was the blood of the angels that makes us love like this."

"Marilyn, I'm going to have to kill people for their blood. I promised never to kill again after Vietnam."

"I know the first time is hard. You are going to have to take blood from humans to live. Prepare yourself for this. The first time will take all your strength. Anne and I will be with you. She will show you what to do, how to kill quickly, and painlessly. These are bad people we hunt, the worst of the human race. You will see this when the time comes, but it must be soon. You were near death when Anne changed you. Anne can give you some of her blood to keep you going, but this will only work for a short time."

"Where is Anne?" he asked.

"She has gone to Seattle to feed and left me here with you."

"Who is Anne? Where is she from?"

"Anne is old and has the blood of the ancients. She lived in Britain in the time of the Romans. You can see she is pretty, so the Roman soldiers gave her a rough time. Unfortunately for you, she's not that thrilled with men. Her vampire blood is almost pure blood of the angels, and she has many supernatural powers. Believe me, I have seen her strength. Our lineage comes from Herit, our covenant is Herit, and we are in the Bryce family. Anne says there are few Herit's, unlike the rest of the covenants, because of the demons and Bricius. There are five covenants, and now Anne leads the Herit Covenant. She also possesses one of the five original swords from Heaven, Deceida. You will spend a hundred years with her, so you will get to know her. Everything we do for the next century, we need Anne's permission. She is our maker and has given you a gift, though you don't believe it right now. You look like you could use a shower. Come on, follow me."

Shawn followed Marilyn to the bathroom, and it was a large room with a big sunken tub and a large, walk-in shower. The bathroom had lilac and white-colored tiles, white pedestal sinks, and a toilet and bidet.

"Can we still use a toilet?" he asked.

"We pee because we drink, but you have eaten your last meal. No more steak. Sorry, I know how you loved steak," Marilyn apologized with a grin. "You don't have a stomach anymore. You have a blood sac. It holds and absorbs the blood you will take."

Soon they were naked. Shawn always loved Marilyn's naked body, and this time was no different. To him, everything on her body was perfect, pleasing to his eyes, and it always made him want her.

"Do you still like my body?" Marilyn teased.

"You're beautiful, and you know it."

The hot water of the shower soothed him, but as he watched the pink-stained water flow down the drain, his fear returned.

"It's all right, you've been through a traumatic time," Marilyn reassured him. "When you feed, you will feel much better."

He couldn't take his eyes off her; he was afraid she would disappear. She smiled at him and gave him a reassuring look.

Shawn advanced toward Marilyn, hesitantly, letting his desires take over. Marilyn placed her fingers on his lips to stop him.

"We can't do that, Shawn. We need Anne's permission," Marilyn whispered in frustration. "She is your maker. She will take you first and give you blood for now."

"She likes women, though, doesn't she?" Shawn replied.

"Most of the time, she is with women but has been with a few men. I don't believe there have been many. She likes sex with men but prefers the emotions and sex of women. Anne is very good to me, and we are lucky to have her as a maker. When in private, she is loving and pleasant. However, you have to remember when she is with other vampires--it will be different. We are her changelings. Vampires have an ancient and rigid hierarchy. Their ways are funny when it comes to young vampires. We cannot speak to older vampires unless they speak to us first. When we meet older vampires, Anne will make our greetings for us. You must remember this and never question or contradict her in front of her peers."

"Have you seen other vampires? Are there more vampires living around here?" Shawn asked.

"There are many vampires in the world. I'm not sure how many. I have met vampires, but most pay me no attention, and most seem okay, but I have met some I'm not sure about, too. There is a big family in Oregon, headed by Hector Nicholas, a 2,000-year-old vampire, and is a new member of the Vampire Council. He is holding a gathering for Anne, and we should travel to his home soon. The Council has selected Anne to be a member, a big honor for her, and probably why I had to beg so hard for your life."

Shawn realized while talking to Marilyn that there was a lot to learn. He knew he had to kill for blood, or he would not be around to learn how to be a vampire. He took the soap, continued to wash, and it soothed him. The water coming off his body was now clear. While they were drying themselves, he became weak and lightheaded again. He saw the concerned look on Marilyn's face.

"Let's get dressed and go for a walk outside, there is still some night left," Marilyn suggested.

They went out a large wooden door on the side of the mansion, and again Shawn noticed the strange carvings on the door.

"What are these symbols?" Shawn asked.

"They keep the demons out," Marilyn said as her voice lowered. "Anne carved them, and these symbols are everywhere in this house. They are a gift from the angels."

"Angels?"

"You will learn about the angels. I'm sure you have realized you don't sleep like before."

"Tell me, when did you start having sex with women?"

"When I met Anne. She was everything I wanted in a companion. I know that now. Yet, I can't wait to have you."

The door led them to a covered patio with chairs and a table. They walked out onto a mowed lawn, and there was a beautiful small mountain lake. Across the lake, Shawn could see eagle chicks in their nest; their mouths were open and pointed toward the sky, crying for their mother to feed them. He turned and looked at Marilyn in amazement.

"That's just the beginning of what you are going to be capable of," Marilyn said. "That is if you survive the transitioning."

He looked back across the lake at the brook and a twenty-foot waterfall.

"How beautiful this place is," he marveled. They were located in the middle of a pine forest. Toward the front of the house was a long, gravel road that led to a paved, county road. The house was a large, two-story, brick-and-stone mansion, its back built into a steep hill. The front and sides had a large, well-manicured lawn.

As they walked around to the front of the house, they passed a large garage with a black limousine inside. A big man with dark hair and a mustache worked on a red Pontiac.

"Hello, Daren. How are you tonight?" Marilyn asked politely.

"I'm fine, ma'am, thank you," Daren replied.

"Who is that?" Shawn asked.

"That is Daren, a Crimmian servant. His wife is our other servant," Marilyn explained. "They come from an ancient society that exists to do vampires business in the human world, and they are paid extremely well." Marilyn laughed and added, "We couldn't afford them."

"What if they tell others about us?"

"They can't, or they would immediately be killed vampire law. Humans can't hide their thoughts from us."

"A lot of talk of killing!"

Marilyn's voice lowered, and she whispered, "We are killers. Something I haven't come to terms with yet. We are Michaels guardians, assassins here on earth, Heaven's killers. Our purpose is to kill evil wherever we find it."

They continued to walk toward the front of the house and toward the gravel road. Marilyn turned and looked up toward the top of the trees. As Shawn was starting to wonder what she was doing, he sensed what she had—Anne was returning.

Anne flew over the trees and came down ten feet from him. As she came close to the ground, she turned and landed, one foot in front of the other, like a gymnast. She was wearing form-fitting black pants with black leather boots that went to the top of her calves. A long, black leather jacket ended at her knees. She also wore a tan blouse that had a small amount of blood splattered on the chest, with few drops of blood on her jacket. She smiled and gave him a look of concern, then walked over to Marilyn and kissed her passionately on the mouth.

"I hope you two have been behaving yourselves," Anne said with a teasing grin. "Have you been catching up with Shawn, talking about old times?"

"Yes, we have been talking all night," Marilyn said. "Thanks again for what you did."

Anne took Marilyn in her arms and brushed the hair from her face. "You left me no choice, love, but he doesn't look good."

Suddenly Anne was in front of Shawn. She startled him, and he took a step back.

"Have you given some thought about feeding? You are going to need blood soon. I don't think you're going to have a lot of time to decide."

"I have been thinking about it. I don't know if I can kill people. I just don't know!"

"Pity, we won't have you around. That would hurt Marilyn very much," Anne said. "I want you to consider this—I will be taking Marilyn to feed soon."

"You're going to feed! You're going to survive for yourself and me!" Marilyn shouted. "I didn't beg for your life so you would die a horrible death. I will pour the blood down you myself. Believe me, Shawn, I can do it."

"Calm down, love," Anne said. "Shawn will have to decide for himself. I didn't choose him in a way that other changelings are chosen, and he will either survive or perish. He might not have the mentality to be a vampire. He might not have the stamina to travel through the centuries as a vampire. In the next few days, we will see, but you don't have much time, Shawn. One week at the most. You can already feel the fire in your stomach, can't you?"

"I can feel it. I don't even know if I have the strength to kill a human and take his blood."

"You must make your decision soon, and then I will give you some of my blood," Anne said. "The sun is going to rise. Take Shawn inside, Marilyn. I am going for a swim."

Shawn's thoughts were in turmoil. What if Anne was right? Maybe he shouldn't be a vampire, he didn't ask for this. He didn't know if he even wanted to be a vampire, just let himself succumb, and that would be the end of all this. But, he didn't want to make Marilyn unhappy; where was that instinct to survive? It wasn't like him to quit. He never used to give up at anything. Since Kristen's and his daughter's deaths, he had lost that will to survive. His final thoughts always came back to survive, though. Learn how to deal with this, he told himself, and live.

He watched Anne glide to the lake, barely above the lawn, not taking a step. There was a small beach with some lawn chairs. Anne started to undress, and then she was standing naked, a beautiful woman with an exquisite body. Her skin looked so soft and supple, almost like it was brand new. He wanted to touch her skin, caress it, but strangely, he felt some force holding him back from her.

"Hope you decide to live," Anne turned and said. "You should go inside now. I want you to sleep in the couch, not on the bed. You can sleep on the other side, away from Marilyn and me if you want. Marilyn, would you tell Linda that I have clothes for her to wash?"

He watched Anne walk into the water, then dive and pierce the water with her beauty. Her formed streaked through the water just below the surface. She then broke the surface, traveled thirty feet into the air, and dove back into the water. *How amazing, and it does look like fun,* he thought.

He went back to the house, and as he was entering, he looked back and saw the sunlight as it came over the horizon. He saw the morning mist that hung over the lake and a beautiful woman swimming in the water. The sun made his eyes burn, and a wave of nausea came over him. Despite the countless years, she has existed, doing whatever she must to live, the vampire was enjoying herself, taking an early morning swim as if she hadn't a care. Maybe he should choose to survive after all

.

Chapter Four

S hawn returned to the bedroom, and Marilyn went to talk to the woman servant. He entered the bathroom to prepare himself for bed and noticed men's clean, blue pajamas and a robe hanging on a hook. One of the sinks had a man's toiletries, including a new toothbrush, but no razor. He splashed water on his face, washed, and brushed his teeth, drank some water, and discovered it still tasted cool and refreshing. His vampire's face stared back at him, when he looked into the mirror, his teeth perfectly white with no cavities, and he felt his smooth face, and realized, still no whiskers. He looked pale and exhausted, his eyes with dark circles, but he did look younger, maybe thirty.

Shawn was careful not to show his vampire teeth and eyes—he wanted to sleep. He dressed in the pajamas, went to the couch, and allowed himself to fall backward, landing softly on the cushions. *How comfortable this is,* he thought. The pleasant scent of Anne and Marilyn filled his nose. Vampire sleep came quickly, and as usual with strange dreams.

It was late morning, and he woke to low moans of pleasure. The top of the couch was down, covering the box in the floor where they slept. This is where people got the idea for coffins. He looked over and saw Marilyn's head travel back up Anne's body, and then emerge from the covers.

Marilyn startled him; she wore her vampire face. Anne took her head and guided it to her neck. Marilyn's mouth closed on Anne's neck, and she fed briefly. Shawn saw dark red blood forming around her lips and trickling down Anne's neck. Marilyn licked the excess blood from her wet, red mouth, and Anne's bloodstained neck, and then lay next to her. He heard her say, "I love you."

Anne held Marilyn and turned her head to look at Shawn. Her eyes were penetrating, always pulling at him, trying to show him what he was, and drawing him into her world. She was still searching his head, seeking to learn as much as she could about him. Shawn forced himself to turn away, to close out their world, and fall back to sleep.

When he woke again, it was early evening, and he was alone. He went to the common room and sensed that Anne was in her art studio. Marilyn was down a small hallway in a sitting room watching television. He continued to explore the house and found a large dance studio with a stereo system and an old saloon piano, with a metal tag that read, "Carson City 1858". He sat down and started to play. It was tuned and sounded reasonably pleasant. Shawn played a couple of old songs from his past. When he finished, he sensed Marilyn and Anne standing behind him.

"That was beautiful," Marilyn said.

"Yes, it was, I didn't know you could play so well," Anne said. "I heard those songs before, but never played like that."

"My mother was a music teacher, and I came from a musical family," he explained, "My sister is an accomplished classical pianist."

Shawn started to stand but felt weak. He quickly sat down, a fever raging inside that burned at him.

"You can feel the fire now. I can sense it," Anne said.

"You have to finish the change!" Marilyn warned. "Anne is taking me to Spokane tomorrow to hunt, and you are coming with me if I have to drag you there!"

"Marilyn, the decision must come from him. Shawn, listen to me, you should decide about the blood—there is little time left. This I can feel."

Shawn had already decided he was going to survive and try to live this new life. When he saw the love that Marilyn had for Anne, and when he realized that Marilyn liked being a vampire—he knew now she would rather be a vampire than human—he had to trust her judgment, there was no choice. Now, he had to face the act itself, to kill a human, a bad one, he hoped.

"I will go with you to kill and take blood!" Shawn said with hesitation in his voice. "I will do my best, but I don't know if I can do this. God help me."

"There is no god to help you with this," Anne said. "The Archangel Michael expects you to use the life force you have been given to feed on evil. That is what the angels expect of you. I will be with you to show you how, and when it's done, you will feel different about blood. You will then realize what you are."

"I know what I am—I'm a person trying to survive," he answered.

Anne gave Shawn a stern look. "You are far greater than a person now, and I don't want to hear you say that again. You are a vampire, a guardian—accept this. Let us have some tea in the sitting room. You can rest there."

"I will be with you," Marilyn promised. "It will only take once, and the next time it will be easier. You will see! I promise, and then you will start your life as a vampire. We will be together!"

The news flickered on the television; the human world went on without him. He was a vampire, and he must learn to kill again, but he felt tired, and he didn't feel like some mighty creature that walked the dark night. He went back to the couch, exhausted. He was going to feed, yet the thought made him sick to his stomach. He could not imagine how he was going to suck the blood from a human. When the time came, would the courage come? Soon he would find out, or he would die. Shawn felt tired, very tired, and went back to bed to hide in his sleep.

He awoke the next evening and went to the bathroom to wash. Anne and Marilyn were showering, and the sight of their bodies didn't arouse him. His thoughts were racing about the coming unpleasant events. Could he accomplish this terrible mission? He didn't know. The idea of biting a person on the neck, with those teeth, seemed like a very uncertain task to undertake.

"Shawn, there is tea in the kitchen. It will warm your insides," Anne shouted from the shower. "You will find it to be a soothing, pleasant sensation. We will be leaving by car soon."

His insides warmed that he did not need — they already felt hot. He went to the kitchen, and there sat a steaming pot of tea. He poured himself a large cup and watched the steam float from the surface and disappear, and then drank a couple of swallows. Anne was right. It was a pleasant sensation for a vampire and soothed his new blood sac. He started to laugh; the absurdity of all this caught him funny.

They drove to Spokane in the limousine and parked in a deserted, industrial section of the city, rusted metal signs, faded white lines, and drab weeds growing from the cracks in the old blacktop pavement. Anne tapped on the window, separating them from the driver's seat. Daren slid the little window open.

"Wait here for us," Anne told him. "We will be gone for a while."

"Yes, ma'am," Daren answered.

The servant was looking at him, and Shawn sensed he was amused. He concentrated on seeing what was in his head, and a thought came through: They are taking the scared fledgling to feed and kill for the first time. Shawn felt a fit of quick, hot anger, and his eyes narrowed. Maybe they turned. He wasn't sure. He was not in the best of moods. The man quickly turned away. Shawn sensed more of what the man was thinking. How stupid he was, young vampires were the most dangerous to mortals.

Anne slid the window shut, turned, and placed her hand on Shawn's cheek, surprising him with a caring and loving voice. "You are going to have to be strong tonight. Focus yourself and control your fear. Allow your vampire instincts to guide you. They will show you the way. See the blood in your mind's eye, the color, the texture, feel the thirst, the need you have for blood. Follow me and follow my instructions. Marilyn, stay with him and make sure he doesn't fall until he feeds."

"I don't know if I have the strength to do this," he countered. His mind was racing, trying to think of excuses so he wouldn't have to drink blood. His thoughts swam in a sea of uncertainty.

"I will help you with that. Drink some of my blood — it will give you the strength you need."

Anne placed her hand on the back of his head and guided his mouth to her neck. He could smell her scent; her smooth skin was so inviting and sensual. He could feel himself change, and his blood-teeth grew. His mouth closed on her neck. He felt his teeth slide into her, his lips pressing against the softness of her skin, the wetness of the blood flowing into him. Marilyn grasping his hand. He immediately tasted the sweetness and the power of her blood. It was sweet nectar to him, and his body came alive.

"You see, taking blood is not hard," Anne whispered in his ear.

They walked down a wide alley between two tall, red-brick warehouses. At the end of the lane, they came to a lower, two-story brick warehouse. The abandoned building was old, all the windows broken, and the sun-bleached bricks of the walls were starting to crumble. Anne jumped to the roof with no effort at all, and then Marilyn did the same. Shawn stood and stared up at them.

"Think of jumping to a point and simply jump! Don't forget to concentrate on slowing down when you land!" Marilyn yelled down to him.

He could tell Marilyn was nervous for him, but he followed her instructions. He was a little high, but it worked. Anne was searching the horizon with her eyes, moving her head, searching for a feeling, a sense she had learned to detect centuries ago. She stopped and pointed.

"We will go this way. Shawn, follow me, and Marilyn, stay next to him," Anne ordered. "We will be moving fast, so concentrate on keeping up. When you jump to the next building, keep your arc low."

This was the seedy part of town, and Shawn looked at the many flat roofs of the old, two-story row houses. Anne started to run, and then Marilyn said, "go."

He gathered speed as he ran. He was running faster than he had ever run in his mortal life. His peripheral vision became a blur as he focused his new sight in front of him. The air rushed by his head and ears. He would jump, land, and keep running. Sometimes he would stumble, but he was learning quickly. Anne slowed—they had entered an area of sleazy bars full of bikers. They stopped on a bar roof; Anne pointed to a roof a couple more buildings down the street. She took hold of Shawn, rose slowly into the night air, and floated to the roof as Marilyn followed.

Anne released him, and he walked to the back of the brick building, looked over the parapet down at the old, wooden back door, the concrete back yard, and the dilapidated shed. They heard a terrible yelling coming from the first floor of the building and he turned to look at Anne, who now had the look of a deadly predator. Never had he seen her like this; there was a frightening beauty about her. She looked vicious, and he would not have wanted to run into her in a dark alley when he was mortal.

She spoke directly to him: "When they come out, we will decide which one will be yours. Listen, think about what you want to do, and then do it. When you jump, use a controlled descent into the human's body, concentrate on your speed, think of slowing, and you will. You will hit the human with just enough force to knock him out, and then you should drain him as quickly as you can. Remember this always— spit the last mouthful onto the puncture points so they will heal." She waited for him to nod in understanding, and then continued. "There are three men in the building. You must always know who is around when you feed. You must account for every human. Always know where the humans are in the feeding area. You never want to be seen feeding by another human. That is how all the terrible stories started about vampires."

Shawn was feeling sick. He looked away, concentrating on the black, roofing tar that covered his shoes. The same shoes he wore the night Anne turned him. He didn't know if he could do this. It didn't feel right—it felt like murder. Shawn looked at Marilyn; she was afraid for him. Suddenly, a couple of gunshots rang out. This startled him and woke him from his daze.

"Now, there's only two," Anne said. "Marilyn, you take one, and Shawn can have the other. You can do this, Shawn."

Two bikers came out the back door laughing about "Stupid Fred." They lit cigarettes and started to talk about shooting Fred in the dick before they shot him in the head.

Anne hissed, "This is what we feed on. Lucifer's children. Sense them, Shawn. You can feel their depraved nature, the evil that permeates them. They care nothing for life—only their needs, their desires, and giving pain in the dark one's name."

43

The first guy had short, blond, greasy hair. He was muscular and had a black, jagged tattoo going up the side of his neck. A rough man in his mid-thirties. The second was older, with long, black-and-gray hair, and a mustache that progressed into a long, stringy beard that ended just above a large beer-belly. Both dressed in regular biker clothes: black, biker boots, blue jeans, black t-shirts, and faded dungaree biker jackets, which were sleeveless — for the summer — bearing an insignia on the back. Shawn could see a pistol stuck in the pants of one of the men.

"You can have the younger one—he's not as foul," Marilyn told him.

"Thanks," he mumbled.

"Are you ready, Shawn?" Anne asked. "Remember to allow your vampire senses to guide you. Do it now! Feed and live!"

He remained frozen, looking at the two men talking, laughing. The older man turned his head, and a brown, shiny glob of thick tobacco juice squirted from his mouth. Shawn looked at Marilyn. She had changed — a vampire ready to strike — waiting for him. He stared at her, marveling at her look, and then a gentle shove to his shoulder from Anne.

Shawn knew these two strangers had just murdered with no remorse. He had to do this for his survival — his precious survival and for Marilyn. He felt himself starting to rise—to stand up!

Anne was on him, moist lips at his ear. "Feed, Shawn, and live for Marilyn. Don't make her suffer. Mortals owe us, Heaven wants this, and you are far greater now than these evil creatures. I want you to live. I want to know you better."

Shawn felt himself change, a bloodlust coming over him. He wanted this man, and he wanted his blood. The need to crush him for the sick evil he felt coming from him, for what the man had brought to his world. Shawn stepped on the parapet and projected his new supernatural senses. A familiar evil came to him, the same darkness he felt years ago in a rice paddy. He fell forward and traveled like an arrow straight toward the blond man, told himself to slow, but he struck the man and drove him into the concrete. The man was unconscious, with a large gash on the back of his head. He heard another thud, then a quick cry. It was Marilyn, colliding into the second man.

The man had no weight at all to him; he could lift this man and throw him fifty feet if he wanted. Shawn held him and exposed his flesh; a scar ran down his neck where he planned to bite. The man smelled of alcohol, cigarettes, and cheap cologne. Everything slowed; the bloodlust was with him. He needed this blood. He could see the pores of his now translucent skin, the veins, and arteries in his neck, as his fangs came down on the biggest one. The blood shot into his mouth and poured down his throat. He could feel his throat widen to allow the thick blood to flow quickly.

At first, it tasted like blood should, thick, metallic, and salty. Then it became a sweet flavor, like pure honey from a beehive. There was a tremendous roar in his head, a feeling of euphoria and power. The blood flipped a switch in him. He felt energized, a quickening of his life force, and so much more alive. The beating of the man's heart slowed, and then it stopped. He sucked on the man's neck until no more blood came to his mouth, and then spit the last mouthful back onto the man's neck and watched in amazement the puncture wounds disappear.

Shawn raised his head and gave a cry to the night to release his built-up tension and fear. He felt himself shift out of this reality and into the heavens, then back again, and saw spirits flowing around him. Anne floated to the concrete, large transparent wings on her back, and the reason for vampire's swift flight. Shawn dropped the man to the ground; his dead prey's eyes stared back. He turned and looked at Marilyn; syrupy red blood covered her mouth and chin, her eyes burning blue, a vampire, a killer.

"You fed! The change is done!" Marilyn cried in relief.

Anne quickly came and flung their lifeless bodies back into the house. She jumped to the roof, leaned over the parapet, and gave the two bloodied vampires orders. "Let's go, we have to leave. Humans are coming."

Marilyn was smiling at Shawn, her look of relief unmistakable. Marilyn jumped to join Anne on the roof, and Shawn followed. They ran after Anne, back the way they had come. Midway, Anne stopped and turned her head to the east. She had sensed something, and after a moment, she whispered, "Wolves. Four of them. A hundred miles to the east."

Marilyn stopped and turned her head, straining to sense what Anne had sensed, her eyes searching the night.

"Yes, I feel them," she confirmed.

Shawn turned and looked in the same direction. "What could be the problem with wolves? What do you mean by 'wolves'?"

Anne then explained, "Shape shifters that have turned themselves into large wolves. For the promise to kill vampires, Lucifer gave them the gift of great strength, quickness, and smell. They must live out their existences as wolves until they die, and then they turn back to their human forms. They can cross from Manitoba into North Dakota and Minnesota. That is where vampires allow them, and no place else. They are too far west."

"Why are they so far west?" Marilyn asked

"They are young males, following the scent of young vampires. I have sent them a message to turn back—they are in my territory. Maybe they smelled you and Shawn. Who knows?"

"How do you know this?" Shawn asked.

Anne looked at him with her vampire eyes; he could feel her enter his mind.

"Many forces are traveling through the planes of existence," Anne told him. "Project your mind outward. Feel these forces. Attach your senses to these forces and ride them. Learn how the different energies feel. Let these energies take you where they go, and then you can start to learn. You can do this. Abandon your human expectations—you are a vampire. Look at me! Sense my life force!" She had opened herself to him, and he could see her completely. He gasped at the immense strength of her life force. It was almost overpowering. "Yes, I feel it!"

"Now stay with it. Ride my mental energy and see the wolves. Can you see them?" Anne asked him as she projected her senses toward the wolves. Shawn could hear Anne in his mind telling him to follow her. He willed himself to stay with her energy, and he did, to his amazement.

"Yes, I see them. This is unbelievable!" Shawn shouted.

"Practice this, Shawn. Experience your new vampire senses. I will help you." The vampires continued to travel back to the car. At the edge of the last roof, Anne spoke again. "Marilyn, go to the car and tell Daren to take you home. Shawn and I will be along shortly. Don't leave the house."

Shawn could sense Marilyn's amusement. "Have fun, Shawn, you're about to find out that Anne's a hands-on teacher."

Anne took hold of him, as if he had no weight at all, put him on her back, and flew through the cool night air. He could see the lights below. They passed almost as soon as he saw them. He felt the wind on his face, whipping his clothes only slightly. Somehow, his vampire body diverted most of the wind around him. He also realized Anne no longer repulsed him. Now, he felt a need for her. They landed on a bluff a half-mile back from a brook at the edge of a pine forest. Four giant wolves trotted around a bend. Shawn could see the wolves were three times the size of regular wolves. The wolves stopped, looked at the bluff, and communicated with each other.

"Use your vampire senses to learn about these creatures. Feel their life force. Feel them so you will always be aware of them when they are near. They are vicious killers—especially to young vampires like you and Marilyn."

"Yes, I feel them!"

"The wolves will not bother you now because I am with you. I sent them a message that they are in my territory. They are to leave and not come back, and if they do, I will take their lives. If I were alone, I would kill one of them to make myself clear."

Shawn looked at Anne. "You talk of this so nonchalantly." Then he briefly sensed anger from Anne. This surprised him.

She told him straight. "I am a killer. I have killed thousands of times in my life. There was a time early in my life I might have killed you. You are a killer now and can be vicious and cruel. Heaven has made us that way. We are the killers of the warrior choir of angels. There will be times you will become indifferent to humans when you realize their lack of interest in the evil in this world." Anne reached out and touched Shawn's cheek. "I'm sorry I scared you. I will always protect you so you can grow and learn what you are. So, you can learn you are a shadow angel made by the power of the angels. I will teach you what those angels expect of you. I will make you more powerful than you can imagine so that you are ready for these dangers. But you must give yourself to me in body and mind." She looked at the wolves. "Someday, when you are by yourself, and still young, if you sense these creatures, you are to get away from them. Never try to engage them—they will run you down. They hunt young vampires in packs. That is probably what they are doing now. You may kill one or two, but they will never attack you by themselves—they are always in a group. These creatures have killed many young vampires. Remember, get away from them, and survive."

The wolves continued along the brook, and then picked up speed until they became a blur. "We are going to run. I want you to follow me. I want you to see for yourself what these creatures are. I will do nothing you are not capable of doing. Stay behind me—understand?"

"Yes, I will do the best I can."

Anne bit her wrist. "Drink a little. It will give you more strength."

Shawn took her hand and took two mouthfuls of blood, and then she pulled her wrist away. Anne stepped off the bluff, and Shawn followed. They fell thirty feet to the ground and landed in a crouching position, one foot in front of the other. Anne's blue eyes flashed at him, and then she started her run, with Shawn following.

Anne slowly increased her speed, and Shawn matched her. Faster, they ran toward the brook. Anne jumped the creek with no effort and Shawn followed. He hit the soft, moist ground, rolled, and sprung to his feet. Anne was following the stream, going in the same direction as the wolves. Watching her silky brown hair flying in the wind, he managed to stay with her, her buttocks tightening and relaxing with each powerful stride.

Objects became a blur, and his vision funneled down to focus only on what was in front of him. He surmised this was a vampire's way of maintaining clarity at high speeds. Anne jumped fallen, rotted trees, and then boulders, and Shawn followed, feeling exhilarated. He never imagined such a thrill running this way. They would leap from side to side, over the brook, following the best path. Soon he saw the wolves in front of them; they had caught the menacing beasts. The wolves stopped and gathered, and Shawn immediately felt their fear.

The grey and white wolf stepped forward and pawed at the ground. Suddenly, he spoke, "Immortal, we were leaving as you asked."

Shawn's mouth fell open, dumbfounded.

"What are you doing here, wolf?" Anne demanded.

"Our apologies, vampire. We got lost."

Shawn could feel they were lying; he also could feel they wanted him. They longed to sink their foul, yellow teeth into him and tear him apart. This was how they gained favor with their leader. Shawn was a delicacy to them, and this was chilling for him.

"You're liars! I would kill all of you if my changeling weren't here. Now leave quickly."

The wolves turned and immediately left. Anne turned to Shawn. "Remember what you saw and felt here! Come, let's go home. You look sick again."

Shawn climbed onto Anne's back and they started their flight back to the house. What a night this had been—he had fed and started to feel better, and then seen the wolves. As they were flying, Shawn realized his face was buried into Anne's intoxicating neck. He felt aroused, her soft bottom next to his groin. He smelled her scent, took her essence in with his vampire senses, brushed his lips against her neck, tasting her, which only heightened his lust. She had made him hard. He moved his hands quickly between her thighs, searching, feeling her, and then thought better of it.

He shook his head and forced a deep breath of air to clear his cloudy mind. He brought his hands back to her stomach as she glanced back and smiled at him. Anne was always in control; she could manipulate him whenever she wanted.

Over the next few weeks, Anne would take Shawn to feed a couple times per week. Sometimes she would feed, and most of the time, Marilyn would feed, but if they only found one victim, Shawn took the nourishing blood. Anne continued her instructions on how to feed. Stealth was the name of the game—never be seen by another human while taking blood, they reminded him. You might have to kill innocents. Anne told him a vampire her age only needed to feed once a month. Once Shawn got his strength, young vampires like him and Marilyn would have to feed once a week.

Marilyn had been right—the repulsion he felt for her, and Anne disappeared after his first feeding. He still slept separately from Anne and Marilyn in the couch, though. Anne would invite him when she was ready. At times, he heard Anne and Marilyn making love. It was apparent that Marilyn loved Anne. She gave her this new, superior life, and she was content living this way. He still had terrible bouts of guilt about killing humans, still felt killing was wrong, and he would struggle with his conscience when he fed on humans. Always trying to convince himself, these were evil people, and the world was better without them.

Two months into his life as a vampire, he woke to a warm, sensual feeling in his loins. He heard a soft whisper in his mind, a siren's voice of a woman calling in the distance. Anne was in his head, stimulating him, telling him it was time for them to know each other in another way.

Shawn turned over, and Anne was staring at him, drawing him to her, the soft lullaby of come to me. She threw her covers back, naked and beautiful, her arms held out to him, inviting him to her. Shawn moved over and embraced her as she took complete control of him. He kissed her long and intensely, and then she directed his head to her neck. He could feel his teeth penetrate, tasting the texture of her skin as the blood flooded into his mouth and down his throat.

Suddenly, he came through a mist and was standing looking at a vampire woman, and behind her was the ocean. He knew her name was Dianthe. The woman wore ancient clothes, and somehow, he had traveled back to ancient times.

"I love being with you, Anwen. The vampire told him as she stroked his cheek.

"I will always love you." It was the voice of Anne, and he was seeing through her. He was her, and she was him. *What now! How could this be,* he thought.

They walked in silence with the woman on the beach and felt the water rushing over Anne's feet. Suddenly Dianthe stopped. "Can you feel it?"

"Yes, I feel it. What is it?"

"Amon is killing Belos!" Dianthe cried. The demon has found us.

He sensed the terrible hurt in Anne's head, the anguish of losing a dear friend, and then the realization that this Amon was an Esmanaa demon.

"No! Anwen, hide your thoughts—cloak your mind!" Screamed Dianthe.

It was too late. A terrible sense of evil overwhelmed Shawn and grew stronger, the closer this demon came.

"The demon knows where we are, my love. He is coming. Use the water to hide from him—go deep. I will distract him!" Dianthe pleaded.

"No, let me stay to help!"

"He will kill you—you can't face him. You are too young, and he is too strong."

Shawn felt the vampire woman take hold of Anne, and amazingly she threw them out over the water. They traveled hundreds of feet before falling into the sea.

On entering, Shawn saw an explosion of bubbles forming in front of their eyes. They traveled underneath for a distance and then came to the surface, the top of Anne's head and eyes rising above the water. Shawn felt wave after wave of intense evil. Nausea that permeated Anne's body. They saw the demon come over the horizon, and Dianthe start her escape into the night sky to lead the Esmanaa away from Anne. She had not traveled far when Amon contacted her. As a vulture strikes a dove, the monster brought the vampire to the ground. They listened to her screams as the demon mauled her before taking her heart and ending her six-hundred-year life. He was a grotesque creature, short and stout with black eyes, smooth greenish skin with no texture, and the creature was now looking for Anne.

Shawn felt Anne's grief and fear, it paralyzed her, and they drifted toward the bottom of the sea. Shawn heard her praying to The Mother. She asked this mother to protect her and hide her from the demon. He felt her grief and heard her scream into the water. Down deeper, they drifted toward the seafloor and the cool darkness. Shawn felt the cold currents catching and pushing Anne's body in different directions as they descended.

When they reached the bottom, Anne dug into the sand, shell, and coral to make a hiding spot—to bury herself in the seafloor. Shawn again heard her praying to The Mother to shield her from the demon, begging this angel not to let the beast find her. Shawn felt that Anne was ashamed that she didn't go back to help Dianthe, but the monster would have killed her. Then another one of her thoughts came to him, was she a coward like they said of her maker Bricius. They laid on the seafloor, and Anne sobbed, her lover gone, and now a young vampire on her own again.

Through the day, they lay in Anne's underwater grave, and at last, she needed air.

Slowly, they rose up through the seawater, broke the surface, and sensed the demon had given up and moved on. They floated just above the surface of the water, moving toward shore, scanning everything with their vampire senses. They found Dianthe's remains. Anne fell to her knees and cried, why hadn't she stayed with her? He heard her sob never again would she leave her lovers, and never again abandon them. And she swore she would kill these demons. They scattered Dianthe's dirt and asked Michael to show her mercy and kindness in her next life.

Shawn woke and was on top of Anne. He had entered her and was making passionate love to her and still could feel her in his mind. He fell off her, rolled, and laid in a fetal position shaking. Anne's powerful arm wrapped around him, pulled him to her and held him. He heard her whisper in his ear, "You are a rider of vampire blood. This is very rare for a vampire—you must be careful. You will have to control this, or you will be taken to places and events you might not want to experience."

For the first time, he felt her long, powerful teeth enter deep into his neck. There was no pain; she took very little of his blood and then licked the wound, so it healed instantly. Then he heard Anne's voice in his mind as if she was talking to him. What did you see?

"It was a long time ago. I saw a vampire name Dianthe and a demon kill her. I was in you!"

"I was a young vampire and lived in Athens. She was my first vampire love. The demon was Esmanaa, and his name was Amon. You must be brave, someday, I think the angels want you to fight the demons."

Shawn then asked, "What did you mean that your maker, Bricius, was a coward?"

"The Esmanaa demons killed Herit, and Bricius was tasked to carry on the fight and to make vampires for the Herit Covenant. The Archangel gave Bricius high power to fight the demons, but it turned out he was afraid of them. He ran from the beasts, and, being so ashamed, he didn't make any vampires in his long life. I was the only one. He fell out of favor with Michael. He disappointed the angels. The only thing he did was give me his powerful blood and leave the rest behind in a gold vase.

Chapter Five

T hree months had passed since the change, and Shawn was
   adjusting to his new vampire life. Mentally, he was also
improving and hadn't taken a drink since his turning. The pain he felt
for Kristen and Christine was starting to lessen, that terrible wound
finally beginning to heal. The vampire life force he now had was
indeed a great healer. One evening, he found that a new piano was
placed in the sitting room of the mansion. Anne told Shawn that a
vampire's life was long, and they must have interests to occupy
themselves.

Shawn felt from the beginning the secure connection between
Anne and him. He had recovered from his experience traveling back
in her life by occupying himself learning the vampire way. He learned
to control those types of travels. Anne could be gentle but was a much
different creature than he had ever imagined walking this world. Her
pure blood gave him strength, and she was very good to Marilyn and
him—but she was definitely in charge.

A few weeks later, Anne informed them that Hector Nicolas was
holding a gathering for her. The Vampire Council had selected Anne
to be their newest member, a very high honor in the vampire world.
An ancient had decided to leave this world and join Michael's legions
in Heaven. She told them they would be going in one week, traveling
there by limousine. This would be the first time Shawn would meet
other vampires. The thought of this made him nervous.

"I will make your greetings for you, and you must be respectful.
Do you understand?" Anne told him.

Shawn gave his standard answer, "Yes, Anne, I will do my best."

"I will help him," Marilyn told Anne. "I will tell him what he needs
to know and how to behave."

Shawn didn't like having to behave in a certain way, but he remembered this was a big night for Anne, so he would be on his best behavior. And he certainly didn't want to upset older vampires.

Hector Nicolas was a two-thousand-year-old vampire with a big family living on a large estate in the middle of Oregon's Ochoco Forest. He was a member of the Vampire Council and was in charge of all vampires in the Northern Hemisphere. Hector's family consisted of eleven living members, and he came from the Barcelona area of Spain. He had two changelings, Adriana and Teresa, and they had changelings of their own and so on, resulting in eleven members of his family.

The night came for their trip and they left early in the evening, so they would arrive before sunrise. Daren and Linda had everything ready for their trip. Shawn's mind was busy thinking about other vampires — what it would be like to be around that many of his fellow beings. Marilyn told him not to worry — that older vampires would ignore him. Anne briefed him more on how he should behave, and Marilyn was giving him tips on the ride to Hector's estate.

"Don't stare at them, or you will invite mind probes," Marilyn said. "And don't flirt with the females."

"I certainly won't be flirting, I promise you. What if they are looking at me?"

"Then smile and gently divert your gaze away from them," Anne instructed. "I know you have been practicing your psychic abilities, but don't try it on the vampires there. That is rude in the vampire world, especially from a young vampire."

"I'll stand behind you, and they probably won't notice me."

"Probably not, but the way I changed you has gathered some interest," Anne answered.

"What do you mean? What's so special about it?"

"Vampires watch humans over time, fall in love with them before we select them," Anne teased. "They don't have an automobile crash and have a changeling beg for their life."

The trip went on with Anne and Marilyn talking about a few eccentric vampires they knew. Shawn raised his window curtain and watched the scenery go by. Colors were far deeper now, and he realized there were so many more layers to colors. Many different hues, he had never seen before. He watched the owls flying in the moonlit sky a mile away. He even focused his hearing on the night animals scampering in the forest as they rode by.

They eventually turned left onto a paved country road and drove a reasonable distance back into the woods. Shawn was feeling anxious in anticipation of the meetings to come. They turned right onto a wide, well-maintained graveled road.

The car continued traveling a couple of miles when he noticed somebody had cleared away the underbrush in the woods. He could see a canopy in the underside of the trees. Then he noticed cleared paths back into the woods and saw two men dressed in black military clothes with assault rifles patrolling.

"Those are Crimmian guards," Anne told him. "All council members have guards if they want them."

"Are you going to have guards?" Shawn asked.

"No, I don't need human males for protection."

"Are we almost there?" Shawn asked nervously.

"We are. Stay with Marilyn and do what she tells you. You will be fine. I won't let anything happen to you."

As Anne finished talking, they left the woods and came onto a big lawn with a circular driveway. The house was a large, three-story, red-brick mansion with a big white porch. There was a large garage to the left, with many limousines already parked inside.

A man with a half-smile stood at the top of the stairs on the porch. He had black, well-groomed hair and an olive complexion—a very handsome, dashing man, and he, too, looked to be around thirty. It struck Shawn how young he looked for an older vampire of his stature, but vampires did not age. The slowness of their metabolism allowed for everlasting rejuvenation.

Daren came around to the door where Anne was sitting and opened it. Anne got out, and Daren gave a little bow. Marilyn and Shawn followed her out of the car and up the porch stairs. Shawn walked behind Marilyn, trying to keep out of sight. "It is so good to see you, Anne," Hector called out. "I have tomorrow eve all planned for you and let me be the first to congratulate you."

"It is good to see you, too, Hector," Anne said. "Thank you! How have you been? I hope you haven't had to deal with too many problems."

"I am doing well. And no, it has been quiet since the Vietnam War," Hector said. "The calm before the storm...who knows? The Esmanaa must be hibernating. No one has seen or heard from them since."

"Hector, you remember, Marilyn," Anne said.

"Yes, I do. How are you, my dear?" Hector said with a flash of a forced smile.

"I am fine, sir. It's an honor to see you again," Marilyn answered.

"Anne, is this male your new changeling?" Hector asked. "I heard about him. You will have to give me the details later. Ahmoss is here and most of the council as well. He also has some questions for you about your new changeling."

"This is Shawn, Hector, and he handled the change quite well."

"That's surprising," Hector said as he turned to walk into the house. "Come. Adrianna and Teresa want to greet you, and then a servant will show you to your suite."

Shawn's first impression of this vampire inspired dislike, but he quickly banished the thought to the back of his mind. They followed Hector into the house onto a grand foyer with three large, white marble statues and two paintings of a young man and woman in medieval attire. There were two more vampires—Latin women who stood ready to greet Anne.

"Welcome, Anne. I hope you are well," Teresa said.

"Greetings, Anne. Your hard work over the centuries has paid off," Adriana said. "I'm very happy for you."

"Thank you. I do appreciate both of you coming to help me celebrate. It is an honor."

"We wouldn't have missed it," Adriana said. "Would we, Teresa?"

"No, we wanted to be here," Teresa said. "Remember, I told you that you would be a council member someday. Are these your two changelings? I heard a beautiful story about these two. You always had a big heart."

"Ah, here's the servant," Hector said. "Take our guest to the red room. I think you will be comfortable. It is a good size room with a large couch. Anne, come to the study when you're settled. Ahmoss and the council are there."

Shawn felt shaken and was grateful that the servant had come. They followed the servant up a flight of stairs to the second floor, continued down the long hallway, and arrived at a pair of ornate, oak doors stained a deep cherry. Entering the room, Shawn saw why they called it the red room.

The carpet was red, and so were the draperies. The vampire couch was large and made of polished oak with carvings etched into the wood and painted gold. Inside the couch was red, quilted bedding and big, red pillows. He saw a sitting area with a white sofa, three yellow chairs, and a large coffee table set in the middle, with a big bottle of red wine.

Their luggage and clothes sat on top of a bed with a red quilted covering. A gold-painted door led to the bathroom. The walls were covered by white wallpaper with red velvet designs, and the lamps in the room were ornate brass, as were the door latches. Two large glass doors led to a balcony, with large, thick, red drapes ready to cover the doors. Where Shawn came from, they would call it gaudy.

"I'm leaving you two in the room. Shawn, you are not to leave, and Marilyn, stay with him. It looks like I have some questions to answer. Surprisingly, Ahmoss, the head of the Vampire Council, is here."

"Anne, can I have some wine?" Shawn asked. "I could use a glass."

"Yes, you can have wine. I will have some more sent up. I will probably need some when I return."

Anne freshened herself and went to her meeting. Shawn poured Marilyn a glass of wine, and then one for himself.

"Let's go out on the balcony. The weather is perfect," Marilyn told him.

"Good idea. Maybe I can relax."

They took their wine and went out onto the balcony, located at the front corner of the mansion. From the balcony, he could see the driveway and front yard. They drank wine and watched vampires arrive for the party.

"Look, a red Fiat," Shawn said.

A red sports car came roaring up the graveled road, squealed around the curved drive, and stopped in front of the big porch. A young, blond-haired male vampire, wearing blue jeans and a brown leather bomber jacket, stepped out. A valet came running from the garage to offer him aid. The man flipped him the keys, fixed his hair, and headed for the house.

"That's Eric!" Marilyn said. "He is one good-looking vamp, don't you think?"

"Not bad," Shawn replied. "Is he one of your love interests?"

"I don't know, but it will be a long time before I have the chance to find out. I am a young changeling, and Eric is a one-hundred-and-two-year-old vampire. He's also a musician like you—he plays in a vampire band."

"Vampire band? I'd like to see that."

"Our kind has many interests—we need to. Most of us live for a long time."

Eric turned, looked up at them, and waved to Marilyn. She waved back. He gave Shawn a friendly look, then walked up the stairs and disappeared into the house. They continued to drink their wine while more vampires arrived in limousines. *How strange all this is*, Shawn thought. His new life was still hard to accept— vampires, wolves, and now this party with his new brethren everywhere.

Two female vampires flew over the trees, turned, and descended feet-first. Seeing people flying was still surprising and shocking to him. Anne promised him that soon he would be able to fly short distances. As the two vampires descended, the blond vampire was talking to her companion. He heard her asking about the clothes that she was going to borrow for the party. Both vampires were beautiful, but the blonde was extraordinary. Her hair was different shades of blond. The wind caught her silk hair and blew it back to reveal a lovely neck and facial features. Her body was exquisite, and Shawn thought she was stunning.

"Marilyn, do you know who those vampires are?"

"The dark-haired one is Abigail. I don't know who the other one is. Abigail likes to tease, like her maker, Teresa."

"You don't know who the blonde is?" Shawn asked.

"No, I have never seen her, but she is an older vampire—that, I can sense."

Shawn leaned out over the rail of the balcony. "Look how she holds herself, how she walks like she was once nobility."

Shawn wanted to know more about her. Then that familiar woman's voice in his head, *know her for what she is.* He decided to see if he could detect her life force. The blond vampire turned and glared at him. He felt a sharp pain, a slap to his mind. The vampire stood and looked at him as if he were an annoying child that had overstepped his bounds.

She turned, started to walk toward the house, and stopped, looked back at him with a perplexed look as if something had come to her, a recognition. Very briefly in his head he could recognize a thought:

You are the one, after all this time. How could it be?

Her look was penetrating, but soon she turned and walked up the steps. At the top, Shawn felt her emerald eyes flash at him, and he could hear in his mind once more:

Who are you, young one? You are a Herit. Yes, I understand now.

She turned and went into the house.

"What did you do?" Marilyn asked exasperated.

"I tried to sense the blond vampire's life force. I thought if I did it briefly, she wouldn't notice."

"Anne told you not to do anything like that," Marilyn said. "You're lucky that vampire wasn't up here paying you a visit."

They had another glass of wine and continued to watch the vampires arrive. He felt Marilyn's hand slide down his back and onto his bottom. He turned to see she wore her lustful look.

"Did Anne give you permission?" Shawn asked.

"No, she hasn't," Marilyn shrugged and sighed. "Let's go to the couch. I'm tired."

They undressed each other and embraced fell back into the couch and floated onto the soft mattress. Shawn could feel everything about her as she could with him. He loved Marilyn; she was his reason to live a vampire's life. They tasted each other's blood, embraced, and fell to sleep.

Shawn woke while Anne was descending into the couch. A couple of hours had passed since she left, and it was now morning, by the sounds of the birds outside. Wearing a silk, white nightgown and smelling of honeysuckle, she pulled the top of the couch down to close out the light rays breaking through the drawn curtains. Seeing he was awake, she slid over next to him and lay facing him.

"Is everything all right?" Shawn whispered. "Have I gotten you into trouble?"

"No," Anne whispered back. "I had to answer some questions regarding why I have taken two changelings. It is unusual for vampires to have two changelings, but luckily, Ahmoss is a romantic. He is an ancient vampire, and I think he doesn't care that much about what goes on anymore. I have seen this before with old vampires."

"Will there be many vampires at the party?" Shawn nervously inquired.

"There will be thirty guests at the party. Renee, my first changeling, the one that looks like Dianthe, has sent me her love, but she cannot attend the gathering this eve. I am disappointed. She took a changeling herself. Her name is Caitlyn, and she didn't want to bring her around just yet. I was hoping she would come. I have missed her. You are also probably a little young for this too. What did you and Marilyn do to occupy yourselves?"

"We drank wine and watched the guests arrive. Marilyn pointed out Eric and Abigail to me. I also saw a beautiful blond-haired vampire with Abigail. Do you know who she is?"

"The blond vampire is Victoria Kenmare," Anne whispered. "She is an artist like me. I see her sometimes at art shows."

"Victoria…she was stunning."

"She is from Ireland, and she is over seven-hundred-years-old," Anne said with a chuckle. "She came from nobility and lived in a castle. Her father was Lord Edward Draper. She is too old for such a young changeling like you. Already trying to spread that charm of yours, my dear Shawn?

"She acted like she recognized me."

Shawn sensed Anne become serious. "That is interesting! Her maker was Erdin Kenmare. The only vampire to kill an Esmanaa demon. He killed Amon, the beast you saw in my past.

"I saw him when you turned me."

"You did! Erdin Kenmare once was a druid priest that committed sacrifices, Michael turned him, and tasked him to fight the Esmanaa Demons to serve penance for what he had done. He and Victoria have no covenant. Erdin Kenmare had a vast knowledge of the Esmanaa demons. He studied them for thousands of years, but they killed him too. He passed that knowledge onto that blond vampire you saw. And it is said she waits for a champion to pass this knowledge onto and to help her destroy the Esmanaa demons."

"This all sounds very serious, but I don't think I will be killing any demons," Shawn chuckled.

"Not a Demon Slayer, are you?"

"Anne, I have wanted to ask you something for a while…"

"I know what you want to ask—did Marilyn consent to sex with me the first time. Yes, she did. She decided to come with me. She has always had a taste for women, which I sensed immediately. She just didn't know, until I showed her, and I would have never turned her if she didn't have a liking for woman, but she needs men, too."

"What do you need?" Shawn asked.

"I have preferred women most of my life. There haven't been many men. The Roman soldiers made sure of that, and sometimes I think my maker had something to do with it, too. I like making love to you. Maybe you can help me with my man problem. We will see." Anne touched his cheek and smiled.

"I'm sure you know that I love you," Shawn whispered.

"I know. I could tell almost from the beginning. It is partly because of the blood we share, but let us be honest. We were always attracted to each other."

Anne's eyes became sapphire blue and hypnotic; they drew him to her. Her open mouth went to his neck—he could feel the wetness of her lips, the caress of her tongue, the gentle suck before the bite, and two sharp points on his neck as her teeth grew. Slowly, her teeth penetrated his skin, slid past the muscle, and found the artery. His blood filled her mouth; she took only a mouthful and swallowed. He could feel her blood teeth slide back out of his neck and the touch of her tongue as she licked the excess from his neck.

"Soon, my love, you will feel comfortable around vampires. You'll see," Anne whispered. "Take my blood and be brave. This time allow yourself to travel. I want you to see why I prefer women." Anne guided his head to her neck, and he penetrated her and drank and immediately found himself in the mist.

Shawn found himself in the middle of a field, clipping sheep, surrounded by a birch and maple forest. The animals had chewed and beaten down the field grass, and a boy stood next to him. He looked down and saw the arms and hands of a woman, and knew his mental energy was in Anne when she was mortal. He saw, heard, and felt what Anne did.

Five men on horseback rode out of the tree line, and he seemed to know they were two Roman officers, one Roman soldier, and two Saxon mercenaries. They were riding big, Celtic horses, and their sloppy horsemanship showed him they were drunk. The men had ridden the horses hard, and he could see steam coming from their backs, heard the snort of their nostrils.

The men rode toward him and the boy. The boy also saw them, positioned himself in front of Shawn, and said, "Stand behind me, Anwen, and let me do the talking."

"Barbarian peasants," slurred one of the drunken officers to the other. "Is that beauty, your sister, boy? She is a fine little bitch, and you look like a strong, young man. Well-developed and clear-eyed. He would make a good soldier, don't you think, Tullius?"

Tullius leaned forward and squinted, his blood-shot eyes scrutinizing them as if he were at a horse auction looking to buy. "Yes, I think he would make a good soldier." He turned and winked at Decimus.

Tullius turned with a sneer and spoke to the two mercenaries, "Take the boy and follow me back to the camp."

The two mercenaries dismounted with small clubs in hand. As they approached the boy, Decimus yelled, "If you fight us, we will beat you, boy. Don't fight us, or we will beat you bloody and drag you back to our camp."

"We have to resist these men, Darryn!" Anne shouted. "If we don't, we will never see Mother and Father again!"

Shawn saw how Decimus was eyeing them, looking Anne up and down, staring at the slight glisten of sweat on her cleavage from the day's work. He saw Decimus give a filthy wink to the other Roman. *My god, they are going to rape us,* Shawn thought.

Anne and Darryn attacked the two mercenaries. The quick action startled the horses, and they reared, throwing the Roman soldier from his horse. The two Roman officers half-dismounted and half-fell from their horses. Tullius helped the two mercenaries beat and bind Darryn. Decimus and the Roman soldier fought with Anne. She swung at them with her fists and gouged at their eyes with her fingers.

"Don't take my brother, you bastards! You sons of a filthy bitch!" He heard Anne scream at Tullius and the mercenaries. They led Darryn away, bounded, half-walking, and half-dragging behind Tullius' horse.

Shawn knew Anne fought as best she could, but she quickly found herself pinned to the ground. It was late afternoon, and the sun had gone down below the top of the trees. Twilight came over the field. The air was calm with that damp spring chill. The livestock had gone to the far side of the field because of the commotion.

Shawn could feel the dampness from the ground seep through Anne's tunic. He felt her lungs burning from the exertion of the fight. He tasted the blood in her mouth from the blows and heard Anne plead with their tormentors, "Honorable sir, my apologies for my actions. My father is good friends with many Romans at the garrison at Suthfulk. Please, sir, many of these animals you see will go to feed your legions. My family has always served the Romans faithfully. Please let my brother go!"

Decimus said with a sneer, "That is all over now in this horrible land. We are leaving here, and before I go, I am going to have you. Don't resist, and I might let you live."

He could smell the horrible breath, the body odor, and feel the sweat. He felt the rough, filthy hand groping between Anne's thighs.

Shawn wanted to wake himself, but he had to stay with Anne. He could not leave her now.

Decimus laughed and said to the Roman soldier, "Grab her other leg, and we'll bring her to that stump over there by the edge of the woods. We'll bend her over it. I mean to wet my cock with her, and if you help me, I might let you have seconds."

Shawn knew Anne was beginning to feel dizzy and sick to her stomach. He felt the men dragging her, the desperation and terror in her, the field grass and dirt building in her fingers as she clawed at the ground. The men lifted her and forced her over the stump. He heard her screams and tasted the bile that came into her mouth. He knew Anne was faint, and then he listened to the Roman say, "If you pass out, I will beat you to death.

Rough hands groped at her buttocks, and he felt her shame, the pain and burning as the Roman raped her. He felt her eyes filling with tears and heard Decimus' grunts coming from behind. Suddenly, a wind blew across her face, and a feeling of something warm splashed across her cheek. A scream came and went like the wind through her hair. Her hands went free, but he saw no soldier. He felt her fall to the ground, the dampness on her bare bottom.

Decimus was running, climbing onto his horse and riding like there was a ghost after him. The blood on Anne's cheek was not hers; she looked around, there was nobody there, and the field was quiet, except for the sound of the animals, but there was something there. Shawn could feel it, a powerful vampire lurked in the shadows. Nausea overwhelmed Anne as she doubled over, what little that was in her stomach came up, and on to the ground.

You have to leave here, Anne, he thought. *Save yourself.* Anne stood up, straightened her clothes, and took off through the thick birch trees. She came to the brook and washed her face, between her legs, and rinsed her cut mouth.

Shawn found himself back in his body with blood tears running down his cheeks and hate for those men who caused Anne such fear and torment. "I am so sorry, Anne! That was a horrible act to bear!"

"I come from a different time than you. Men were brutal then, especially to women." Anne turned over, moved against him, and pulled his arm over her. "See? I'm much better now."

He felt Marilyn move against his back. Anne pulled the covers over their heads, and sleep took them. Wrapped together, but sadness held him at what he had just experienced.

Shawn woke late. Anne and Marilyn were in the bathroom, getting ready for the party. Arrival time was 11:00 p.m.; he stretched, and reluctantly levitated himself up and onto his feet. That was the extent of his levitating skills. Two silk gowns, one red and one light blue, were on the bed, along with a black suit, white shirt, tie, shoes, and socks. Shawn realized he was naked and slipped on some pants.

His nerves were as tight as piano wire. Anne showing him her early life hadn't helped. He poured himself a glass of wine, went out onto the deck and drank half a glass right away. It was late autumn, and the air was crisp. There was a slight mist in the air, and the smell of pine was strong. He saw no clouds in the sky, and the stars sparkled on this night. A large, full moon hung in the air, a halo of mist surrounding it, marking the moon for this special occasion. He drank the other half of his wine, looked at the silver moon's corona, and turned to go back inside.

"You there!"

Down the side of the building, twenty feet away, was another balcony. The vampire Abigail was looking at him with puzzlement on her face.

"I am Abigail," she informed him. "You are Anne's changeling— Shawn—are you not?"

"Yes, I am!"

"I am part of Hector's family. I heard about Marilyn and you. Foolish, Shawn, almost getting himself killed. Tell me, are you glad that Anne was there, pretty vampire?"

"I don't know the answer to that yet," he blustered. "I'll tell you in a couple of years."

"You're a proud one," Abigail said. "And you have not learned how to talk to an older vampire."

"Someday, maybe! You are with the blond vampire?" Shawn asked with a little too much excitement in his voice.

"Yes, you have an interest, I can tell. That was rude of you, touching her mind, but you have a powerful vampire as your maker. Victoria was right. I can sense Herit in you, very strongly. I have to get ready for the party. Maybe we will see each other later. Would you like me to say hello to Victoria for you?"

"Yes, if you think it's proper."

"Someday, maybe! We'll see," Abigail teased, and then gave him a seductive smile.

Anne was putting on the red gown, and Marilyn, the light blue as he came back inside. Anne gave him a quizzical look.

"Have a conversation with Abigail?" laughed Marilyn. "I knew you would flirt."

"Yes, I did, and you can stop the teasing—I'm nervous enough."

Shawn went and poured himself another big glass of wine and went to get ready. He still felt nervous and hoped he didn't draw attention to Anne on her big night.

"Shawn, relax, you will do fine," Anne assured.

He proceeded to ready himself for the upcoming event. Still, there was no facial hair to shave on his young face. Anne told him he would have to will his hair to grow if he wanted long hair. He showered, brushed his white teeth, combed his hair, and poured himself another glass of wine.

"Take it easy on the wine," Anne warned. "You wear that suit well—you're very handsome."

The hour was drawing near when there was a knock on the door; Marilyn opened the door. Waiting outside was an older Crimmian woman, dressed in a white shirt, ballooned, gold pants, a red cummerbund around her slim waist, and red slippers on her feet. Anne walked to the door; the woman gave a bow and a nervous smile. It was an honor for Crimmians to work for this party— only the best was there.

"Madam Vampire, I am here to bring you to the festivities."

"Marilyn, follow behind me, Shawn, behind her, and you are to be on your best behavior."

Here we go, he thought.

They proceeded to the party and arrived at big, white double doors that the woman pushed open. Inside were vampires dressed in their most elegant clothes, sitting at many decorated tables with silver candelabras, crystal wine glasses, and white tablecloths. A small band played a minuet from centuries past. The vampires turned in recognition and started to tap their drink glasses with the rings on their fingers. Hector stood up and motioned for quiet.

"I would like to introduce the council's newest member, council member Anne Bryce of the Americas."

Then loud applause and cheers. Anne bowed and gave a grateful smile. This must be a great night for her, Shawn thought. He felt proud and happy for her and knew it had taken Anne centuries of work to receive this honor. Marilyn gave her a hug, and the servant showed them to their table, which took some time because of the greetings she received along the way. Anne took a glass of champagne, told Shawn to stay at the table, then began her rounds to greet the vampires and take her place at the council table. Shawn could tell she knew most of the vampires that attended the festivities.

"Would you like some champagne, sir?" asked the waiter.

"Yes, I'll have a bottle, thank you," Shawn said. "And don't be a stranger."

"Easy with the drink," Marilyn warned. "You don't want to do anything to embarrass, Anne."

"I'm not going to embarrass, Anne. I'm just trying to calm my nerves. I'm in a room full of vampires."

The surreal feeling had come back as he looked around the room at the vampires attending the festivities. Where is the beautiful blonde vampire? There she is at the table with Abigail. Shawn continued to scan the room. Most of the vampires were centuries old, and many were over a thousand years old. All of them looked young and beautiful. The older vampires had aged a little. Shawn still had trouble accepting this reality. Never would he have imagined (how could he) that he would find himself in this world.

"We won't be doing a lot of dancing with this band," he told Marilyn.

"They change music as the night progresses," Marilyn replied. "Keep your dancing shoes on. Maybe you could play the piano and sing for all these old vampires." Marilyn pinched him and gave him a teasing laugh.

"Please, Marilyn! You're not helping."

Shawn spied Eric, making his way to their table.

"Marilyn, how are you?" Eric asked.

"I'm fine, Eric. And yourself?"

"I'm doing well, still getting used to being on my own."

"How has it been going? The last time I talked with you was at your emancipation party," Marilyn said with a smile.

"Not bad. I still live here at the house, and I've been traveling a little," Eric replied. "Teresa still keeps a close eye on me, though. She says she will always watch out for me, and I'm not surprised. We grew to love each other, and she has done so much for me... making me a vampire."

"This is Shawn," Marilyn said.

"I've heard about you," Eric replied. "I'm sure you had some rough months. I still remember what it was like those first months...bizarre, to say the least."

"It's been a challenge, and tonight has shown me that I still have some ways to go," Shawn answered.

"It will get better, you'll see," Eric said. "Marilyn and I have had a couple of long talks over her first years. She told me how you two went to school together. I never had a beauty like Marilyn in my school, but then, my school had one room."

Eric looked to be a little fidgety; Shawn could sense he had feelings for Marilyn. Shawn also sensed he couldn't act on them because of her age and the fact she was a changeling.

"I hear you are a musician," Shawn said. "What instruments do you play?"

"I've played them all. Guitar, bass, piano, organ, and drums...I had plenty of time to learn over the last hundred years. What do you play?"

"The piano. My mother taught me," Shawn said.

"Your birthmother? Well, I'm sure we will be seeing each other over the coming years. Try to have some fun, Marilyn."

"Have a good time tonight, Eric. Come visit us at the house," Marilyn said with a smile as Eric walked away and joined a group of younger vampires.

Shawn took a couple of good swigs of his champagne and noticed that the music had improved; it was slowly working its way toward something recognizably modern. Vampires were slowly coming to the dance floor and displaying their many different dance steps. He smiled for the first time that evening.

Looking around, he noticed Abigail watching him. The blonde vampire Victoria was standing with her. Abigail turned and spoke to her. Shawn used his vampire ears to hear what she was saying. "There's Anne's newbie that tried to get into your head. He's a pretty boy, don't you think, Vic? He told me on the balcony to say hello to you."

Victoria turned and looked at him. She still carried the puzzled look, then turned back and said something to Abigail he didn't catch.

The band had started to play contemporary music. Marilyn got Anne's attention and asked her if she and Shawn could dance. Anne smiled and nodded, yes. Marilyn was an excellent dancer, and Shawn followed her lead. Shawn was aware that they were being watched and heard the whispers, and the name "Herit" came through. Marilyn was using her newfound vampire skills to improve on their dance steps. They danced and twirled while they floated just above the floor. Shawn was beginning to have fun at the party.

They came back to the table, and Shawn poured the rest of the champagne into their glasses. A look of concern spread over Marilyn's face, as Abigail was walking toward their table.

"Looks like we are going to have some fun now," Marilyn said.

"How have you been, Marilyn? Well, I hope?" said Abigail in a playful voice.

"I've been all right. I haven't seen you in a while. It's been four or five years since we've seen each other."

"Yes, I've been in Europe," Abigail said, "Staying at Victoria's place. I'm a traveler these days. This handsome man must be Shawn Bryce?"

"This is Shawn. He's been a vampire only four months," Marilyn said.

Abigail approached him. Shawn felt her vampire presence immediately, braced himself, and felt her slight secret probing of his mind; the sensation still felt alien to him.

"So, how is your new life going?" Abigail asked, leaning toward him. "Has it been rough? I have trouble remembering that far back, but I think it was rough for me."

"I'm working my way through it," Shawn said, leaning away.

"Such a young vampire. I bet you taste delicious with that Herit blood in you. Would you like to dance? I'll let your hands roam," Abigail said with a wink.

"I believe I would have to get permission to dance with you," Shawn said.

"He is not ready to dance with you, Abigail," Anne said coming from behind.

"He is still too young to deal with your shenanigans." Unexpectedly, Anne was standing by the table. Abigail's sensuous expression changed quickly as she backed up a couple of steps.

"I meant no disrespect," Abigail said. "I thought he looked like he could use a little fun."

"I'm sure you didn't," Anne replied. "He hasn't had a lot of fun lately. I'm hoping that will start to change."

Anne and Abigail walked off together, then split and went their separate ways, and Shawn had to deal with an empty champagne bottle. Twenty feet away was a long table with two Crimmians acting as bartenders; on that table were full bottles of wine. Shawn steadied himself and started toward the table.

"Where are you going?" Marilyn giggled. The wine was starting to take effect.

"I'm thirsty. I'm going to get a bottle of wine for us," Shawn answered, walking to the table and asking one of the men for a bottle of wine.

The man said, "Yes, sir," and proceeded to uncork the bottle.

"This must be the brand-new vampire, Shawn Bryce, I presume?"

Shawn turned. It was from Victoria. She was even more beautiful close-up, her eyes a stunning, light green, twinkling yet penetrating. As with Anne's, he immediately got lost in them. Her lips were moist and sparkled. Her blond hair was like silk; her eyebrows, light blond as well. Her skin had a slight bronze glow, which almost hid the small number of freckles sprinkled on her cheeks, the tip of her nose, and on her chest, where they made their way to her cleavage. It looked as if she spent some time in the sun, but of course, she hadn't. She smelled like a freshly flowered spring meadow.

"Yes, it is…er, I am," Shawn stammered. "I'm sorry for that mishap earlier. I didn't mean to bother you."

"I'm sure you didn't," Victoria said, smiling, "but you must be careful, young Shawn. Not every vampire is as forgiving as me."

"Well, I'm learning. I'm still unsure of this new existence," he said.

Victoria smiled and gave him a soft laugh. "Yes, I'm sure you are and well protected."

Victoria glanced across the room where Anne was watching. She smiled at Anne and nodded to her.

"Since our little mishap, I have asked about you. You are American, not European, and you come from the state of New York?"

"That's right."

Victoria looked into his eyes and held his gaze for what felt like an eternity. He could feel her touching his mind looking for something. What, he couldn't tell, and then she stopped and looked in Anne's direction. She was using stealth to peer into his mind, and she did not want Anne to know. Vampires did not allow others to look into their changeling minds.

"You were a soldier once and almost died. You know war," she said.

"That's right. I hope that's not the most obvious thought in my mind. War is a horror, something I wouldn't want to experience again."

Victoria drew close to him and he took in her scent and was near her beautiful wet lips. Her voice was like sensuous music. She entranced him, made his head swim in lust.

"Yes, it is, of course, you're right, but war always comes to this world, and it will come again. The Esmanaa demons will make sure of that. You were a warrior of this age—that, I can see."

Shawn knew she was right—war always came, and the thought bothered him. He also felt a little disappointed that she saw only a warrior in him. War was a hell he did know, seen it like few people, and he wanted no part of it again.

Victoria started to leave. "Take care, Shawn Bryce. I wish you success in your new life. You are an excellent dancer. Maybe you can teach me someday, young Demon Slayer."

Shawn watched Victoria walk away and saw her long, form-fitting white dress. Her bottom was firm, with only a slight jiggle. He loved the sight of her.

Shawn felt a tap on his shoulder, and the Crimmian handed him a bottle of wine and two clean glasses. Walking back to the table, his mind replaying their conversation, and he couldn't help but wonder what she was looking for in him. Young Demon Slayer? What was that about? Vampires — it was going to take some time to understand them.

"So, was she as terrific as you thought?" Marilyn asked.

"Yes, she was. There are many beautiful women here. Are all vampires good looking?"

"I think that's one of the criteria. Oddly, I haven't seen an unattractive vampire," Marilyn giggled.

Shawn poured the wine into the glasses, and they sat, talking, and watching the party. Finally, Anne came back, and they left to go back to the room. He changed and went right to bed. Tonight, he learned, he could get quite drunk as a vampire.

The party had excited Anne, and they talked for a good while as they lay together in the couch. This had been a very successful night for her. She told them how she had worked on becoming a council member for centuries, and now she was going to open her house in Amsterdam. They would be making trips there when the council convened. They fell asleep together as they had the previous night, and such was the way it would be for the next hundred years.

The next evening, they left to go back to the mansion in the woods by the lake. It was raining, and Shawn watched the scenery as it went by. The leaves had changed into their vibrant oranges, yellows, and reds; the smell of pine and forest musk was strong.

Shawn would project his sight across a large lake to see the loons standing and sleeping with one leg raised. He could hear the harsh cries of the eagles on the treetops a mile away with the same clarity as he listened to the rhythmic thumps of the windshield wipers doing their best to keep up with the rain.

He saw the oncoming headlights reflected off his rain-streaked window, and it cast a soft glow on the faces of Anne and Marilyn as they talked about opening the house in Amsterdam. Deep in thought, Shawn wondered what it would be like to live for centuries. Would he get bored? Would Marilyn and Anne tire of him

They arrived back at the house, and with a couple hours of night left. They went swimming in the lake. It was a cold, autumn night, the leaves were turning, and there was an explosion of color around their home. Grey clouds covered the dark sky, and it had started to rain again. They swam naked near the falls. Shawn noticed Anne holding Marilyn, kissing her, caressing her face, and talking to her in a low, soothing voice. Anne was also looking at him—he could hear her clearly.

"It has been long enough, my love. Do you want him? Do you want to feel him inside you again, taste his blood? You can't take much, he is too young."

"You know I do. Are you giving your permission?" Marilyn said in an urgent whisper. "I thought you never would."

"Yes, my love, you have my permission. You and Shawn can make love when you want. I have done this for you because I love you, and I know you need men. Go to him if you want."

Marilyn turned and looked at Shawn with a look he had seen before, a look of desire. She swam toward him, and when she arrived, she wrapped her smooth legs around his waist and her strong arms around his neck. This was the first time he realized that Marilyn was stronger than he was. Shawn felt the passion rise in him; they kissed long and hard to make up for all their years apart. He could not tell who was more passionate, Marilyn or him.

"Do you want me?" Marilyn gasped. "It has been so long since you have been with me."

"You know I want you!"

Marilyn had changed; her blood-teeth closed on his neck, her mouth pulling the blood from him.

"Not too much," Anne warned.

Marilyn guided him into her, lifted him, and flew him into the tall grass. She was on him, and then he was on her. Shawn took her sweet blood and made love like the old days, but the feelings were far more intense. Anne joined them in their lovemaking, and then they talked until the soft light of the new day started to show itself.

Anne would tell them about her past. It was times like these that he heard pieces of her long life. It would take centuries for Shawn to piece all of her life together, a task he loved. The vampires lay together in the dew-soaked grass by the lake. The morning light started to rise, and Shawn looked at Anne as she told him, "It is all right. You can see the daylight for a short time."

The low-intensity light filtered through the clouds, casting a soft white over the lake. He saw a layer of morning fog covering the lake like a wrinkled, white blanket. He heard the sounds of the birds and animals welcoming the new morning. He was lying in the soft light of a chilly early morning.

Chapter Six

V ictoria liked walking the streets of different cities. She loved walking amongst the humans; it had always connected her to the times she found herself in. She would probe their human minds to learn about what was important to them, how they lived, and the politics of their age. She was always careful not to get too close or to become too engaged with them, unless they had Lucifer's seed of evil in their souls, and then they became food for her. Some vampires liked to interact with mortals, but she preferred to observe. She knew her looks always attracted the eyes of male humans, and she knew what was in their minds. It had always been this way with her and men.

It was hot and humid this night in Amsterdam. She could see a glisten of sweat on their human skin. The smell of sweat and human body odor filled her sensitive nostrils. She did not mind, for it stirred long-forgotten memories of her own age when she was human. In this kind of heat, the smell of human blood was also strong.

She liked watching the lights of the city, flashing, and people and machines moving with the hustle and bustle of the mortals. Victoria was there to buy a painting, one she felt would be worth money in a couple of decades and had just purchased the art and shipped it home. Also, The Vampire Council was in session in August, and she knew Anne and her changelings were there.

It had been fifty-two years since she discovered Shawn. Victoria was on a mission this night—her destination, the lower canal area of Amsterdam where the streets grew narrow, and the alleys smaller. She had left her lover of a century, Andrew, at home, and now traveled to a vampire disco on Einsstraat in a dark and almost abandoned area of the city. A vampire told her that the Bryce changelings frequented the establishment and had been seen dancing there while the council was in session. She was hoping to connect with Shawn to see if he was still the vampire Erdin told her to watch and knew she would have to be careful. The blood of Herit had made Anne a mighty vampire, and she was very protective of her changelings.

Victoria also knew a man followed her tonight. She had entered a less populated area of the city and had just turned onto Roerstraat. This man was a rapist; he was a Slavic soldier and had raped before — she could feel the hate he harbored. The evil flaw in him that made him think that all people were his to torture, and tonight, she was his target. The soldier was waiting for her to cross the canal and enter a more deserted area of the city. Prostitutes stood on the corner dressed in their scant, colorful clothing, selling their sex to a group of sailors. She laughed to herself—there will always be ladies of the evening. Victoria had fed a week ago, so she was not hungry and didn't want to bloody herself before her mission. If the time came, she would just kill the man.

Continuing her walk, she crossed two more black water canals toward Einsstraat. She had considered taking a changeling herself, and then she had stumbled on Shawn. She knew that vampires used changelings as steps of connections through the ages.

"Maybe someday," Victoria whispered to herself.

She now heard the man's steps quicken as he came toward her; she could sense no other humans. The man was making his move. She sensed the evil in him and the long blade of the knife in his hand. Tonight, she would do Michael's work.

The man lunged at her. With blinding speed, she turned, caught him by the throat, and lifting him, watching his eyes bulge, noticing his missing front tooth and the ugly scar on his chin, the veins becoming pronounced as his face turned blue. She caught his knife hand as he brought it around in a try to slice her face. Her grip tightened, she twisted her hand, and his neck snapped. Victoria threw him back into the alley where he was going to rape her, turned, and continued her walk. Arriving at Einsstraat, she went right and followed the canal for a couple of blocks.

The streetlights were few in this area. She listened to the sounds of her steps on the cobblestones, echoing off the walls of the warehouses, and heard the wail of a lone ship's horn in the bay. The darkness grew with her every step. She thought of how her kind lived in the shadows, always hiding from the humans. Now, she heard the pulsing techno music of the day coming from the disco.

She continued her walk; there, she could sense him, stronger now than when she first discovered him. Victoria leaped four stories to the top of a warehouse so she could take in the surroundings. Since her vampire beginnings with Erdin, she had always been careful, had always used stealth.

Her mission over the centuries had been the Esmanaa. This had limited her in the number of lovers and friends she had taken. There were times she had led a solitary life. She had learned much about the Esmanaa but had avoided the Vampire Council. Victoria felt they showed little interest in confronting the Esmanaa. They would give her only platitudes and promises.

The disco was in its secret place in a dark alley. This was an industrial area next to the bay, "The Ijmeer," where ships came to unload their cargo. She walked off the roof, floated to the ground, and continued across the street to the alley that was home to the disco.

A couple of vampires stood outside, talking about the evening's events. The scent of humans also came from the disco. She always wondered what type of human would feel comfortable being with vampires. Were these mortal thrill-seekers? People who had to live on the edge, who needed more in their short, uneventful lives? A few mortals were aware of vampires; most still thought vampires were folklore, though.

Power was changing in this world again. The Americas were fading, and the nations of Asia were rising. She had seen this before, and usually, it brought war to the humans' world. Victoria could tell that most of the vampires at this bar were young, a couple of centuries old at the most. The door to the bar was thick wood, sanded, and varnished to a golden glow. There was a little, metal, sliding cover over a small opening, which made a clicking noise when used.

"You have to knock for them to let you in," said one of the vampires. "I haven't seen you here before."

"I've come just for this evening to listen to the music," Victoria answered.

"A vampire your age? I wouldn't think you would like the music."

78

"Yes, a vampire my age," Victoria spat back, "and I like all kinds of music."

Victoria knocked on the door, and the cover slid back to reveal the face of a male vampire. She dropped her defenses for a second to allow the vampire to judge her for entrance. The vampire opened the door, motioned for her to enter, and gave her a pleasant look, smiled and nodded to her.

There was a large bar to her left, and to her right, a large area with tables. In the middle, a dance floor, and a vampire playing music from an elaborate, state-of-the-art mixing device. The lights were dim, and the pulsating, colored lights and music filled the senses. The loud music did not bother her, maybe because it reminded her of the pounding drums and fiddles of her Irish past.

Mostly vampires occupied this place, but she could smell human. She could smell wine, spirits, and marijuana in the air. The younger vampires were in their modern-day paints and clothing, trying to achieve that mysterious, Gothic look that had come back into style.

Victoria could sense Michael's victor. The signs were becoming stronger to her as he aged. She went to the bar and ordered a small bottle of wine and a glass. Her sharp senses were active, and she started to search the room for the Bryces. There they are in the back, dancing, but who is that young female vampire with them? Caitlyn Bryce, Renee's changeling, she surmised.

Victoria and Renee were about the same age. Renee came from the pauper streets of medieval Paris. She had lived a hard life and had been a thief of necessity. Some had wondered why Anne had made her a vampire. Renee was a lesbian and extremely loyal to Anne, and they had always been lovers. Renee was a tall, dark-haired beauty, with sharp features, and was known for her skill in using a slayer.

The Bryce changelings were by themselves this evening, trying to keep a low profile. Anne was probably at the council, and Renee, who was now acting as her assistant, was probably with her. It was not unusual to see a fifty-two-year-old changeling on his own in a limited way. Many younger family members of the council came here. Anne must be comfortable with this establishment, and few vampires would be that stupid to bother the Bryce changelings.

Victoria sipped her wine and watched the Bryces dance. She could tell that Shawn had grown stronger in his abilities since she last saw him. His progress surprised her. However, she could tell that he was still a young vampire, and was of little use to her now. Many years would past before a human could totally adapt to their turning and being so aware of the supernatural forces that surrounded them. The reason they spend a hundred years with their maker, and the reason only older vampires can change a human. She knew the angel's plan would take centuries to unfold. Vampires had not heard from the Esmanaa since their meddling in the Middle East wars forty years ago.

Again, Victoria smelled human; she could detect their scent and their blood. Females—their blood always stood out because of what was between their legs. At the end of the bar, she saw two females with two young male vampires. She could tell by their blank looks that the two vampires had mesmerized them. The vampires saw Victoria's harsh look and ushered the human females back to their table. This was a taboo, but young male vampires think it is exotic to have a human female, while female vampires thought little of human males.

Shawn suddenly turned and looked at Victoria. They stared at each other, and then Shawn leaned over and spoke to Marilyn. Victoria turned back to her wine, surprised that Shawn had suddenly sensed her.

Victoria heard a male vampire down the bar talking to the bartender. "Those Bryces think they're special. Why are you letting changelings in here?"

"Take care, friend; they are Bryces. They aren't hurting anyone, and they spend money here," replied the bartender.

Something was not right with this vampire, she turned her powerful senses on the man and found he was a rogue. Even the bartender was becoming suspicious of this vampire. "You need to move on, friend!"

Rogue vampires were turned by young vampires too young to make vampires, and these vampires did not have the strength other vampires had and quickly succumbed to evil. Most rogues were controlled by the Esmanaa demons. When they did show themselves, their vampire eyes were yellow. This one had sensed Herit and Shawn and company were in danger. If a rogue killed a Herit, they would be in good favor with the Esmanaa.

Victoria knew that Shawn was now standing next to her. Unaware of the danger he was in.

"I hope you don't think I'm out of bounds talking to you, but I remembered you from a party a long time ago."

Victoria turned and looked at Shawn, thought how attractive he was, his light blond hair, his bright light blue eyes. Rarely in her long life had she seen such beautiful eyes. His perfectly proportioned facial features blended into the face of a very handsome man. He had lips that begged to be kissed, and clear, smooth, light brown skin, with a muscular body that was not too much. She found herself thinking about what it would be like to make love to him. He had been dancing, and she could smell his Herit blood.

Victoria brought her eyes back up to meet his. She attracted him; he was a child; she, sugar. He could not help himself, and that was what she wanted.

"Young Shawn Bryce, you may speak to me anytime you like— and I do remember you. Maybe we can become friends."

"Yes, we can!" Shawn answered quickly, excited by the idea. "Do you like places like this? I am surprised to see you here."

"I like many types of music, and sometimes, if I am close, I will come to a place like this for a drink."

"Yes, maybe—there's something about you—I'm not sure what it is," a quizzical Shawn replied. "You are the most guarded vampire I have ever met."

"I don't know what you mean. I have only met you twice. Is this how Anne taught you to talk to an older vampire, changeling?"

"My apologies. I didn't mean to be disrespectful," Shawn said. "Do you like Amsterdam?"

"I have always loved Amsterdam. You should've seen it during the Renaissance."

"Unfortunately, I wasn't alive then."

"How have you found vampire life? Does it suit you?" Victoria asked.

"I grew into my vampire life, and now I rather enjoy it. I have everything I need, Anne protects me, I live with beautiful women, and I have these amazing abilities. Being a vampire suits me just fine. There is still some strangeness to it, though."

"Most humans come to love their vampire life. I forgot when I started enjoying this life. It was a long time ago."

Time, another strange concept these days."

"It can be especially for the young. Do you come to Amsterdam every year with Anne?" Victoria asked, trying to lead the conversation elsewhere.

"Yes, we both do. First, we stop in Paris and visit Renee and Caitlyn, and then we all come here."

Victoria could see Marilyn and Caitlyn giving Shawn a look of displeasure, a look that said he was not following the rules.

Victoria leaned over and placed her lips by his ear, letting them brush his flesh slightly. She knew Shawn would take this opportunity to draw her scent, her essence, into him, and knew Shawn's vampire senses were working very hard to find out everything he could about her.

"You cannot enter my head if I don't want you to, young one. I think your friends want you to come back to your table."

"I had better go. Maybe we will meet again," a flustered Shawn said. "Something tells me we will."

"Do you think so?" Victoria laughed. "If we do, remember, you must teach me to dance."

Shawn turned and walked back to his table. What stood out for Victoria were his psychic abilities—they were very sharp for a vampire his age. She knew she had to have more contact with him, and she needed to take some of his blood. Victoria watched Shawn walk away. This time she sensed strongly that he was the vampire Erdin spoke of so long ago. Shawn attracted her, and she wasn't sure why. She also wondered if the angels knew why. She became aware of Marilyn's intense look toward her, and knew, she too, was protective of Shawn—that, Victoria could sense strongly. Marilyn is a beauty. Anne knew how to select her changelings, but then, she didn't really choose Shawn.

Victoria turned back and continued drinking her wine. Shawn had only been with vampire women who liked women. He would find sex very different with her. A smile came over Victoria's face; her eyes flashed an emerald green. She liked men, had sexually devoured some, and the thought of making love with Shawn excited her.

A loud crash brought Victoria out of her daydream. The rogue vampire from earlier had thrown Marilyn into a wall. The path she took clear by the overturned chairs and tables. The vampire now standing over her yelling, "Watch where you're going, Herit whore!"

Shawn and Caitlyn were immediately upon the vampire. Their fists were pummeling him, and the rogue took on a look of rage. The vampire grabbed Caitlyn, spun her, and rammed her head into the brick wall; she crumpled to the floor in a daze. He was not that successful with Shawn.

Shawn was on the rogue's back with his left arm around the vampire's neck, giving blows with his right. The rogue tried desperately to get him off. Finally, he got a hold of Shawn's head and flipped him over his shoulder, sending him smashing through a side door and riding it into the alley.

Victoria had to intervene and followed them out into the alley. The vampire was on top of Shawn, picked him up, and threw him down the alleyway, where he landed against a brick wall.

The assailant had taken his hand and extended his fingers into a point, ready to run Shawn through. Victoria changed immediately, her eyes a brilliant emerald green, a vampire prepared to attack. She let out a hiss and was on the attacker. She had him by his throat and arm. "Filthy rogue here to do the Esmanaa work. You will not leave this alley, fool."

Then in an instant, Anne shoved Victoria aside and tore the vampire from her grasp. Never had she seen a fiercer creature. Her eyes were large and dark blue; her face had shapeshifted slightly into a menacing form, which only a vampire of her age and strength could do. Her fangs had grown long and razor-sharp. She squeezed the vampire's neck like a vice clamp. He gasped, and blood ran down Anne's extended arm. Victoria thought she was going to rip his head off.

"How dare you attack my changelings?" Anne hissed. "I know who you are! You are walking filth of the demons. You will die for what you have done! In the name of the Vampire Council, I sentence you to death!" In a flash, Anne's hand disappeared into the vampire's chest. The thrust was followed by the vampire's scream. Victoria watched her tear his heart from his chest and throw the bloody lump of muscle to the ground. It turned grey and disintegrated into a pile of fine dirt, as did the body when Anne let him fall. She turned, changed back to her normal form, and started to walk toward Victoria and Shawn.

"Thank you, Victoria, for helping. I appreciate what you have done. I thought they would be safe here. Are you all right, Shawn?"

"Yes, I'm all right, no permanent damage, but he attacked Marilyn for no reason," Shawn said as he pulled himself to a standing position and brushed at his clothes.

"I'm going to check on Marilyn and Caitlyn," Anne said as she turned and walked back toward the bar. "Don't leave this spot."

Shawn had two cuts, one on his head, and the other on the side of his neck. Victoria saw the wounds healing, but the gash on his neck was still bleeding.

"Well, it looks like we meet again, much sooner than I thought," Shawn said.

"Yes, it looks that way. Are you all right?"

"I'm all right," he said as he brushed the dirt from his clothes.

Victoria saw the blood on the side of his neck. She sensed with all her psychic abilities that nobody else was watching, and she knew that now was her chance to take some of his blood—to make the connection. Victoria reached out with her two fingers, wiping a good amount of blood from his neck and placing it into her mouth. And then she saw the look of curiosity spread over Shawn's face.

"Do I get to have some of yours?"

"Our secret," Victoria whispered. "Anne would not appreciate me giving blood to her changeling."

"Or taking it," Shawn said. "Again, you guard yourself."

"You fight very well," Victoria told him, again trying to change the subject. "I can tell you are truly a warrior."

"I'm sure you know there was a time when I was a soldier. A time I wish to forget, but even as a vampire, it still comes up."

"Unfortunately, there are going to be times you will face evil and have to fight. It is what being a vampire is really about. That is why we exist here in this world. All gifts come with a price."

Anne's voice came from behind them: "Shawn, I want you to go back to the house."

Victoria saw Anne and Marilyn standing in the alley with Renee, who was carrying Caitlyn. Shawn nodded and floated into the air over Victoria and then straight up into the night sky. Marilyn and Renee—with Caitlyn—vanished in the same way.

Anne was suddenly in front of Victoria, an arm's length away. "You cloud your mind very well, Victoria, but I can still see that you want something from Shawn. I can tell by your words, and I know your pass. You have many layers of defense, and over time, you have learned to use them quite well. Why? What do you want? Why are you here, vampire?"

"I am sorry, I do not mean to offend you," Victoria spoke in a cautious voice. "I was nearby and sensed Shawn."

"I love and care for Shawn very much. I would not want to see anything happen to him. You understand me, Victoria?"

"I would never harm him, Anne, but sometimes, as vampires, others have tasks for us to accomplish."

"Yes, that is true, but for a vampire, your age to take notice of a young vampire like Shawn is unusual. Would Erdin have anything to do with this, I wonder?" Anne did not wait for an answer. "Take care, Victoria. You had better be sure of what you do. Thank you again for your help." Anne turned, took a couple of steps, and then lifted into the hot, dark sky and then as an afterthought she heard. "I hope you liked the taste."

Victoria felt shaken by her talk with Anne. Anne had warned her, knew she had taken some blood, and she had mentioned Erdin. She knew that Anne had also battled the Esmanaa and that her covenant was that of Herit. For thousands of years, Herit's blood covenant had only one vampire, Bricius, a powerful vampire that only cared about himself. It had been a covenant that did not grow because of the

Esmanaa demons and Bricius. She would have plenty of time to think, but for now, she wanted to return to Andrew. She had a thirst for him and wanted to quench it.

Victoria slowly rose into the dark sky. She drifted above the tallest building and looked out into the night sky, sparkling stars spread out upon its canvas. She saw the lights flashing on the ships in the bay as they were leaving with their cargoes to destinations known only to them, the humans scurrying around on the well-lit docks, loading the moored cargo ships. She stretched her arm above her head, arched her back, and pointed her hand toward her home in Ireland. The night's activities had tired her, and so she started her trip home with ever-quickening speed.

Chapter Seven

S hawn was in his ninetieth year as a vampire, and long ago had learned to embrace his life and the ways of a vampire. He had learned it was common for Anne to travel the open roads with a backpack on her back. She would seek secluded, peaceful places in forests and mountains. And there were times she would seek out the bizarre. They would walk through the inner cities, spy on the humans that felt hopeless and the ones that thought they had no one to answer to.

Shawn knew Anne to peer through their windows in stealth, and watch them live their lives, fight across their dinner tables, or embrace with passion in their bedrooms. She brought them to a secret room on top of a Giza Pyramid filled with the treasure she had discovered centuries before, doing council business. Over the years, Shawn had pieced together her long life, knew she had come to this country before the Europeans. Anne had spent years exploring this continent and had lived on deer blood. He learned that she had owned saloons in the wild west, and at times humans had discovered what she was and chased her from her property.

Over the years, Anne had given them many lessons. She taught them how to use their senses, and supernatural powers, taught them how to fly, and once taught them how to bury themselves in The Mother's earth. She told him, vampires bury themselves to hide from their enemies, to escape the sunlight when necessary, and to allow the energies of Mother Earth to heal them. This was when he had learned of the Lesser God Eos. Heaven has many angels, the older and more powerful of the angels are the Archangels and Lesser Gods. There is no god, only angels of varying power. Archangels run the choir of angels, and Lesser Gods inhabit the physical planets that hold intelligent life. Eos is known as The Mother in this world, and her enormous energy flows through the earth and water. Vampires bury themselves to receive the healing power of The Mother, and she is the reason vampires love the water.

A few years ago, the angels started coming to him as he slept. Vampires do not sleep like mortals; their spirit leaves and floats above their bodies while they sleep. The angels would come when he was in the light. They formed dark spaces, shadows etched in the light, shapes barely resembling a human form. He could see flashes of lights of different colors, and sometimes he saw what used to be their mortal faces appear and disappear. The angels told him they did this so his life force could be near them, and so their life force didn't overwhelm him.

At first, they made him comfortable, sung to him, praised him, and told him stories of battles of great warrior angels. Then they started to teach him about his kind and his choir of warrior angels in Heaven. The angels said Guardians were sent to earth to be heavens killers. They warned him about the Esmanaa demons. That they would try to kill him. The angels told him to remember the demon's senses were weak. Michael had robbed them of much of their psychic abilities when they made their escape to earth. He also could feel the presence of another angel watching him. Marilyn told him it was probably Herit.

They were traveling again, and Shawn knew by the change in Anne's demeanor that they were on a learning trip. Anne had changed from loving and nurturing to matter-of-fact and commanding. It was winter, he saw a fresh coat of snow blanketing the ground, and a large, full moon low in the night sky and the moonlight gave a warm, sparkling glow to the new-fallen snow. He saw millions of stars crowding the dark, clear sky; the Northern Lights shimmered in the distance. Anne had brought him and Marilyn to Northern Canada to teach them about the shapeshifters, Lucifer's dark wolves.

He knew the trip would be dangerous because she wore her sword, Deceida, on her back. He had asked her once about the sword, and she told him the Archangel Michael had given the sword to Herit when he made her a vampire. There were five swords given to the five original vampires. Deceida had come from Heaven, and nothing on Earth could destroy its blade. They had fed in Edmonton and traveled to this location. Now, Anne had sprung her lesson on them, delivering them amongst Lucifer's dark wolves.

Shawn looked across the clearing and saw the bright eyes, and then the bodies of two mountain lions crossing the field. He heard the call of wolves far off in the distance and knew these were the dark ones, the dark wolves, tools used by Lucifer to kill his kind. Shawn turned and looked easts sensing more dark wolves than he had ever in his vampire life. Tonight's lesson would be wolves, and in his mind's eye, he saw them gathering. *That explains Deicida.* There were fourteen, fifty miles away, and they were starting to come toward him. Anne and Marilyn had taken the road further and were now coming back at a quick pace. Shawn sensed two leaving the pack and traveling to the southwest. They were trying to close off their route in that direction.

The wolves cannot detect Anne—they must think we are alone, he thought. Anne and Marilyn approached Shawn's location; excitement was on Marilyn's face while Anne had on her poker face. Wolves can be extremely dangerous for young vampires since not all young vampires can levitate as well as Shawn and Marilyn. Most young vampires tired quickly when flying.

"There is a pack of wolves coming for you," Anne warned. "They don't know I'm with you. I have hidden from them. You are young vampires, and now you need to escape them. As I speak, they have come closer. It is time for you to act."

"We have to start running," Marilyn said. "We can follow the logging road west and then turn south."

"Right! We'll outrun them, and the sooner we start, the better," Shawn replied.

Shawn and Marilyn started their run down the logging road. Anne did not follow; she stayed back, allowing her changelings to be independent in their escape. There was a foot of new snow on the road; it was forming a cloud around them as they ran. They increased their speed, and their low body temperature caused the snow to cake their faces. They would have to slow and constantly clear their vision.

They came to the end of the logging road and stopped to decide the best way to proceed. There was a small creek off the road, which flowed to the southwest. Shawn saw a trail that looked as if it ran northwest. Shawn and Marilyn were losing time, stopping to make their decisions. To their dismay, the wolves were much better at running in the forest. They knew the territory and the shortcuts.

"The wolves are closing in on us! We have to make better time!" Shawn said as he wiped the caked snow from his face.

"I know!" Marilyn said. "Which way do you think we should go?"

"The creek goes in the right direction, but it will slow us down. I'm not sure where the trail goes. We had better take the creek."

Shawn knew they had to make better time, but he didn't know where the trail went, and worse, they had lost track of six wolves. He felt they did not have time to stop and sense where the missing wolves were. The dark wolves were dogging them, relentless in their pursuit. This was much harder than he had ever thought. He thought himself a powerful creature, but now he was running for his life; he had become the prey. The terrain was becoming a factor he hadn't counted on. Shawn soon realized why Anne had always warned him about these creatures.

Anxiety was in Shawn's voice. "We have to take the creek. I'm not sure about the trail, but we need to leave here—that, I know."

"Well, let's go then—I can't sense all the wolves!" Marilyn shouted. "Where did they all go?"

"I don't know! If they overtake us, we must come together and fight back-to-back. Do you understand?"

"Yes, I understand!"

Shawn and Marilyn plunged into the creek and started to make their way southwest. They were beginning to tire, their clothes were frozen to their bodies, but they were holding their own. The wolves had run into rough terrain themselves. Ice was forming on them, and they were exhausted, but finally a trail came alongside the brook that traveled in the right direction.

"Finally," Shawn yelled. "We can take the trail!"

Shawn was trying to fight off a feeling of panic. They stopped again to make plans as to what was going to be their final escape route. The trail turned south, and then Anne suddenly reappeared.

"You have stopped too many times, changelings. Do you know where all the wolves are? This is very important to know."

"Yes, we think so," Marilyn answered in a shaky voice.

"Well, think again and sense again, changelings."

Shawn let his senses move outward, to take in their surroundings, and his face suddenly wore a mask of fear. He found the six missing wolves. They worked their way down from the north and were now slightly ahead, cutting off their westward escape route. The other six wolves were now heading toward them from behind and were probably fifteen minutes away. The two from the south were slightly behind them and moving to close off their southern escape route. Their situation had suddenly turned desperate. The look he saw on Marilyn's face also showed that she was aware of the new situation.

"What do you think, Shawn?" Marilyn asked while trying to remain calm.

"We're going to go south, through the two wolves. We will follow the trail south. That is the only way we can go. We are going to have to fight, and two is better than six, but we have to do this quickly."

Shawn glanced at Anne, hoping she would now call off this lesson, but her poker face was still in full force, and she said nothing. Shawn could hear deer running fast through the forest and could see some jumping across the trail. The dark wolves were driving the frightened deer in their direction.

"You're right, that's what we have to do," Marilyn said.

"The deer are running for their lives, something you might want to start doing as well," Anne said sternly. Anne had a hard look; Shawn could tell she was not pleased with their efforts to escape. He could sense her disappointment. Anne told them, "Remember, break their necks and take their hearts from their bodies."

This was Anne's answer, she wasn't going to stop the wolves. Shawn gave Marilyn a kiss and wiped her snow-covered cheeks. "Follow me. I will hit the first one, and you take the second. We will break their necks as soon as possible. Form your fingers into a deadly tip, to spear them. Fight like I taught you."

Marilyn nodded, biting her lower lip, and then said, in a shaky voice, "I'm ready, let's go."

Shawn and Marilyn started their run down the trail that went south. It was easygoing, and their speed increased rapidly. Shawn knew this would help them when they made contact with the wolves. He could sense the wolves had reached the trail and turned northward to meet them. It would not be long now; he was anticipating contact, and it would come soon.

"There they are, and they are big!" Shawn shouted over one shoulder.

Two large wolves sprang into the air, saliva dripping from their long, vicious teeth. One was black with white streaks, while the bigger wolf was light brown. Shawn turned to his vampire form, a fierce sight, as he flew into the air and made contact with the larger wolf. The force from his speed and strength drove the wolf back into the trees. Loud popping and cracking sounds from the breaking tree branches disturbed the peaceful silence of the forest. Vicious, loud growls from the wolves echoed through the woods.

Shawn's arms only went halfway around his foe, so the wolf bent around as they flew backward. The wolf gave a loud snarl as he sunk his teeth into Shawn's shoulder. Shawn screamed from the searing pain as they landed in the snow. His shoulder burned from the wound. Shawn rolled, flipped the wolf over his shoulder and brought his fist down on the wolf's chest with a crushing blow. Except for his own kind, the wolf was the strongest creature he had encountered in his ninety years as a vampire.

Shawn knew he was the stronger, and clung to its fur, wrestled the snarling wolf onto its back. He wrapped his right arm around the wolf's head, held its snout with his left hand, and twisted its neck until he heard a loud snap. Then he plunged his hand deep into the wolf's body, found the monster's pounding, slippery heart, and ripped it from the beast's body.

Marilyn killed her wolf in the same way. Shawn looked down on the lifeless wolf. He saw the wolf starting to change into a dead, naked human lying on the white snow, its visceral organs hanging from a large, gaping wound in its side. An ever-growing bloodstain formed around him, its border expanding outward toward Shawn's feet. The wolf was a young human with red hair, black, lifeless eyes, and a fair complexion. Marilyn had bitten her in the thigh, and Shawn felt anger building, a hatred for these creatures.

Shawn was torn from his trance by a screaming Marilyn, "We have to go! More wolves are coming!"

They continued their run, Shawn trying to fight off feelings of panic. He had lost track of some wolves. They stopped again to decide on what was going to be their final escape route. The trail turned south, and then Anne suddenly reappeared.

"You have stopped too many times, changelings! Do you know where all the wolves are? This is very important to know."

"We think so," Marilyn answered in a shaky voice.

"Well, think again and sense again!"

Shawn let his senses move outward, to take in their surroundings, and to his shock, there were wolves all around them. Then Anne quickly led them and ran them south for miles. Finally, they could sense the wolves had turned back. The three then continued until coming to another brook, and they followed it for a couple of miles, arriving at a large rock formation. There, they found a small cave.

The sun suddenly came over the horizon. The cloud cover and the trees kept the light low. Shawn felt excitement as he stood and watched the sunrise through the mist. The light-filled his eyes and he felt the drain on his energy, but that did not matter.

"Thank you, Michael," Shawn whispered.

"Amen to that," Marilyn added.

Anne smiled and looked at the horizon. "I love to see you two watch the sunrise."

Anne stood there with Shawn and Marilyn, and they allowed the daylight to engulf them. It was magical to Shawn; he was standing in the day with a big grin on his face.

"Let's wash in the brook, and then I'll tend to your wounds," Anne said.

They took off their clothes and walked onto a sheet of ice and into the water. Shawn couldn't help but notice that it wasn't often that he followed behind Anne and Marilyn naked in the daylight. As they stepped into the brook, he saw them sparkle and shimmer in the light.

They washed, and Anne tended to their wounds cut her wrist slightly with one of her fingernails. She applied her blood gently, lovingly, to Marilyn's thigh, looked up, and smiled. Anne had her caring nature back, and Shawn knew the lesson was over. Anne waded toward him, took his face in her hands, and kissed him, and applied her blood to his shoulder.

He saw Anne take a couple of steps back, facing them, standing naked in the brook. Frozen ice droplets had formed on her hair, eyebrows, and pubic hair, her skin a subtle pink, and again, he saw her shimmer in the light of the frozen world, but then she made her point.

"Never stop when it comes to wolves. If you hadn't stopped, you wouldn't have these wounds. You two could have communicated with each other's minds directly—you do it all the time. Let us take shelter. We can use that cave in the rocks."

They dressed, gathered their belongings, and then flew to the ledge that was in front of the cave. They went back into the cave, laid out their bedrolls, and huddled together in the cave to spend the rest of the day. Shawn nestled himself against Anne's back and placed his head at her neck. Marilyn laid on her other side, facing toward her maker.

Marilyn spoke first to Anne. "Would you have let the wolves kill us?"

"No, my love. If the wolves had become too much for you and Shawn Deceida and I would have struck them down. I told you long ago that I would never let anything happen to you. As you saw, one wolf was no match for you. At your age, three or four would kill you. I have made Shawn and you strong so you will survive these dangers, but you also have to know how to handle these perils by yourselves. This is why I put Shawn and you in these situations, so you can learn by experience. It breaks my heart, but soon you will be on your own, Marilyn."

"I will never leave you for long, I love you!" Marilyn whispered to Anne. "I will always come back to be with you."

The weather had turned for the worse again; the snow swirled and howled outside.

"It looks like we will have more snow to wade through on the way home," Shawn said.

"We aren't going home," Anne answered. "We are headed east, to Chicago."

"Why are we going to Chicago?" Marilyn questioned.

"I must go there on council business. The Pandora Witch has asked for a meeting, and she has requested my presence. She also requires me to bring you, Shawn."

"A witch! Now we have to meet a witch!" Shawn replied, exasperated.

"She is a mother's witch and one of the most powerful. She has great power to know the future. First, we have to stop in Casper. Rebecca McCall is bringing a sealed message from the council, and I must meet her there. Let's get some sleep. We'll start our trip tonight."

To the north, Shawn saw in his mind's eye the shapeshifters, Lucifer's dark wolves, burying two human bodies. Anne had told Shawn about Rebecca McCall. She was a red-haired, fair-complexioned beauty. She came from the hard streets of London, where a young, rebellious vampire changed her in the year 1602. Rebecca's maker had little use for the laws of vampires and killed a vampire out of spite, and for his money. The council eventually sent an eliminator to kill him.

Rebecca was fifty years old at the time and in a weakened state. She had the sense to throw herself at the mercy of the council. The council promptly turned her over to Anne for the next fifty years. Anne taught her the ways of vampires and gave her blood to make her strong. Rebecca and Anne eventually grew to love each other, and Rebecca became fiercely loyal to Anne.

Rebecca left Anne eventually, but they had kept in touch through the years. She hadn't taken the Bryce name, and this was something that bothered Anne. There were plenty of stories about the brazen vampire, Rebecca McCall.

Chapter Eight

S hawn stood at the corner of Cheyenne and Rockridge Street in Casper Wyoming outside a large, rowdy saloon. The snow had melted from the streets, and the pavement was wet. He watched the anti-gravity cars go by, pulling the water droplets a foot off the road. The water would then fall back to the pavement as the car passed by. On the large, public viewer, he saw news of food riots on the newly-formed Martian colony. These viewers would project their images into the air so all could see them. He waited and took in the sights while Anne and Marilyn continued their stroll down the street to meet Rebecca. The human race had come a long way in ninety years.

He heard the country and western music playing in a saloon behind him and found himself tapping his foot to the beat. He easily could hear country dancing, and boot heels hitting the wooden floor inside. The smell of alcohol was strong and mixed with fragrant soaps, perfumes, and colognes. The workers from the large cattle ranches that surround Casper wore cowboy hats, boots, and blue jeans. Many ranch workers crowded the modern speakeasy. Humans loved their steak; even he could remember the taste of steak. It was Saturday night, partying and sex were on the minds of the mortals.

Shawn considered going inside but he didn't have Anne's permission. Then he felt a poke to his shoulder and hard shove. He turned to see a large man with a brown, handlebar mustache, black, cowboy hat, and cherry, polished red boots. His face was weatherworn due to years of labor. His breath smelled of alcohol, and his eyes were bloodshot.

"You shove like my sister, pal," Shawn growled at the man.

The cowboy drew his arm back with a fist and propelled it toward Shawn's face. With lightning speed, Shawn grabbed the man's hand and squeezed until his face turned bright red, and he fell to the ground in agony and yelled, "Oh, shit!" He released the man's hand, and the cowboy quickly got up and staggered away.

Shawn turned to see Rebecca, Anne, and Marilyn staring at him. Rebecca's hair was fire red, with smooth, cream-colored skin, and a perky, freckled, upturned nose and a strange, light blue symbol tattooed on the side of her neck. The logo wasn't pronounced; he had to look closely to see it. It traveled around to the back of her neck and proceeded down her back. Marilyn was shaking her head, Rebecca was laughing, and Anne was plain mad.

Anne walked over to Shawn and demanded, "Follow me."

Shawn shoved the man away and followed Anne across the street and up Rockridge Ave. He knew Anne was upset with him; he could feel it strongly. They came to a small, narrow street named Elm, turned right, and walked for a distance.

Marilyn came up and walked alongside him, and Rebecca walked behind them.

"You shouldn't have done that," Marilyn whispered to him.

"I know, but I didn't think it would hurt."

"Soon, our lives as changelings will end. You must obey Anne— you know this. We must always obey her."

"She will always have my love and loyalty — you know that," Shawn answered.

"So, that's Rebecca?" He asked, trying to change the subject.

"Yes," Marilyn whispered. "She's all right, but she didn't kiss me like a family member. I'm not sure she cares for changelings. Anne and Rebecca love each other, that's obvious, but it isn't a physical love, and she never took our family's name."

Anne finally stopped, turned, and looked at Shawn. He could see that she had calmed down.

"Shawn, you shouldn't have done that in front of all those people."

"The man was a jerk and needed to be taken down!"

"I'm a council member, and I must follow the laws of vampires. We cannot expose ourselves to mortals, and that is what you almost did. You need to behave much differently in large crowds of mortals. It's not like being with a few. You should have never grabbed his fist. Escape, that's what you should have done." Anne shook her head.

"You are too flippant sometimes. You know what you are, but sometimes you do not act it. Fun is all you're about! Evil is coming for you! I have sensed it in my angels, and Herit has hinted at it. That is why Victoria shows up. That is why she hides from me."

"I have only met Victoria twice," Shawn said.

"Enough, Shawn—I'm not a fool!" Anne told him sternly as she turned and nodded to Rebecca to come closer. "This is Rebecca; she is very special to me."

"Hello, Shawn. So, you like to have fun like me? I bet the ladies like to have fun with you. Well, what have you to say for yourself, young vampire?" Rebecca teased.

"Nothing but hello, and I'm glad to finally meet you. I've heard so much about you."

Rebecca walked over and kissed Marilyn. "My apologies. I forget protocol sometimes." She moved next to Shawn. She smelled him long, and then she kissed him.

"I'm so happy to see you again, Anne, and to meet your family."

"Our family, Rebecca."

"Remember, I told you, Anne, I want to stay a McCall. I know I have Herit blood, and I speak with her often. She understands. Soon there will be two families in the Herit Covenant. I will bring honor again to the McCall name."

Rebecca handed Anne a message on heavy paper, folded twice with a large glob of red wax, and stamped with the vampire seal.

"Here's the message I came to deliver," Rebecca said. "Try to understand."

Shawn looked down the street, saw a red-and-blue neon sign flashing the name Jaspers, and watched festive mortals come out the door. Rebecca was next to him again, and he could sense she had an interest in him. Her eyes turned the blue of the Herit covenant, and then she winked at Anne. There was no doubt that Rebecca was a fierce creature.

"Anne, since I have been here, I found two humans five blocks to the east. You will find them suitable for feeding. Two more are to the north in a cattle house. Let me take Shawn to feed. Nothing will happen to him. We will all meet back at Jaspers."

"All right. Since Shawn is feeling so independent this evening, maybe it would be a good idea for him to hunt with you. Shawn, go with Rebecca."

"Follow me," Rebecca said.

Rebecca led him into an alley and took his hand. They floated four stories to the roof. "Let's go get some blood, handsome."

She started to run north, and Shawn followed, watching her run— her perfect bottom, her body moving in rhythm with her strides, and her shiny red hair flying in the wind.

She accelerated, and Shawn lost sight of her. He jumped to a higher roof expecting to see her, but she was not there. Suddenly, she was on him, holding him, and driving him onto the roof with far greater strength. Rebecca sat on him, and he was helpless.

"What will you do when you're by yourself, and you meet a vampire like me? Who will take you like I'm doing now—helpless, young vampire."

"I would do my best to stay away from a vampire like that."

"Would you hide? Is that what you would do? I don't think so. I know better. We share the same blood, you and I. Anne made sure of that." Rebecca leaned down and kissed him hard and long. "Do you want to taste me? Go ahead, it's okay. Anne won't care. Suck the blood from my neck, taste me." Rebecca reached back and stroked Shawn's hard cock. "You want to. I know it, and I can feel it."

Shawn sank his teeth into Rebecca's neck as deep as he could and passionately sucked. He drank three mouthfuls and then tried to pull her pants down, but she held him.

"No, not here, young vampire!"

She had excited him, and he wanted her---a safe danger, which he loved. He felt her wet mouth against his neck, and two sharp points enter his neck. He could feel her squeezing his cock as her blood-teeth entered deep in his throat. He pushed his hips into her to give himself relief from the lust he felt for her. She drank his blood and then smeared it on his lips, kissing him passionately. Shawn's loins exploded with an intense orgasm as the two rubbed against each other.

Shawn cleared his head and saw Rebecca sitting on him, watching him.

"Why did Anne decide to change you? I tried once to get her to take a male, but she would have none of it. Shawn Bryce...Herit has spoken to me about you."

She freed Shawn and stood, pulling him up.

"Follow me—let's go feed," Rebecca told him.

They continued on following the roofs northward. When they ran out of rooftop, Rebecca lifted into the air, and Shawn followed. Soon they came to a large corral filled with cattle. A long building stood next to the corral, where the workers cleaned and slaughtered the animals. There was dark, packed dirt between the buildings, and more corrals with abandoned train tracks running past them. The animals had settled for the night, and steam rose from their backs. Rebecca flew to the middle, landed between the cattle, and reluctantly he followed. Shawn knew she had done this on purpose, as the potent smell of dung reached his wrinkled-up nose. Rebecca shook her head and laughed at him.

"It's easy to see what age you're from. You should have smelled the pauper streets of London, where I grew as a human. Can you sense the human in that long building?"

"Yes, there's only one."

"The second man has left. Follow me. We will share this one."

Shawn followed, pushing cows aside until he reached the fence by the long building. Suddenly, Rebecca crouched and pulled him with her.

"Shroud your mind quickly."

"Sure," Shawn said.

"Quiet!"

Shawn now sensed four rogue vampires and knew these four were older rogues. They waited a few minutes, and eventually, he saw the rogues flying low across the flat grasslands that surrounded the facility. Rebecca turned and held a finger to her lips. The rogues flew thirty feet, passed them, and landed in front of a side door that gave entrance to the building.

They wore dark slacks that went over black cowboy boots and differently colored long winter parkas. Their hair was dark and slicked back with some type of hair grease. Their fingers were adorned with many rings. Then one stopped and looked where they were hiding. He pointed his finger and said to the others, "Vampires, over there."

Rebecca turned and gave Shawn an annoyed look. "Anne is going to kill me! You stay behind me—do you hear me?"

"Why don't we run?"

"I'm not sure you could escape! These are old rogues, stronger than most. And, dammit all, I sense the stench of Esmanaa Demons on them."

They stood, floated over the fence, and landed facing the rogues, and the four vampires started walking toward them.

"Why are you here?" the leader asked. "What goes on here is of no concern to you."

"Why are you so afraid that we will find out what goes on here?" Rebecca demanded. "Your idiot partner tells me what I need to know."

Even Shawn could tell from the weak-minded one that they were here to collect money from the male mortal inside and deliver it to the Esmanaa. The human had a slave operation, and the rogues provided him with women. Shawn looked toward the building and sensed him. He was the owner of this cattle business and scurried to hide. He also could tell the rogues were making up their minds whether to attack or leave.

Rebecca must have sensed this, too. "I will let you leave here, because of the young one that is with me."

The leader turned to the others. "She is afraid for the changeling. She is not sure if she can protect him. He has a strong scent of Herit. The demon Horsa would look on us favorably if we killed him. He would pay us quite well for the head of this Herit. Let's kill these vampires and be done with it."

The rogues took off their jackets and spread out, preparing for their attack. Rebecca said over her shoulder, "I'm sorry I got you into this. We are going to have to fight. Hold out as long as you can, until I can get to you. Stay close to me. Anne will be here soon."

Rebecca changed immediately to her vampire form as Shawn stepped out from behind her and transformed. The rogues attacked; the two older, stronger rogues went for Rebecca, and the other two came at Shawn. He caught the reluctant addled brain, one with a kick to his face, and drove him into the side of the building. The other was on Shawn and sunk his teeth deep into his arm.

Shawn wrestled with the rogue, but he was stronger. Shawn flipped the rogue over his shoulder, throwing him through the air. The rogue hit the ground and skidded to a stop, jumped to his feet, and came at him again. The reluctant one landed on his back and sunk his teeth into his neck. Shawn flipped this one onto the ground, plunged his hand into his chest, and tore his heart from him.

The remaining rogue hit him with the full weight of his body and slammed him back into the building. He was on Shawn and drove him hard against the building. Shawn felt dazed; never had he been hit this hard and now saw, for the first time, a vampire slayer in the rogue's hand. It was a dagger with a silver spike for a blade and a burr at the tip for ripping a vampire's heart from its body. Carved into the shiny metal were strange symbols, and it came with a bloodstained white, bone hilt.

The rogue knocked Shawn to a sitting position. Shawn grabbed and held the spike hand of the rogue. Slowly, the rogue pushed the spike closer to Shawn's heart. Shawn tried with all his strength to keep the spike from his chest, but the dagger slowly came closer.

Shawn did not see the blade as it moved too quickly. He did see the rogue's head lifted off his neck and felt the blood splatter his face. The head fell to the ground, rolled a couple of times, and then the body and head disintegrated into fine dirt. Anne had saved him again.

Rebecca killed the last rogue while Anne quickly pulled him to his feet. His situation had scared Anne; it was a feeling he rarely sensed from her. She turned immediately for an explanation from Rebecca.

"They came out of nowhere. I am so sorry," Rebecca said. "Are you all right, Shawn?"

"Yes, I'm fine."

Anne gave him a glance, and then she turned to Rebecca. "These rogues belong to the demon Horsa. And he is not far away!" He saw the fear spread over Rebecca's face as she nodded her head in agreement.

Shawn then remembered the human. He flew to the door and kicked it open, went down a hallway and into an open area with pens holding cattle ready for the slaughter. He could sense the man hiding in a room on the other side of the pens, went to the door, and forced it open.

From behind him, he heard Anne's desperate shout, "No, Shawn, we have to leave here!"

The man was standing across the room with a revolver and fired it once. Shawn felt pain and heard the thud of the bullet when it hit his stomach. He fell back out the door and felt his stomach skin harden, pushing the slug out. Shawn, in an instant, was up and on him, tore the gun from his hand, held the man by the throat, and pushed him up the wall.

"Tell me, filth, what makes you think you can enslave other humans so you can have more money? What is enough money for you? You will pay the price now, but it will not be with your money. Now, your money will do you no good!"

"Wait!" the man choked. "Spare me, and I will tell you where we keep the women!"

Anne took the man from Shawn. He sensed her enter his head. I know where they are Anne hissed."

"Will you spare me?"

"I do not spare human filth like you. The angels demand I take your life, and Lucifer awaits you." Anne did not take the man's blood. She broke his neck and threw him to the feet of Rebecca.

"This should not have happened, Rebecca!"

"I should have been more aware. I should have known about this man's evil ways. My attention was on Shawn. Like him, I like to have fun sometimes." Rebecca was the protégé again, explaining her actions.

Shawn's first clue that something terrible was coming was the ringing of Deceida's metal. Anne drew the sword from heaven with its metal humming and glowing. He had never seen the slayer do this, but Anne once said the sword had a mind of its own. Fear spread over Anne's face, and this to was something he rarely saw. "Quiet Deceida!" Anne said tensely. "The demon will kill my changelings!"

"Horsa is coming!" Anne gritted out. "Follow me; there isn't much time!"

Shawn knew that Horsa was one of the Esmanaa Demons, and if he remembered right, he was one of the more powerful. Anne had told him that Esmanaa Demons had weak psychic senses when they operated in the physical world. When they were in the dark realm, their senses returned, but still, wherever an Esmanaa was, they always were stronger and quicker than the strongest of vampires.

Shawn, with the others, followed Anne out the door down the large open bay with the cattle pens set in the middle. Anne stopped and looked off in the distance, searching, and then she said, "The demon is almost here! Through this door!"

Anne forced the door open, and they went into a room. The room was cold and enclosed by concrete walls and a floor, and it held bins of discarded scraps from the slaughter of the cattle. In the center of the room was a metal handle embedded into a large, round, concrete cover that fits into an opening in the floor. Anne lifted the concrete lid and said, "Quick down this pipe!"

One by one, they went through the opening with Anne being the last. Shawn helped her slide the concrete cover back over the opening. They all slid a reasonable distance down a large concrete pipe and then stopped deep underground and listened. Humans used the pipe to flush the animal waste out to the vats that were then loaded on trucks and taken to the fertilizer factories. The stench was unbearable, and the inside walls were slippery from animal fat, blood, and visceral.

They hid in the pipe and waited. Shawn and Marilyn huddled together, Anne in front of them, and Rebecca behind. An overpowering feeling of nausea overcame him, and Marilyn squeezed his hand as she too became ill. The ground and pipe shook when the demon landed. The Esmanaa entered the building, and the closer it came, the sicker Shawn felt. A grinding noise of a thousand insects filled his head, and when he looked down, maggots covered his hands. Marilyn clutched at him and held him tight.

"Hold me, Shawn," Marilyn gasped.

Shawn knew Anne had no choice but to hide from the demon she might survive, but she knew her changelings wouldn't.

"Be strong," Anne whispered. "Cloak your minds."

And for the second time, he heard Anne pray to The Mother not to let the demon find them. This time it wasn't for her, it was for them. Easily, Shawn could sense the demon location, as it moved through the building. Thank the angels; the monster couldn't detect them. The horrible noise in his head would rise and fall the closer the demon came. He and Marilyn held each other as Horsa went down the bay and moved over top of them. The beast gave off a sickening stench that overcame the smell of the pipe. Maggots covered all of the surfaces. Then the demon stopped momentarily, and Anne drew Deceida close and grip it tightly. And again, Shawn heard Anne asked for The Mothers help. Points of light formed in the darkness swirled and came together to form a large ball of light that moved over them enclosed them. Shawn heard a woman's voice in his mind. *I will protect you, Shawn, you still have far to go.* Then the demon moved on down the bay out of the building, took flight, and the light subsided.

They waited for hours and eventually crawled out of the pipe and flew back to the hotel. They slept that day, huddled together. The message had to do with Pandora, and Anne never shared the contents with him. The next evening, the vampires said their goodbyes, and Rebecca traveled back to Amsterdam to tell the vampire council that they had seen Horsa and the Esmanaa were active again. Rebecca took Shawn to the side and told him, "You did well last night. Someday you will be a powerful guardian. Herit has told me this."

Shawn, Anne, and Marilyn left for Nebraska to the place the demon rogues kept their slaves.

Chapter Nine

S hawn, with Anne and Marilyn, stood at the edge of a cluster of trees looking across a small field at a typical, old-time, two-story Nebraska farmhouse. The snow had just melted, and the brown field grass ran to the faded brick foundation of the house. The night was clear and cold. Shawn heard the traffic from the nearby road, along with an occasional bark of a dog off in the distance. He saw the white paint of the farmhouse had worn off years ago and now showed grey, weathered-wood siding. A light came from the shuttered windows, but no lights were visible on the outside. They had been there for a couple of hours, and Anne had stared into the night, sensing the darkness looking for any signs of an Esmanaa demon. They knew Horsa and his rogues had been there. His stench was still heavy.

Shawn sensed the evil coming from this place; he knew there were three men in the house, but only one woman. The men were holding the woman hostage. He felt the woman was in a back bedroom on the second floor. The fear coming from her was as intense as the evil coming from the men.

"One woman in the back," Shawn informed.

Shawn had sensed the rage building in Anne all night. She was in this world to fight demons, not to be another Bricius. Hiding from Horsa had upset her. That was the reason she would risk bringing her changelings here. Anne had already changed to her vampire form. He knew they would show no mercy to these men. Anne had Deceida at the ready, and rarely did she use her sword against a human. Already, he was unsettled from the horror he was about to see. He had seen and felt enough the night before.

Anne started to float to the back of the house. "Follow me!" She commanded. "And make no noise!" She had become deadly serious, a heaven's killer

They levitated to the back porch and landed quietly. Shawn peered through the door and saw one man in the kitchen, stirring beef stew on the oven, and a stack of stew cans on the counter. He was a large, young and muscular man, with a tattoo of a bare-chested woman on his arm. The man wore tight, black pants with a cut-off white t-shirt to expose his muscular stomach. Lipstick and make-up adorned his face, his hair was black, slicked back on his head, and he had shaved all his body hair. He was humming and drinking whiskey from a bottle. The man would grab his crotch and give it a squeeze as he attended the stew.

"Can you believe him? What a creep!" Marilyn whispered. "His cock fascinates him."

"I'm going to check on the girl," Shawn said quickly.

"Marilyn, we will go to the front and check the other two," Anne said.

Shawn drifted to the back corner of the house and followed the sidewall to the back, first-floor window. Slowly, he rose to a second-floor window and peered through the glass and saw a naked woman with her hands and legs handcuffed to bedposts. Her mouth was duct-taped. The woman had long, black hair and light brown skin. The last man in had thrown a blanket over her that only covered a small part of her body. Make-up streaked her face from her crying. Shawn was aware that Anne had come up behind him and heard a hiss come from deep inside her. The hair stood up on the back of his neck.

"It's time to remove this filth from this world," Anne raged.

"I'll take the man in the kitchen," he said quickly.

He knew it was going to go badly for the mortals, so he wanted to be by himself in the kitchen.

"Wait by the back door until you hear us enter the front, and then you enter."

"What are we going to do with her?" Shawn asked.

"When we are done, we will mesmerize her and take her home. We will fade her memory of what is going to happen to these pigs. Be ready!"

Shawn went to the back door and again looked in. The pretty boy was spooning stew into three bowls, then set the pot on the table and licked his fingers. A bang came with shouting, struggling, and then screams. Shawn placed his hands on the back door and shoved. The door ripped from its hinges and flew across the room, hitting the man as he was walking toward the hallway that led to the front of the house. The creep fell forward and landed on the floor with the door on top of him. Shawn was on him, blood was running down the man's face from broken glass. Grabbing his arm, he yanked him to his feet.

The pretty boy screamed, and then pleaded, "Please, don't! Who are you?"

"Justice!" Shawn sunk his teeth into the man's neck. He found the artery and tore it with his teeth, draining him of his blood quickly. He threw the man against the wall, watching him fall to the floor, rolling to a facedown position. Shawn then said aloud, "You're lucky you're not in the front."

Bracing himself for the gore he expected to see, he followed the hall to the front room. Anne and Marilyn did not disappoint him; blood covered them. Anne had used her sword and decapitated both men. There was a torn arm lying on the sofa, blood splattered the walls and ceiling, and covered the floor, which made walking slippery.

"How are we going to get the girl out of here now?" Shawn questioned. "She will lose it when she sees you two."

"Be quiet," Anne demanded. Her eyes were afire. "Those bastards deserved what they got. Go upstairs and take care of the girl. Marilyn and I will wash and change our clothes. Hurry this place reeks of Esmanaa!"

Shawn followed the stairs to the second floor and went down a dark hallway. He looked into the room. The woman's eyes were wide and showed the terror she felt. She was squirming on the bed, and he could hear muffled screaming through the duct tape. There was a bed and a dresser with a small lamp on top, a yellow light that gave the room an eerie glow, and dead bugs of summer lying around the base.

"I mean you no harm," Shawn said. "I'm here to help you." Shawn moved and instantly was beside the woman. He waved his hand in front of her eyes to draw her attention to him.

"Look at me and listen. You are being saved—quiet yourself."

Shawn looked into the woman's eyes and brought her to a deep trance. He then took the duct tape off her mouth, broke the handcuffs, and freed her arms and legs. He found her clothes thrown in the closet and helped her dress.

"What's happening?" the woman asked in a dreamy voice.

"I'm here to save you and take you home," Shawn whispered. "But nobody can know who we are. Do you understand?"

The woman replied in a wistful voice, "Yes, I understand. Are those horrible creatures gone?"

"Yes, they won't bother you anymore."

The big red-haired man is he gone?

"Yes, Horsa is gone," Anne said from behind.

Marilyn and Anne were standing in the door, cleaned and changed.

"I found these tranquilizers downstairs," Marilyn said.

She had a pill bottle and a glass of water. She gave a couple to the woman and a drink of water.

"We'll take her down the stairs and out the back," Anne instructed. "Marilyn, get rid of the body in the kitchen."

"Dear woman, you are safe now," Anne said to her in a caring voice. "Calm is taking hold of you. Do you feel the calm, the release of your fears?"

"Yes, I feel it," the woman sobbed.

"Where do you live, dear? Tell me so I can take you home."

"I live on Park Street in Holdrege, Nebraska," the woman said. "I live in a white house with my husband and my baby."

"Sleep now, and we will take you home," Anne said to the woman. "You will forget the horror you saw here. This place will be a distant memory."

They cleaned and flew the woman home when they arrived, three police cars were parked in front of her house. They took the unconscious woman to the back, second-floor window. Anne held the woman, and Shawn forced the window open and quickly entered. He took the woman and laid her on the bed. Shawn turned and saw a baby standing in its crib, holding onto the side rail, staring at him.

"Hello, little baby. I've brought mommy back."

The vampires left as quickly as they came, went back, and set the farmhouse on fire. The day was coming, and they flew east, where they found a barn in which to take shelter. They spread their bedrolls in the loft and used the straw for a mattress. Shawn put his lips next to Marilyn's ear and whispered, "Did you get any blood in you? There was so much blood on the walls and floor."

"Those men were evil," Marilyn whispered. "That brought out a tremendous bloodlust in me."

"It exhilarated you," Shawn whispered back.

"It did. I'm not the woman you knew one hundred and twenty years ago, and you're not the same man."

"Shawn has never released his bloodlust—totally," Anne said. "He hasn't found anything to disgust him enough. Brutal rape of a woman didn't do it."

"They got their punishment," Shawn whispered, "but mutilating them, maybe that was too much."

Anne drew Shawn close to her. "Kind Shawn, you give mercy so easily. We are the Archangel Michael's warriors on this earth. We are the angel's sword, Guardians, the dam that holds back the evil that comes to this world. You cannot show these people mercy. The evil that was in those humans is only a part of the darkness in the Esmanaa demon that controlled them. The angels made us predators and killers, and you need to harden yourself for the day you confront this hideous evil. The angels have seen that someday we will fight these demons together. Let's sleep—next eve we will arrive in Chicago."

She drew his mouth to her neck, allowed him to drink from her, to receive her strength, her will, and to help build his. Anne was his maker, and he loved her dearly.

The next night they flew to Chicago. Anne had opened her throttle more than usual. The lights and buildings were a blur; Marilyn and Shawn could barely keep up. They arrived in Chicago around midnight and rented a hotel suite in Orland Park. They had plenty of wine and tea sent to the room and promptly went to the large walk-in shower. They washed the road dirt and blood from their bodies, and Shawn watched it swirl down the drain.

He was feeling better, and lay with Anne and Marilyn, naked, on a big, round bed with large fluffy pillows and a thick green quilt. They drank wine, talked, and then Anne kissed him passionately, took blood from his neck. He sensed her passion; he knew she needed this intimacy after the violence they had experienced. He felt Marilyn use her mouth on him, getting him ready for them. Anne straddled him and then Marilyn. Shawn would bring them to orgasm, and they would do the same to him. They made love for hours, and in the end, Anne gave them her sweet blood.

This time he allowed himself to travel the blood and went to a time long ago to Anne's first changelings Renee's turning. He was Anne on a roof high above, seeing, hearing, and feeling what Anne did. He saw a woman he knew to be Renee. The woman was having a heated discussion with four other women. The argument intensified, and he saw three men come up the connecting street. The peasant men were around the corner, out of Renee's sight—two had clubs, and one had a knife.

He saw one of the women shove Renee and heard, "You cheated my man out of his money. Your special ointment didn't work, and my son's wound still festers. You have cheated others. People have told me this! They say you lie with women, and you are immoral!"

He saw one of the women step out and slap Renee in the face. Another punched her in the side of the head. The woman that was talking shoved Renee and made her fall back onto the dirt street.

Shawn felt Anne instantly change to her vampire form and sensed the peasants had finally discovered Renee's deceptions. Renee leaped up and ran down the street, but the men ran after her. He felt Anne rise into the air and travel quickly to a roof where he saw Renee run around a corner and slip on a patch of mud. He saw her fall and get up again, but he knew the men would now catch her. Renee ran into an alleyway to hide, but the men saw her and gathered at the entrance to close off the exit.

They floated across the street and came down quickly between Renee and the men. "Leave now, and I will let you live," he heard Anne say, but he knew she didn't mean it. Anne wanted to kill these men, and he could feel the desire in her.

"Witch! God save us!" one of the toothless men yelled.

The man with the knife charged. Anne's hand moved with a flash, catching him around his throat and snapping his neck. He watched the man crumple to the ground and saw the knife land next to him.

"Witch!" the filthy men yelled as they ran away.

They looked at Renee and saw her deep fear. Renee was a tall woman for the age she lived in, jet black hair, sharp, beautiful facial features, but her teeth were stained, and dirt-streaked her peasant's face. Her husband had caught her with another woman and had thrown her out. Now she had to fend for herself.

"Are you a witch?" Renee asked in a shaky voice.

He heard Anne say, "No, I am not, my love. I am a vampire."

"A bloodsucker! I think I would rather face the men," Renee said as her light grey eyes darted, looking for some way to escape.

Shawn could hear Anne speaking again: "You will want to face me. I offer life, not death. Happiness, not sorrows."

"You're a bloodsucker—you only bring death," Renee answered.

Again, he heard Anne tell her, "No, you don't understand my kind. What you have heard is not true. I have watched you, and now I want you. I want to change you. I will turn you tonight and teach you how to live as a vampire."

He saw Renee get to her feet and try to force her way past Anne, but she took hold of her and pushed her gently back to the ground.

"You can't escape me, my love," he heard Anne whisper into her ear. "Someday, you will be happy I did this for you. You know you will not live long as a human. I offer you a much greater life. A life in which you won't have to spend every waking minute searching, lying, and stealing to survive. I will give you my love and teach you how special you really are. Someday maybe you will love me."

He heard Renee say back, "You smell of Jasmine, and your body has no heat. Why is my head so clouded? Where has my fear gone, vampire?"

"I'm helping you stay calm. Can't you feel me in your mind? Feel that I mean you no harm?"

"Are you going to make me a living corpse, vampire?"

"No, my love, I will not. You will have a greater life force. You will sleep. When you wake, you will be like me. Far more alive than you are now."

Shawn felt Renee cease her struggling, and suddenly she looked into Anne's eyes. "Do what you must. I'm ready. I'm tired of this life!"

Shawn felt Anne's metabolism speed up as it sensed the change. He felt Anne's teeth enter Renee's neck. He tasted her blood. Renee's life as a vampire started that night.

Shawn woke, and Anne came, sat next to him, and spoke softly to him. "Have you been traveling? I can sense your powers are increasing, and I think Victoria knows the reason. Be careful—I will always be there to protect you. I want you to know that."

Anne then told them, "We are going to meet Pandora on the north shore of Orland Lake. Let me do the talking, and do not get trapped staring into her eyes for any length of time."

"Is she an old witch?" Marilyn asked. "An ugly old witch?"

"She is close to five hundred years old. When I first met her, she was young. She is a tall woman and has always looked young to me, but she does age. She has long, flowing, blond hair, and she looks Nordic."

"Do you trust her?" Shawn replied.

"I have met with her four times. The first was in Salem, at the witch trials, and since then, once a century. We have always gotten along at these meetings. Pandora is a powerful witch. She has great abilities to see into the future, and usually, that is what the meetings are about."

Shawn left the hotel with Anne and Marilyn, flew a couple of miles, and landed by the shore of Orland Lake. When they arrived, Shawn immediately heard a woman's voice in his head singing a riddle in a soft, hypnotic melody. The energies of The Mother flowed through him, and he sensed there was a mighty creature up the trail. Never had he felt so much power in one place.

"Pandora, stop, or we won't come any closer," Anne demanded.

They continued down the trail and came to the shore with a boat dock traveling out into the water. He saw a plain-looking woman, large, with long, blond hair, floating a foot above the end of the pier.

She had a well-formed nose, too large for her face, and her ears stuck out of her long hair. She wore the clothes of a friar, with a rope tied around her middle, and her feet were bare. Shawn could feel tremendous power coming from her. She smiled and floated back to the dock. A pleasant smile with a mischievous twist was what Shawn first noticed. He felt no evil—if anything, she liked vampires.

"Anne, we meet again. It's been so long. I thought your brood would like a little song," Pandora said. "A little riddle." Floating just above the surface, she came down the dock toward them. Marilyn grabbed hold of Shawn's hand.

"I apologize for the high energy, but The Mother is near. It seems she has an interest in these proceedings. So, you have been raising vampires since our last meeting. I wish this meeting would be as easy as our last. These are your brood, and you must be proud of them. How pretty they are—but we all know how vain vampires are. Vampires love beauty—how could they not, with the blood of the angels in them." The witch gave a loud laugh that echoed across the lake.

"This is Marilyn and Shawn. They are coming to the end of their time with me, I'm sorry to say."

"Yes, the beautiful Marilyn and the male, Shawn. Angels hide this one. They have a destiny for him."

"What do you mean?" Anne asked.

"A favor I will give you. The angels hide a secret about this one. Shawn's name doesn't even show in the hall of records for your kind."

"Would the vampire Victoria know about this?" Anne asked.

"Yes, she knows. She is the only one that knows, but she hides this secret from everyone. Shawn is beginning to know, but he hides this from you. Young Shawn is very good at this."

Shawn quickly looked to the ground and could feel Anne's hot gaze on him. This witch knew about him and had called him out. Shawn looked up and watched Pandora as she concentrated on him. He was careful not to look too long or deeply into her eyes. She was probing his psyche, for what, he did not know. But then courage came to him, and he looks at the witch and thought, *what are you?*

A strong force entered his mind and made him stagger back. *Pandora serves me, and so will you.*

He shook his head and again was staring at the witch.

"I was born a witch. My mother was a witch doing Eos business. The mother is very interested in you." Pandora let out another hearty laugh at this remark. "Anne, if your changelings ever need my help, they may ask me. Now it is time to discuss why we are here tonight."

"The council has sent me to receive your message," Anne said. "The council always wants to know your predictions."

"I have always worked with your kind because The Mother requires it. You stand against the darkness. You slow its grip on this world. Understand this warning—the Esmanaa is active again, and in a hundred years, they will plunge this world, these humans, into a terrible calamity. A great dark age will take over this world, and humans will suffer terribly."

"The mortals will endure a great war, and then a plague will wipe out a large part of their civilization and their population. It will take centuries to recover, but only if your kind protects them from themselves and the demon's evil that will spread."

"Are you sure about this?" Anne said. "You have seen this?"

"This is coming! I see it strongly!"

Shawn could not believe what he was hearing. A great war was coming, and then a terrible sickness spread over him as he looked at Marilyn, and blood tears filled her eyes. He put his arm around her and drew her close.

"The council will stop this," Anne said. "We will have to prevent this from happening."

"The Mother knows the council will not stop the Esmanaa. The council is afraid of the Esmanaa—Mother knows this. Prepare yourselves. When the time comes, vampires must protect the humans from the demons." The witch then drifted in front of Anne and said, The Mother watches Shawn. She, too, has a destiny for him. We will meet again, Shawn." Pandora then drifted back over the lake and then into the night sky and disappeared.

The meeting ended, and the vampires went back to their hotel room. They drank a lot of wine and talked for hours about what they had heard. The next night they made their returned trip back to their home in Washington.

Shawn spent the rest of the winter working on his favorite hobby: researching the locations of specific antiquities. His current project was the Crown of Kilkenney, a crown that was solid gold, adorned with large diamonds, rubies, and emeralds. The pieces were worth a fortune in this age.

The following spring, they took an anti-gravity airliner to Amsterdam. Anne was going to brief the Vampire Council on her meeting with the witch Pandora. They had opened the Amsterdam house and planned to spend some time living there. Anne had been in a melancholy mood of late—Marilyn was spending her last year as a changeling.

The spring chill had left the air, and the evening was warm. Shawn was working on his Crown of Kilkenney project, Anne had left for a meeting at the Vampire Council, and Marilyn had gone to a disco with Eric. Shawn's head suddenly rose from his studies—he could sense the vampire Victoria. She was by herself and had landed a couple of miles to the south in the canal district: near the place, he had last seen her. *She is hunting and must sense me,* he thought. Shawn decided to cloak himself and see how close he could come to her. He went to the back balcony, lifted into the air, and flew to a roof a block away from Victoria.

He traveled slowly along the rooftops until he came upon her walking, wearing form-fitting red pants and a tight-fitting, white halter-top. Her skin looked as smooth as cream, and her long, blond hair was slightly curled, streaked with light brown highlights, and laid on her beautiful bare shoulders. Shawn watched the ever-so-slight jiggle of her bottom as her black boots hit the pavement as she walked.

Two young men were following her, and the tattoos on the side of their necks showed they were in one of the Amsterdam gangs. Shawn continued to follow from behind. "What is she up to?" He whispered to himself.

She knew he was behind her; he could feel her in his mind now, and then she told him, *Be ready.* The two men were making their move on Victoria. They grabbed her and dragged her into an alleyway. Shawn was immediately at the parapet, looking down on the scene below. Victoria had turned, grabbed both men by their necks, and held them in her sturdy grip. This had taken but a second to play out. Shawn stepped off the roof and floated to the alley. Victoria threw one of the men to Shawn. "This one is for you, young vampire."

The man landed at his feet and started to stand to make his escape. Shawn was on him and exposed the man's neck, sank his blood teeth deep, took his time, and held him so he wouldn't struggle, savoring the man's blood. Victoria finished with her man and turned to him with blood covering her chin and lips. In an instant, he found himself in her powerful embrace. She flew him to a secluded shore on the west side of the bay, landed, and was on top of him, pinning him to the ground. She licked the blood from his face and then sank her fangs slowly into his neck.

He felt her caressing soft lips, and her blood teeth sink deep into his neck. Slowly, she drank a small amount of his blood, only a couple of mouthfuls, and licked the punctures until they disappeared.

"Remember, our secret," she whispered. "I wanted to come for a brief visit. It's been a long time since we last saw each other. Soon you will be on your own."

"Eight more years, and I will be responsible for myself again. Do you think you could let me up?"

Victoria released him and asked, "Does Anne know where you are?"

"I'm sure she does. She allows me to go out on my own, but I can't leave the city." Shawn leaned over to see if Victoria would let him kiss her. She did, and her lips were soft and lush. He took his time with this first kiss and savored her.

Shawn watched her stand and remove her clothes, wade into the water, and wash the blood from herself. Mesmerized, Shawn stood still and watched her. He was looking at her naked body for the first time, and the thrill of her shot through him. She was the most beautiful woman he had ever seen, and he wanted her—and he was going to have her.

She looked at him, and Shawn saw into her mind. She had opened herself to him, allowing him to see her for the first time, smiling and motioning him to come to her. He removed his clothes and went to her. Her eyes glowed an emerald green, and he could feel her desire, her passion. He couldn't believe she was letting him get close to her in this way.

He took her in his arms, and she allowed him to control her. He kissed her passionately, ran his hands over her body, and pressed them between her legs. The lust built in him. Shawn knew that he was not going to control his desire for her and sensed that she had become aroused as she pushed him away.

He watched Victoria walk away and heard her gasped, "That is all we can do. I don't have Anne's permission. Anne would never allow this, and I cannot risk her anger. She is too powerful. You will be on your own soon, and I will come to you. There is much we have to talk about."

"Your maker Erdin Kenmare told you someday you would find me. But why do you still try to hide the reason from me? I know it's about Esmanaa!"

"My maker told me I would find you someday, and we would fight the Esmanaa together. You must be careful with this knowledge and always hide these thoughts from others. It is dangerous for you to allow others to know any of this. When you are on your own, I will explain all of this to you."

Shawn approached her again and embraced her. "I want to make love to you. I will hide it from Anne."

"I want to make love to you, but she would know. I can't risk making an enemy of Anne. I will need her support in the future, and so will you. I can hide taking blood from you, but she would know immediately if my blood was in you, and she certainly would smell my sex on you."

Shawn kissed her again, and she still pushed him back, walked to her clothes, and dressed, turned her head, and looked into the distance.

"I must leave, and you should go home. Anne has come home, and she knows where you are." Victoria laughed and said as she rose into the air, "You must be a handful for her, young Shawn. I will find you when you are ready."

Naked, with a frown on his face, Shawn stood in the bay. He waded to the shore, dressed, and went home. Victoria had plans for him that he knew. *Fight demons,* he thought, *maybe he should have told her about the coming disaster.*

At the end of that year, Marilyn left with Eric to travel with his band. Before she left, they went back to their home in Washington. Anne went to the room in the cellar and brought the vase of Bricius' blood to the parlor. Shawn watched her pore two small glasses for them to drink. The blood seared its way through his veins, pulled at him, and made him follow its power. Shawn drifted in the light and felt the energy of his life force. Slowly, the vibration changed, the light faded, and he was at the tree in the green field. Shawn knew that heaven was near and looked into the distance and saw the light coming across the field toward him. The brightness made Shawn want to move away but knew he shouldn't. The orb stopped some distance from him, and he saw a woman in the light. He knew immediately who this woman was.

Shawn heard a soft familiar female voice. Finally, we meet. I have watched you since your mortal mother gave you birth. I was with you when you were near death in the war. You felt me. I hid you and kept the rogues from you.

You are... Herit.

Yes, I am Herit, once the leader of our blood covenant, the covenant that has fought demons and will become the slayer of demons. You will become a demon killer, but that will take time. Anne, Victoria, and you will kill the demons. There will be another, but that vampire is not apparent. The angels have seen this. The angels sing of Anne, the greatest of vampires, made by the blood of Bricius. After his failure with the Esmanaa, Michael demanded him to make Anne a vampire and leave in her possession the strength of my earthly blood. The angels hide your real purpose from Anne; they must, the Esmanaa know of her and watch her. The angel Erdin Kenmare wants you to follow Victoria, to learn from her about the demons. To receive her vast knowledge of the Esmanaa. She knows what the angels want from you. Victoria knows the way, but be careful of the dangers.

The angels have picked the wrong vampire—I'm no demon killer.

You have been destined to be a vampire since your mortal birth, to exist in the Herit Covenant, to be a demon fighter. You were not—as you say—picked. For now, listen to Anne when she teaches you how to deal with evil, how to handle darkness. You have not really experienced the Esmanaa yet, but you must prepare yourself for this. It will take all your strength. My time with you is up. We will meet again.

The light moved away, his vibration increased, and he woke to Marilyn staring at him. She told Shawn how she had gone to the next world, and Herit had met her. Herit said you would need me someday, and I should be ready. She asked him what he thought Herit meant, but he told her he didn't know. The one thing they both agreed on was their strength and senses had surged from the blood.

Shawn spent eight years with Anne, and most of the time, they traveled alone together. Anne took him to Cairo, where she showed him a secluded room she had discovered abandoned at the top of a Giza Pyramid. She often spoke to him about the Esmanaa—never when Marilyn was around. She told him someday the bloodline of Herit would have a great battle with the Esmanaa.

Shawn spent the first two years of his freedom living at the house in Washington. His first trip on his own was to Dalton to find his human parents' graves. The town had seen better days and wasn't the place he remembered as a young human. He found his parents' graves in the old section of Dalton Cemetery, their gravestones old and starting to fade. Next to them was his sister, Susan Nelson.

"Why didn't you marry, Susan?" Shawn whispered. He was sad that she had never shared her life with someone, but he knew Susan, and she usually did what she wanted. He had so much love from his vampire family, and it seemed Susan had so little. There was another small stone almost buried in the tall grass. It read Shawn Nelson, We Miss You. The hundred years of his vampire beginnings had gone by so quickly. He still could remember his parents, but for the first time, he felt an overwhelming grieve for their deaths, and then in his guilt, he looked away from their grave and wiped a bloody tear from his eye.

He knew that human life had nothing to do with vampires, witches, and demons, yet in this life, the angels expected him to be a demon killer. He then felt fear wondering when the time came for his death would humans still bury their dead in this way. He would never be buried this way—he would just fall apart. Would he have any memories of his human family when he died? Sometimes immortality stilled scared him.

When he returned to Washington, he took night courses at a college in Seattle to study archaeology and to continue his research on the location of the Crown of Kilkenney. Finally, with the help of Anne, he secured interviews with vampires who were alive at the time and tracked its location to a small mountain area on the northwest coast of Scotland. Soon after, Shawn informed Anne and began to prepare for his first extended trip alone, away from Washington.

Chapter Ten

S hawn took an anti-gravity airliner across the Atlantic and spent much of his time in the lounge drinking and playing the piano, or in his cabin, buried under his bed covers. How strange it was to sleep by himself, to be on his own, a vampire in a human world. Already he felt lonely and missed Anne and Marilyn. It surprised him how quickly this feeling came on. Shawn had become a strong vampire for his age and had superb flying skills. Thanks to Bricius blood. While in Scotland, he planned to use his flying abilities wherever he went. After all, flying was his favorite vampire skill.

He rented a small house outside of Inverness, twenty kilometers northeast from his search location in the northwest highlands of Scotland. With the help of Anne, he contacted the Crimmians for this effort. Shawn pinpointed the coordinates for his crown and now had to find a passageway into the mountains. He would use his flying skills to search the mountain ranges. This would prove to be a challenge for him due to the continually changing air currents.

Shawn spent his days sleeping alone under the big bed in his bedroom. He moved the mattress and the covers under the bed. He felt foolish doing this, but it soothed him. Anne had always slept next to him.

At first, he wanted to experience his vampire life alone, but now he wasn't so sure. He remembered how Anne told him about her early years; how alone she'd felt. Shawn longed to see Anne, to see Marilyn, but he must live on his own for now. He needed to take care of himself again.

One evening he felt especially lonely. Victoria had told him she would contact him, but he decided he would fly to Victoria's estate in Ireland. Knowing her home was on the North Shore of Clare Island, he flew to the location where he sensed Victoria, and there found a large house on a large, secluded estate. Slowly he descended onto the lawn, the proper distance from her home. He did this so she could decide whether to greet him. This was a typical vampire custom when approaching another vampire's house unannounced. Shawn could sense Victoria, but there was also a male vampire in the house, and Shawn's arrival did not please him.

Soon Victoria came out of the house, walked down the porch stairs, and out onto the lawn, wearing an emerald-colored silk robe. She always excited him when he saw her, her legs showing as she gracefully walked toward him.

"Young Shawn, all by himself," Victoria said. "How does it feel… all of the new possibilities for you?"

"Terrible. I didn't count on the loneliness. I'm used to being with other vampires."

Victoria smiled and said, "Your whole vampire existence has been with other vampires, and now you will learn about the loneliness, the solitude that sometimes comes with our long lives."

"That's why I'm here for your company."

"I'm sorry, Andrew is here. Come back in a couple weeks, and we can spend some time together." Victoria reached out, touched Shawn's cheek, and warned. "Be careful!"

Shawn went back to his little house and continued his search of the mountains. He spent the next week searching for an opening and did his best to put Victoria out of his mind. He should have known that Victoria had a lover; she probably had many. All vampires have different lovers. Who could spend an eternity with the same vampire?

He had finished his second week searching when he decided to travel to Edinburgh to a vampire bar. It was the closest vampire bar, and he wanted to be with his kind. Anne had warned him to be careful when meeting older vampires. Some would use his young age to take advantage of him. He probably was too young to visit this type of place, but he was lonely and felt he could take care of himself.

Shawn arrived in the city early in the evening and walked the remainder of the distance to the bar. He had cleaned himself up and worn what he thought would be respectful clothes for the evening.

It was a crisp autumn evening, and in the distance, a foghorn let out its lonely moan. The vapor was slowly rolling in off the ocean and creeping down the avenues, hiding the buildings one by one. Deserted streets marked this area, typical for the location of a vampire bar. He could hear loud shouting from humans off in the distance, so he slowed his pace and expanded his senses.

Shawn turned the corner onto Lenox Row. Off this street was a dead-end known as Knox Lane. This was the location of the vampire bar. Five young men full of alcohol were standing down the lane, boasting and talking loudly. The streetlight, through the fog, cast a sinister glow around the men. Where did they come from? Shawn wondered. They certainly didn't come from the vampire bar.

He could sense the bar at the other end of the street. The humans turned and yelled at him, "Stay there, we want to talk, ya bastard." The men started to walk toward Shawn, expanding their chests, making fists with their hands. He remembered what Anne had told him about these situations.

He walked around the corner, checked for humans, and floated to the roof above. Squatting at the edge of the roof, he watched the men walk by.

"Where did he go," Shawn heard them say. "He must have gone into one of these buildings."

The men continued to walk down Harbor Way, feeling the alcohol, drinking whiskey from the bottle they carried. The young males were not evil. They were drunk, stupid, and looking for a fight; they were looking for trouble. They almost found it tonight.

Shawn floated over the peak of the roof and came down on the sidewalk that led to the bar. The closer he came, the louder the music was to his vampire hearing. Arriving at the bar, he knocked on the door. The door opened, and a vampire peered out. Shawn could tell he was hesitant to let him in, but finally stepped aside and allowed him to enter. He drew attention immediately as he walked toward a table. He could hear surprised murmurs from some of the vampires: "He's young. He's a Herit."

Vampires had always had a strong hierarchy, and some seemed to have a problem with age. This had always annoyed him.

"The tables are for older vampires, young one. You can sit at the bar," the bartender told him with a sharp voice.

Shawn looked at the man. He was human and a Crimmian. He narrowed his eyes at him, and the man turned away. Shawn took a seat at the bar and ordered, "Whiskey and soda. Make it a double, and don't ever talk to me like that again. I can hurt you quicker than these older vampires can save you, Crimmian."

As he looked around, he could sense he was the youngest vampire in the place. He also could detect humans. There were a few human females with some of the male vampires, but they did not look mesmerized. They wore beautiful clothes and jewelry, and their vampires took good care of them. They kept them for their warmth and blood.

The smell of blood coming from them was strong, and he saw marks where the vampires had taken blood. The male vampires noticed him looking and placed a warning in his head to mind his business. Turning away, he sipped his drink; the smell of blood was delicious, coming from the kept human females. He had not fed in weeks. How sweet their blood smelled. Discipline, Shawn thought but knew he would have to feed soon. To Shawn's surprise, Abigail, a friend of Victoria's, came into the bar. She was with a group of older vampires, but she noticed him right away.

She spoke to her friends and then approached him. "What are you doing here? You need to be more careful."

"I'm fine, Abigail, I can take care of myself now. Anne was an outstanding teacher."

"I'm sure she was, but be careful. I have to join my friends. I would ask you to join us, but some of them would not understand. Take care, Shawn."

"Have you heard from Victoria?" Shawn quickly asked.

"No, not recently. She has been spending all her time with Andrew. I am going for a visit next month. However, she mentions you from time to time. Maybe, young vampire, someday you might work your way into her couch." Abigail gave him a laugh, a wink, and went to join her friends.

Shawn had hoped that Abigail would invite him to sit with her, but obviously, some of her friends would not like that. He finished his drink and ordered another. Some of the vampires were still looking him over. He could sense his Herit blood confused them. He sat and listened to music and drank his whiskey. He hadn't had that much whiskey over the last hundred years, Anne preferred him to drink wine, and even that wasn't too often.

He felt a tap on his shoulder, turned to see a female vampire standing and smiling at him. Her hair was black and fell to her shoulders. She had a slight Oriental look to her beautiful face; one of her human parents must have been Asian.

"Hello. What can I do for you?" Shawn asked.

"Greetings, young vampire. I'm Malene Vinther from the blood covenant Zavan. I sensed you are a Herit. My maker told me about the Covenant of Herit. He told me he knew Bricius."

Shawn could tell she was an older vampire, but not as old as Victoria. He also could tell she wanted something.

"Can I buy you a drink?" Shawn asked.

Malene took a seat next to Shawn. "Yes, thank you, I will have red wine. Such a young Herit. I heard Anne had changelings, but I didn't think it true. She had two, a male and a female. You are the male?"

"The female's name is Marilyn, and I'm Shawn Bryce. Pleased to meet you."

Malene smiled at Shawn. He could sense she was pondering an idea but was hiding it from him. Malene slightly touched Shawn's cheek. "Let's have some drinks together."

"Where are you from?" Shawn asked.

"I'm from Copenhagen. I have lived there my whole life, but I travel a lot. Being a Herit, your blood is close to that of the ancients."

"I have been told that. However, tonight, I am here to have fun and some drinks. And my family is not on my mind right now."

"My covenant has many families, but we are strong vampires. The blood of the angels only dilutes so much."

They continued to drink, and Shawn started to relax. He was feeling the whiskey, and Malene made him feel comfortable. She would touch him and probe him with her eyes. She would brush her lips to his cheek and ear as she whispered her secrets to him.

Malene turned and nodded toward her table. "These are my friends. They are from different families, but we are in the same blood covenant."

Shawn sensed the women were friendly, but the men were indifferent to him. The men eventually left, leaving the two women vampires by themselves.

"Let's go and sit at my table. I want to introduce you to my friends."

Shawn was drunk when he found himself sitting with three older vampires. Malene introduced him to the other two females. "Shawn, this is Athala and Mia, two of my closest friends. I'm staying with Athala while I'm in Edinburgh."

"Glad to meet you. Let me buy us a bottle of champagne." Shawn knew these women vampires were attracted to him, but he still felt they wanted something from him. They continued to drink, and Shawn got drunker, but he was having a good time.

"Would you dance with me, Shawn?" Mia asked.

"Sure, but it's been a while for me."

Mia was the youngest of the three and a good dancer. A thought came through to him—a slight thought stolen from Mia's mind. They want to taste my blood; that is what they want from me. He didn't care; they allowed him to forget his loneliness. He was on his own and having a good time. Shawn kept drinking, and soon it became time for the sun to rise. He left with the women to go to Athala's home.

Shawn found himself naked in Athala's couch, making love to the three female vampires. He felt such pleasure from the vampires, as they all made love to him, felt their bites, each taking their turns, tasting and taking his blood. He saw the crimson glow of their eyes, the blood-teeth, his blood dripping from their mouths, as they took his blood and continued to make love to him. When he felt too weak, they would guide his head to their necks to replenish him. All three paid attention to his body and gave him pleasures he could never have imagined.

Shawn woke to Athala and Mia, leaving the couch. He turned, and Malene was next to him, smiling.

"Good eve to you, young vampire. Did you enjoy your day with us? You are looking a little peaked. Take some of my blood, young lover."

Malene rolled on top of Shawn and guided his head to her neck. Shawn was weak, so he took her blood. Again, she made love to him—moved passionately on him. Malene eyes were crimson her blood teeth long, and still, he felt their sting.

When she finished, she looked into his eyes. "I'm sorry, Shawn, my lover, will be here tonight, and he would be upset catching me in a couch with a vampire as young as you. You must leave, but I hope we will see each other again. Come see me when you're in Copenhagen. I would prefer to spend more time with you, but he is coming, and that won't be possible. Take care, my young vampire."

Shawn dressed and left. He went to a part of Edinburgh where Malene had told him he could find humans to feed on. He felt weak and had an intense thirst for blood. Shawn sat on a warehouse roof, taking in the city, waiting for that sense to tell him his nourishment was there. Towns in this age were different. Flying vehicles were everywhere, and vampires had to be careful when flying in a modern city. He would watch as the lights of the cars arced, then traveled and floated gently down on the rooftops, or the high-rise parking decks. He then pushed his memory to picture the cars of his time.

There it was, the dark evil he had been waiting for! He floated into the air to sense more, and then went to his prey. Two assassins waiting for their victim, leaning on an expensive air car that had landed on the street. The men dressed in fine clothes of the day, gold rings on their fingers and gold watches on their wrists, sleek revolvers hidden in their elegant jackets. They would not see their prey or kill tonight. Tonight, they would become Shawn's prey. Shawn descended, killed both, and took their blood. Full of blood, he traveled back to Inverness, ready to continue his search for the Crown of Kilkenney.

Shawn searched for the next month. He was following a mountain valley southwest until it opened onto a large area of flatlands. The high mountain grass, purple heather, and patches of snow were scattered everywhere. He landed and immediately sensed the two dark wolves. He was concentrating on the side of the mountain and missed them. They were ten kilometers away and started to head toward him.

"Bastards!" Shawn yelled. "Can't you leave me alone?"

Anne would be upset with him. Shawn felt he could handle two wolves, but he didn't want to face Anne if he stayed and fought. He didn't want to get hurt, and he didn't want to go back, but he had no choice.

He flew back up the mountain valley. On his return, he noticed an indentation on the North mountain wall and saw snow pulled into an opening and then puffed back out. Immediately he flew to the entrance fifty feet from the valley floor, landed on a thin ledge, and looked into the large opening.

"Damn, is this it?" Shawn whispered to himself.

Shawn saw a decaying, ornate, brown wooden chest back in the cave. The wind was howling, and the wolves were coming, but he had to see what was in the chest. He crouched and walked back to the wooden crate. The rotted chest fell apart when Shawn touched it, and inside was the Crown of Kilkenney, a golden, roman scepter, and a gold dagger with rubies embedded in the hilt.

Shawn shook his head as if he couldn't believe what he was seeing. He had found his treasure at last. He turned his head toward the opening.

"Damn!" he whispered.

He had underestimated the wolves' speed. They were on the valley floor directly below the opening of the cave. Shawn gathered his booty, set it at the cave opening, and then looked over the side. There were two dark wolves, one black and one brown, with saliva dripping from their mouths and were pacing back and forth on the valley floor among the boulders and snow. He heard the howl of the wolves and the rush of the wind. Anne was going to be livid with him.

Shawn then heard plainly in his mind the wolves: What will you do now, vampire—fly away? Face us, vampire. Show some courage. We know your kind has little of it. The winner will leave this place.

"Filthy beast, I'm going to give you one chance to turn and leave," he yelled at them. Shawn really didn't think this was going to have any effect on them. Dark wolves always showed such bravado.

Tonight, he was not going to fight; he would make his escape, straight up, and would not need his courage.

"Filthy wolves can't jump this high. That's too bad!" Shawn yelled over the howling wind.

This riled them, and the black wolf jumped within ten feet of Shawn. Shawn decided to end this; he gathered his treasure and made his escape, flying out the cave opening. While he was turned away, the black wolf jumped twenty feet to a ledge. The wolf used this advantage to leap and sink his teeth into Shawn's thigh, bringing him crashing to the valley floor.

Shawn let out a scream, grabbed the wolf, and slammed him into the ground. He was drawing his arm back to pierce the wolf when the second wolf's mouth came down on his side. Shawn screamed again at the searing pain. Dark wolves were Lucifer's beast, and their nasty bite always came with great agony. He then pierced the chest of the wolf that was lying on the ground, found its slippery heart, and crushed it with his hand. He suddenly grabbed the wolf on top of him and flipped him into the mountainside. The wolf slid down the side. Shawn flew at the wolf, and the wolf leaped at him. They made contact, and Shawn drove the wolf back, but the wolf's teeth sunk into his upper left arm. Shawn grabbed the wolf's head twisted and heard a snap come from the beast's neck. Two wolves lay dead, changing to their human form.

Shawn was angry with himself. He had allowed the wolves to outsmart him and had underestimated them. Anne had taught him and warned him about the wolves. Now, they had caught him. The wolves had badly hurt him; three bites, and he had two large gashes on his head above his eyes. The beasts had badly bitten his side, thigh, and arm. He was losing blood, and it flowed into his eyes, blinding him. What should he do? He would fly to Victoria's house and get help there.

Shawn gathered his treasure and then flew above the snow-capped mountains, heading southwest across the narrow Irish Sea into Ireland and on to Victoria's estate. Exhausted, he landed on her lawn and immediately fell to his knees, his bloody treasure spilling from his arms. He had healed enough for the bleeding to stop, but he had lost a lot of blood.

Victoria was immediately at his side. "What did you do, Shawn? Look at you!"

She helped him into her house, where he saw two female, Crimmian servants, which Victoria immediately started to give orders. "Bring warm wet towels and bandages. I will be upstairs in the front bedroom."

Abigail was visiting and talking to Anne on the communicator. "He is all right—he has bite wounds," she was reporting. "We will take care of him. Victoria will not let anything happen to him. Yes, I promise he is all right. No, I don't think he can talk right now, but I will have him call you as soon as possible."

Victoria took Shawn upstairs to a bedroom with a large, four-post bed and a canopy. She helped him onto the bed and removed his bloody clothes, took the wet towels, and cleaned the dried blood from him. She slit her wrist, applied her blood to the bandages, and then placed them on Shawn's wounds.

"How did you let wolves get so close to you? Anne is upset over this. You are going to have some explaining to do. She might call you home."

"How did she know?" Shawn whispered.

"She called as you arrived. She knew immediately that you had gotten yourself into trouble and where you were going. She is your maker."

"I found my crown, got distracted, and lost track of the wolves. I underestimated them when I was trying to escape, which I will not do again."

Victoria reached for Shawn's head and guided his mouth to her neck. "Drink and rest for now."

Shawn's fangs slowly sunk into her neck; he bypassed her vein and went deeper for the artery. He allowed the blood to fill his mouth slowly and flow down his throat, took his time, and savored the sweet nectar that was her. Shawn had waited since he first met Victoria to taste her luscious blood. He felt her blood move through his body, and the blood made him feel sexually aroused. Victoria pushed him away, and he fell back onto the bed.

"That's enough, Shawn. Thinking of your cock when you are hurt like this," Victoria scolded him. "Allowing wolves to catch you. You are too careless, young vampire. Why am I not surprised?"

Then he went through the mist, and was on a horse, riding at full gallop. He looked down and saw female hands, arms, and legs—he was Victoria when she was mortal. She pulled up on the horse, and Shawn could hear her say, "Whoa, easy Star." They rode through an opening in an old wooden fence and out onto a field. Peasants had crudely turned the ground by the looks of the dark soil and clumps of grass thrown into a pile. Soon they came upon a group of wretched-looking people dressed in medieval peasants' clothing.

"You must have these beets planted by sundown," he heard Victoria order in a loud, commanding voice.

Shawn heard the harsh "yes," and they called her Lady Draper, and he knew she came from nobility. Victoria turned the horse, and Shawn found himself lying on the bed again, looking up at a smiling Victoria.

"Where did you go?" Victoria said. "Your eyes turned a deep blue. You need to sleep. We will hunt for blood when you are better."

"I take it this isn't your room."

"No, this is the front bedroom. You haven't made it to my bedroom yet."

Shawn fell asleep and slept for two days. When he woke, his wounds had healed, except for red marks where the cuts and punctures were. He immediately called Anne and let her know he was all right. She wanted him to come home, and he pleaded that he needed to stay. The conversation did not go well, but Anne agreed to let him continue on his own.

*****

Victoria had come back to check on Shawn. It was daytime, and she could see the light breaking around the curtain's edge, barely giving view to the room. She liked looking at Shawn's naked body. His wounds were already healing. Her cat, Lourdes, jumped on the bed and licked at the wound on his side. Shooing him away, she said, "Does his blood taste good, Lourdes? I know you like vampire blood."

Shawn was lying on his side, and she smiled, looking at his chest, stomach, and his buttocks, his nakedness. This incident had been a loud warning to her. Shawn was such a young, undisciplined vampire, and he took too many risks, certainly not yet able to help her with the Esmanaa. Now, she knew she would have to stay close to him, to protect him from the evil coming for him. It was only a matter of time before the Esmanaa knew of him.

Victoria felt confused, about falling in love with Shawn. This was not like her; this was not how love was for her. Love for her was different from this. Victoria worried she would lead the young vampire that she was falling in love with to his death.

She contemplated informing Anne about her mission, maybe enlisting her. She would have to tell Andrew she wanted a break from their relationship. Victoria knew that Andrew was also ready for a break, accusing her of wanting a young vampire. He didn't understand, and she couldn't tell him.

She watched and pondered while Shawn slept. He had a rare talent, a rider of vampire blood and he had developed strong psychic abilities, she also knew his strength was that of a vampire twice his age. He was too trusting; she had seen this before with young vampires. Anne had protected him, sheltered him, while he was a changeling.

Abigail had seen him with older vampires in Edinburgh and told her the vampires wanted to taste his Herit blood. Abigail told her Shawn was drunk and went with these vampires. She must teach him to be careful and spend his early years with him. He was young, careless, and she wanted him to survive. Victoria also decided that she would give him a lesson when she took him.

Victoria was saying her goodbyes to Abigail in the sitting room, Abigail was leaving to meet her vampire friends in London. She watched Shawn enter the room and smiled at him. He looked recovered but was pale. *He needs blood,* she thought.

"You look better than the last time I saw you," Abigail said.

"You look pretty good, too. I like the dress," Shawn replied, trying not to stare.

"That's sweet of you," Abigail said as she slipped her shoes on. "Now try not to chase Victoria around the house. I'll see you two later." She laughed and winked at Victoria as she left the room.

Victoria slid onto the green, velvet sofa, patted the spot next to her, and told Shawn, "Get yourself some tea and come sit down."

Shawn poured the tea, set the delicate teapot on the table, and slid next to Victoria.

"How do you feel?" Victoria asked as she brushed his hair out of his eyes.

"I feel fine—a little embarrassed that I got caught like that. I talked to Anne, and she is upset with me."

"You have healed well, just some red marks left," Victoria said as she lightly brushed his cheek with her hand. "I was hoping we could spend some time together. I gathered your treasure and put it in the vault. You realize the crown is a historic treasure and is worth a fortune."

"Yes, I'm aware of its value. This is my hobby. It's how I fill my time seeing how nobody wants to be with me."

"Poor Shawn! When I was your age, I spent a hundred years in the Green Isle by myself hiding. I believe your maker led a lonely existence at first."

"She did. I'm taking the pieces to a secret place in Cairo. And if you ask me to spend time with you, I would love to."

Victoria knew Shawn had become excited at the thought of staying with her. She leaned over, allowing her lips to touch his ear as she whispered, "I will go to Cairo with you, but first, I'm going to take you to Dublin to feed. You are pale, and you're going to need some blood for what I have in mind."

Shawn and Victoria landed on a rooftop in the Ringsend area of Dublin. The spring evening had a slight chill in the air. They were close to the bay and could see the lights in the distance from the ferries heading toward Liverpool. The area was dark and deserted, with narrow streets. They checked the area to see if it was clear, and then they floated to the alley below. Victoria opened her jacket and unbuttoned the top buttons to her blouse.

"This is to arouse the bad guys, not you," Victoria told him. She could feel his sexual tension, and soon, she would give him what he wanted, maybe more than he wanted. "Follow me. Down this street is a gang hangout. We will walk by them and see what happens. I know what you are thinking, but you need to concentrate on the hunt."

"I'll be ready."

She walked with Shawn slowly down Brewster Street, it's stone buildings and steep roofs covered with weathered slate. This was the old part of the city and where the wrong people hung out. She heard the bravado coming from around the bend. The gang had built a bonfire in the dead-end alley showing their large, bizarre shadows dancing on the sides of the buildings. Victoria and Shawn approached the group from the opposite side of the street and saw both men and women dressed in their gang attire with their insignia tattooed on the sides of their necks. The gang members tilted their bottles of liquor to the sky and took their gulps. The catcalls started, and as expected, two men began to follow them. She quickly sensed they were the enforcers of the gang, the bad ones of the group.

"Let them follow us. They might turn back. Their whiskey courage might not be enough for them," Victoria whispered.

"They want you—I can feel that," Shawn replied. "And they are not good people."

They continued walking toward the bay, and the two followed, drinking heavily. Victoria looked back and saw their puffs of moist breath as they hurried toward them.

"Where are you going with that bitta fluff, lad?" snarled one of the men.

"Keep walking," Victoria instructed as she hurried her pace and gave a quick glance over her shoulder.

Suddenly, she heard the bottle shatter against the stone. The men charged her and Shawn. The vampires turned and grabbed the men by their necks and flew them into the alley. Victoria pinned her man against the stone, sank her teeth deep in his neck, and took his blood.

Since her very first feeding, she had always loved the taste of human blood.

She saw the other man draw a laser knife from his sleeve and tried to slice Shawn's face. Shawn caught the man's hand, and his blood teeth tore at the man's neck. The knife fell to the pavement and went out. She saw his brilliant blue eyes, his blood-teeth, and lips coated with the man's blood. She saw the killer in him, her protégée now, a vicious vampire doing the work of the angels. They left the men in the alley with their blank, lifeless eyes, and pale, bloodless faces, and flew back to her home.

Victoria led Shawn to her shower. She undressed slowly, allowing Shawn's eyes to take her in, and then watched Shawn undress. She entered the shower, and Shawn followed. He immediately came to her, kissed her, and caressed her. They lathered and washed each other, both feeling the anticipation of the first time they would make love. Victoria could feel the desire for Shawn to grow, and Shawn's passion for her.

She led Shawn to her couch, and placed her naked body on top of his, wrapping her arms and legs around him to immobilize him. She penetrated Shawn's neck with her blood-teeth and drank. She continued to drink and could feel Shawn briefly struggle to free himself. She was much stronger than Shawn and held him firmly in her bed and continued to drink. She could taste the purity of Shawn's Herit blood.

She sensed Shawn's panic as his strength slowly left him. Then she felt him relax, the fear leaving him. Victoria released him and pushed him to the side. She watched him slowly try to sit up, but he was weak from the loss of so much blood. Victoria pushed him back down, straddled him, and guided him into her. She made love to Shawn for a long time. She made sure his lips had kissed, and his tongue had tasted every part of her body.

Lying next to him, she whispered in his ear, "I'm more than eight hundred years old and can do what I want with you. Again, you could have lost your life. Older vampires can do what they want with you—remember that—there are evil vampires in this world. You must be more careful! There are many evils in this world, and a time will come when they will seek you out—and your Herit blood." She then guided his mouth to her neck. "Take back the blood I took from you."

She felt Shawn's teeth enter her neck, then forcing her down onto the bed, pressing himself against her. She saw his eyes glow like sapphires, his fangs covered with her blood. He lay on top of her, entered her, and made love to her aggressively, rolled her over, and forced himself onto her again. He left bite marks on her and took back his blood as he brought her to orgasm.

Victoria allowed herself to be submissive to Shawn. She let him do what he wanted with her. She knew he was a proud, young vampire and was going to show her he could be dominant. They lay on bloodstained bedding in her couch, exhausted from their lovemaking.

"I knew you wouldn't kill me," Shawn said. "I know Erdin, too, Lady Victoria Draper. I know more about you than you think."

Victoria had suspected that Shawn had somehow contacted Erdin. And he knew her mortal last name, but he was a rider of vampire blood.

"It is time we bring our secrets out into the open, my love. How do you know Erdin? How do you know my mortal name?"

"I met Erdin in the spiritual world, in a sunny, green meadow under a large tree when Anne turned me. Herit was also there." He continued. "When I drink vampire's blood, I can travel back in their lives. I become them. I can see what they see and hear what they hear. Usually, I don't do this. It can be dangerous, and it made Marilyn mad. Since Anne changed me, I've had this ability. My psychic abilities grow stronger the older I become. I know my strength is increasing much faster than other vampires'."

Victoria placed her lips next to Shawn's ear and whispered, "You and I have formed a connection now. We exchanged a large amount of blood. I will always know when you are happy or sad. I will know when you are hurt or in trouble, and you will know the same about me."

"What do the angels want of me? Why do they come in my sleep and talk of killing demons?"

"I have much to tell you. Michael and The Mother want you to help me destroy the Esmanaa, to cleanse this world of their dark and evil presence. We must grow stronger to accomplish this, and you, more disciplined. They make you stronger while you're in the spiritual world. The angels do not allow most vampires in the spiritual world—only the light. Herit will give you great strength, and with Anne's help, we will rid this world of the Esmanaa. We must keep this a secret until you are strong enough to face them. You must always cloud your thoughts when it comes to this. The Esmanaa must not know that you are here to destroy them."

"Anne has told me about the Esmanaa—Lucifer's demons, terrible creatures that have turned against good and deceived their way to Earth. I once saw Amon traveling Anne's blood and hid from Horsa with Anne and Marilyn as the monster passed over our hiding spot!

Victoria kissed Shawn passionately. She loved the feel of his lips, his taste, and his smell. "Let's sleep, we will talk more of this later. You have tired me, young vampire."

Chapter Eleven

S hawn sat next to Victoria on a large limestone block two-thirds of the way up a Giza pyramid. The desert sand had, over thousands of years, blasted the filler from these ancient stones and left perfect perches to sit and lie upon. Shawn and Victoria brought his treasure to the secret room in the pyramid. They now shared a bottle of wine and sat in front of a hidden crevice left long ago between two mammoth stones of the pyramid. The crevice was two feet wide and six feet tall. The opening ran twenty feet into the tomb and ended at a large rock that, with great strength, turned on a pivot point. Past this stone was Anne's ancient, treasure-filled, hidden room.

The air was hot, and the night sky clear. He had used his vampire eyes to blanket the night sky with bright white stars. A hot, dry wind blew against his face and blew Victoria's hair back to expose more of her beautiful face and neck. He saw a large, full moon projecting a yellow path across the desert sand, only to be lost when it met the lights of the city.

Victoria spoke softly, "You leave yourself so open when you are with me."

"I have nothing to hide. Unfortunately, you're not quite that giving."

"At the lounge tonight, I enjoyed your performance at the piano," Victoria said, "You are a talented musician."

"My mother and sister were musicians. My sister was a concert pianist. My mother was a music teacher at the school. I have to concentrate now to see their faces. I'm afraid to say I have forgotten their voices."

"When we were in the bar, did you think the human girl was pretty?" Victoria asked. "I saw you watching her. Do you seek her warmth?"

"No. Sometimes I watch the mortals, but she looked like Herit. I can still remember being mortal. I don't know if you can."

"Some… only flashes. I think long ago, I chose not to think about my mortal life. A time came when I was not sure what it was like to be mortal. Sounds and smells will trigger feelings and thoughts of when I was human. I have lived a long time as a vampire and have been with many vampires, but never a mortal. I prefer to hide my true self from the mortals. I am cautious with humans. When you kiss a human, they will know what you are, unless you hide yourself from them. Anne must have taught you this."

"Yes, she did mention that," Shawn said. "Can you remember having sex when you were mortal? Your time was much more proper."

Victoria took a drink of wine and then started to laugh. "Yes, I think I did once, but I'm not sure. Eight hundred years is a long time. I have learned in my long life that people have always had plenty of sex."

"You are the only one I want to be with," Shawn confessed, then leaned and kissed Victoria passionately.

"What's that for?" Victoria whispered.

"I kiss you now because you will let me."

"You will live a long time, and you will want to be with other vampires," Victoria told him. "I'm sure you have realized this by now. At the cabaret, you attract humans. You like being with humans. I can tell, and humans like being with you."

Shawn took a sip of wine. "Humans have come a long way since you were mortal. They aren't peasants anymore for nobles to abuse and look down on."

"You kill them with no hesitation, though," Victoria whispered.

"To me, killing evil is what makes the most sense in this world. This is my purpose now, something the angels won't let me forget."

They sat, drank wine, and watched the flickering stars, the silver moon watching them with its pocked-marked surface. Shawn saw a small sand twister formed and traveled its erratic path across the desert and then disappeared.

Victoria broke the silence. "I want to talk to you about the Esmanaa. I have spent centuries tracking them to where they live."

"You know where they live? Did you tell the Vampire Council?"

"I have never told anyone what I know about the Esmanaa," Victoria said. "The council tries to ignore the Esmanaa. They have no interest in my knowledge. Besides, my maker told me to hide from the Esmanaa. Nobody can know until we are ready. Esmanaa have many spies, some are vampires, and you never know who their spies are. When you talk about them, you must always shroud your mind. There are times they sleep and become inactive, but they are awake now and scheme the enslavement and destruction of the human race. The Esmanaa plot to start a great war."

"You know this?" Shawn said.

"Yes, I have heard them speak of it. I want to take you to observe Charun. He is the weakest among them, but still, if he discovers us, he has the strength to kill both of us. He lives in Russia, west of Saint Petersburg, in a stone mansion on Lake Ladoga, just south of Priozersk. We can get near him, but he still has the means to sense us if we get too close. That is why we must cloak ourselves—never allow your mind cloak to drop. I know you have these abilities. I wouldn't take you there if you didn't. This is how you can hear what they say."

"How do you know about the distance?" Shawn said. "Why should we take such a risk?"

"My maker, Erdin, taught me. The Esmanaa can sense a vampire within ten miles of them. One mile from them, cloaking won't work."

"I have met your maker in heaven. He killed the Esmanaa demon Amon."

"He was more daring, and he was stronger than me. He took more risks than I would. You must start learning about the Esmanaa and experience its evil. They are much stronger than you are, but their psychic abilities are fragile. When you have the strength to face them, you must know them and be ready for them."

Shawn pushed Victoria back onto their bedrolls. "Right now, I want to learn about you." They made love on their perch on the side of the pyramid while a warm desert wind blew over their naked bodies.

Shawn arrived in St. Petersburg with Victoria three days later and took a suite in an expensive hotel in the city. Victoria, like Anne, had gained a great deal of wealth over her life, and he soon found out she liked staying in nice places. They hunted and found blood in St. Petersburg, and then made their way east to the shore of Lake Ladoga.

They traveled north, following the shoreline of the lake. The night was cold, and a mist hung over the lake. The moon was barely visible through the clouds. Shawn and Victoria used care and stealth as they made their way north. They arrived at a large marsh that surrounded the estate of the dark angel Charun. Human mercenaries guarded the two roads that led into the estate. At this point, they were ten miles out from the compound.

"Careful now, we must keep all our thoughts secret. Stealth is essential now," Victoria whispered. "We will take the marsh. It will give us the best view of the house. When daylight comes, we will hide in the marsh under our bedrolls. There is a cloud cover, so we should be all right. Our bedrolls will protect us."

They traveled into the marsh, always using the high grass for cover. One would proceed a short distance, then the other would follow. They would take cover together and repeat the movement. Frost covered the clumps of marsh grass, and the dark, rich dirt of the marsh—slightly frozen at the surface. Ice crystals were forming on the many pools of water. The morning had come, and the day's light came over the horizon and spread over the marsh. Ducks flew overhead, honking their morning arrival. Victoria was beautiful in the light of the day with the streak of mud across her cheek. Patches of fog drifted off the lake, carried along by a slight morning breeze, and a rich, earthy smell made its way into Shawn's nose.

Soon they came to a higher, drier patch of ground that offered cover. Now the vampires were within a couple of miles of Charun's house.

"This looks like a good place to take cover," Victoria said. "It's the driest place I've seen. We are close now, and we must keep our thoughts hidden."

"I can sense microwaves up ahead. They're probably coming from their security cameras," Shawn warned.

"We will have to avoid the cameras and sensors when we proceed this eve. Let's rest here. From this point on, we have to be sure of our path," Victoria warned.

They lay on the cold, damp ground, huddled together under the bedrolls. Shawn moved close to Victoria; she draped herself over Shawn, between him and the sun.

"We could bury ourselves."

"We'll be all right. We don't need to bury ourselves," Victoria said. "I don't want to get dirty. Let's try to get some rest."

Shawn was restless and wanted to talk. "Anne once told me the Esmanaa attacked her. She said they were heavy creatures."

"They are very dense beings. Three of the demons weighs over three thousand pounds. Horsa and Zepar weigh close to five thousand pounds. Esmanaa uses its speed, weight, and strength very effectively."

Suddenly, Shawn shook his head in an attempt to rid it of this new sensation. A terrible sense of evil came over him. "Victoria, what is this, what has possessed my mind? The smell is terrible."

"That's Charun. He has come home," Victoria whispered. "We must be careful now. We should try and sleep. This eve will be a perilous time for us."

Shawn sensed the fear in Victoria. He tried to sleep, but his thoughts kept going to how fate had led him there. He would much rather be at a pub having a good time than spying on these horrible creatures. He finally drifted off to sleep and dreamt of hiding in the arches of some medieval cathedral, and heard the priest chant a mass. He saw the nobles and priests of long ago gather underneath him, and the smell of incense hung in the air. He saw a part of Anne's life. Shawn often dreamt of Anne's life, especially when life stressed him. She was his maker, and her blood was his.

Shawn slowly woke and sensed a terrible evil, far stronger than when he had fallen asleep. It brought a melancholy with it. It engulfed him and wrapped itself around him as if it were a dense, dark cloak. It was suffocating. Then came the horrible smell—a smell of death—

but far more intense. Shawn knew this smell from a time when he was human. It was the same smell of a dead, bloated corpse under a hot, Vietnam sun.

Shawn shook his head, and it disgusted him. He perceived maggots crawling on his hands, arms, and face, the buzz of a million insects grinding in his head. His instinct made him dig at the ground. He wanted to bury himself, and then he heard Victoria whisper while she stroked his face and held him still.

"The remainder of the Esmanaa have arrived at Charun's house. This is very unusual. Lucky for me—bad for you. I know this is terrible for you. Only vampires can sense this evil so intensely, and it will affect each of us differently. Our keen senses work against us sometimes. We sense this evil far stronger than humans do. This power is what they used against the humans and the leaders of this mortal world. A demon will slowly project this darkness into their consciousness to make them think there is only chaos in their world. They slowly manipulate humans, giving them pain and doubt, which makes them worry and despair. It brings a terrible emptiness, and this turns them to drugs, crime, murder, and war. We can go forward or back, I will leave it up to you, but I would like you to see more. The angels want you to see more."

Shawn wanted to go back, but he could not admit this to Victoria.

"We'll go on," he said reluctantly.

"Try to dampen the sensations you're feeling," Victoria instructed. "It can be done."

"I'm doing better. I'm starting to control it better."

"We'll levitate just above the ground and move slowly through the marsh," Victoria said. "When we get to the lookout spot, we will cover ourselves with the bedrolls."

"Remember, located ahead of us are cameras," Shawn whispered. "Are you sure about this?"

"Follow me, I know a place about a mile and a half out from the house, just ahead of the cameras," Victoria said. "We can see and hear the house from there. Remember, keep yourself hidden—it's crucial now."

The night was cloudy and cold. Shawn followed Victoria, floating in a horizontal position just above the ground. He slithered around the clumps of frosted marsh grass and over the slushy, soaked ground like a field snake moving through the reeds. A half-mile away from the cameras and sensors, they came to Victoria's predetermined location and quickly covered themselves with their bedrolls.

Shawn could easily see the mansion in detail with his vampire eyes. The estate was secluded by the lake and needed no surrounding walls. A perfectly manicured green lawn ran its way to a stone-and-brick, three-story building with a steep, Victorian roof. The house had a large white porch and large glass windows that reflected the outside lights.

At each end of the house was a towering steeple that rose higher into the sky than the building. Heavily armed, paramilitary guards were inside the tower and throughout the compound. A hundred feet out on the lake was an anchored yacht, while onshore, speedboats tied to a dock...at the ready.

Shawn and Victoria quickly became soaked with cold water from the damp ground, but the bedrolls allowed them to blend into the dark dirt of the marsh. They peered around clumps of marsh grass, watching and waiting. Shawn was having some success controlling the terrible feelings and smells of the Esmanaa.

"How are you doing, love?" Victoria whispered.

"I'm doing better. You've been here before, haven't you?"

"Yes," Victoria said. "I've watched all of them through the centuries."

Suddenly, a large, middle-aged man with blond hair walked onto the back patio of the house.

"That's Zepar," Victoria whispered excitedly. "He is the leader and the strongest."

"He's the one that attacked Anne."

Two short and stocky, black-haired men came out, followed by a large, stocky, red-haired man.

"The first, black-haired man is Charun, and the ugly, dark-haired man is Shenti. The red-haired man is Horsa."

"The demon we hid from," he whispered. Shawn watched the demon's light cigars and heard them talk about a Chinese ambassador. The demons gave the ambassador money to mislead his government. Shawn could sense deep and powerful evil from these creatures, darkness with many layers. Anne had taught him the Esmanaa had tremendous strength, and move with unbelievable speed, could fly through the sky, and live forever, but that was all they could do. He knew this now. He had gotten close to them, and they were completely unaware. They had little ability to detect vampires.

Shawn watched how intensely Victoria observed the demons. He whispered to her, "They don't know we are here."

"No, they don't," Victoria whispered back, "as long as we block our thoughts. They are active now, I can tell. They are weaving their webs of evil again. They want to start a great war. They are buying influence in governments, instilling darkness in crucial government people, so they can lead them to disaster."

Shawn lay there and listened to the Esmanaa discuss bribing and manipulating a Russian government official. He heard the talk of a great war. Chills went through Shawn's spine. He heard them talking about gaining the ability to raise the dead by using modern electronics. They spoke of vampires they had killed. Finishing their cigars, they started back toward the house. Shawn's blood turned to ice when Zepar stopped, turned, and looked in their direction. He stood there for what felt like an eternity, then turned and followed the rest into the house.

Shawn felt sick, his hands shaking. The constant sense of evil and sadness from these demons wore on him. He felt his cheeks get wet, could taste his blood as it reached his lips. Shawn wondered how the angels could possibly expect him to destroy these creatures. He felt hopeless now; he could never be near these monsters. He felt pitifully weak next to these demons. Again, he heard the buzzing of flies in his head looked at his hands and saw maggots crawling on them.

Victoria stroked his cheek with her hand and wiped his tears. "You will get better at this. It was hard on me at first."

"The angels have made a mistake. I can't stand being near the Esmanaa," Shawn said in disgust. "Now, I understand, Bricius."

"They are evil beings and hard to be near, but we will have to try. It will be a long time before we are ready. Only the angels know when. Let's leave. We will move to the lake and use it for cover."

They slithered to the lake, entered the water, and swam with great speed westward. They went deep, along the bottom of the lake in darkness, seeing with their vampire eyes, using their vampire strength to propel them. The bottom of the lake was sand with large boulders, long blades of grass, and vines of vegetation swaying in the deep, cold currents of the lake. He saw a sunken ship, with rusted military vehicles strewn around its hull. When they had gone a couple of miles, they turned south and swam toward the southern end of Lake Ladoga. Five miles from Shlisselburg, they broke the surface of the lake and took flight to St. Petersburg.

They landed a couple of blocks from their hotel, dirty, tired, and disheveled. Shawn was feeling better, but the experience had left him shaken. They went straight to their hotel room, closed the curtains, hung a "do not disturb" sign, showered, and went to bed. Shawn lay next to Victoria, as close as physically possible.

He had sensed evil before, but nothing like this. This evil was so strong that it brought on a sadness that took hold of his mind and clouded his thoughts. A feeling that enslaved his being. The next time he met with the angels, they would have a talk. Shawn moved his leg over Victoria and tried to move closer to her.

Victoria kissed and caressed Shawn. "You will be all right. Once out of their presence, these feeling will leave you. It was a rare occasion to see all four together. That's why the sensations you felt were so strong."

"How do you kill beings like them?" Shawn asked.

"You take their heads off. That is how Erdin killed Amon. With a sword that has a blade made of the hardest metals and is sharp as a razor. Remove their heads, and Hell is where they go."

"I am not ready as a vampire to take on the likes of the Esmanaa," Shawn whispered. "I will certainly tell the angels this the next time I meet with them."

Victoria turned and placed her backside into Shawn's stomach and pulled his arm over her. "Hold me tightly, young vampire. Our confrontation with the Esmanaa is in the future. We are vampires, and we have time."

"Did you hear them talk about raising the dead by using modern science?"

"Yes, that was disturbing news," Victoria replied. "They must have a strong connection with Lucifer now. We should try to find out more about this. Erdin came to me in my sleep and warned me of a new development with the Esmanaa. This must be what he meant."

"You see Erdin in your dreams? You have contact with him?"

Victoria turned, took Shawn's head, and looked directly into his eyes. "When I am asleep, I have limited contact with him. I learn, like all vampires, from the angels in the light. They teach me about Heaven and Earth. They are my friends, and like yours, have been with me throughout my life. I can travel to the astral plane whenever I want, but I have never been to the spiritual world. Most vampires cannot travel to the spiritual world like you, we have great strengths and psychic powers, but only here in this world, on this planet. Our power is here, forever, if we wish, but vampires have minimal access to the upper spiritual worlds." Victoria then guided Shawn's head to her neck. "Take some of my blood to soothe yourself. Drink, and then we will make love and sleep. You're tired. You will feel better this eve."

Shawn's teeth entered Victoria's neck, and the sweet blood flowed down his throat. Her blood strengthened him. He loved the taste of her blood, her flesh, as much as he loved her. He lay on top of Victoria, kissed her neck and breasts, made slow love to her, and fell asleep in her arms.

Shawn drifted in the light and soon felt a pull—a calling from Herit. He was sitting against the tree in the green field, with scattered white clouds in the sky, and more trees, to give his spot a wooded feeling. Far off in the distance, he saw a large, glowing light that took up a section of the horizon. He was in Heaven and at the gates of the Archangels Michaels city. There was immense energy coming from the light. Then, a smaller light came out of the bigger and traveled toward him. It was Herit. The light stopped a distance from him. He realized why vampires didn't come here. It was the immense amount of energy.

Welcome, Shawn, I see you struggling as a young vampire. You will find your way, you will see. I have faith in you. You have now experienced the Esmanaa.

They are horrible creatures, and the angels have made a mistake with me. I am not the one to fight these demons. Flesh and blood cannot kill those evil creatures. I cannot stand to be near them.

I know you are still a young vampire, but you will be ready when the time comes. A vampire's life is as long as the Nile, and sometimes it flows quickly, and sometimes it flows slowly. You are a vampire, and you have time. Your battle with these demons will come. The angels have made no mistake when it comes to you.

Herit, when the time comes, will I have the strength to face them?

Yes, but you will need far more than strength. You will need cunning and, more importantly, faith in Michael and the angels. You must learn from Victoria all you can about these demons. Even now, they strengthen the connection between your world and the darkness known as Lucifer and Hell. Soon they will start a great war. Over the centuries, the Vampire Council had no stomach to face these demons. They have allowed the Esmanaa, by their complacency, to weave a dark plan that will plunge the world into chaos. The council did not accept that mortal weapons are far stronger now. Far more destructive. This occupies the angels and The Mother. Guardians must help the human race survive. They must protect them from themselves and from the evil that will come. The destruction of the Esmanaa will come after the coming apocalypse. The angels will soon make their plans known to the Vampire Council.

The Mother's witch Pandora told Anne about Victoria and me.

My beloved Anne, who has lived her vampire life with strength and cunning, the most powerful of vampires. No vampire will ever surpass her. She has sensed your purpose. And now knows her destiny is also yours. You and Victoria will need her strength for the coming battles.

Is there any way I can escape this destiny?

No, Shawn, this is your fate—have courage. Remember this guardian, The Mother also watches you. Now, I must leave but we will meet again. Herit moved back toward the bright light on the horizon.

Shawn allowed his life force to drift through the astral plane, back to his physical body, lying next to Victoria.

Shawn spent the next seventy-five years with Victoria. He traveled with her and lived at her home in Ireland. His strength and psychic abilities continued to grow at an accelerated pace. He made trips to the spiritual world to gain mental strength and talk with the angel Herit.

He took many trips with Victoria to spy on the Esmanaa and learned to deflect their evil, but the horrible smell remained. Over time he learned the habits of each of the four Esmanaa, including their likes and dislikes, and what he perceived their weaknesses were.

Unfortunately, their age difference as vampires were beginning to show as the years went by. Shawn liked to go to the vampire bars and the mortal discos where he could drink, dance, play the piano and socialize. On occasion, he would dance and talk with human women. This was entertainment for him. He would ask about the latest politics, learn the social norms of the times, and listened to the different types of slang as the years passed.

In his vampire family, this was normal. Anne had taught him to deal with mortals. Victoria liked to travel, buy, and sell paintings and did not feel the need to socialize with mortals. The ending of their first period together began when they were returning home from one of Victoria's art trips.

Shawn had sensed a group of bad men in a small, well-guarded compound in the Kashmir Province of Pakistan, and wanted to investigate. They had not fed for two weeks, and Shawn felt the need for blood, but Victoria wanted to travel on to a more familiar place to find blood.

He had convinced Victoria to come, but now she wanted to leave. There were too many mortals throughout the camp. The compound was back in a valley where the hills on each side rose sharply. The ground was rocky, mixed with fine, brown dirt, and scruffy pine trees scattered along the hillside, with no clouds in the sky, and no moon, only the stars blanketed the sky. There was one fortified wall built across the steep valley to connect the two hillsides, and behind the wall were the many buildings.

"Shawn, I can tell an older vampire has been here," Victoria warned. "This could be his territory. We should leave."

As Victoria was saying this, he sensed four rogue vampires flying directly to them. On their arrival, the rogues attacked them, trying to drive them from the compound. He was getting the better of the rogues as Victoria quickly overpowered them. During the heat of the fight, Shawn mistook the rogues, thinking they were demon rogues and killed one. This drove the rogues away, but immediately, an old vampire arrived. The ancient vampire was in a surly mood and instantly overpowered Shawn holding him off the ground by the throat.

"You have destroyed my property—vampires. This place is where I keep my belongings, and these humans and vampires guard this place. I will kill this male. It will be just retribution for your crime."

Shawn saw Victoria change to her vampire form and circle the old vampire. He knew she was preparing herself for the attack—an attack that she probably would not survive. Shawn heard her voice turn to ice, and she hissed her reply at the vampire.

"Our apologies, sir, but we didn't know this place belonged to a vampire." Victoria became desperate. "I will not let you harm him. I cannot allow it. I will fight you."

"You will not survive your attack, vampire, but I see you care very much for this one. And I sense the angels do, too. I can see in his mind. He has given you away with the Esmanaa—your secret. Maybe we can work something out. What do you say, young vampire, or should I just tear off your head and then take care of your lover?"

"I'm for working a deal," Shawn gurgled. "We can pay you for the rogue. Also, the Vampire Council would not look kindly on you killing us."

The old vampire threw Shawn to the ground. "Do you think I care about your worthless Vampire Council, stupid young vampire?"

"Please, sir, he is young, and sometimes his tongue and actions get the better of him." Victoria was close to begging. "I would be grateful to you if we could work out a deal. What is your name, master vampire?"

"My name is Jawid. You will pay me one million dollars for my property, the young one killed. Pay this amount, or I will kill you both."

"I will pay for our lives—one million dollars," Victoria promised. "I will guarantee it with my word. You can trust me. You can sense that. I will send the money to any place you choose."

"Then we have a deal, I will trust you, and if I don't get my money, I will find this young, stupid vampire, and tear his heart from his chest. You're lucky—I, too, hate the Esmanaa, so I will spare this one."

Victoria and Jawid worked out the details, and the old vampire let them go. Shawn was aware Victoria was upset with him, disappointed in him, and knew she thought his response wasn't necessary—they should have left. She felt he did not use his head again.

"You almost got us killed. You have to stop being so reckless if you are going to survive as a vampire. You take nothing seriously. You should listen to me more. I sometimes wonder what Michael was thinking of sending you to me."

"I'm sorry!" Shawn pleaded.

"You gave us a way to the old vampire. He saw the Esmanaa in your mind."

A couple of months later, Shawn slept with a mortal woman. He was drinking heavily and wondered what it would be like with a human woman. He let his lust for this woman get out of hand, and knew Victoria would feel differently, she would feel betrayed. A couple of days later, she came to Shawn.

"I can sense and smell it in you. You have been with a human woman. I have never felt it was right for vampires to be with mortals. You are a vampire, and you have betrayed me! You have betrayed my love!"

Shawn had never seen Victoria so mad. She took hold of him with a sturdy grip and flung him through the door, out into the yard. "I want us to go our separate ways!" Victoria yelled at him. "I want you to go back to Washington!"

He tried to stand, but Victoria was on him and drove him back to the ground. She turned him over, and he felt the hard slap of her hand against his face, a mighty blow that stunned him. He could see Victoria was beside herself. She bit him on the shoulder, not to drink blood, but to hurt him. Suddenly, he saw her start to sob.

As Victoria fell off him, she sobbed, "I love you. I'm sorry I hurt you. I never thought I could hurt you. I want you to leave. I don't know how you could have sex with humans. I'm disappointed in you."

"I love you so much, but I do love other vampires," Shawn pleaded to her. "I was curious with the human girl—that's all. That is how I am now. When I was human, I wasn't like this. Now I realize you will not be my only love."

Victoria sat on the lawn and continued to cry with her head down, blood-tears falling from her face. "I have spent centuries preparing to fight these demons, and Michael sends me a playboy. I love you, Shawn. I love you deeply, and I have never understood why. Leave me now!"

Shawn was hurt and angry with her, something he thought would never happen. He had spent his life as a vampire longing for her, and she did not understand how much he loved her, how committed he was to her. Now she had attacked him and asked him to leave. As a vampire, he realized almost immediately his immense ability to love. He loved Marilyn, Anne, and Victoria. He loved and cared for the humans, the race he came from. Victoria was different from him. She did not give her love as quickly and as much as he. She was from a different age and did not think of humans the way he did. Maybe too many years separated them after all.

Chapter Twelve

S hawn wore a wide-brimmed, white hat, a white, seersucker sports jacket, and pants. Underneath the coat was a blue t-shirt, and on his feet were brown loafers with no socks. He walked along a sandy bayou road lined with small palm trees and swamp brush. Scattered about were Majestic Cypress trees covered with grey, hanging, Spanish moss. The air was hot and muggy, heavy with insects, and all the sounds associated with them. This did not bother him. He did not sweat, and the insects had no taste for him.

Shawn had cleaned himself and was taking his weekly trip into town to meet and drink with his mortal friends at the Blue Bayou Lounge. He came to the bayous of Louisiana ten years earlier. He knew the local population talked about him, the blonde, good-looking young man, a scientist who had moved to the bayou. The man who walked the back roads of the swamp, always at night.

It had been twenty years since Shawn had left Victoria. He was now almost two centuries as a vampire and had been a vampire for far longer than he'd ever been human. Now being a vampire was mostly what he knew.

He bought—with Crimmian help—a small, abandoned research building made of a rusted, metal roof and green-painted cement blocks covered with algae and moss. The building was at the edge of the bayou and came with a long, L-shaped dock that traveled out into the green soup that was the swamp. Shawn had local workers remodel the building for a living area and a large garage to store the long, flat-bottomed swamp boats, electric boat motors, batteries, and marine mining equipment.

He spent most of his time traveling and living with Marilyn since he left Victoria. Last year she went to Rio with Eric and his band, bought a house with him, and stayed. Shawn knew she didn't care for swamp life. She would complain to him about the constant, grating buzz of insects and the croaking of frogs at night. He was on his own again.

Depression had its grip on Shawn when he came home from Ireland. Anne told him a story about two brothers she had known in Manassas during the Civil War to cheer him up. They were known as the Benoit brothers, Jack and Roy, and had lived in Iberia, Louisiana. She explained to him that they were spies for the Confederate army, and the Vampire Council had sent her to Antietam to protect the battlefield from rogue vampires feeding on the dead.

She told him she met the Benoit brothers in a tavern at Manassas, and her beauty had clouded their judgment. They allowed her to drink and play poker with them, always bragging how they stole fifteen tons of Federal gold from a train wreck outside Chattanooga. They bragged one night over cards, with their alcohol-soaked brains, how they hauled it south in two wagons to the bayous of Iberia, Louisiana, while laughing and winking at each other.

Anne laughed at the memory and admitted to him how this had finally piqued her interest. She became especially seductive, fanning their male egos, drawing them in slowly, mesmerizing them, and gradually loosening their tongues. They dropped the gold into a deep pool of swamp water, and only they knew the location. While mesmerized, they drew her a map that showed the site of the gold.

Anne informed him that she never saw the brothers again but heard one year later that Union agents had killed them at Vicksburg. The location of the gold—now worth two hundred million dollars—died with the brothers. Shawn knew Anne never went looking for the gold, she was not the type to go digging in a swamp, but knowing how he loved treasure hunting, she gave the map to him to cheer him up.

The brothers drew the map poorly on a piece of old rough canvas, but after eight years of research, he located the general area marked on the map. Tonight, deep in thought, Shawn walked toward town. The political situation of the world was becoming grimmer as the years passed. The Chinese and Russians had formed an economic alliance and were now courting India to join. They were imposing their ever-increasing demands on the Europeans and the Americans.

Anne told him it was the work of the Esmanaa and probably was too late to stop them.

Shawn had arrived at the Blue Bayou Lounge, and, upon entering, heard the familiar voice of the bartender. The bartender had an exceptional reputation with the ladies, and they called him Johnnie Love. "Good evening, Shawn. The usual?"

"Yes, a bottle of that grocery wine, John. And how are you this evening?"

"Doing fine. Hope this heat breaks soon," John said. "The rest of us sweat, but you look as cool as a cucumber."

"I always could handle the heat. That's why I didn't mind coming here for my research."

Shawn liked coming to the Blue Bayou. They were friendly, he could drink, and they would let him play the piano and sing. Sometimes, he would dance with the human girls, but never went home with them. Someday, Victoria would return, and he wanted to be sure that he could tell her he had not been with a mortal woman.

A couple of evenings later, he was back at work, traveling into the bayou on his long swamp boat. He had located two deep pools with his sonar alongside a small island and was sure this was the spot marked on the old map. He had just come to the surface after searching the bottom of one of the deep pools for the gold. To his disappointment, he had found nothing.

"Damn it," he muttered to himself, spitting the brackish water out of his mouth. He climbed back into the boat. As he was picking the leeches off his skin, he heard the enchanting melody of the witch Pandora.

Shawn looked across the swamp and saw her floating just above the water, coming through the mist toward him. She was wearing a long, light green linen tunic, was barefoot, and had a brown rope tied around her waist. In her hands, she held a short, brownish rod. The hairs stood up on the back of Shawn's neck. It was her, the witch, and no Anne this time.

Pandora landed at the end of the longboat, and Shawn took a couple of steps back. He realized now how big she was, a tall, majestic woman. Her blond hair blew slightly in the breeze, and she had beautiful green eyes. "Greetings, vampire. I trust you have been well since we last met."

"Good to see you, and I have been well," Shawn replied with a hesitant voice. "What brings you to this place?"

"This is my part of the country. I live on the Texas side of these wetlands. When I realized you were here, I came to see you. The Mother also wanted me to pay you a visit."

"What's the small stick for?"

"This is my rod, my weapon, to attract and cast The Mother's energy. Some mother witches use a staff, and some push the energy with their hands. I prefer this rod and always take it when I travel through the swamp. You never know—you might run into a vampire." Pandora let out a loud laugh that echoed through the swamp. "I'm afraid I have some bad news for you. The Esmanaa have learned your name. The dark angel Lucifer detected it from the cast of angels the demons came from. They have become suspicious of you. They know you are from the Herit Covenant, so beware."

"They have learned of me? That's not good," Shawn said. "I should tell Victoria."

"Yes, tell Victoria," Pandora said. She started to drift toward him. "The gold you are looking for is on the other side of this island." Pandora then gave him a mischievous look. "Do you think this witch is pretty?" The witch's body wavered, and Shawn felt his body lose its weight. He heard a beautiful melody in his head as if it were coming from a music box. Pandora's face was in front of his. He felt dizzy, and then strangely had a desire for this witch. Pandora had him; he couldn't clear her from his head. He tried to get away, but the witch grabbed him before he fell into the swamp. He heard her voice, but it sounded so far away. "I'm sorry to trick you, vampire—The Mother wants your seed."

She pulled him into her and kissed him deeply. He raised her tunic and felt her buttocks and between her legs, and then they collapsed to the boat floor where he made love to her.

Shawn woke naked and alone, lying at the bottom of the boat. The witch had taken over him, mesmerized and seduced him, and had done this so quickly, so completely, before he could react, or muster his defenses. He remembered what Victoria had said about trusting. He would have to be more careful with this witch.

Shawn returned the following night to the other side of the island, located another deep hole, and set his equipment. He dove into the swamp and descended to the bottom. The suspended dirt and algae swirled as he swam by. The shadow of a crocodile hidden by the tall weeds, swam past him moving off to a more secluded spot. He was perfectly capable of seeing in this darkness. He only breathed once a minute, so lack of air wasn't a problem for him.

The bottom was a mix of fine silt, sand, old logs, and sticks, with vegetation dancing in the currents made as he swam by. He only had to dig a couple of feet down through this muck to find his treasure. Shawn broke the surface and gave a yell of elation. Finally, he had found his second treasure. He spent the next three months, bringing the gold to the surface and moving it back to his building. Shawn stored the gold in an underground vault installed during the remodeling of the building.

Another month had passed, and Shawn was close to salvaging all the gold from the bayou. Loneliness had its grip on him this night. Anne had just left from her annual two-week visit. He always felt lonely after Anne left him. Anne would spend two weeks every year with each of her changelings, no matter where they were. She told him she was traveling north to Memphis to attend an art show, where she was going to meet Renee.

Shawn had put on his seersucker clothes and the old, wide-brim Southern hat he had found. He was walking the sandy back road from his home to the Blue Bayou Lounge, thinking of Victoria. He had received a strong sense of Victoria two days ago; she was in New Orleans with her art. Shawn had missed her, thought about contacting her, to tell her what Pandora had told him, but he was a proud vampire, and she had asked him to leave. Shawn also knew she was with another man. He decided to wait, afraid she would ask him to go again.

The sensation came on quickly—an overpowering evil that escalated rapidly. Then came the smell. Shawn had detected the demon, but he was moving so fast it didn't matter. The ground shook when the beast landed twenty feet in front of him. It was accompanied by a hoarse blast from a trumpet that vibrated his skull, and a cold arctic chill. Shawn shook his head, trying to shake the evil from it. It was the one called Charun, short and stocky. He stared at Shawn and tilted his head from side to side like a vulture, an evil smirk on his mouth.

His face then changed— his nose flattened into his face to show two large holes—his nostrils. His skull and body grew, and the crown of his head thickened with bony protruding knobs. His eyes bulged and turned black as night. His mouth stretched longer at the corners, his lips thinned out, and his hands grew large, with long fingers and thick, yellowish nails at the tips. The monster had a ghoulish look of evil, and his skin lost texture and took on a smooth, greenish tint. Shawn had learned over the years observing the demons with Victoria, if you could call any of the demons foolish, Charun would be the one.

Charun giggled at Shawn. "You are the vampire Shawn Bryce, are you not? A vampire of the Herit Covenant. Yes, that is who you are. I can tell you hide your mind from me. That is very rude of you, vampire."

"What do you want from me? How did you know where I was?"

"We may not have your psychic abilities, but we have many rogues and mortal spies."

Shawn knew Charun planned to kill him. The angels had missed something. He was not strong enough yet to defend himself against this demon. He thought of sending a psychic "SOS" to Anne and Victoria, but he did not want them killed.

"Why the angels speak of you so much, I wonder. You tell me the answer to that, and I will tell you what I want from you," cackled Charun. The demon chuckled at everything he said. He seemed mad to Shawn. "Oh, I know you aren't going to tell me the answer, but I will be gracious and tell you the answer to your question. I am going to do what I would do to any Herit I meet. I'm going to kill you." The demon gave out a loud, cruel laugh that sent a chill through Shawn's body. "I'm going to kill you, vampire! I'm going to kill you slowly and cause you pain—and I will enjoy it." Charun giggled and kept on laughing in a crazed way. "I will tell you secrets, vampire. We are going to kill your precious Anne. When humans are done destroying themselves in the coming war, we will enslave the rest of mankind in this world."

"You are a pathetic, evil creature!" Shawn shouted. "Why do you search for me!"

"You occupy the same world as me, vampire, and I cannot allow that. We know your kind plot against us. To kill us and send us to our father, Lucifer. The warrior angels of Michael humiliated us, drove us from Heaven. Now we will kill all warrior vampires on earth. This is our revenge on Michael."

"Get over it! That was a long time ago!" Shawn spat.

"Why do you hide your mind from me? Let me hear your thoughts if you have nothing to hide—I hear nothing from you, vampire. I didn't think you would let me into your mind."

The first attack was sudden and with a speed that Shawn could barely detect. The demon lowered his head and charged, trying to ram his chest with his thick knobby skull. Shawn pivoted his body to avoid the strike, but the monster caught him in the right shoulder, spinning him like a top and sending him flying down the road.

The blow stunned Shawn and broke his shoulder. Charun giggled at him as he quickly got to his feet. He flew at the creature with all the power he could gather and struck him, barely moving him back. The blow sent waves of pain through his body and underlined the gravity of the situation. Shawn pivoted around the demon and wrapped his arms around the demon's neck, flipping him over his hip and propelling him down the road. The beast regained control, hovered above the ground, and started his giggling again.

"Is that the best you can do?" Charun taunted. "You are no threat to me. You are too young and weak, vampire."

Again, the monster lowered his head and charged at Shawn, this time catching him in the chest with a crushing blow. Shawn flew into the woods, plowing through thin scrub pines, and finding himself half-buried in the sand. The demon had crushed his chest, and he was bleeding from his eyes, ears, and mouth. He started to lose consciousness but told himself not to, or that would be his end.

"Your smell makes me sick," Shawn cursed at the demon, blood spurting from his mouth. "It always has--- every time I've watched you." Again, he flew at the monster, but the demon caught him by the throat. The monster's fist repeatedly struck Shawn in the head and side, breaking his bones and sending him flying into the underbrush. The blows had distorted his face, and now he crawled helplessly back toward the road. Darkness was trying to take him. *I am going to die,* he thought. He would not live long as a vampire, after all.

He now sensed Anne, Renee, and Victoria coming to his rescue, but they were too far away. The demon was standing over him; he picked Shawn up by his throat and plunged his filthy hand into Shawn's side. *Now death is coming,* Shawn thought. *Death is here. Where are you, angels? Don't let the demon have me.* As that last thought left him, Charun turned his head, dropped him to the ground, and kicked him to the side of the road. Shawn was quickly losing consciousness; he raised his head to see Pandora standing thirty feet away with a look of rage and disgust on her face and her rod in hand.

She then began a chant, "Power above, fire below, Mother Earth send your wrath to kill this demon foe." Pandora raised her arm to the sky and stomped her foot and again yelled, "Send me your power, Blessed Mother! Send me your might for this fight! Help me, Mother, to save this chosen vampire and rid yourself this night—of this blight!"

A deafening boom and then a crack sounded as the air filled with an electrical charge that Shawn could feel throughout his body. The electricity danced on his skin, and his surroundings came alive with it. His hair stood on end, and then the electrical charge condensed around the witch and formed a sphere of electricity. The energy channeled into her, down her arm and out her rod, shooting toward the demon a white plasma beam, pulsating and surging with power.

The beam hit Charun, bending around him like the flame of a blowtorch surrounding a metal rod. Sparks flew off the demon as he held his arms in front of his macabre face. This kept the beast in place and stopped his advance. The witch was trying to save him, Shawn realized. He sent a mental message to Pandora, which told her Anne, Renee, and Victoria were coming. She turned her head, looked at

Shawn, and nodded that she understood. A terrible smell and taste of ozone were in the air, and then he lost consciousness. Darkness overtook him, and everything went quiet.

Chapter Thirteen

V ictoria was in New Orleans—her painting The Lost Boy had won a significant award. She had worked on it since asking Shawn to leave and painted it in his likeness. Now, The Society of Artists had selected it as one of the top pieces of art for the last decade. She had easily sensed that Shawn was only a hundred miles to the west, but she was with her vampire lover, Blake, and decided she was not ready to contact him. This evening she was attending a banquet to honor her and four other artists.

Sitting in the back, she requested not to speak at the podium. She could not help thinking that Shawn would have no problem talking to the mortals in the room, but he was much more comfortable with humans.

The society displayed her painting. She rose to the accolades, took her bows, smiled at all the mortals, and repeatedly mouthed, "Thank you."

"You look beautiful tonight," Blake said. "I love how you did your hair, with the sparkles and the tinted streaks."

"I have to keep up my artist's look, you know," Victoria laughed. "Besides, how do you expect me to keep your interest? A man with so many lovers."

Victoria was raising her champagne glass to take a sip when it hit her. A horror that she had not expected to sense this soon. She dropped the glass to the table, and it shattered, sending a sharp crackling sound throughout the room. "He is dying—it is the Esmanaa! How did they know?"

"Who's dying?" Blake questioned.

"It's Shawn. I have to go." She quickly rose from the table, sending it sliding across the floor, tipping over the candelabra, and startling many of the mortals.

"Victoria, are you going to leave me here? I'm here for you—this evening is for you!"

"I will contact you as soon as I can!" She answered over her shoulder as she made her way toward the exit.

"Victoria, you can't be serious!" Blake pleaded. "I'm going back to the hotel. I won't wait long for you!"

Victoria made her way outside and hurried down the street to an alley where she found cover from the humans. She tore the bottom of her dress off, kicked her shoes to the side, pulled a dagger from her purse, and tossed the bag to the ground. Then rose into the night, heading west at a speed that taxed her vampire powers. Their blood connection was strong, so she knew his location.

Ten minutes later, she arrived at the site to see large bursts of white light pulsating and lighting up the night. Maybe this will attract some mortals, and the demon will have to end his attack. She also sensed that Anne and Renee were coming from the north. Unfortunately, they still were a distance away.

Victoria circled the area and saw a witch firing her rod at the bastard Charun. She saw her using the energy beam to push the demon away from Shawn, protecting him. Shawn was lying motionless on the side of the road near the witch. Blood soaked his clothing, but she knew he was still alive.

She pulled her dagger from its sheath and prepared to make her first run at the monster. If she and the witch could hold the demon away from Shawn, maybe when help arrived, they could drive him off. Victoria began sending telepathic messages to the witch. "When I strike, stop your attack." She continued to repeat this message as she circled and aligned herself for the charge. While preparing to dive toward the demon she received a reply.

I understand, vampire. I don't know how long I can keep the demon back.

Victoria sent a message back to Pandora. More help is on the way. Be strong. She then dove at the demon at a speed that no human could see. She straightened her flight path, approached Charun at a blinding pace. As she arrived, the plasma beam stopped, and she drove her dagger deep into the back of Charun's neck. She tried to severe his spine but missed. The knife did not have enough metal. The monster turned and caught her with a mighty bash to the side of her head, sending her crashing into the brush. She tumbled through the swamp brush, which slowed her speed. A tall, thin pine tree finally stopped her flight, and then came crashing down on her.

The blow had stunned her. She quickly rose, cleared her head, and whispered to herself, "Erdin, please, we are in trouble." She saw the witch resume her attack on the demon.

Charun again leaned into the plasma beam and slowly advanced toward the witch. "You tax me, witch, but soon I will have my hands round your neck."

"Will you, demon? You won't find me as helpless as that young vampire!"

Victoria flew at the demon again, hoping to pull the dagger from its neck. She pulled and took possession of her only weapon, but the monster caught her by her leg, swung her, and flung her again into the swamp, crashing through the trees until halted by a large cypress that shook from her impact. She, as well as twigs, moss, and dead leaves, fell to the ground. How she wished she had her slayer.

She wiped the blood, caked sand from her face, retrieved her dagger, half-buried in the dirt, and attacked the demon again, plunging her blade into the front of his neck. She took too much time trying to make a cut in Charun's neck. The knife broke at the hilt, and the demon caught her by the throat. Charun held Victoria in front of him. She tried to break his grip, but did not have the strength, and looked into his bulging black eyes and spat at him. "Someday, demon, your time in this world will be over."

Charun giggled and replied, "Maybe, but it won't be by you this night. I recognize you from long ago, a Kenmare, the vampire of Erdin's making, and you are protecting this Herit. He must be something special, a weapon the angels are making to use against us. No matter, I will kill all of you before this night is through." Charun ripped what was left of Victoria's dress from her and he raked his long, thick yellow nails across her chest. He gouged her, tore her flesh, and ripped a breast from her. The monster beat her face and body and then threw her at Pandora as if she were a ball and he the pitcher.

Pandora was ready and ducked as Victoria flew by, landing on the sandy road and rolling to a stop. Pandora began her attack again, lowered her rod and fired, but the demon came closer.

Victoria knew she couldn't take much more of Charun's assault. She was losing strength, and her mind was becoming cloudy. Shawn and Victoria's blood stained the sand around Pandora. Victoria forced herself to her feet and propelled herself at the demon. Flying over Pandora and into the beast, she drove him back. She landed on top of Charun and plunged her hand into his stomach, only to hear his demonic giggles.

He then stabbed his hand into Victoria's chest in return. She screamed, flew back off Charun, and fell to the ground. The demon was on her. He rolled her over, and with a mighty stomp, landed his foot on her back, breaking her spine, making her legs useless. He grabbed her by the hair, pulling her up, her feet dangling, and tossed her to the side of the road. "I will kill you and that Bryce as soon as I'm done with this witch," Charun snarled.

"Again, Mother, again, for help is almost here. Send me more of your power!" Pandora screamed as she lowered her rod and fired at the demon.

Victoria fought to stay alert, but she was losing that battle, too. She raised her head and saw Shawn lying in front of her, used her arms to crawl toward him, trying to be near him. As she reached him, he opened his eyes briefly, looked at her, and then closed them. She thought he saw her, but with his grotesquely battered face, she could not be sure.

She turned her head and looked back at the demon as a flash went by him, and the monster screamed. Help had arrived at last. Victoria laid her head back down on the sand, and darkness overtook her. She had done all she could.

*****

Anne became aware almost immediately that Shawn was in trouble; it had stopped her cold. It was the Esmanaa trying to kill him. She was preparing to leave Memphis, packing her belongings after attending an art show. Anne had displayed paintings and artifacts that she had collected over the millennia.

The trip was successful until that moment, with the sale of two of her paintings. She and Renee had just changed into their travel clothes and were waiting for the Crimmian servant to return with the limousine.

A terrible fear had come over her. "It's the Esmanaa, Renee. They are trying to kill Shawn."

"Yes, I can sense it, too. Shawn is to the south of here," Renee answered.

"This is Victoria's fault, I know it." There was anger in her voice. "I warned her about this!"

Anne immediately retrieved a large, polished, mahogany case. She had brought Deceida and another slayer like it. She found the sword in the catacombs of Paris centuries ago. The slayer lay next to the remains of a dead vampire, probably killed by one of the Esmanaa. She had been a little jealous of the swords. The slayers had received more attention than her paintings.

Anne hurriedly took the swords from the case and gave the copy to Renee. "I always intended to give you this. You don't have to come if you don't want to."

"Of course, I'm coming, Shawn, and you are my family, and without you, I have nothing."

They went to the balcony and propelled themselves into the night, proceeding south at an impressive speed. Anne took the lead, while Renee flew alongside and slightly back from her. The lights below passed by at a blinding pace.

As they drew closer to Shawn, doubt started to enter Anne's mind. Could she reach him in time? Blood tears came to her cheeks. She wiped them away and told herself she must keep her thoughts pure for the coming fight. She thought of how she had found him almost two centuries ago, a damaged human in a car wreck. How her love had grown for this male and the mischievous look he always gave her. She also knew it would crush Marilyn if there were no Shawn.

Anne would do everything she could to kill the Esmanaa that had taken her Shawn's life. No, he is not dead yet, she told herself, and then she detected the witch, Pandora. Maybe she can help Shawn and, then—yes—Victoria is there, battling this demon. The two of them would give her the time needed to save Shawn. She strained even harder to increase her speed at this newfound information.

As she approached the fight, she could see a pulsating, white light surrounding the area. It was the witch Pandora, barely holding the demon back with the energies of The Mother. She saw Shawn lying motionless and a badly beaten Victoria crawling toward him with her useless legs. Anne received a message in her mind from Pandora.

When you strike, I will stop my attack.

Anne and Renee slowed their descent, circling around to approach the demon from behind, warrior vampires guiding themselves to their target. Anne yelled at Renee, "You strike first to distract him! I will hold back and then strike! Use your sword and go for the neck! Don't ever let go of your slayer, or you will end up like Victoria!"

Anne thanked Michael that this demon was Charun and not Zepar. Renee started her dive toward the monster, swooped by, and delivered a slice to the back of the demon's neck. The demon screamed at this new indignity.

Anne had positioned herself in front and flew at him like an arrow shot from a bow with a glowing Deceida in front of her. She plunged it into the demon's chest, rolled around him, and twisted the sword to create a large, open wound. Charun swung at her and slammed his fist into her side, driving her to the ground. Anne rolled away and then retook flight, slayer in hand.

Renee struck again, thrusting her sword through the demon's shoulder and into his chest. The beast turned and caught her in the head with a blow from his fist, sending her into the pines and brush. She slid to a stop, shook her head to clear it, and wiped the sand and blood from a gash on her cheek. Renee rose into the air for another attack. Anne came around the monster in an arc and delivered a deep wound to the side of the demon's neck.

The evil, sadistic smirk had left the monster's face, replaced by a look of fear. The two vampires took turns attacking him repeatedly. Charun was starting to lose this fight, and the vampires he faced were stronger than any he had ever come across. Renee dove at the demon sliced him across the throat, and immediately accelerated straight into the sky to avoid another blow. Anne landed fifteen feet in front of the monster, holding her slayer with both hands and sidestepping to circle the beast. Deceida glowed a white light, and its steel rang with anticipation.

"Another Bryce, the elder Anne, I see." Charun turned his head and spit a foul load of brown blood from his mouth. "It will be a pleasure killing you."

"You are not dealing with a young vampire now, demon, and you will pay for what you have done here this night. You will pay for attacking my Shawn. The angels are my witness!"

Charun charged at Anne, but this is what she wanted; she knew he would do this. Sidestepping, she pivoted, brought her slayer around, and severed his right arm from his body. Charun screamed and shot into the air to make his escape, his brown, thick, putrid blood splattering the ground.

Anne and Renee followed the monster. The demon was weak now, and they quickly caught him. Renee grabbed hold of his right leg as Anne landed on his back, wrapping her legs around him and riding him like the filthy animal he was. Renee brought her sword around and plunged it into his stomach. Twisting the blade, she made a large gash, allowing his insides to spill out. The demon let out a terrible shriek, kicked Renee loose, and sent her flying toward the ground.

Anne took hold of Charun's head, pulled back, brought Deceida around, and slashed his neck. His dark blood started to spark and sizzle. A terrible stench came from him—the smell of sulfur and rotten flesh. She struck his neck with her razor-sharp slayer again and repeated until finally taking his head from his body.

She fell off him, head in hand, until it, too, started to burn and sizzle with an intense, dark blue flame. The evil stench was terrible, and she flung it away. She watched his body fall to the ground, burning in the same way. Renee returned to Anne's side, and they circled to return to where Shawn and Victoria lay.

Pandora was barely standing; Anne could see how exhausted she was.

"The woman vampire saved us. She saved your young one."

"You also saved him," Anne said as she hugged the witch. "I will always be grateful for this. If there is ever any way I can repay you—ask."

"I'm fond of this male vampire, and The Mother wants him to live. He will live and be pretty again. Now there are only three Esmanaa, and that pleases Eos. She knows a great darkness is coming and now prepares for it. Farewell, vampires, you must stay strong." Pandora rose into the air, headed west to her home, and a much-needed rest.

Anne kneeled by Victoria's head. "Can you hear me, Victoria?" She saw a slight nod of her head. "I'm going to take you to my home and bury you with Shawn. I will watch over you and protect you while you heal. I thank you for what you have done. You saved him for me."

A siren sounded in the distance and traveled up the bayou road. The fight had attracted mortals, and it was now time for them to make their escape.

"We have to leave here," Renee warned. "Shawn is alive, but we must bury him as soon as we can."

"You take Victoria, and I will take Shawn," Anne sobbed.

Blood tears came to her as she looked on her changeling's mutilated face. She could barely tell it was him. His beautiful face…look what the demon did to him. She would kill the beast again if she could. They took the disfigured vampires and flew to Anne's home in Washington.

Before she left the hotel, Anne had quickly sent a message to Marilyn, telling her to hurry home—an Esmanaa had attacked Shawn. On arrival, she met Marilyn and Caitlyn on the front lawn of the Bryce's home.

"For the love of The Mother, what has happened to him?" screamed Marilyn. "Look at his face! A demon did this?"

"An Esmanaa attacked him," Anne answered, trying to control her voice. "The angels were with us. We killed the demon, but we must be on alert and careful."

"Is that Victoria?" asked Marilyn. "I should have known it would be Victoria."

"Shawn would be dead, a pile of dirt by a road in Louisiana, if not for her. She and the Pandora witch saved him. Now we have to bury them, and you need to calm yourself!"

Anne knew Marilyn was going to react emotionally. She also knew they had to remain calm and bury Shawn and Victoria. "Caitlyn, would you get linen strips? The Crimmian servants will make them. Tell them to hurry, or they will answer to me. Then bring them to the basement."

"Yes, Anne," Caitlyn said.

They went to the bronze basement door, down the spiral stairs, lit the proper candles, and placed Shawn and Victoria on the marble cleansing table.

"Marilyn and Caitlyn, soak the linen strips with your blood," Anne told them as she and Renee removed the remainder of their clothes.

Anne used the water hose with Renee's help to clean their bodies, and then they dressed the wounds with linen strips soaked in vampire blood.

"Demons are after Shawn, and we need to find out why," Marilyn sobbed.

"The Esmanaa are always after Herit blood," Renee sighed. "They despise us. They know we are a danger to them."

"We will find out, but first, we need to get them into the ground," Anne said, "Marilyn and Caitlyn, prepare the grave."

Anne and Renee cut their wrists and allowed the blood to pour into Shawn and Victoria's mouths. This was the last step before burial. Victoria's eyes flickered open briefly, and Anne spoke to her.

"We are going to bury you next to Shawn. You will be safe. Heal yourself. All the Bryces are here. We will protect you. We will talk when you come out."

Victoria gave a slight nod and closed her eyes. Shawn had not regained consciousness since the fight.

The vampires placed them in the ground and put linen strips over their eyes. Anne saw Victoria's hand move slowly to touch Shawn when sleep overcame her. They filled the graves, graded them, and lit two large, burgundy candles. They placed the candles in two large, gold candleholders at the head of the pit. Anne then drew two large symbols in the dirt to protect them from the demons. The wait started for the vampires to emerge from Mother Earth.

The rest of the vampires went upstairs to wash, except Marilyn, who stayed to watch over the pit. Anne was in her room, cleaning herself. She and Renee had only received superficial wounds. Victoria and Pandora had weakened the demon before they arrived. Anne was not surprised to see Marilyn's travel bag in her room; she wanted her maker to soothe her. Anne knew she would react this way; she and Shawn always had a special closeness. They had known each other since they were mortal children.

She loved both of them and did not want to think of this existence without them. Anne felt tired this night—she had lived for so many years. She finally realized what Bricius had told her about the melancholy of a long life almost two millennia ago. The centuries now ran into each other. She felt like she was becoming lost in time. It was hard for her to remember the beginning, and she could not see the end. She needed changelings—the ones she already had and maybe a new fledgling to anchor her to this age.

Anne made her way back down the curved stair, stopped, and looked at the gold blood vase from Bricius. Maybe it was time they all took a large drink. She floated over the floor, hugged Marilyn, and kissed her.

"Shawn has left his body. Can you sense it?" Marilyn whispered. Anne could hear the fear in her voice.

"Yes, I can, but he has left a little behind to show us he is all right."

"He thinks of the Esmanaa, this I know," Marilyn sighed. "When we lie together, as he drifts off to sleep, I slip into his mind without him knowing. I could always do this but never told him. Victoria has a lot to do with this. We have to find out what this is. What is going on?"

Anne could tell by Marilyn's hurried talk that she was distraught. Anne embraced her, kissed her, stroked her face, and soothed her. "Calm yourself. Shawn will be all right, and we will find out what is going on."

Anne sensed the arrival of two council members, Hector and Stephen, and knew they were waiting upstairs. Stephen was newly elected to head the Vampire Council. She had given him her support and vote. It had been a close election, and he had won.

"I'm wanted upstairs," Anne whispered. She went upstairs to find Stephen and Hector waiting for her in the sitting room. "Stephen, Hector, why are you here?" Anne asked. "I'm sure this isn't a friendly social visit?"

"No, it isn't," a worried Stephen replied. "The angels sing praise for you, your family, and Victoria Kenmare."

"We have killed a demon. You must believe that is good," Anne told him as she tried to see what was in his mind.

Stephen looked at Hector and then back at Anne. Hector spoke first.

"The angels sing to all vampires of a great battle between the warrior vampires of earth and the demons. They sing to all the courage of the Bryce and Kenmare clans, the reemergence of the Herit Covenant, to take the battle to the demons, and they disparage the council. How a young vampire fights the demons and the Vampire Council runs from the demons. We cannot have this, Anne. We have lost respect amongst our kind. The vampires must see the council as the leaders of our kind on Earth—not the Bryces. You must control your changeling."

"The vampire rogues of the Esmanaa have contacted the council. They arrogantly believe they know all the facts about this incident. They believe that Shawn and Victoria are dead. As I stand here, I know this is not true. They told us a witch was there."

"They did not mention Renee or me?" Anne asked as she felt a wave of exhaustion come over her.

"No, they did not," answered Stephen. "We should allow them to think Victoria and Shawn are dead for as long as possible. The demons have threatened to kill all the council members. What happened in that swamp?"

"The demon came to kill Shawn. The Pandora witch, along with Victoria, protected Shawn until Renee, and I arrived and killed the demon known as Charun. Charun did not hurt Pandora, but the demon seriously hurt Shawn and Victoria, and we buried them in the cellar.

They are under my protection, and nothing will harm them while I'm here."

"Why are the Esmanaa after Shawn?" Stephen asked, trying to probe her mind. "It has to be more than his Herit blood. It did not surprise the council that Victoria was there. When it comes to upsetting the Esmanaa, she is always near."

Anne shut her thoughts off from the vampires, hid her mind, and cloak herself deeply as no other vampire in this world could.

"I don't know why they are after Shawn," Anne lied. "We should have been more involved with the Esmanaa. By our lack of action, the Esmanaa are going to plunge this world into war. To protect the council's name, we need to become much more active in fighting the demons. We must protect humans—and vampires—from the demons. The council must lead the way in the fight with the Esmanaa, not just have meetings about it and talk of it."

"We first have to survive the human assault on civilization," Stephen said. "I have ordered shelters built around the world for vampires. We must protect the humans. Keep the evil that is coming away from them as best we can."

"We will need to arm ourselves," Anne replied. "All vampires should have slayers. Stephen, you should convene the council to decide on these matters. To decide on how much, we expose ourselves to humans." Anne sensed Marilyn going to her room, so she excused herself, showed the vampires to the door, and went to be with her. She took Marilyn to her couch, held her, caressed her, and whispered to her that everything would be all right, made her feel safe like she always did until she fell to sleep. She knew Shawn's narrow escape had terribly upset her, and the coming events were not helping.

The council convened and sponsored an edict to inform vampires on how to prepare for the coming war and what they expected of vampires in the aftermath. They also gave a promise to all vampires of this world that they would do better handling the Esmanaa.

Chapter Fourteen

V ictoria was becoming more aware. She was floating in soft, white light. It bathed her, penetrated her, and soothed her, giving her a feeling of well-being. Her angels came to her, sang to her, and praised her. How long she floated, she did not know or care. She knew the light was to heal her spirit, and the earth, her body. She remembered Erdin's spirit reassuring her, talking to her, telling her how proud he was of her. She had fought a great battle, brought about the death to one of the Esmanaa, and saved Shawn. The angels sang her greatness as a warrior.

He told her the attack on Shawn caught the angels by surprise. She must prepare for the coming apocalypse, and for the great Dark Age that would come after, to be more understanding, to stay with Shawn, and to prepare herself to help the humans.

Victoria heard Erdin tell of how Shawn gave encouragement to the angels by the way he handled the fight. How he showed courage and soul that resisted extreme evil. The angels felt they could give him the strength to defeat the Esmanaa. They thought he could handle this power when the time came. Victoria had her doubts, but the angels must know something she didn't.

Time passed, or so she thought. Erdin came again and told her it was time to leave the light. The light changed to a mist, and soon, the mist faded. She was awakening, coming out. She could feel the warm earth and The Mother's energies surrounding her. It made her feel safe as if she were in a healing cocoon. Victoria wanted to lay there and sleep. Then she felt the strength of the bloodlust; rarely had she felt it so strong. She could see blood in her mind, dark red, a river of blood flowing—coating her—how red it was! The texture, the creamy thickness, and the sweetness—the bloodlust drove her up and out of her grave. Her instincts told her to rise up and satisfy this need.

Reality crashed upon her, blurred her sight, and left her senses slight. She could taste the dirt in her mouth. There was a face in front of her, but she could not make it out.

She sensed it was Marilyn, and then she heard her say, "She is trying to rise."

"Hold her, I'm coming. She's trying to fly and find blood," Anne warned.

"I'll try, but she's a nine-hundred-year-old vampire," Marilyn pointed out.

"Of course…" Anne grabbed hold of Victoria. "Let's bring her to the table. We will clean her and give her blood."

Victoria tried to keep her dry eyes open. They brought her to the marble table. She felt the warm water on her body; they were washing her. She could feel Marilyn's lips cover hers, kissing her. "Sorry, Victoria, but you saved Shawn. So glad to see you healed."

Victoria tried to say blood—that she needed blood—but she didn't know how successful she was. She could see another face over her. It was Anne's.

"I know you crave blood. Renee and Caitlyn are coming to help with that," Anne said. "I'm going to give you some of mine. It will help!"

Victoria felt the blood flow into her mouth. She knew it was Anne's blood. Victoria could feel the energy pulse through her body. She felt herself coming alive. "Thank you," she heard herself say.

"You have healed nicely," Anne told her.

"You will be happy to know that you again have a beautiful breast," Marilyn laughed.

"Shawn," Victoria whispered. "How is he?"

"He has not come out yet," Anne answered with concern. "He is alive, that we know, but where his spirit is, that we don't know. So, we wait."

"I need more blood—please!"

"Marilyn will give you blood, and then we will take you to Shawn's room. He has a big, comfortable bed for you to rest and regain your strength."

Victoria was tired, a feeling that went right to her bones. She closed her eyes and fell back to sleep, a sleep that would come and go for the next few days. She woke, sunken deep into the soft mattress, and wearing a white silk nightgown. They had covered her with a crisp, linen sheet and a thick, goose down quilt. She was better, and then she noticed the tube of blood running to her arm. Victoria looked up, and she could sense someone standing in the doorway.

Marilyn came through the door, walked over, and checked the blood tube and needle in Victoria's arm. "Hello, Victoria. I hope we can be better friends. Thank you for saving Shawn. I don't know how I can repay you."

"Yes, I hope so, too," Victoria whispered.

"I'm checking on you. You are looking much better. You and Shawn were a mess when you got here."

"Is Shawn still buried?" Victoria asked.

"Yes, he's still buried. You were the first to come out," Marilyn replied. "Anne thinks he should come out soon. I'm getting worried, but she reassures me."

"He will be alright."

"I have to go," Marilyn sighed. "You should sleep anyway."

Victoria woke for the second time and sat up with little effort. She was feeling much better. Looking around the room, she could tell it was Shawn's—she had been there many times. His scent permeated the room, and there was an old piano of a long-gone saloon against the wall. There were maps spread over the top of his desk, and she saw drawings of vampire slayers.

He had a large couch with a burgundy top and comfortable bedding. She left the bed and went to the desk to snoop, and found an invoice showing Shawn had ordered six swords. She went into the hallway and could sense Marilyn, Renee, and Caitlyn in the front, watching the news. The Russians were threatening war against the Europeans. She sensed Anne in the basement. Her feet were bare, so she floated over the floor, went to the bronze door, and found it open. She slowly floated down the stairs. They had filled in her spot and raked the dirt smooth.

Anne was standing next to the burial pit. She turned, her face drawn and worried, but smiled anyway. "Glad to see you up. You're looking much better."

Victoria had often wondered how Anne, whom she hadn't seen with a male in her life, had fallen so deeply in love with this one.

"I knew the demon hurt him," Victoria said, "but don't despair! His spirit is gone, but that's not unusual with him."

"Yes, Charun badly hurt him. He damaged many of his organs. You and Pandora saved him—I'm so grateful."

"I love Shawn! I spent many years with him. I would do anything for him, but sometimes he takes nothing seriously! He is such a handful! The angels prepare him to lead the destruction of the Esmanaa, yet much of the time, I don't understand their decision."

"How do you know this about Shawn? And if this were true, why would you leave him so exposed? If we had not been close to him, he would be dead! I warned you a long time ago about Shawn. How I felt about him. If he had lost his life without me knowing what was going on—you could have lost yours!"

"It was a mistake," Victoria replied. "I should have never left him by himself without telling you the truth. My maker spent his existence in this world fighting the Esmanaa. At the end of his life, at his final battle, knowing he was going to lose his life, he buried me to hide me from them. His final words were that the angels were going to send another warrior and that I should look for him."

"Your council induction party is when I felt him. Shawn, standing on the balcony. His first hundred years, I watched him and observed him from afar. The second hundred, I tried to teach him about the Esmanaa, but he wasn't serious about it, and that confused me."

"He didn't tell me about this," Anne said.

"I told him not to. I allowed our love to grow, so he did what I asked. Erdin told me to keep the Esmanaa secret. I had to keep it secret until we were ready, and I certainly didn't think we were ready, not with Shawn's behavior."

"I always knew my covenant would fight the Esmanaa again. But not how or when," Anne told her solemnly. "I will protect my changelings."

"I understand, but the angels are the ones that have brought this, not me. The angels gave me this task. I had no choice, either. Shawn talks with Herit, so you must, too."

"Yes, I talk to her, but she hid this part from me. I remember Erdin's death and the talk about him killing an Esmanaa," Anne said with a far-off look. "I remember vampires believed you were dead, but you were in hiding."

"I was in hiding for a long time. I need to tell you Erdin came to me when I was drifting between this world and the spiritual. He wanted me to know that soon, Shawn would be different. Michael has decided to give him the power to defeat the Esmanaa. He also told me we should prepare for the coming Dark Age."

"The world will change soon," Anne agreed. "The council is meeting in a couple of months to deal with the coming events. I am thinking of building a shelter in the mountain behind this house. You should decide on what continent you are going to live on during this Dark Age. You are always welcome here. I will need my family here—at home."

Victoria saw Anne's concerned look for her family.

"You're tired," Anne said. "You should sleep more, and then we will talk again. Remember, you have an ally with the Bryce family."

Victoria nodded her acceptance and made her way back to Shawn's room. She looked at the big bed, and then the couch smiled and went to where Shawn slept. Her body went horizontal as she drifted down to the soft bedding and pulled the covers over her head. She took in the scent of Shawn and fell back into a deep sleep. She had made her decision.

*****

Shawn had stayed with his body until the death of Charun. His last memory was Victoria crawling toward him, her face badly disfigured. He had sensed Anne and Renee's arrival, and the desperation coming from Pandora. He felt ashamed that he wasn't able to put up a better fight against the demon. Shawn sensed the moment of Charun's death; he could feel a tremendous evil enter the spiritual plane, an evil disruption for all spirits to feel. He waited for Charun's essence to pass, and then he left his body quickly, matching the vibration of his soul to his spiritual place. The greenfield he had discovered so many years ago, and now found himself there, sitting under the tree. He felt worn, tired, but he was safe, and he soon fell into a deep sleep. The sleep was a spiritual sleep that restored his soul, removed the fear and sadness from his soul.

When he woke, he saw a yellow glow off in the distance. A spirit had always been there to greet him, but this time nobody came. Shawn had a strong inclination to follow the beacon of light, and cautiously started down a dirt road toward the light. This world was bright, but then it was always bright. The sky was clear, and the field went on forever, with blades of bright green grass.

Shawn thought how beautiful it would be with colored flowers and white clouds in the sky. The flowers and clouds immediately appeared, he imagined mountain peaks, and they came into focus far off in the distance. He looked closely at the vibrant, shimmering colors that flowed and oozed in a world that was not quite solid.

In the distance, he saw a large city. With the look of a Renaissance city with many steeples and domes with gold roofs that reflected their brightness far into the spiritual sky. Smooth, pastel colors of its buildings shimmered in the light. No walls were surrounding this city.

Shawn thought of walking along the cobblestone path to the city, but the world started to fade. He could feel the vibrations again and reassured himself that everything was all right and concentrated on staying in this world. When he did, the world came back, and the vibrations stopped. A light appeared and traveled quickly to the road, came to him, and a beautiful, Egyptian woman emerged. Shawn knew the spirit was Herit. You cannot enter the city. You are not of the spiritual world, and you cannot stand the energy and brightness of the city.

I can finally see you. How beautiful you are, Shawn projected.

That has no importance in this world. You only see me this way because I will it. It takes a lot of energy for you to see me like this. I cannot stay long. I wanted to see you and talk to you. You will recover from this and grow strong. The angels did not see this; The Mother knew, and she warned us, but it was too late. Much of your life is now clouded to us. The apocalypse has made the future uncertain. You will have other encounters with the Esmanaa. That, we know.

Will I be at the final battle with the Esmanaa?

Eos still sees you at the battle. The death of Erdin Kenmare made the angels searched the future. In the haze that is the future, they see Anne, Victoria, and you at the final battle with the Esmanaa. There is another—we believe that vampire is Marilyn, but we aren't sure. The Esmanaa knew of Victoria and Anne, but they knew nothing about you. You will need Anne and Victoria's strength to accomplish your task. Make good use of their power and knowledge. It is time for the Bryces and Victoria Kenmare to drink the blood of Bricius. Great power will come to the ones that take his blood. I will go to Anne and tell her. I will soothe her like I always have. She is angry with me for hiding our secret from her—my beautiful, courageous Anne.

You love Anne very much.

I love all vampires in my blood covenant. I love you. Herit's hand reached out and touched Shawn's cheek. He could feel the energy leave her and spread through his spiritual body. It gave him courage and hope.

The Esmanaa are aware of me now. They will come for me.

For now, they think you are dead, and they are starting a war. The demon's plans are coming to fruition—the chaos they have woven these past centuries while your Vampire Council ignored them and tried to wish them away. Your days of having a good time are ending. The Great War will mature you, and Victoria will see this. You must stay with her, she teaches you, passes Erdin's knowledge to you, and, most importantly, she gives you direction. The angels expect vampires to protect the human race from themselves and the coming apocalypse.

Shawn saw Herit's brightness increasing, and her human shape losing form. He heard her say, *I must leave, but we will talk again.* Herit moved back toward the city, and the immense light of the city absorbed her radiance. Then Shawn thought of going home and his vibrations started, and the spiritual world dissipated as he traveled back to his body.

He could feel the warm, healing earth around him; the soft purr of Mother Earth welcomed him back. He became a part of her enormous energy, it traveled through him, absorbed him, and then he would return to his own identity. He felt a thirst for blood; the bloodlust hit him with full force. The panic for blood made him move up and out of the ground. He felt Anne grab and hold him. His instinct was to take flight and find blood. He was weak, disorientated, but he knew Anne and Marilyn were there to help him.

"I'm here, Shawn. I have you! You're all right!" He could hear Anne's emotional voice as she wiped dirt from his face. "Look at you—healed. You have returned to us! We are going to wash you and give you blood. Marilyn is here!"

"You look much better," Marilyn sobbed, trying to talk. "Victoria went to London to meet a vampire. We have sent a message to her. I'm sure she is on her way back."

Shawn felt Anne place him on the marble table, followed by warm water flowing over his body.

"Marilyn, give him blood," he heard Anne say.

He tasted her blood as it poured into his mouth and down his throat. He felt his healed body, starting to wake from its deep sleep. Sensations started to come back, and his vision improved. He was tired, but his first overwhelming need was blood.

He must have tried to rise again because he felt Anne push him down. "I know you need blood. Renee and Caitlyn are coming with blood. Let us finish cleaning you, and I will give you some of mine."

He slipped into a deep sleep and woke in his couch. It was mid-afternoon, and Anne and Marilyn were with him. There was a blood tube running to his arm. Anne's lips cover his, she kissed him, and it made him smile.

"My savior," Shawn whispered.

"You better believe it," Anne said. "That was too close—you almost died."

He felt Marilyn wrap her arms around him, and she, too, kissed him. "You keep this up, and you'll have me with you all the time. What have you gotten yourself into?"

"The angels believe I will lead the fight to destroy the Esmanaa. They are deciding if they are going to make me as strong as the Esmanaa."

"You can't be serious," Marilyn responded with disbelief.

"They see in Shawn what I have always seen in him," Anne replied. "His kindness, his fairness toward others, and a determination to find good in mortals and this world. He is poison to these demons."

"Herit is coming to you, Anne," Shawn said. "She will tell you everything. The angels want the council to do better. The Vampire Council has disappointed the angels. They feel the Vampire Council has performed badly over the last a couple of centuries."

"Ahmoss was old and distracted by his preparation to leave this world," Anne told him. "This went on for centuries, and the council became mired in their ways. The angels are right, and the council must do better. Stephen has called the council to action. We meet in a couple of months and will do better—that, I promise."

"Herit also told me it is time for the Bryces to drink Bricius's blood, and Victoria should also drink the blood," Shawn said with a sleepy voice.

"We will talk more of this," Anne said. "You are tired and can hardly keep your eyes open—sleep, for now, my love."

Shawn felt sleep take him, but as long as he had Anne and Marilyn with him, all was safe.

When Shawn woke, Anne and Marilyn had left. Somebody had removed the blood tube, and he sensed Victoria immediately. He felt excited, a little hurried, as he raised the lid to his couch and levitated onto the floor.

Shawn drifted barely above the floor, toward the bathroom, and to the door of the shower. Victoria was naked and wet. The water made her skin glisten. She was smiling at him with a look of seduction. "Hello, my love—awake and all better. Still a looker, you are. You take a girl's breath away."

"You're looking good yourself. Much better than the last time I saw you." Shawn took off his pajama bottoms, walked into the shower, embraced her, and kissed her. "How long are you staying?"

"As long as you let me," Victoria whispered into his ear. "The next time I leave, it will be because you ask me."

"I have not been with a mortal woman since we parted. I haven't! If it bothers you that much, I will never do it again!"

"I understand that Bryces think differently about mortals than I. Your family likes to have contact with them. I like walking with them, but I keep my contact to a minimum."

"I knew you were in New Orleans," Shawn said as he kissed her again. "Pandora came to me in the bayou. Told me the Esmanaa had learned of me. Lucifer detected the angels speaking of me. He heard my name."

"You should have told me," Victoria said. "I'm sorry I made you feel that you couldn't talk to me. We were fortunate that both of us weren't killed."

"I was no match for Charun. He would have killed me if you and Pandora hadn't come. He would have killed all of us if Anne and Renee hadn't been in Memphis."

"I know. I am sorry. You look tired, my love." Victoria guided Shawn to her neck. "Drink, so you can regain your strength."

He allowed her blood to flow slowly over his tongue, tasting Victoria's sweet blood again—her distinctive taste that always excited him. He leaned on her for support and then found himself in the body of a little girl. He saw the childlike arms and hands—Victoria when she was twelve. She was hiding at the entrance to a medieval, banquet room.

It was a large room, and there was a great deal of commotion inside. The castle was primitive, with walls made of large, irregular stones, log rafters in the ceiling, uneven boards for covering, and a slate roof exposed through the cracks in the planking. He saw a large fireplace with an animal on a spit. A dirty, peasant man, with soot on his face and a large carving knife tied to his waist turning the beast.

The room smelled of burning wood and roasted meat and thin tendrils of smoke wafted through the air. There was a long banquet table with men eating and drinking, a burly man, with red hair and a beard to match, rise and point his finger at a man he called Lord Draper—Victoria's father. The man yelled, "You're a robber baron, and I should take my sword to you." Drunken men, dressed for a fight, jumped to their feet with hands on their swords to protect Lord Draper. Two large dogs lay under the table, chewing on large, meaty scrap bones, oblivious to the noise.

Suddenly, a woman grabbed Victoria's arm and dragged her through a wooden door that still had the ax marks from the shaping of the wood. Down a long, dim hall that felt cold and damp, she tugged them. There were windows with rough glass that he could barely see through, and some had no glass—only weathered, wooden shutters. "You should not spy on your father," her mother scolded. He could hear Victoria say, "Mother, I wanted to see what all the yelling was."

"Do you want him to beat you?"

"No, Mother!"

"Then, don't spy on your father!"

Shawn could easily see where Victoria's looks came from. The woman had radiant, red hair, fair skin, a freckled face, and light green eyes with cinnamon eyebrows. Victoria's mother rushed her through a door into a room with medieval wooden furniture and a wooden bed with a rough, faded, red bed cover and a coarse, lumpy pillow.

"Stay in your room and work on your drawings," Victoria's mother scolded as she pushed her daughter into a chair and handed her a piece of coal and old, white linen. "Do not come out until those men leave."

Shawn felt the pull on his spirit, and then Victoria was carrying him toward his couch.

"You're back! What did you see about me this time?" Victoria whispered to him. "I'm taking you back to bed."

They lay together in his couch. He could feel sleep coming, but he wanted to talk about the coming war.

"The Esmanaa are going to plunge this world into a terrible war. I know Anne expects me to remain here to help the mortals, but what are your plans? Will you live here or in Europe?"

"Five years ago, I bought land in Colorado, secluded, back in the mountains," Victoria whispered to him as she caressed him. "I decided to build a house on this land. It is a beautiful place, wooded, and there is a pleasing brook close by. I've always lived in Ireland, but times have changed, and my life must, too."

The vampires spent the next five years in hurried preparation. Anne and Hector took control of North America and all the vampires that lived there. Anne built a secured, underground home in the mountain behind the house. Shawn then moved the remainder of his Louisiana gold to a vault in this new bomb shelter.

True to Victoria's nature, she built a majestic, stone house in Colorado that resembled a castle, with large, stonewalls and a metal gate. Back in the woods, she, too, built an underground shelter. She sold her property in Ireland and moved all her belongings, paintings, and wealth to Colorado.

Shawn stayed with Victoria; they made their preparations and tried to enjoy what little time they had left amid a civilization that soon would disappear.

When the war was imminent, Shawn received an invitation from Anne for the drinking of Bricius's blood. Shawn knew Anne had sent messages to the entire family, and to Victoria. A room was prepared for the drinking and instructions given to the Crimmian servants not to enter the room. Shawn stood in the room next to the small table with the gold vase that held Bricius's blood. Another table held six large crystal goblets, five for the Bryces, and one for Victoria.

Anne divided the blood amongst the glass goblets and then spoke. "You should know that when you drink this blood, you will go into a trance. You will become unconscious. This could last for days. I have drunk small amounts through the centuries, and each time I have lost consciousness. Each time I have traveled to a different place, a different event—this is also unpredictable. The blood will change you. It will make you far stronger than you are now. Are we ready?"

"I'm ready," Victoria replied.

"Cheers!" Marilyn added.

The blood was thick, like syrup, in Shawn's mouth, with a slight sweetness and an old, musky taste. There was a good size portion given to each. Shawn finished his share and set the glass down on the table. As soon as he did this, a loud roar grew in his head. Incredible energy traveled through him, and it felt like it would rip him apart. He fell back onto the floor and found himself floating in the white light.

He could feel his angels around him; he felt them touching him, caressing him. They would pass through his spirit, and he felt an unbelievable bliss, almost orgasmic. Their voices were soothing as they sang their words. They called him a great warrior vampire, a demon slayer.

Their form slowly dissipated, and Herit appeared. She drew him into her and took him to the bank of the Nile River with tall river reeds growing at the edge of the water. It was midday with a large bright sun set high in the vibrant, cobalt blue sky, sparkling and reflecting off the flowing river water. Along the side were huts made of mud bricks and thatched roofs. Herit sat next to him. She was beautiful, and her hair was dark and braided. She wore a blue shroud made of coarse cloth and a necklace of polished white stones. The sun had given her a rich, dark glow. Now he heard her voice plainly, and she told him that she was once the priestess of this village.

She explained to him, "I have taken you to my past so you can sit and be next to me." Smiling, she stroked his cheek and looked at him as if he was her child. "Beautiful Shawn, my blood is in you, vampire. I received this blood long ago from Michael. I am one of the original five. Michael came to this world and took physical form. He traveled the world and changed five humans by draining them of their mortal blood and giving them his blood—the power of the angels. I was bathing in this river, and suddenly the angel was there. He took my blood on the sand next to the river and gave me his. The angel kept company with me for ten days and taught me how to be a guardian. How to handle my powers here on Earth. He gave me a sword so bright I could hardly look at it. I buried the sword and waited until the brightness went away before I took it home." Herit turned and gazed out of over the river.

"I asked him about the gods. He told me that God was the combined love and wisdom of all the angels in Heaven and that I should look to the angels and Eos for help. He said his choir of angels were warrior angels and told me, 'now is the time on Earth for warrior angels to halt the spread of evil.' He taught me to give this blood to others in the same way he had given it to me. Vampire, I am the original member of our covenant. Unfortunately, I only made Bricius before the Esmanaa hunted me. When they discovered me, they chased me for days, and then they surrounded me and killed me."

"The Esmanaa killed you?" Shawn asked.

"Yes, this is the connection you have with the Esmanaa and why they hunt your family. Heaven has always known our covenant will destroy the Esmanaa. Avenge me and rid your world of these demons."

He felt her deep in his spirit; he thought he saw blood come to her eyes. "I'm sorry! You will pay a terrible price for their destruction. Lucifer will seek his revenge."

Shawn felt a cold fear spread through his being, and he whispered, "What scares me is that they will take my soul to Hell. I never speak of this, but it frightens me."

Herit touched his face and gave him a tender smile. She replaced his fear with a feeling of serenity and strength. "Don't be afraid. If that happens, I will follow you to Hell and fight for you—that, I promise!"

"I'm going to hold you to that. Why don't I ever see Bricius?"

"Bricius is not in Michael's choir of warrior angels. He has gone on to another choir of angels. He was not a warrior, and the Esmanaa terrified him. I selected him for his charm, gentle ways, and how he made me feel when he held me—I made a mistake. Being a vampire was new to me, as it was for all vampires at that time."

Shawn watched Herit reach into the water and bring out a small vase. There was nothing in the opening, and only river water filled the vessel. "What is that?" he asked.

"Blood of the angels," Herit said. "Listen and remember what I tell you. When you drink, you will receive the power to face the Esmanaa. You cannot face all of them at one time. Remember this! You must fight them one at a time—use your quickness and agility. You can defeat them. But be careful with this strength and use it for good. If you do not, there will be no warnings. The angels will kill you here on Earth and send your soul to limbo. Remember, use this power only for good."

Herit handed Shawn the vase. He knew it was river water from the past, but he drank. He had only taken a couple of swallows when he felt intense surges of vibrations and energy. He found himself spiraling through a tunnel and heard a hum that rose and lowered very quickly. The noise vibrated his being, and soon his vibration matched the hum of the tube. When he stretched his arms, he could touch the side of the tunnel—it felt elastic and made the waves stronger in him.

Two days later, he woke. The others also talked about experiences, but all of the lessons were different. None of them wanted to give all the details of what happened. There were still secrets about the future that their angels wanted them to keep to themselves. Shawn decided to keep his new strength to himself. He hid it from the others, but they knew. His powers were immense. Now, he could shapeshift and turn himself into a fierce creature or a vapor to penetrate the smallest opening. The angels lead him to believe he was the most powerful vampire on earth.

Chapter Fifteen

S hawn sensed the start of the war. The despair that went through Heaven and the cries of The Mother! It was a Wednesday morning, May 9th, 2198, civilization's last typical morning. He and Victoria had just gone to the couch for a day's sleep. He knew this was coming but still watched the news in disbelief and shock. Russia and India had launched massive, conventional bombing raids and missile attacks on the League of European Nations.

Shawn knew the Esmanaa had set this trap over the last century. Herit and the Pandora witch had warned him of this. The demons convinced these countries to expand outward because of their large populations. They had sown the seeds of domination in the Chinese, Russian, and Indian governments. Economic and military supremacy was what these governments coveted now.

Shawn and Victoria watched the news nightly as they went about closing Victoria's house in Colorado. He watched the three days of bombing, and a massive Russian and Indian army move across the Russian border into Lithuania, Belarus, and Ukraine. He watched and listened to the news as this immense army moved quickly through Eastern Europe. Finally, an equally massive United European Army engaged them.

Shawn and Victoria would hold each other and view the horrific ground battles playing out in Europe. The two armies had fought themselves to exhaustion, neither able to gain an advantage nor push the other back. The Russians, seeing the chance for a quick victory disappearing, became desperate, and launched a nuclear attack on the Europeans. The insanity of such a strike enraged the Europeans, and with the realization that the end had come, they retaliated with a complete nuclear attack on Russia, India, and the Middle East.

Shawn deeply felt the pain and sadness from the many millions of humans dying and The Mother weeping. A third of the world had gone silent, and desperate survival was all they knew now. He took the lull in the war to travel with Victoria to his home in Washington.

Again, he watched, through a technology that soon would be extinct, a great naval battle in the Pacific Ocean that lasted for five days and at great destruction to the United States, Japanese, and Chinese fleets.

One week later, he watched the news flashes, how the Chinese had prevailed in the Pacific, and moved a million combat-ready soldiers across the South Pacific, landing a massive army on the shores of Puerto Vallarta. He heard through the civil defense warning that the Chinese had turned northward and were now invading the United States.

It was mid-autumn. Shawn and Victoria had traveled south to be near the fighting, to see the events for themselves. The Chinese were in full retreat. He learned on arrival that the worst hurricane season in a century had settled in the South Pacific, sending most of their supply ships and anti-gravity transporters to the bottom of the ocean. The Chinese had run out of supplies, and ammunition was scarce.

Shawn and Victoria were close to Freeport, Mississippi. They hid in the trees to watch a division of the Chinese army retreat westward along Interstate 20. This part of the army had pushed into Louisiana until, finally, the United States Marines and citizen soldiers had stopped their advance.

Shock and fear were on the faces of the Chinese, and he heard it in their voices as they desperately tried to make their way back to Waco to join the main army. He sensed in the soldier's minds how they wished they could leave this horrible land and go home to be with their loved ones again. Despair filled the Chinese when they realized they would never leave this place. He saw the many lights from the long retreating procession of army vehicles.

All night Shawn watched the pilotless flyers come and fire their missiles at the Chinese. Sleek, silver machines shaped like arrowheads, with the new ion engines. Horrific explosions shook the ground and hurt his ears. He heard the screams and cursing of the soldiers as they panicked. The Chinese would fire back, and some of the flyers would explode and rain down their burning debris.

In the flyers' wake, the Chinese left many dying soldiers by the side of the road. Shawn heard their cries for help and their pleading for water. This kind of agony he had felt once before, long ago, the desperation of lying wounded, the thirst, and intense pain clouding the mind. As he made his way to help the soldiers, he saw fires burning everywhere—he was in Hell again.

Shawn and Victoria brought water to some of the soldiers. Some begged him to end their suffering, and he told them not to despair—he would send them to Heaven as he broke their necks. Early that morning, when they were taking shelter in an abandoned farmhouse, a massive ground attack ended the long, wretched procession of Chinese soldiers. The survivors scattered and later joined the Americans in a desperate fight to survive the Hell the Esmanaa and humans had brought.

Shawn and Victoria traveled on to Midland and Waco to watch the final land battle of the war. Millions perished in this massive battle. The earth shook and moaned under the tremendous explosions of the R486 bombs, conventional bombs many times stronger than anything used before. The badly beaten Chinese eventually retreated to southern Mexico to live out their remaining days.

Shawn sensed the first nuclear strikes hitting the East Coast. He and Victoria quickly flew north to the shelter in Washington. He learned that China, in a final desperate move to save their army, launched a massive nuclear attack on the eastern and southern United States and South America.

He heard through sporadic transmissions an exhausted and collapsing United States unleash the largest nuclear exchange of the war. He felt a terrible sorrow that in just six months, modern civilization had ended, and starvation and influenza had spread throughout the world. The Great Dark Age had begun.

After the war, Shawn, Victoria, and the family stayed close to home for the next five years. The war destroyed the house in Paris, and Renee and Caitlyn now lived at the Washington house. At first, Shawn listened to humans try to begin emergency procedures. The transmissions soon stopped—he knew they were far beyond the help of emergency procedures. The world would fall silent, and few broadcasts would be heard for the next fifty years. He saw famine and disease further reduce the world's population.

Shawn stayed with Victoria and spent his time in Colorado or the Bryces home in Washington. He socialized with other small groups of vampires or pursued his hobbies and interests. The fallout from the nuclear blasts was slight in the Northwest because most of the atomic weapons had landed on the East and West Coast and the Southwest before the United States destroyed China's nuclear capabilities. Ash from the war had moved north and hung in the air for the next two years.

Shawn watched as the world population formed into small enclaves or towns spaced sparsely apart. Primitive, feudalistic society had begun.

Eight years had passed since the war. Shawn was standing on the fifth floor of a bombed-out office building, located in San Fernando, north of Los Angeles. The massive explosions had blown the sides of the building off, but the floor structure and charred steel supports were still standing.

Evening had come—the round, orange ball that was the sun was setting, covered by dirty, orange-streaked clouds and the mud-colored haze that permeated the sky. He was watching four human, male wretches, hiding in a large, broken section of concrete drain piping. The nuclear blasts had heaved and exposed the piping on the side of what used to be a paved boulevard. Now vegetation grew in the multitudes of cracks and gaps in the crumbling pavement.

Looking out from the building, he saw the massive destruction of what used to be Los Angeles. He was traveling with Anne, Marilyn, and Victoria—their destination, an abandoned government laboratory in Simi Valley. Shawn had gone ahead and was expecting the others shortly.

The Vampire Council had decided to secure human technology and safeguard it until the humans were ready to use their centuries of advancements again. Their targets were the plans and knowledge of cold fusion; their prize was the storage device that held this information.

Shawn saw a family about a mile down the road, pulling two small carts with all their limited belongings. There was a man and a woman with two teenagers, a boy, and a girl. They were dirty, their clothes old, faded, and worn. Their hair was long, stringy, and dry—there was no more shampoo. Their faces were worn and aged from a hard life and the worry of survival. Radiation sores covered their arms and faces.

Shawn, with his vampire eyes and senses, saw the humans pulling their youngest, lifeless child in a cart. The child had died from the radiation, and they were trying to escape west, away from the city and the fallout. This had left them exposed to the new dangers of this world, bad people with nobody to stop them, evil ones who wanted other people's belongings, or their lives. Humans that had succumbed to Lucifer's and the Esmanaa's evil.

The wretched family headed toward the concrete pipe to take shelter for the night. A blood tear came to Shawn's eye—he was human once, and he sometimes cried for the mortals.

Shawn sensed the harm the four evil men wanted to do to this family. He could feel their depravity, their lust for evil, the loss of good in them. *You're going to rape and murder this family for their belongings,* he thought to himself. Shawn immediately changed to his vampire state, gave a hiss, and crouched. The family came closer, and he watched the men with anger building in him.

He could see in the distance two glowing domes of purple, orange, and red light radiating from the blast areas. The city of Los Angeles had flattened in the center and now surrounded by the ragged skeletons of the destroyed buildings. All he saw was the destruction of what used to be a majestic city. He felt the hot, dry air from the blast zones drift by his face, smelled the scorched earth and the decay—here, the devastation was immense. Shawn could sense nothing but despair in this place, and it made him edgy. The family talked to each other, and he heard no joy in their voices, only a desperate tone of survival.

From this point south along the coast, past San Diego and into Mexico, the war had left uninhabitable. The radiation was still too concentrated. Shawn wore a radiation monitor that gave off a verbal reading of radiation levels. Vampires could withstand more radiation than humans, but it was like sunlight to them—it drained their life force. They were following a boundary, a safe zone of low emissions, into Simi Valley.

Anne, Marilyn, and Victoria flew into the opposite side of the building and landed behind him.

"What's the matter?" Marilyn asked.

"Shitheads!" he cursed as he motioned them to crouch.

"The human family is walking into a trap," Victoria surmised.

Shawn looked at Anne and said, "What do you think? Can't we do something?"

"The humans will start to learn of us. They will have to if we do what needs to be done for them. We don't need to feed. Besides—they smell of shit and piss. We will take their heads and meet on top of the building across the street."

They drew their slayers from the sheaths on their backs, spread their invisible wings, and took flight, landing on the concrete pipe that hid the attackers. Shawn smashed the tube with his foot and dragged a filthy man out of the hole. He held him up, quickly took his head, and threw him to the ground.

Then he turned and looked at the family, allowing the humans to see him for what he was. Horror replaced their looks of despair. They saw strange creatures easily take the heads of these men. Shawn changed back to his human state. When he smiled, their looks of horror turned to bewilderment. He flew to the building on the other side of the boulevard and regrouped with the others. There was a spike in radiation readings, so they decided to travel north, then turn and go south to Simi Valley. Later that evening, to their surprise, they came upon a large shantytown.

"Why do they stay here?" Shawn asked in bewilderment. "They are too far south. They should move north."

"The humans don't know any better. Eventually, they will just become sick and die," Victoria answered.

"We should try and find the leaders," Anne told them. "We should risk it... warn them."

"Are you sure we should expose ourselves to the mortals?" Victoria asked. "I'm not sure. They will want to know why we look so different. And I sense an Esmanaa demon to the Northwest!"

"The humans are in trouble. The council has talked about this. We are going to have to come out of the shadows for now. I have the authority of the Vampire Council to use discretion. We will enter and warn them."

Victoria looked at Shawn, and he smiled at her. He knew she was cautious when it came to humans, but he agreed with Anne. The humans were in bad shape, and they had to take risks. He also was aware that Victoria knew instantly how he felt. He had always disagreed with Victoria on how to handle humans, but they now accepted this from each other.

Three roads traveled parallel through the camp, with shanties spread between them. They picked the middle lane and entered the camp, fires were burning everywhere; a haze of smoke hung in the air. There was no breeze—only a stillness to the air that didn't feel natural. In the distance, Shawn heard loud booms in the sky from intense weather, gone crazy by the effects of radiation. The shantytown smelled of cooked meat, burnt wood, unwashed humans, and sewage.

The shanties were small and made of scrap wood, boards, plywood, and sheet metal cobbled together to create a shelter that barely offered protection from the wind and rain. Shawn could hear the muffled talk of humans through the flimsy walls of the shanties. They talked about survival, where to find food, and how to make life better. He heard moans of agony and sickness and could sense an overwhelming feeling of desperation and hopelessness. These people did not know what the future held for them. The war obliterated civilization in this part of the country— human survival was doubtful here.

Soon they started to draw attention from some of the people and looks of surprise and wonder at their condition. "Who are these people? Where are they from?" Shawn could hear this talk spread through the camp.

Suddenly, four big men with rifles were standing in front of them. They had a look of mean fear. By their clothing, Shawn could tell they had been soldiers once. Anne quickly sent a telepathic message.

Do not hurt these humans. If necessary, we will escape this place.

"Who are you people? Where do you come from?" the leader of the men asked. "Why are you dressed so well?"

"We are peaceful people, sir," Anne said, trying to calm them.

"Why do you carry swords on your backs?" Another man sneered and asked.

"For our protection," Marilyn answered.

Shawn could sense the stress and fear in these men.

"We are from the north," Anne said. "Life is better there. We want to speak with your leaders if that is possible, and we don't want any trouble."

"There's something about you people, something not right with you," one man said. "You look too good to be living in this world."

Shawn sensed Anne was trying to replace their fear with thoughts of peace and well-being. She ever-so-slightly started to calm them.

An older man came and spoke from behind the four big men. "I'm the leader here," the elder said as he walked to the front. "What do you want here, strangers?"

"We mean you no harm. We are here in peace," Anne told him.

"That's what you say, but few people come in peace anymore," the elder said.

"Why shouldn't we just shoot you and get rid of you?" A couple of the men half raised their rifles.

Sir, I hope you don't decide to kill us. We are here to help. You need to take your people farther north. The radiation is still too intense here, and it's making them sick by staying here. Look at the sores on these people."

"Why go north? The bombs fell on San Francisco, too," the leader replied.

"They were neutron bombs," Shawn answered. "They gave a burst of radiation that killed the population. Little destruction happened, and the radiation cleared much faster. You must take these people north and east to the mountains and the forest. The chance of survival is much better there. You will find more food and little radiation. This is a wasteland here. There is only death here."

A crowd started to gather around them. The vampires could hear talk of killing, and some discussed taking their belongings.

"Listen to me—take these people out of here. We have warned you," Anne shouted to the leader. "It is up to you. Now stand back, and we will leave you in peace."

One of the men raised his rifle and pointed it at Anne. "You have swords! You're here to kill us." Shawn quickly caught him by the throat and threw him back into the shanties. The man rolled through a campfire, sending burning embers into the night.

They heard gasps come from the people, and then a yell: "They're not human! They're mutants!"

"This is not going well," Victoria warned. Then she yelled into the crowd. "We are here to help you. Foolish people!"

"We want no trouble!" Anne yelled at them. "We are going to leave. Remember, move north and east."

"The crowd has surrounded us. We have no place to go," Victoria told Anne.

"Then we shall fly out of here," Anne said. "Straight up!"

"In front of all these people?" Victoria questioned.

"Yes, unless you want to stay and visit."

They shot into the air, leaving the shantytown and the stunned people behind. They headed northwest to Santa Barbara to take shelter for the day. Shawn still could sense an Esmanaa lurking. The vampires selected a large, abandoned mall for shelter and made their way deep inside. Survivors stripped the mall of all its wares and furniture years ago. Scattered about were broken glass and piles of garbage. It was dark where they laid their bedrolls. Down the walkway between the shops, light rays penetrated the dark through a large hole in the roof.

They huddled and slept together for the comfort it gave them. The trip had become very emotional, and Anne was the first to speak. "Victoria, I know you don't agree with me, but we have to start exposing ourselves to the mortals."

Victoria faced Anne and said, "I'm not sure. I can't help thinking if the mortals know of us, someday, they will find a way to destroy us. I prefer hiding from them."

"We will have to expose ourselves to humans. How much, I'm not sure, but it could be a lot. The humans will realize someday they aren't the only creatures that inhabit this world."

"You represent the Vampire Council, and if that is what the council believes, then I will accept it." Victoria then turned, faced Shawn, and kissed him lightly. "You feel so much for these mortals, much more than the rest of us."

"We must help them...take the risk," Shawn said. "We came from humans... they are in such bad shape."

"That's true, but you have been a vampire far longer than human," Victoria said sleepily.

"She's right—you care too deeply for the humans," Marilyn added. "You need to be careful. You take too many risks. Humans can turn on the ones that try to help them. You saw how that man raised his gun at Anne. Mortals can be unpredictable."

"This is a time for risk-taking, and we better learn how," Shawn said. "A time is coming that our lives will depend on it. I am tired. I'm going to sleep."

Shawn woke first, sat up, realized it was late afternoon, and sensed humans close by. The light still came through the hole in the roof. Slowly, he rose and flew to the opening, looked out, and saw dark white clouds with a tint of orange against a dirty sky. He drifted up through the gap and landed on the burnt, cracked, rubber roof, walked to the edge and looked out over the densely vegetated parking lot. A brown haze always painted the horizon in this part of the country. Shawn could see the large, blood-red sun through the clouds and haze, setting into the radiated, fluorescent-green waters of the Pacific Ocean.

Across the parking lot, he saw two young boys. One boy was talking to the other and pointing to the back of an overturned cargo truck. Copper gravity pads on the bottom of the vehicle reflected the dim, red light. The boys were around twelve years old. Shawn walked the edge of the roof until he was behind the boys, then he stepped off the roof. He floated at an angle toward the parking lot, landed some ways from the boys, and walked toward them.

"Good evening to you," Shawn called out.

He had startled them. When they turned, he saw fear on their faces. He knew they wanted to run but did not want to leave the cargo behind. Shawn touched their minds, and they believed there was food in the truck.

"I won't hurt you. I'm harmless. Do you think something is in the truck?"

The boys had the look of hard-living, despite their young age. They both had old pairs of designer sneakers that now had holes in them, worn soles, as well as faded and torn dungarees, and worn jackets.

"No, mister, there's nothing in the truck," the fidgety one said.

Shawn saw the bolted and locked door on the back of the vehicle. A large steel lock guarded the entrance.

"I'm Shawn. What are your names?"

"My name is Pete, and this is Ricardo."

Shawn sensed the boys were scared of him. "Are you alone?"

"No, we travel with a group. They're close, mister. My people are looking for supplies. How is it, sir, that your clothes are so fine and you wear a sword on your back?"

"I'm a different person than you are, and the sword is for protection."

"Why wouldn't you have a gun?" Pete asked.

"A sword is all I need."

The boys' eyes widened. Victoria had appeared and was floating to the ground. She held her cloak and hood pulled around her.

"Young boys—I could smell their sweet blood when I woke," Victoria said with a wicked smile. "Are you good boys? Lucky for you, you are—I'm hungry this evening."

"You're beautiful," Pete said. "Are you an angel?"

"Kind of—aren't you clever? Can't your friend talk?"

Pete pulled back the long, stringy black hair of the other boy and exposed a large scar on his neck. "Bad men caught him, slit his throat, and left him for dead. He has no voice, so I talk for him."

"That's too bad," Shawn said. "We won't harm you. Now, let's see what's in this truck." Shawn walked to the back door, pulled the door off, and threw it to the side. "Looks like you boys are in luck—there's food." Shawn saw boxes of canned food in the truck. Some crates had broken open, and he could see cans of beef stew and spaghetti lying on the side of the vehicle. The boys looked in and gasped, their eyes widened. This was a treasure to them—in this destroyed place.

"Ricardo, go get the others. I'll stay here to guard the truck. Please, mister, we'll share some of the food with you. Just don't take it all. We're starving."

"We don't need this food. You can have it all. But you must tell the rest of your group to go north. Life is a little easier there. There is more food there."

"We have to go back," Victoria told him. "Anne has a map she wants you to look at."

Shawn was walking back toward the mall when Victoria landed on his back and sank her teeth into the side of his neck and drew a mouthful of his blood.

"Thank you, kind mister." She laughed and playfully shoved him.

Shawn grabbed her, forcing her around to the front of him, held her, kissed her long and hard, and then let an amazed Victoria go.

"You're stronger than me, aren't you?" a surprised Victoria asked.

"No, I'm not," he answered. "Come on, I want some tea."

He hid his new strength from them. Shawn did not want the vampires, he loved to treat him differently, but he knew they would eventually find out.

They returned to find Anne and Marilyn studying a map that Anne had taken from her pack. Shawn poured himself hot tea—he loved the heat from the drink, especially when he woke in the evening. It was soothing for him as the warm liquid hit his blood sac.

The map showed the location of the government building they were looking for and provided a detailed layout of the building. Shawn saw the stamp of the Vampire Council on the map and could see the exact location of the installation on Long Canyon Road.

"How did the council come by this information?" Shawn asked.

"A few years after the war, the council sent agents to find and capture key scientists," Anne explained. "One of these humans was a man in charge of this data storage area. The council questioned the man, and his mind searched for the information that you see here. This information will allow us to succeed in our mission."

Shawn studied the map and then placed his finger on their destination. Lucifer's evil came from there that he could feel, and they would have to be careful there.

"What is it, Shawn?" Anne asked.

"Esmanaa, but he has left. It's something else. Can you sense it?"

"No, I can't," Anne said as she exchanged a perplexed look with the others.

"None of us can," Victoria replied.

"I don't sense anything," Marilyn added. "But I'm not surprised you do."

"You lead, Shawn—we will follow you," Anne said.

They finished their tea and left. Shawn followed a path that had the lowest radiation readings. They soon picked up elevated readings coming from Oxnard. They made a slight detour and landed on the roof of a building on the perimeter of the government installation.

"Can you feel it now?" Shawn asked.

"Yes, I can. It's not the Esmanaa, but close," Anne answered. "We need to find out what this is."

"Let's go slow. We don't know if we can be detected," Victoria added.

"The evil is coming from the building we are going to," Marilyn warned.

They flew from roof to roof and made their way toward the lab that held the storage device. Shawn floated to the parapet of the building across the parking lot from their destination and saw four humanoid creatures moving with a slight stiffness. They had ashen skin, no emotions, and a blank stare in their eyes.

Shawn focused his vampire eyes to see what looked to be some type of electronics attached to the sides of their heads. The leader had a bigger circuit board than the rest. Down the parking lot was an anti-gravity flyer. He knew they had to be careful, all anti-gravity flyers had locators on them. The zombie-like creatures were attaching a square package to the steel double doors that entered this section of the building. The box contained explosives and a detonator.

Shawn turned and looked at the others, saying, "They're going to blow the doors off the entrance to the building."

"They are not aware of us, and they don't have the strength to tear those doors off," Anne pointed out.

"The electronics attached to their heads could alert the Esmanaa of our presence," Shawn warned.

"Do you think there is a camera on the electronics?" Victoria asked.

"Most likely there are cameras. We need to get closer."

"That's going to be risky," Marilyn said.

There was a loud explosion. Dust and smoke blew into the parking lot. The bomb exploded the doors open, and a battery-powered alarm sounded, which quickly stopped working. The zombies walked into the smoke and then went through the opening.

Anne had a worried look as she spoke to them. "We are going to have to follow them. Stay behind them, but we have to get as close as we can. Do not let the leader see you. When the time comes, kill them from behind—don't say a word."

They moved further down the building so they could cross the parking lot out of sight of the anti-gravity flyer. They flew toward the entrance at a blinding speed and quickly entered the blown doorway. The four traveled down the hallway until they came to an intersection that they had pinpointed on the map.

"The storage room is down this hallway," Anne said.

They slowly made their way, came to a right turn, and a short distance away were the zombies. One of the strange creatures was shining a light on a door. The others were attaching another package to the first of the two steel doors that led into the room.

Shawn whispered to Anne, "They can't see in the dark, and they still don't know we're here."

Shawn was close enough now to sense the signals coming to the zombies. The leader was sending and receiving instructions from the flyer and then sending the directions to the others. Shawn could tell they were simple microwave signals that were not complex enough to carry moving pictures. Again, the Esmanaa hadn't covered all the bases—it had to be arrogance. He knew they could quickly kill these creatures, and the Esmanaa wouldn't know who did it.

Shawn whispered to the others, "The flyer is receiving the instructions and sending them on to the lead zombie. We must stay away from the flyer. Only the flyer can detect us."

"And you can sense this?" Victoria questioned.

"Yes, I can," Shawn answered. "Or we could let the Esmanaa know we are here and he will come back. All four of us can attack and kill him!"

Both Shawn and Victoria looked to Anne for her approval.

"Not yet," Anne quickly answered. "The time will come when we will go on the offensive."

"Then we have to kill them before they set off the explosives," Shawn said. "The force of the explosion could damage the storage device. Remember, stay behind them, destroy the circuit boards first."

"Are we ready? Slayers out," Anne commanded. "We will smash the electronics and take their heads."

They floated toward the zombies undetected until it was too late for the creatures. Shawn hit the lead zombie's circuit board with the hilt of his slayer, and the small blinking lights of the electronics went out. Twirling with slayer in hand, he severed the monster's head from its body. The creature crumbled to the ground. The vampires quickly dispatched the other zombies in the same way.

They discarded the explosives, and Victoria tore the two doors from their hinges. Entering the room, Shawn saw a slim, black box inside a glass-enclosed office. Victoria forced the glass door open, and they entered the clean room.

Shawn quickly located the storage device. The device was four inches thick, and one foot wide by three feet long. Humans had stored years of research on cold fusion in this device. The war had silenced its electronic hum, but the valuable secret was still there, lying dormant inside its electrical circuits, waiting for humans to discover the knowledge again. A docking bay held the storage device. This interface allowed the information to come from the multitude of lab computers that were located throughout the building before that fateful morning.

Shawn pulled the device from the interface and carefully secured it in a transport case that humans had left in the room. They went out into the hall and heard a crackle. The head of the demon Zepar grew from one of the circuit boards on a lifeless zombie, became a hologram, did a full turn, and then sputtered out.

"Thank the angels. It's the board with no camera," Shawn gasped.

"Let's go home. I have had enough of this place," Anne said

"I'm certainly ready," Marilyn replied.

They left the building with their prize and made sure they went the opposite way of the anti-gravity flyer.

The four took to the air and started their trip back to their small sanctuary in Washington.

Chapter Sixteen

A hundred years had passed since the war. Shawn now heard shortwave radio transmissions as the towns started to communicate. He knew the mortals were raising their heads and looking around. Shawn had spent some time with Victoria at her house and traveling overseas to see the destruction of the war. They often traveled the world for a couple of years at a time.

The mortals had plunged themselves four hundred years into the past. Humans had lost their science and technology. Every year, Shawn would receive an assignment from the Vampire Council through Anne.

It was a mid-autumn night, Shawn and Victoria lay in a hammock on a back lawn in desperate need of a cutting. He had just made love to Victoria, and both were lying entwined in the hammock, feeling a cool breeze blow over their naked bodies. Shawn was deep in thought. He had lived as a vampire for more than three hundred years and would sometimes think back through those years, trying to remember his long life. Now recalling his beginnings was not an easy task for him, and he was becoming afraid of forgetting his memories as the number of years grew.

He loved the feel of Victoria, lightly caressed her soft skin, and asked.

"Victoria, can you remember the years of your life?"

"No, I can't, but I can remember some of it," she said sleepily. "I don't remember too much about my mortal life. I do remember when Erdin turned me, and my years with him. Strangely, I remember that clearly, but I cannot remember being a child."

"I'm forgetting my mortal life, too, but I try to remember," Shawn said. Victoria moved on top of Shawn, kissed him, and told him, "I like it when you take my blood and go back in my human life. What you tell me helps me remember those lost times."

"I cannot remember the faces of my family anymore," Shawn sighed to her. "This bothers me sometimes. My beginnings are a haze to me now, and I try to look back, but my memory won't go back that far."

"Try not to overthink this. Your mortal memories will be the first to go. Time is different for us, and as the years go by, our beginnings fade in our memories. This is one of our burdens... the burdens of eternal life."

The following eve around midnight, Anne and Renee arrived with an urgent assignment to help the mortals. A transmission from a fortified town had been repeating nightly for three months. The settlement was Rawlins, located in what used to be Wyoming. Anne informed him the transmissions were a call for help, and that strange creatures were infiltrating the settlement, kidnapping humans. The human broadcasts were different this time, they were asking for help from the Guardians. Word had spread through the settlements in the Northwest. The humans talked of strange beings that looked like people but had tremendous strength and could fly through the air.

Anne told him this had brought a renewed debate among the Vampire Council. The council ruled to have limited discretionary contact with the citizens of Rawlins.

The next evening, the four vampires landed at the edge of a field that led to logged walls that surrounded a section of what used to be Rawlins, Wyoming. Shawn saw the humans had scavenged materials from other parts of the town for building material for New Rawlins. Surrounding the village were large fields used for farming and corrals to hold cattle and horses.

The sun was setting behind a lone mountain chain that stood sentry over the long stretch of flatlands, and brown prairie grass that made its way to the town. The Great American Prairie was ending its vast stretch to the west. The wind blew cold dust, and the land was stark, which reflected the mood of this place.

Shawn walked toward the main gate and noticed one side of the gate was open, with people coming and going. Located at different stations on top of the walls, he saw men with rifles. The people were dressed in makeshift fabrics and leathers of different colors, large wide-brimmed hats stained with sweat and dirt, which made their dress colorful and interesting. They wore old leather shoes or boots, scuffed and worn—sneakers had disappeared years ago. They had weathered faces forged into stern looks by years of survival and hard work.

Suddenly, a shot rang out! The bullet hit five feet in front of Shawn, throwing a small amount of dirt into his face. He spat and sputtered the soil out of his mouth and glared at the men.

"Halt!" a man shouted. "Who are you?"

"Steady…let me reason with them," Anne whispered. She then yelled out, "You broadcast a message asking for Guardians—we are here! We want to talk to the people in charge!"

"Why do you have swords on your backs?" the guard yelled.

"The swords are for our protection. Sir, take care—do not fire your weapon at us again," Anne yelled back.

"We have sent for the marshals—stay where you are!" yelled the guard.

Soon, four men on horseback with rifles rode out and surrounded the vampires.

"We are here to talk to the leaders of this village," Anne requested. "Who are you?"

"We are the law in this town," one of the riders barked. "The mayor is on his way."

Shawn knew that Renee and Victoria were losing patience quickly with these men. Renee was worse than Victoria when it came to tolerating mortals.

Shawn warned the men. "Don't raise your rifles at us. This will be the only time I will tell you."

No sooner had he spoken then one of the men raised his rifle, and faster than any human could see, all four men had their guns stripped from their hands. The weapons now lay at the feet of Anne. The men, wide eyed, backed their horses away from the vampires, forming a line across the road between the gate and the vampires. Shawn could sense a strong feeling of fear coming from the men.

"We aren't here to hurt you," Shawn shouted, trying to calm them.

Some uncomfortable moments passed, and then three men, wearing worn clothes, old, leather, brimmed hats, and pistols in leather holsters strapped around their waists, walked out of the gate. They looked in desperate need of a shave and a haircut.

"This reminds me of the Old West," Anne whispered.

The men stopped a respectful distance from the vampires. With a nervous voice, one of the men spoke: "Greetings to you, strangers. I am Bob Thornton, mayor of this town. They told me you identified yourselves as Guardians."

One of the riders muttered, "Mayor, they took our rifles from us, and we didn't see them do it."

"We are the beings you think of as Guardians," Anne said. "You must instruct every human that has a gun not to point them at us. We will not allow that. We have come in peace and friendship. We expect you to treat us the same. Now, tell us about your troubles."

A small crowd had gathered, and someone yelled: "Do you drink blood?"

Bob gave a nervous smile and a quick lick of his lips. "Some people here say Guardians are vampires. There are people here that come from another town, and they have seen what you can do."

"We are also known as vampires. What we really are is warrior angels sent to help you during this time of great trouble," Anne yelled to the crowd, "If you harbor no wrong toward your neighbor, you have nothing to fear from us. If you are evil, follow Lucifer, lust to take property or life, look at mankind as something to abuse, take care, because someday you might meet us in the shadows and we will take your blood."

"They say you come from Heaven. Is that true?" asked a small woman from the crowd.

"Like you, we come from Heaven, but unlike you, great power is given to us," Shawn revealed.

"We will trust you! We have no choice," a man shouted from the crowd.

Anne then spoke to Bob. "Now, tell me what is coming over your walls."

"They come over late at night, shoot their way into our town, and take our citizens. They take them east—to where we don't know. The last time was about a month ago. They came, and we killed two of them. One of them was a man named Jack Caracalla. The strangers took him in the first raid. We tried to keep the bodies, but the smell was too bad, and they became covered with maggots."

"What do these creatures look like?" Victoria asked.

"They look human, with a grayish color and blank looks on their faces. They are strong, but we can kill them with a rifle. These creatures have better guns than us, though—they have automatic weapons."

"Do they move stiffly?" Victoria asked.

"No, they are agile when they scale the wall."

"Zombies from the Esmanaa," Victoria advised. "They have switched to live humans rather than dead ones. Maybe live humans make better zombies."

"We want to enter your town and see where they came over the wall," Anne informed Bob.

"Is that necessary? It could upset the people even more than they are," Bob said.

Suddenly, Renee was in the middle of the men with her arm around the shoulder of the youngest of the three. "You call us here and ask us for our help, but we can't enter your town? This one looking us up and down, thinking sexual thoughts about us." Renee grabbed hold of the man's crotch. "Oh! Don't you want me now? Look at me! Take a good look! Do you really want me?"

"No!" the man stammered. "I'm sorry. I didn't mean to offend you."

"Well, you have. Let us in this town, or we shall leave you to the zombies."

"Renee, come back," Anne ordered. "Stand with us."

Bob sent the other two men back into the city to inform the armed men to keep their guns away from the vampires.

"I'm sorry. Of course, you can come in. Please, follow me. As you can see, the guards are closing the gates for the evening."

Bob escorted the vampires into the town. Shawn saw people riding on horses or in horse-drawn wagons, and the scent of livestock hung in the air. They had entered the settlement directly onto Main Street. Gas lanterns were burning on posts with a small, steel tubes feeding gas to the lamps.

"You have gas," Shawn said.

"When the end came, there were natural gas wells drilled and capped close to Rawlins. Some of the survivors knew about these wells. We have been fortunate to bring this gas to our town. It lights the town and keeps us warm. We are luckier than most."

The old storefronts held the shops of today. Shawn saw wood and metalworking shops with bicycle-driven lathes, a shoemaker's shop with leather hanging to dry, along with old leatherworking tools. The town's people ate from many different types of food stands. Street food was the way humans ate now—no more home kitchens. If humans didn't use the buildings for commerce, they used them for shelter. People were living in old, anti-gravity cars, vans, and trucks scattered between the buildings.

Shawn walked alongside Bob and asked him, "Do you use money here?"

"No, we allow people who work two meals a day from the food stands. For supplies and clothing, they have to go before the Commerce Council or make it themselves. As you can see, they don't grant many requests."

"Bob, would you take us to where the attackers came over the wall?" Anne asked.

"Sure, follow me."

They followed Bob down side streets, past scattered wreck cars and barrels holding lit fires, and proceeded to the east side of town where the zombies were scaling the wall. It was a cold autumn night, and Shawn could see the puffs of Bob's nervous breathing, the smoke hanging in the cold air from the open fires. Shawn jumped to the top of the wall to survey the terrain. Only the prairie ran east, and there was no cover for the zombies to use on their approach to the town.

Shawn raised his head slowly as a look of recognition spread over his face, and he whispered, "There you are. I sense you. This time will be different." The other vampires joined him on the wall. He whispered to them as if he dares not speak it. "One Esmanaa, to the east, about three hundred miles—just one. The zombies are there with the demon. Can you sense the dark angel?"

"Yes, Shawn. There's an Esmanaa there?" Anne answered. "Can you feel him, Renee?"

"I feel the demon—Lucifer's spawn. Are you sure we want to proceed?"

Shawn saw the worry on Anne's face. He knew it was not her safety—it was his and Renee's safety. Anne met his gaze and smiled. "Yes, we will proceed carefully." He sensed Anne knew the time had come to fight the demons, to fulfill her destiny. The reason Bricius came to her so long ago.

"I can feel his evil, but I can't tell which one it is," Victoria said. "We can get close if we're careful. If we do it right, we have a chance to kill another Esmanaa."

"You lead us, Victoria—you have the most experience with this," Anne said. "I will make the final decision on what to do when we arrive."

They bid their farewells to Bob and told him they would do their best to rid him of the zombies.

"You are amazing creatures," Bob announced for all to hear. "God sent you to us in our time of need."

The vampires flew east until they reached a small mountain range and came upon an old mining shaft. They sheltered from the day, spread their bedrolls, and slept close to each other.

"There is only one Esmanaa there, and I can feel who the demon is now—it's Horsa," Shawn said.

"He will be formidable," Victoria said, "but we should do better than our last meeting with the Esmanaa."

"We will do better, you'll see," Shawn assured.

"Will we? I've heard you are much stronger now," Renee said. "You're stronger than any of us, blood brother."

Renee had always been with women, never a man, and preferred their relationship to be that of brother and sister.

"Who told you that?" Shawn asked quickly.

"I'm not going to tell you, but they say it's in your blood. The vampire tells me you can taste it." Renee's eyes became as blue as a sapphire, and her blood-teeth grew long. "Let me taste for myself, brother."

"Maybe this isn't the time for this," Victoria whispered.

"This is a family matter, Victoria! No concern of yours!"

The bite came quick and hard. Shawn's body shook, and Victoria reached over to grab his hand. He could feel Renee's blood-teeth pierce his artery, held his neck tight, and the pressure as his blood flowed into her mouth, then her wet tongue licking the excess from his neck.

Renee kissed Shawn and stroked his face. "I can taste it—there is a difference. Something has happened. Tell me, brother."

Shawn was torn but finally decided to tell them. They would fight this demon with him and should know. "When I drank Bricius's blood, I went to Herit, and she gave me the blood of the angels, or what represents the blood in their world. This has given me great strength and abilities. Since my beginnings as a vampire, the angels have always made me aware that they expect more from me. The angels made me strong, to give me the best chance of ridding this world of the Esmanaa demons. If we fight this demon, it will be different than the last time."

The following evening, they continued onto Horsa's lair. They arrived on the outskirts of what was once Falls City, Nebraska, a small agriculture and dairy town. Victoria told them to cloak themselves, and from this point on, to remain cloaked. The humans had abandoned the village a century ago. The buildings were in extreme disrepair, and many of the homes were collapsing into their basements. Vegetation and weather had done its best to reclaim the town for The Mother.

The vampires found an old residential house on the outskirts of town and took shelter for the day. The house was a one-story, old-style ranch with a basement. They settled in a dry area in the damp, musty basement. Tree roots had penetrated the foundation, and in the far corner was a recently vacated fox den. The foxes wanted nothing to do with vampires. Sleep did not come easy for Shawn, and when it did, he soon awakened. He sat up and saw Anne holding a finger to her lips. Anne whispered, "Zombies."

"They're outside and coming this way," she added.

Shawn floated up the stairs to a large opening that was once a living room window. It was a crisp, clear day with a brilliant blue sky and white, billowy clouds. The ash from the war had dissipated in this part of the country a few decades ago. He saw four zombies with automatic rifles coming down the old residential street. They were working their way through foliage that now covered the worn pavement of the road. The zombies didn't have the stiffness associated with the earlier zombies.

"Look how they walk," Shawn pointed out.

"They don't know that we are here," Anne told them. "Look, they have electronics on the side of their heads."

Then, a light beam came from the electronics, and a hologram appeared in front of the leader's face. It was the head of Horsa, giving the leader orders. Shawn immediately ducked away from the window.

"Are we sure we want to do this?" Renee whispered from behind.

"For now, we will observe," Victoria answered.

The vampires returned to the basement to wait for the evening and to discuss their next move. Shawn exchanged glances with Victoria and knew she planned to attack Horsa. Maybe Anne and Renee had not committed yet, but he had taken Victoria's blood for two centuries, knew what she was thinking, and she knew the same with him. He thought they could be successful in their attack, and he sensed Victoria was thinking of a way to tell Anne and Renee.

Victoria hesitated and then spoke. "For thousands of years, the Esmanaa have brought heartache and destruction to the human race. Look what they have done now—they have brought mankind close to total extinction."

"We know this, Victoria," Anne said. "This is a dangerous game you're asking us to play."

"I want to attack Horsa! The time is right now!" Victoria called out. "I think we can beat him. We can kill another Esmanaa. I believe the time has come to attack the Esmanaa, one at a time, and destroy them. Rid this world of them and their evil. Erdin has told me this—Shawn knows this to be true."

"We saved you once before from the Esmanaa," Renee reminded her. "Now you want to attack them again? I'm not as confident as you are. Sometimes I think you will get my family killed."

"I thank you for my life, but we all have Bricius's blood, and we have Shawn. Shawn agrees with me—I can feel this—I know this. We must test ourselves!"

Anne looked at Victoria, with a worried look on her face, and said, "My family and I will attack Horsa with you. The time has come for the Bryces and the Kenmare to rid the world of the Esmanaa.

"Michael, be with us," Renee whispered. "Horsa is a powerful Esmanaa, only Zepar is more powerful, but I'm sure you know this, Victoria."

"Let's try to sleep," Anne said. "We will continue into town when the evening comes. If we do this, it has to be now, before we need to feed."

That evening, they prepared themselves for the fight and left their packs and bedrolls behind in the house. Falls City once had the look of small-town America a look now long gone. The vampires now made their way to the center of the town where Horsa made his headquarters in the old city hall. The sense of evil had increased tenfold, and the smell was becoming unbearable. They came upon a group of zombies clearing brush from a street that led to the main section of town.

"The Esmanaa are trying to establish a stronghold in this area," Victoria pondered. "They're trying to spread themselves out to take control of the humans."

Anne whispered, "We will attack the zombies, which will bring Horsa. Remember, do not lose your slayer, or you will lose your life—stab, remove the sword quickly, and move on."

The vampires attacked and quickly killed the zombies. They continued down the cleared street toward the center of town. They walked four abreast, one hand on their slayer, ready for a terrible fight. Soon, they came to the center of the village. The flies became thick, their sound piercing, and maggots covered the surfaces of the streets and buildings.

A course, deafening trumpet sounded in their heads, and the demon shot through the roof of the town hall and into the night sky. Dark energy propelled the monster upward, debris and plaster blew off the beast and left a trail behind like a rocket filled with death as he traveled and arced to turn for his attack. Horsa circled and came down twenty feet in front of the vampires. The ground shook and the monster had already changed to his real look—eyes as black as night. His size and weight had increased, and this demon was much bigger than Charun. His head tilted from side to side in an unnatural way.

He walked over to an old street light, pulled it from its base, and made a club from the metal pole. He swung it back and forth like a baseball player warming up for his turn at bat. He then walked back to the center of the street, stood, and let out a loud laugh that echoed off the buildings. The vampires spread out to form a half-circle in front of the demon.

Horsa stopped and looked directly at Shawn. "You are the vampire Shawn Bryce, I thought we killed you." He hissed his words; there was clumsiness about his speech and movement. "And the Kenmare is also alive. You come to kill me like this? No matter, you will not leave here alive. I'm Horsa, and none of you has the strength to defeat me. I take vengeance on the Archangel Michael and all that he leads. You will die tonight, and when you see Michael, make sure you tell him Horsa sent you to him."

Shawn knew the demon was preparing to charge. Horsa looked at each of the vampires, sizing them up for his attack. Suddenly, he charged Shawn; he had chosen his target poorly. Shawn could still see the demon despite the extreme speed with which he moved. He shot into the air as the creature passed under him. Landing behind Horsa, he brought his slayer around, delivering a deep gash to his side. Horsa quickly turned and bellowed at him, took a swing, but Shawn shot again into the air, and the demon missed.

Victoria attacked next and plunged her sword into the monster's stomach. The demon swung his club and connected, propelling her into the front window of an old hardware store. Victoria exploded back out of the store, in a cloud of debris landing on the street. Anne and Renee attacked at the same time, circling him with vampire speed, slashing him with their slayers.

Shawn propelled himself and hit Horsa with full force, driving the monster through an old corner store and out the back. He wrestled with Horsa, but the demon threw him off and jumped to the roof of the building with Shawn in pursuit. The monster turned and connected his fist with the side of Shawn's head, driving him to the roof's surface. Shawn jumped to his feet and shot himself at the demon, trying to force the beast back. Horsa grabbed Shawn in a bear hug and, with tremendous strength, squeezed Shawn until he thought he would lose consciousness. Finally, he worked one of his hands free and took the slayer from the other and drove it into Horsa's side. The demon screamed his indignity and threw him over the front of the building to the road below.

Horsa walked the roof to the front of the building and had a perplexed look on his face. He no longer had his club. Shawn knew he realized that they were not the typical vampires he had dealt with in the past. He certainly could see the glow of Deceida. The monster was still stronger, but Shawn was more agile, and his practice at swordplay since his last meeting with the Esmanaa was paying off. He knew as the years passed, he would become more powerful than these demons.

The Esmanaa stood on the roof, looking down at the vampires. His foul, brown blood was oozing from his wounds. He wiped it from his face.

He then spat, "We were powerful angels, but your beloved Michael always blocked our authority in his choir of warrior angels. He felt contempt for us; we were not pure enough, as if he was so much better than we were. He shamed us, so we left, and he even tried to ruin our transition to this world. This world will be ours, and we will kill every vampire that occupies it. There will be no warrior angels in this world—only darkness, only Lucifer. And to show you, I will kill one of you before I leave."

Horsa pulled a silver spike, a vampire killer, from his sleeve; he flew at Victoria with the speed of a bullet. She was quick enough, thanks to Bricius's blood, to save herself, but the demon still penetrated the side of her neck, leaving Victoria screaming and collapsing to the ground.

Shawn flew at the demon. "Bastard!" he yelled.

Swinging his slayer in an arc, he repeatedly struck the demon on his arms and chest. Horsa fell back, arms crossed for protection. The Esmanaa bobbed his head and moved his body low then came back up, catching Shawn in the jaw with his fist driving him back. Deciding he had had enough, the creature shot into the air, heading east. Shawn followed Horsa, but he could not overtake him. He circled back to where Victoria was lying.

He saw Anne dripping her blood into Victoria's neck, trying to heal the wound. Victoria could not talk, and blood was pouring from her mouth. He took Victoria from Anne, bit his wrist, and started to apply his blood to her neck.

Anne kneeled next to where Shawn was sitting, holding Victoria. "She will be all right. You have to stay calm. She will heal. A couple of days in the ground will help her."

"Well, this didn't go the way we'd hoped," Shawn told Victoria. "I'm going to take you to my home and bury you."

Bullets started to fly. The remainder of the zombies had launched a frontal assault.

"Take her home," Anne said. "We will take care of the zombies."

Cradling Victoria in his arms, he flew her home and took her to the burial pit in the basement. He stripped her blood-soaked clothes from her and cleansed her. The bleeding from the deep gash on the side of her neck had stopped. Victoria was conscious, but the spike had penetrated her throat, so she could not talk.

"Sleep now, I will watch over you." Shawn bit his wrist and gave her blood. He buried Victoria in the grave, he had dug.

Chapter Seventeen

It was the year of our Lord 2402, and the Great Dark Age still had its heartless grip on the human race. Shawn finally could see bright spots—people were slowly coming back to the northern cities. The towns were communicating with each other and had set up a primitive mail system. Shortwave radio transmissions were becoming common. He saw travelers on horseback or in wagons on the old roads again.

He knew humans were starting to rebuild old motors—smaller pieces of machinery with scavenged parts. Towns were trading information on how to build motors, photovoltaic cells, generators, and other technologies. He saw bare, copper wiring on insulators, strung on old-time telephone poles. Health conditions were starting to improve, but human births were still close to the number of deaths.

Shawn heard of a new American government forming in what was now New Chicago. He would pen lengthy letters to the men starting to occupy these high places and leave them in their bedroom windows to find, pleading with them to show compassion for the weary human race, and told them they needed people of vision to show them what could be. He told them The Mother was angry, and they needed to start protecting the earth. Shawn worried about the humans; he wanted this new civilization to have more of a heart and always signing the letters, "A Guardian."

He saw life starting to improve for humans, and soon realized when humans were not busy trying to survive, they always went back to trying to conquer each other. Armed bands of marauders on horseback were starting to form, raiding the towns and enslaving the people, trying to stake out their little empires.

Shawn sat on a roof in the fan district of Denver. Marilyn was seated next to him. Victoria had gone ahead a couple of blocks to bring three lawless men their way. Marilyn had come for a visit, and they had gone to Denver to feed. Shawn knew Marilyn had something to tell him. She was hiding a secret from him. After all, she loved hiding secrets from him. She would play with him until he finally had enough, and only then, would she give in and tell him with a teasing laugh.

People were coming back to live in Denver. Shawn saw small, independent communities forming throughout old Denver. The fan district was where the robbers, murderers, and thieves hid and planned their criminal acts. It was an eerie place with old, dilapidated buildings, faded paint, worn signs that were hard to read, broken glass, old rusted cars, and fire barrels burning, giving off a cloud of smoke that drifted through the streets and alleys. It was late autumn, and a crisp cold had its grip on the night. Frost covered every surface. Only the sporadic yell of a human or a bark of a dog could be heard.

"I have a message from Anne," Marilyn said, trying to be as coy as possible. "Anne wanted me to tell you this."

"What does she want me to know? Tell me right away! Don't play with me!"

"Brace yourself, Bryce. Anne has taken another changeling."

"You're kidding!" Shawn said. "Anne has a changeling? Is it female?"

"Of course. You were her only male changeling, and if you remember, it took a lot of begging on my part."

"What's her name?" Shawn asked. "Have you seen her?"

"Her name is Juliette Durand, from a French-Canadian family. She has been a vampire for six weeks, and she is taking blood—I have met her. Anne sent me to tell you to come home and meet her."

"I'll go tomorrow night," Shawn said. "Victoria is talking about taking a changeling. She feels the time has come for her. She hesitates… she's not sure."

"Anne wants you to come by yourself. You know how she is, wants to keep it light for the first couple of months with a fledgling. Nevertheless, she wants you to meet her. I'll stay here with Victoria for a couple of nights, and then come home."

Victoria was now in front of them with a baffled look on her face. "Where were you? They are lying in the alley. I suggest we hurry."

"Anne has taken a changeling," Shawn said. "She wants me to come home by myself and meet her."

"I'm not surprised. Recently Anne told me that I should take a changeling. She said it is something I need. I have lived too long not to have had a one. Marilyn, will you be staying?"

"For a couple of days. I hope you don't mind."

"No, we should get to know each other better."

Shawn arrived at the Bryce family home at midnight; he flew a circle around the house and sensed ten Crimmians living in the front of the house. Anne had taken on more Crimmians to give shelter and allow for the survival of their society. He sensed Anne in her art studio with the new vampire. Her changeling was anxious about something.

The house was starting to look rundown—it had been two hundred years since the renovation. Cloaking himself, he landed next to the house and went through the side door. He floated down the hallway and into the art studio without making a sound. Anne immediately sensed him, embraced him, and kissed him passionately. Shawn could see Juliette standing in the far doorway watching them.

"I wish you would come home more," Anne said.

He saw the excitement in her. Taking a changeling had made her happy... much more alive. He knew Anne needed changelings.

"Make love to me! Take me to the sofa!"

Anne pulled Shawn to the gold sofa, the one with scattered paint stains, and pushed the sketches to the floor. They hastily took each other's clothes off and made passionate love. It had been a long time since he felt this much passion in her. They ended up wrapped together, lying on the cluttered rug.

Shawn sensed Juliette leaving the doorway and go to the kitchen. "Where did you find Juliette?" Shawn asked Anne as he kissed her soft lips.

"She came from Seattle. Her family had a fishing boat and lived off the ocean. She lost her parents and two brothers at sea three years ago. She has been on her own since, so I made friends with her to help her."

"You helped her all right—you made her a vampire," Shawn laughed.

"We fell in love. She won't be lonely anymore, or hungry, wondering where her next meal will come from. I gave her the gift, and our family to make it safe for her. She loves women, but she needs men, too. She is like Marilyn. I want you to sometimes satisfy that need for her, take her on little trips—teach her—have a relationship with her. She will need to feed in a couple of nights. I want you to take her by yourself."

"What made you take a changeling again?" Shawn asked.

"I'm more than two thousand years old, and sometimes I need a human to anchor me to this world. To connect me to the age I live in. Maybe even to give me a reason to live. I get tired, sad, and sometimes I feel lost in time, so I take a changeling, like you, the man I grew to love so much."

"She is doing well—she is smart and used to surviving. Humans are different now. Surviving is all they know. Humans are very skilled in surviving. They have two hundred hard years behind them."

"I'll do what you ask of me. You are my maker, and I love you."

"Go meet her now—go by yourself. I'll be by shortly. Go meet your new blood sister."

Shawn shrouded himself and floated, so he made as little noise as possible. Juliette was in the kitchen, making tea, and he slowly made his way to the entrance and peered in. He sensed her thoughts about her new life and meeting him—this is what had brought about her anxiousness. The changeling had light brown hair, with a beautiful, feminine face, a slender, fit body, and creamy white skin. Shawn slowly released his shroud until she became aware that he was standing in the doorway.

She turned and said with a nervous smile, "You are Shawn. Anne told me you were coming tonight."

"Yes, and you are the new vampire, Juliette. How are you? I heard you made it through your first feeding."

"I was scared, but I fed."

"The first time is frightening."

He floated into the kitchen, into the light, his feet just an inch above the floor. Juliette was brave; she didn't back away but gave him an unsure smile. He could read her thoughts: *My, he is handsome.*

Shawn drew near to her, placed his nose against the nape of her neck, and traveled up to her ear. He took in her essence and smelled the sweetness of her blood—she was strong of heart, with courage and intelligence. There was a kindness of spirit that he sensed, but she could be tough if need be. He backed away from her to give her space.

"I thought you were going to take my blood like Marilyn?"

"Not yet. I won't bite you until you feel more comfortable with me," Shawn laughed. "When I do, you can bite me back."

His remark brought a smile and laugh from Juliette. "I saw you with Anne. It's strange to me that family members have sex. I'm confused about this."

"Why? Anne didn't give birth to me—my mother long ago did that. Vampire families are much different from human families. Vampires create families for love and a common purpose. Humans create families by giving birth. Family is a word we use to explain our gathering and living together. Mothers and fathers do not exist in our world. Makers and lovers are what exists for us. The love between Anne and me is not that of a mother and son. It is two lovers, a teacher and her protégé that are on an incredible journey together. She has given me a great gift, has watched over me, taught me how to live as a vampire, protected me from the dangers, and has given me amazing sex. Anne turned you because she loves you and found you worthy. Anne has an immense ability to love, and you feel love toward her, I can tell. I feel the same love for my other blood sisters, and hopefully, we will feel this love between us someday."

"I do love Anne. It was a shock to me—my changing—to find out she was a vampire. Anne made me feel safe. She made me feel special. Since our first meeting, I wanted to be with her."

They took their tea into the lounging room and sat on the couch. Shawn noticed her eyes right away—they were a stunning, light grey, almost a very light blue.

"You had a family in Seattle?" Shawn asked.

"I had a great mother and father, but my brothers were not kind people."

Shawn could sense there was something about her brothers, but she hid it well. She had practice hiding these thoughts even before she became a vampire. He gently probed her mind. She loved her parents but felt nothing for her brothers. He could feel her trying to look into his head—it was clumsy.

He smiled and said, "Careful, trying to enter vampires' minds. We are family—it's fine for you to practice on me, but other vampires would consider it bad manners coming from one as young as you. How did you come to meet Anne?"

Shawn watched Juliette stare out the window, and she squinted. He smiled; she was experimenting with her new vampire sight.

"It was spring," Juliette said. "The weather was bad that day, and I was not feeling well. My parents felt they had to go out in the boat to fish. Our food was running low, and we needed fish to trade for supplies and pay our rent. My mother decided to leave me behind to do light chores. Everything changed in a day, my parents and brothers took the boat to fish in the bay, but they never returned."

Juliette looked out the window with a far-off gaze. "I waited for a month, and then our landlord threw me out of the house. I went to work on a farm and worked long, hard hours in the fields, but I had to leave. The men wouldn't leave me alone. So, I found an old building in the city, down a narrow street, hidden away, and I lived in the attic. I would go to the food stations once a day to eat and scavenge for tools, clothing, soap, and candles — anything to trade for food or use in my dingy attic room. It was a hard life. The undesirables were constantly after me, and despair was starting to color every aspect of my existence." She stopped for a moment and thought, then a smile came to her face. "That day I left my little room in the attic, it was early morning, and the fog was dense. This was the only time I left my place—when I could use the fog or the darkness to travel without others seeing me. I was walking on the side street where I lived. For the first time that morning, I thought I would be better off dead, that this life was just too hard. I was hungry all the time. I felt so defeated, so useless!" She frowned, looked to the floor, and then met his gaze.

"I heard a whisper in my head, saying, 'you will be all right.' I felt someone was following me. I thought maybe it was another bad person, and I was getting ready to make my escape, when I turned to look over my shoulder—Anne came out of the fog. She was clean and well dressed, unusual for these times, and walked with a powerful stride. She handed me a cloth sack that had bread, jam, cheese, some soap, and a brand-new toothbrush. She was beautiful, with a smile on her face that gave me a feeling of warmth, a feeling that everything was going to be all right. These were feelings I had not felt in a long time. Every time she came, I always had these feelings. I would look forward to the times she would come."

"She made contact with you that morning because of your despair," Shawn surmised.

"I asked her, 'Who are you? Where did you come from?' At first, I thought she might be another danger, only in a different package. She told me she was a friend and noticed I was having a hard time. She said she had plenty—far more than needed—and she wanted to share with me. Anne would always come early in the evenings, bringing food, wine, and clothing. We started to make love, and one evening after making love, everything changed. She let me see her for what she was. Her eyes turned a deep blue. I tried to run, but she grabbed my hand and pulled me back down on the bed. She said I was not going to live very long as a mortal. A beautiful, defenseless woman like me in this world—somebody or something was going to kill me. She told me she knew this because of how long she had lived. She had seen this many times in her life and had decided to turn me— make me her changeling, a vampire. Anne said she could not leave me anymore like this. She would give me her blood and make me special. She changed me and brought me here, and life is much easier for me as a vampire."

"You don't mind being with a woman?" Shawn asked.

"I like having a close relationship with a woman. I like the type of intimacy you can have with a woman, but I also like the type of sex I can have with a man. I'm like Anne in that way. I'm sure that is one of the reasons I'm here."

"Your sex was part of the reason, but you drew her attention, probably because you always traveled at night. Anne became interested in you and watched you longer than you realize. You should know that you are fortunate to have a maker like Anne. She is a powerful vampire. She will teach and take care of you. Take her blood as often as you can—it will make you strong. Be prepared to travel and learn by experience."

Anne came into the room with a cup of tea in hand and slid next to Juliette. Shawn could see how alive Anne was. She was beaming like someone who had just found a new lover. "She is doing wonderfully. She fed for the first time very quickly."

"She's a great addition to our family," Shawn said.

"Juliette, you will need to feed in a couple of days. I want Shawn to take you—just you two. You will be in good hands."

"If that's what you want, but I am still learning."

"You will do fine," Shawn assured.

Two nights later, Shawn brought Juliette to Seattle. People were populating in different sections of the city. Large parts were still deserted. They landed in an uninhabited area, next to their destination, a part of the city that held a seedier individual. Seattle, in this time, was a lawless place, of bleak, harsh survival.

It was pitch black, with only a groan from a drunk human, crouched next to a building, unable to go any further. There was a raw coldness to the air. As they drew close to their destination, the smell of cooked food, burnt wood, and garbage hung over the area.

"We'll go to that roof and see what we have to deal with," Shawn said.

Shawn took Juliette's hand, and they jumped to the roof above. Skeletons of skyscrapers stood in the distance, empty for two centuries, ghosts of what used to be. To his surprise, he saw construction again around these old behemoths. Shawn also saw the flickering lights of many fire barrels and a haze of drifting smoke over the city. A gunshot rang out somewhere out in the dark, followed by screams from a man.

"Shawn, you're sad, I can feel it. What's the matter?"

"I feel sad for the humans," Shawn said, looking at the decaying buildings. "I remember what they once were—their greatness. You can see that in these tall buildings, the ones that are still standing."

"I know nothing of that time—the technology age, or their greatness. I don't believe they could have been that great. Look what the old ones did to the world. These buildings have always been bleak, dark, and empty to me."

"They are from a lost time," Shawn said. "The humans are building again, and you can see the signs."

"Life is so hard in this world. Survival is day to day. We have lost the ability to trust each other."

"Survival is different for you, now—you aren't human anymore. You need to realize that," Shawn said. "You are a vampire, and now you must help humans."

Shawn turned away and looked down the main street, to the section of the city that was going to be their feeding ground. Street food vendors were closing their stands for the night. The cold kept most people inside, but a few were walking about. Gas lamps and fire barrels lit the street.

Bars with pianos, trumpets, coronets, and saxophones playing blues and jazz flowed out of the speakeasies to mingle with the yells from two drunken men arguing over a bottle of whiskey. There was a brothel, with men, gathered around the front door, yelling obscenities at the two heavily armed guards who wouldn't let them through the door. Gaunt, unwashed faces, and dirty clothes—that was the image of humanity now.

"Are you ready?" Shawn took Juliette's hand and floated back to the street.

"What if people recognize us?" Juliette said as they floated to the ground.

"There are some people who know about vampires. There are many stories of vampires saving towns."

"Act like you belong here, and don't make eye contact for too long. Project the thought you are human and sense their minds. You have the ability... practice at this. You will know when they become suspicious, and when you're older, you can change that thought in their heads."

They walked up the street, where a kaleidoscope of smells invaded Shawn's nose. They went a block and saw a prostitute having sex in an alley, and criminals exchanging drugs and money. Shawn thought how the world had changed over these two centuries and how this always made him sad.

"You leave your mind so open to me. You are the first vampire that has been like this with me. You think about how the world was in your time, and you let me see this in your mind. That's what makes you sad is what we have become. I mean, what humans have become. What you see is all I know."

"The humans are coming back— you will see. They need law and order now. They also need help and a lot of luck. And for the Esmanaa demons to leave them alone."

They soon entered the area of criminals, looking for their next victim. Juliette walked close to Shawn. He could feel she had become comfortable with him. She liked him, and now the time had come to take her blood.

"Marilyn told me something about you," Juliette said.

"What did she tell you?"

"She told me when you and she were mortals, you were lovers."

"That's true," Shawn laughed. "We have always loved each other... high-school sweethearts. It's one of the few things I remember from my long-lost, mortal life."

"She said that you are a powerful vampire. Few vampires are as powerful as you are. The angels made you that way."

"The angels have a mission for all of us. As vampires, we deal with darkness and evil all of our long lives. That is why you should always try to live in the light. You will learn this as you grow and live with your new family. You will learn of the Esmanaa Demons and your families fight with them."

"She also told me when you take a vampires' blood, you can see into their past."

"Yes, that is true, and now it's time for me to take your blood, to see your secrets. Beautiful Juliette..."

Shawn pushed her into an alley and pinned her against a wall. He sensed she was not afraid of him—she had a look of expectation. He kissed her, captured her eyes with his, and drew her into his mind. He took her to the light that rejuvenated vampires, mingled her force with his, and told her how beautiful she was.

Shawn placed a vision of a warrior angel in her mind to show her what she really was. He allowed her to wake, and then he brought his lips to her neck; his blood-teeth grew. He slipped his razor-sharp teeth into her neck slowly, penetrating her, tasting her, and allowing her sweet blood to flood his mouth.

He traveled back in Juliette's life and now was in a large beer hall, drinking beer. Smoke hung in the air from the fire barrels. The people at her table were drunk, and two young men were trying to squeezing her breasts and trying to put their hands between her legs. He could smell the alcohol that saturated their breaths. Shawn sensed these were her brothers, and they were doing this in front of other people. Shawn could feel Juliette humiliation. That was why she had asked about sex in vampire families. He quickly came back to the present. He kissed and suckled the remainder of her blood from her neck.

"Yes, I can see a vampire's past, and I saw your brothers."

"Well, you have already found out my dirty secret. When I developed, my brothers wouldn't leave me alone. I was glad they died. I never liked my brothers—they were pigs—and they are why I learned to like women."

Juliette pushed past Shawn and continued to walk up the street.

"I will say nothing," Shawn said as he ran after and took her hand. "Anne has made it, so you will never be at the mercy of humans. You don't have to be embarrassed with me. We share the same blood, and I will always protect you. I will never think badly of you."

Juliette suddenly stopped and pulled Shawn toward her. "Those two, the man and the woman, they are Bloody Al and Dirty Mary," Juliette hissed. "They are killers, assassins for hire, even I can feel the evil coming from them. Those are the two we want."

A large man with a pasty complexion, rotted teeth, and curly, dirty red hair stood with a homely woman with an overbite, messy face and stringy, brown hair. Mary dressed like a whore, and it made her look worse.

"We'll see. Let's wait and see what they do," Shawn said as he pulled Juliette into the shadow of the building.

Shawn and Juliette waited, and soon Al and Mary started to walk up the street. They crossed the road and followed a block back.

"Sense them, Juliette. Tell me what you see."

"Darkness, hatred toward people, no heart for this world. Human suffering is a pleasure for them, especially if they inflict it."

"These are the people we feed on. This is the reason the angels put us on earth. We feed on bad people, and maybe we can feed on these two."

They continued to follow the two into a darkened area of the street. Al and Mary stopped to talk to a man standing in an alleyway. Shawn and Juliette walked past them on the other side of the road. Shawn saw that Juliette immediately drew Al's recognition. "Do you know Al?"

"He chased me once, I barely got away," Juliette said.

"You should have told me. Let's keep walking. They are starting to follow us."

They walked another block when they heard Al shout, "You two, stop right there! I know you, sweetie. Yes, it's you. What a fine piece you're going to be."

Al and Mary were crossing the street, and Al had a pistol in his hand. "Get into that alley—now!" Shawn knew they were going to kill him.

"Sure, friend. Relax!" Shawn said as he placed himself between the pistol and Juliette. Shawn didn't want Juliette shot on their first outing together. This would not please Anne. Al put the gun against Shawn's back and pushed him into the alley.

"We meet again, precious—and this time, there is no escape. I am going to have you for a while," Al said. "Then I will make a good living with you lying on your back, but first I'm going to get rid of pretty boy."

Al raised his pistol and pointed it at Shawn. A fraction of a second went by, and the gun was in Shawn's hand. He forged the steel of the gun with his hands, forming it into a ball, and dropped it at Al's feet.

"What's the matter, Al? Looks like you miscalculated," Shawn said coldly.

Shawn turned, plunged his hand into Dirty Mary's chest. As she collapsed, he grabbed her hair, pulled her up, sunk his blood teeth into her neck, and then turned with a bloody mouth and hissed at Al. He did not drain her but threw her body out into the street for all to see. Juliette had Bloody Al by the throat and up against a wall.

"The devil—you are a bloody vampire," Al choked out.

"That's right. Don't you find me attractive anymore?" She hissed as her face changed to that of a vampire. "Looks like your luck has finally run out." Juliette threw him twenty feet to the back of the alley and was immediately on him. She stomped on him, pulled him up, punched him in the stomach, and threw him to the front of the lane.

She flew at him and again jerked Al to his feet. Eyes full of fear and as big as saucers, he gasped and spit blood from his mouth. She placed her hand over Al's mouth, squeezed and hissed, "Don't you spit your filth on me. Now you know what fear is. Are you ready to die?"

Shawn had sensed that Juliette could be tough; hardness was in her.

Juliette sunk her teeth into Al's neck and drained him of his blood. His face became lifeless, and she tore at his throat out of anger. She threw him out into the street to join Dirty Mary in death just as he had joined her in murder.

They walked out into the street, still showing their blood-smeared vampire faces. Shawn looked down the road at the criminals watching. He flashed his blue eyes at them and yelled, "Change your ways, or you will be next!" Taking hold of Juliette's hand, he shot straight into the night sky, arced east, and headed to the Bryce family home. A cold wind blew on their faces, as cold as the reality of this age, but they had fed, and felt the warming energy of the blood.

They landed by the little lake, undressed, and swam out into its cool waters. Juliette would come to him, embrace him, and kiss him passionately. He would break away, float her into the air, and drop her into the lake. She would scream and laugh when she came back to the surface, which brought Anne to the balcony.

They swam, flirted in the water; Shawn brought Juliette's mouth to his neck so she could take his blood for the first time. Shawn felt her wet mouth as she hungrily penetrated his neck, and his blood flowed into her. He could hear her moan, and then she released him, bent her head back, shuddered, let out a loud moan, and fell back into the water.

"Your blood exploded in me," Juliette gasped. "My senses became so alive as if I could see and hear everything in this world."

She swam back, embraced Shawn, and wrapped her legs around his waist. She licked the excess blood from his neck, then brought her hand down and guided him into her.

"We should wait for that," Shawn said.

"I was at the door. Anne gave you permission. I may be a young vampire, but I do have vampire ears." She lowered her body down on him and moved with the rhythm of the water. She would kiss him, take small amounts of blood in her mouth, and moan with ecstasy.

"I have never been afraid of you," Juliet whispered breathlessly in his ear as she held him, thrusting into him. "Strange, I feel drawn to you. Soon after I woke for the second time, I knew to be a vampire— and being with Anne—was what I wanted. I love her. She saved me, and she shows me vampires like you."

"Anne loves you," Shawn whispered as he felt Juliette climax. "She is our maker, and we must always obey her. They floated in the water, and soon after, Shawn said, "Let's go in. The sun is starting to come up."

Shawn left a week later, but he came back many times while Juliette was a changeling to take her on trips. He would show her his unique places and the areas where the earth was healing and where people were building a new beginning. Special love and bond developed between them.

Chapter Eighteen

E ighty years had passed since Juliette's turning. Shawn was with Anne, Marilyn, Renee, and Victoria. Vampires led by Anne had been successful so far in checking the advance of the Esmanaa and their efforts to control this world. But vampires had suffered significant losses confronting the Esmanaa, and still, the Vampire Council did little to help in this effort.

They had taken shelter east of St. Louis in a ruined farmhouse, waiting for council member Hector to arrive. Renee left Caitlyn back at Victoria's house with Juliette and Peter. Shawn remembered how Victoria found Peter in Denver, forty years ago, working as a carpenter. He was Peter McGuire, the epitome of tall, dark, and handsome, with black hair, a masculine, chiseled face, and a short, black beard. Peter was six-feet and four-inches tall, broad-shouldered, with a muscular body. He was personable, friendly, outgoing, and the Bryce women swooned over him.

Deep in thought, Shawn peered out of a large hole in a wall that was once an active stable, the animals had left days ago. The land was flat, brown farmland; much of it, the workers had turned over after the harvest. There were areas of scattered field grass and clumps of trees that stretched to the horizon. It was late September, and the days were starting to grow short. Large farms were finally returning to produce the food humans desperately needed. Herit had sent Shawn here to stop a marauding army.

The humans had abandoned the farm in this area because of the fighting and some left midway through their harvest. To his left, about a half-mile away, was the wreckage of the battle. He smelled death in the air from the bloated bodies that littered the battlefield.

Shawn learned a cruel potentate named John Brown, better known as The General, who had taken control of Memphis. He had formed an army of twelve thousand men and marched up the Mississippi, following old Interstate 55, subjugating all the cities and towns along the way. They were eight thousand armed men on foot and four thousand on horseback. Following behind were supply wagons and horses pulling canons left over from the Great War. The General turned northeast, to St. Louis, and headed toward New Chicago to install himself as supreme dictator. It also was reported that the General had been seen many times with a large red-haired man with dark eyes. The Esmanaa Horsa was making a push to take control of this part of the world.

Shawn knew the government in New Chicago had hastily formed a new Army of the Americas and sent them to intercept John Brown's Army. Shawn watched them meet on the flatlands just outside of St. Louis. A better-trained John Brown Army routed the Army of the Americas in two days of fighting. The shattered army was in full retreat back to New Chicago.

Shawn felt Victoria wrap her arms around him and kiss his neck. "Hector will be here soon. He has a message from the council."

"I know what he is going to say already," Shawn said solemnly. "Wait and watch them march into New Chicago. The council never confronts the Esmanaa, and Hector has no heart for the humans. We cannot let this army reach New Chicago. This will squander many of the humans' gains over these past centuries and give control of this land to the Esmanaa. I will not let that happen! We have to stop them—make them turn back."

"That will be a bloody job," Victoria said. "Many of his men follow him for something to eat, to be given any purpose to live."

"The angels command me—those men chose wrong. They will die and take their chances in Heaven!"

Marilyn joined them and asked Victoria, with a chuckle, "What do you think the chances are that Juliette and Caitlyn are going to keep their hands-off Peter?"

"They better, because he is still off-limits," Victoria teased back. "You Bryce women will have to wait."

"We'll see if they do," Marilyn laughed. "I'm sure they're having a little fun with him." Marilyn gave Victoria a playful shove and left.

Shawn smiled, and his thoughts were drifting back to the time Victoria had asked him to go to Denver with her. She had watched Peter for two years, approaching him in taverns. Victoria told Shawn, "I would talk with him, but he always was leery of me. I remembered what you told me about talking to the humans." Victoria finally came to Shawn and told him she was going to take a changeling. She was leaving to turn him the following evening.

"I have to go tomorrow because he is going to marry," Victoria told him. "I want you to talk to Peter. You are better with humans. He is proud and used to being the strongest in the room, used to commanding men. He will fight me. I want you to ease the way. Tell him what is going to happen—explain it—then I will come in, and you leave."

"You are really taking a changeling?" Shawn said in disbelief.

"The time has come. You can come for visits, and we can still sleep together. Not with Peter, of course. He is very masculine."

"It's all right—I knew this was coming. This is something you must do. I know this has been a longing you've had for some time."

Shawn and Victoria now stood outside of Peter's home at the beginning of Clear Canyon, on the outskirts of Denver. Shawn's head suddenly turned. He could sense the dark wolves back in the mountains. The dark wolves would never dare come close to Shawn and Victoria.

Peter had built a house of logs—he'd shaved off the bark to give the house a lighter appearance, and had put new glass in the windows, finally acquired from a local glass manufacturer. It was close to midnight. Peter and his fiancé had been planning their wedding in between bouts of sex. Her brother had just picked her up in a rebuilt anti-gravity car.

"Are you ready?" Shawn asked with a wink.

"Yes, I'm ready. It's now or never. Go to the door and knock. I'll be outside."

"Relax, you'll do fine," Shawn said. "I've never seen you so nervous."

Shawn walked to the front door. A large, full moon hung in the sky. It was a windy night; leaves and pine needles flew by and danced along the ground. He heard the roar of the wind through the treetops. He knocked on the door three times before Peter answered with an old, battered rifle in hand.

"Can I help you, mister? Why are you here this late? You had better have a good story."

"My apologies. My name is Shawn, and I have come to tell you about your new life."

Peter raised the rifle, stuck it in Shawn's face, and warned, "You had better back yourself away from my door."

Shawn quickly took the rifle from Peter and shoved him back into the house. Peter swung a right hook at Shawn's head, only to have his fist grabbed by him.

"Now, Peter, that's not going to help you," Shawn told him as he set the rifle in the corner of the living room and continued to hold his fist.

"You're one of them—a vampire?" Peter growled.

"You are right; I am a vampire. Let us sit on the sofa. It has been a long time since I sat on a sofa with a mortal in their living room. We can talk, 'visit' as humans say."

As they sat, Peter asked Shawn, "Are you going to kill me?"

"No, Peter, I'm not allowed to kill you. Vampires cannot kill good men. But the angels do allow us to make someone like you into a vampire."

Peter bolted from the sofa, and Shawn was immediately on him. He threw Peter back onto a chair and sat on top of him.

"Relax, Peter, you can do nothing now. Here, let me help you relax." Shawn waved his hand in front of Peter's eyes to draw his attention. "That's better. Your heartbeat is slowing. I'm going to get off of you. I'm feeling a little silly sitting on you."

"Are you going to make me a vampire?"

"Not me, but she is outside. Her name is Victoria, the beautiful blond woman that talked to you occasionally at the tavern."

"I remember her! I knew there was something about her! I'm not going to let her do that to me!"

"You have no choice. Victoria is a hundred times stronger than you are. She is a noble creature and my lover of four hundred years. This will be your fate tonight—she will certainly make you a vampire."

"Why is this happening? She doesn't know me."

"You drew her interest, and she liked what she learned about you. Victoria has been watching you for some time. And believe me, she is very picky."

"I don't want or need this. Doesn't she understand? I'm going to marry. That is what my life is going to be!"

"Listen to me, Peter, I'm telling you this because I can see you are a proud, strong man. Your life will be that of a vampire. There is no changing her mind. She found you, and now she is in love with you. In the next few weeks, you must think of survival. You must do everything you can to survive. Someday, you will like being a vampire. After the first time you take blood, you will like blood. Your maker is a decent and powerful vampire, and she will teach you well. She will protect and take care of you until you are ready to take care of yourself. It is time for me to leave, but remember Peter—survive and live, a glorious life awaits you. We will meet when you are a vampire, and you will feel different."

Shawn rose to leave. Peter stood and took a defensive stance with his fists clenched. "I will fight her. I will not let her do this to me."

Shawn turned back. "I've known you briefly, and you will fight. Bravo, Peter Kenmare, bravo. Goodnight, and good luck."

Shawn opened the door, and Victoria entered. As Shawn left, he heard, "That will do you no good, my love. I will make you a vampire tonight, and you will be mine for a hundred years. That, I assure you."

It had been rough for Victoria and Peter that first couple of months. Soon, Peter realized his situation was not the horror he imagined, especially when the alternatives presented themselves. Peter realized that Victoria could be strict, but she had a tremendous ability to love, and she certainly loved him.

Shawn chuckled, thinking of that night. His attention went back to the scared and cratered battlefield. Where humans were moving among the wreckage. It was some of the General's men, going through the dead men's pockets, scavenging supplies and weapons. He watched the soldiers turn stiff, lifeless corpses over, and rummage through their pockets and backpacks. Their death masks were frozen on their faces. Some of the dead were young boys, who would have done anything to earn coin so they could eat. The smell of death was becoming overwhelming.

"Hector is here," Victoria said, jarring him from his thoughts.

"How many are with him?" Shawn asked.

"Three—Adriana, Abigail, and Eric. At least Marilyn's pleased that Eric is here."

"And you're pleased that Abigail is here." Shawn felt himself getting angry. "Only three—that's not what I asked for. The council is going to do nothing again! Don't they understand the Esmanaa could control a large area of this continent if we don't do something!"

"You must accept what the council has decided. It's the same issue again—how much to expose ourselves. Come on, let's go back."

Shawn and Victoria returned to the farmhouse. Hector was already speaking. Hector still treated Shawn the same way he had the first time they met. Hector never showed respect to anyone.

Hector droned on, "We will observe events, help where we can, and without exposing ourselves. The council feels this is the best way now. The humans will survive this Dark Age. We must return to the shadows and prepare to fight the Esmanaa."

"How many council members decided this?" Shawn demanded.

Hector turned, his eyes narrowed, and he glared at Shawn. "Hegamar, Adrian, and myself."

"That's not a majority," Shawn challenged. He could feel the blood rush in his head. He was becoming mad, and he felt the anger his anger build.

"That's not your concern, Shawn Bryce," Hector warned. "You will do what I tell you."

"It is my concern! This human army will not reach New Chicago!" Shawn assured. "And I will not do as you say!"

"Shawn, that's enough," Anne demanded.

Shawn felt himself continuing to change as his anger seared through his body. He was growing bigger---fiercer. His eyes turned a brilliant blue, and his blood teeth grew. Shawn's strength was now on display for the other vampires to see.

Shawn hissed his words at Hector: "The world is in this predicament because of the inaction of the council. The council ignored the Esmanaa and allowed them to manipulate the humans into this calamity. This whole situation reeks with the Esmanaa influence. I will not stand by and watch their gains destroyed by the Esmanaa. I will do something—that, I promise you, Hector! The angels want this, and you cannot stop me! I am going to pick a fight with this army!"

Shawn shot through a large opening in the roof of the dilapidated farmhouse. He flew straight up, further and further into the night sky, trying to burn the anger off. Finally, he stopped his ascent like an arrow that had lost its battle with gravity. He wobbled, arced, and then fell back toward Earth, drawing his slayer from the sheath on his back.

He saw John Brown's men robbing the dead and turned toward them. He targeted a few, flew by, and sliced their heads from their bodies. He landed in the middle of a group and swung his sword, slashing through some more, and followed some of them, those trying to escape, and cut them down. Panic took over the men as they ran for their horses.

Shawn screamed at the men as they rode off, "Tell John Brown he will never make it to New Chicago! He will have to fight us first!"

Anne landed behind him. "Shawn, stop this. You cannot talk to Hector like that. He is a council member and more than two thousand years old." Anne took hold of Shawn in frustration and shook him. "Do you understand me?"

"Yes, I understand …" As he pulled away, Shawn changed back to his human form. "Your council does too little. They allow the Esmanaa to spread their evil and do nothing about it. This time I will do something; this time, I will stop the Esmanaa. Michael demands this from us! Remember what Herit told us!"

"I remember…Hector and Adriana have left. You will have to apologize to Hector someday. He is furious at you, and he is not used to vampires talking to him in that way. Eric and Abigail have stayed.

All of us will help you. You were right—there is no majority from the council on this matter, and now there is no time to have a ruling. I will take responsibility for this, but do not put me in this situation again!"

"I don't fear Hector," Shawn said with a cold voice. "He has never cared for me, and I have never cared for him. He is a jealous vampire and always has been. He schemes for power."

"Morning is coming. Come back to the house, and we will rest. Our thoughts will be clearer when we wake."

When Shawn woke, it was three in the afternoon. He sensed humans, many of them. Taking his hooded cloak from his sack, he pulled it over him, then went upstairs and looked out the large opening in the wall. It was a sunny day, with billowy white clouds that hung in a crisp, blue sky.

The General's army had surrounded the farmhouse. Men were marching onto the field in front of the house, forming lines across the field, trampling the unharvested wheat. The men moved around the dead bodies and cattle that lay scattered from the last battle. The cavalry was forming in a line in front and to the side of the infantry. They were positioning cannons behind a far stone wall.

Marilyn had come up to Shawn and hugged him from behind. "Good thing for you; they don't know much about vampires."

"No, they don't. The mortals must think we will fight like an army would. I'm going to stop them. I will destroy this army if I have to. The government in New Chicago is almost strong enough to govern this part of the world."

"Shawn, you can't talk that way to Hector. He is a member of the council, and he could make trouble for Anne."

"He's worthless as a leader and thinks a silver tongue is all he needs. He is always trying to find the easy way out. And I would never allow anything to happen to Anne."

Victoria came up the stairs, pulling her cloak around her. "It looks like they came to us. How nice of them. I see, unfortunately, it's going to be a bloody night, and the council will certainly have something to say about it."

The rest of the vampires came up the stairs. Shawn sensed distaste in them for the upcoming activities, but they held their slayers.

"Never a dull moment with you, Shawn," Abigail said as she looked out at the army. "They should have come in the morning."

"The angels sent me here to stop this army from reaching New Chicago," Shawn told them, as he looked each in the face. Any help you give I will appreciate it."

Anne looked out at the gathering army. Shawn could see she was playing out all the scenarios in her head. "We wait for the first cannon shot, which will be their first move. We will then go through the opening in the roof and attack from the air, dive into their ranks, sweep through, killing as many as we can. We can't kill all of them but we can terrorize them and send them running back to Memphis. Get your slayers and be ready for the first shot. Target their leadership."

Shawn knew the General had made a grave mistake; he had taken too much time bringing his army to the farmhouse and positioning them for the attack. It was past five o'clock, and the sun was low in the sky and gave the horizon a brilliant, red hue—an eerie omen for the soldiers. Shawn knew The General wouldn't leave his army exposed at night. He would have to start his attack before sundown.

The humans fired their first cannon shot a little before six. The vampires immediately flew through the opening in the roof. They separated like bats and entered the ranks of the army at different locations, cutting a swath through the humans with their slayers. They flew back into the sky to repeat the attack. Heads, arms, and legs were falling to the ground in pools of blood. Men were screaming and cursing, "Where are they? I can't see anything! God help us!"

Horses were rearing up on their hind legs, panic in their eyes, kicking wildly in the air, and letting out whinnies of terror. Some would fall to the ground, their throats cut by a misplaced slayer's blade. Chaos and shock spread through the soldier's ranks. Horses with no riders were breaking formation and running into the woods. Then came a roar of gunfire as the humans panicked and fired into themselves.

The small army was starting to lose formation, breaking up as terror spread through the men. Shawn repeatedly flew through their ranks, cutting a path of death in John Brown's Army. Men were running in fear from the battlefield.

Again, the humans fired into their ranks. The blood was becoming thick on the ground as horses and men fell with death in their eyes. Shawn heard the cursing and praying of the soldiers as the line of destruction and chaos came closer to them. Horses bolting, men screaming, body parts falling—this heralded the vampires' approach. A stricken soldier's blood would spatter the man standing next to him and spread fear like a disease. In a panic, men raised their rifles and fired into the backs of the men in front of them, only to have their superior shoot them dead with a revolver.

One hour into the fight, a little before seven, after the last officer was killed, Shawn watched the humans break and flee the blood-soaked field, leaving behind their weapons and cannons. They had enough of this hopeless fight. They could not fight what they could not see and fled in many different directions cursing, crying, and wiping blood from their faces. Their great leader John Brown was missing and had fled during the fighting.

The seven vampires stood in blood, staring at each other.

"Is this what you had in mind, Shawn?" shouted Renee. "Is this enough death for you?" Renee then faced Anne and yelled, "Why don't you do something about him!"

Shawn saw the rest of the vampires looking at him, waiting for him to speak.

"Yes, this is what I had in mind. These deaths were worth it. We have to give the humans a chance to make a new society. One that is more forgiving, one that has a heart, and is allowed to thrive in a world without the Esmanaa and their corruption. Michael commands it of us. We have to give the humans this chance—they are so close. The angels make me behave this way. The Archangel gave me no choice. Why can't you understand this? I will find this John Brown and see who put him up to this, where he got the weapons. And I will bet it is the Esmanaa."

They left the bloody field and found a small pond to clean themselves. All the vampires had sustained gunshot wounds. There was no talking as they washed each other—only a solemn cleansing of their bodies. High above their heads, breaking through the clouds, was a blood moon marking this night. They parted company and went back to their homes. Shawn left to go on his own to track down John Brown.

Months later, a ruling reached Shawn from the council, stating that vampires were to return to the shadows. Humans would again rule the world and suffer the consequences of their actions alone. The vote of the council exonerated Anne for her efforts at St. Louis. The council ordered Shawn to return and appear before them. He never did.

The events of that bloody evening would grow and live on in folklore. The people in that part of the country told the story for generations, how the guardians destroyed John Brown's Army. How the mysterious protectors gave them the chance to return to decent lives and to a civilization of modern comforts and prosperity.

A year later, Shawn finally tracked down John Brown. Shawn was never able to get a precise scent of The General during the hostilities at St. Louis. He found him living in a row house near the old railroad yard in Nashville. Shawn arrived at the house around midnight. The street was narrow, and there were no lights, except for the occasional flicker coming from the brick row houses. The quiet night was warm, and all he heard was the sound of his footsteps. Shawn had gone down an alley and was standing at the back of the house. An Esmanaa had been here but had left a few days ago.

A light was coming from the back door, and Shawn knew that John was on the other side. He went to the door and peered through the glass. A well-dressed, large, bald man with a perspiring red face sat at a table drinking whiskey. "There you are," Shawn whispered. A revolver was lying on the table, keeping company with the bottle of liquor.

Shawn heard music coming from a music player and knew John Brown was the only human in the house. He reached and pulled the doorknob from the door, then pushed it open and stepped inside. John went for his revolver, but Shawn was on him, throwing him against the far wall. Shawn grabbed the man, dragged him back to the chair, and sat him down hard.

"Do you know what time it is, John Brown?" Shawn said as he gave him a slap across the face.

"No, I don't!" John Brown cried.

"It's time for you to pay for your sins."

"Please don't kill me, vampire. I have gold I can give you," he begged.

"You don't look like a man who could put an army together. Tell me, how did you do it?"

"Spare me—please, vampire," John whimpered. "Life was hard, and I was the mayor of Memphis. The people of Memphis showed me no respect. All they did was complain about conditions in the city. A large man with red hair came to me and told me he could make me the supreme ruler of the Americas. He had a strange name, 'Horsa,' he said. He gave me gold coins and weapons to form an army."

Esmanaa, Shawn thought. "This man told you to go to New Chicago?"

"Yes, he did. He had a plan. He had every detail laid out for me, but he didn't tell me about the chance of vampires attacking."

"Did he tell you where he came from?" Shawn asked.

"Yes, he was on a communicator. I heard him say 'Norway'— he had a fortress there. Please, don't kill me, I will tell you where the rest of the gold is hidden."

Shawn looked into John Brown's mind and knew the gold was in the basement. "I know where your gold is, mortal. What about all the people you killed? Did you show them mercy? No, you didn't—you just wanted power and wealth."

Shawn bent John Brown's head backward. "Lucifer awaits you." He sank his teeth deep into the man's neck, with such force, it shattered his spine and collapsed his windpipe like a roll of dry parchment paper. Shawn drank John Brown's blood until the life went out of him. He then took the lifeless general by his left foot and dragged him out onto the street. He dragged him a block, leaving a trail of blood, until he reached a large garbage pile, and threw him on top. Shawn knew the council would never allow him to help the humans again on this scale.

Shawn left Nashville and spent many decades traveling on his own. He went back to the bayou in Louisiana and had his old house rebuilt by the local Chinese. There was a small population of Asians, remnants from their failed invasion centuries before. Their ancestors were soldiers, trapped, and unable to retreat with the main army. They lived in relative peace with the small, local population that returned to the area.

The population remained low because of the heat and lack of reliable electricity. The town and the Blue Bayou Lounge were long gone, but there was a new town, and a little bar owned by an old, Chinese man. Shawn had become friends with him while frequenting his establishment, as he had with the locals.

Shawn knew some of the town's people whispered he might be a vampire, a Guardian, a protector of civilization, because of his strange comings and goings. Shawn lived in the bayou, spending his days researching the antiquities of Egypt. At the end of the Great War, robbers sacked Egyptian museums and buried the antiquities in different locations in the nearby deserts, and now, after twenty years of living in the bayou, Shawn left for Cairo.

Shawn used his psychic abilities to locate many of the buried treasures from Egypt's past. He mined only a few of the sites and returned the antiquities to the Egyptians. He kept the gold and jewelry for himself. Most of the places he left alone, only mapping their locations for future retrieval.

He spent much of his time tracking the Esmanaa, and finally located them in a fortress built into a side of a mountain in northern Norway. The Esmanaa now stayed together and had many guards at their stronghold.

Shawn would also visit the house in Amsterdam. There, he renewed his bond with Renee. He had strained their relationship because of his beliefs in fighting the Esmanaa, and because of the battle at St. Louis. He spent a hundred years abroad, and finally, overtaken by loneliness, came home to Washington.

Chapter Nineteen

S hawn was six centuries a vampire when he brought Victoria to northern Norway to show her the Esmanaa fortress. She had left Peter and Juliette at her home in Colorado. Peter was no longer a changeling, and Juliette was spending an increasing amount of time at Victoria's house, with Peter returning her interest.

They worked their way around the side of a mountain, carefully avoiding the keen eyes of the security cameras. Using their levitating abilities, they crawled on the vertical, rock face of the mountain, covering themselves with their cloaks to blend in with the stone. This was the best way to get close to the fortress.

On a large ledge, they hid inside a crevice on the east face of the mountain. The ledge gave a perfect view of the Esmanaa fortress, and good cover to hide. They huddled together in the crevice and waited for dark. Shawn certainly could feel the three demons somewhere deep inside the fortress.

There were two colors here—grey in the rock and the white of the blowing snow. The light level was low due to the heavy cloud cover and snow. Down the mountain from the fortress was a smaller building that was the power station. From this building, piping ran to the main building. Puffs of steam came from the many vents at the power station, but there were no smokestacks. They were using atomic energy to operate the power station. The use of atomics was illegal in this age. The well-lit fortress had many cameras and searchlights that were always looking for an intruder.

"What a fine vampire Peter has become. He is very skilled in using a slayer," Shawn commented while probing for information. "He adjusted well as a vampire and has embraced this life. And you became the center of his life. He loves you very much—that I can see."

"I have never regretted taking him as a changeling. I love him more than anything in this world, and we have developed a deep bond. It was long ago that I had that bond with my maker. I forgot the feeling. Anne was right. We do need changelings to help us live through the centuries to remind us about that kind of love."

"He turned out to be a terrific vampire," Shawn replied. "All the Bryces think the world of him."

"I'm certainly aware of that. I think Juliette has moved in with us. Why the talk about changelings? You have an interest in changelings. I can see it."

"I have been watching this human girl. She lives in Tacoma, Washington, and runs a street food stand. The parents are dead, and her only family is a brother and sister. Her name is Katherine Adair."

"How long has this been going on?"

"I've been watching her for a year," Shawn said. "And I have bought a lot of meat pies. We have talked, and she likes me—that, I can tell."

"How old is she?"

"Twenty-eight and her brother and sister are a couple years younger. She's in charge of the stand, you can see that."

"Sounds serious. What attracted you to her?"

"I was hunting, and I smelled cooking meat. It reminded me of this long-lost smell of meat at the fair. I must have felt nostalgic that night and went to investigate. I saw Katherine cooking lamb soaked in vinegar and spices. You could tell cooking lamb was a rare event, the way the crowd gathered. I watched her—how she directed her brother and sister, and her mannerisms. I followed her, and then I just kept going back."

"You've fallen in love with her like I did with Peter."

"I'm too young for a changeling," Shawn said, trying to sound convincing.

"Vampires have changelings at six hundred years," Victoria said. "Most vampires don't wait as long as I. It is a lot of responsibility. That I can tell you. And it is hard at first. Newly turned vampires that still think as mortals can be scary, especially if your love is strong for them. They don't want to feed. They look at you as if you are a flaming banshee. It's difficult in the beginning, so prepare yourself. Now, let us get some sleep. I'm tired from crawling around this mountain. Next eve, we'll get this over with so we can leave this horrible place."

That evening Victoria sketched the exposed facade of the fortress. She noted the location of the main entrance, a smaller side entrance, and possible entrances from balconies and air vents. Victoria sketched an anti-gravity port and finished by adding notes to the drawings.

They left as soon as she was done, and took their time returning home. They spent three months at the house in Amsterdam. Victoria was briefing the vampire council on the drawings and plans of the Esmanaa fortress. When they parted, Victoria made Shawn promise to come see her more often and to let her know what he was going to do about Katherine.

The following week, Shawn found himself standing across the street, concentrating on the odd dialect of this age, and watching Katherine at her food stand a block from the newly rebuilt Port of Tacoma. He could not help himself; he wanted to see Katherine, the beautiful young woman who waited on customers, selling them meat pies.

She had beautiful facial features—perfectly shaped lips, brown hair, green sparkling eyes, a woman's fit, well-proportioned body, and tanned skin from spending most of her time outside. She had pulled her unruly hair back and tied it in a pigtail. A couple of beads of sweat sparkled on her forehead from the hot oven. Shawn stayed out of her sight and watched the young men try to steal a little conversation with her. Katherine had no shortage of male suitors. It always pleased her to see Shawn, and she would spend more time with him. Tonight, he waited before standing in line.

In her usual, friendly manner, she waited on customers, but tonight Shawn could sense irritation in her. He followed her quick glances across the street to a tall, slender, dark-haired man. A bad man, Shawn, could tell, and he wanted something from her— money.

Shawn walked down the street, found a secluded place, and flew to a roof above the stand and watched. Katherine was closing the food stand for the evening, directing her brother and sister. They were discussing what meat would be available for the following week. When they finished, she told them to go home then started to walk across the street toward the man.

The man turned and walked up the street with Katherine. Shawn followed them from the roofs, not letting her out of his sight. He did not like this. Had he made a mistake with her? No, the man scared her, and she wanted to get rid of him. Shawn was touching her mind repeatedly to find out what was happening. The stranger wanted money from her—extortion money for her food stand. Shawn probed her mind deeply and then quickly withdrew. Suddenly, she stopped and looked around, with a curious look on her face. She had felt him in her head.

The man stopped three blocks up the street and leaned against a building. She approached him and said, "Good eve to you." Shawn saw her pull a bundle of cash from her pants pocket. The man snatched it from her hand and put it in his back pocket.

He spoke while his eyes roamed her body. "You're looking really fine this evening." He stroked her cheek and then brushed his hand across one of her breasts.

Katherine backed up and told him, "I work too hard to look good, and you take my money. I have to go home."

She hurried down the street the way she came. The creep called after her, eyes fixed on her bottom and a sneer on his face. "I'll see you in a couple of weeks. Maybe you will be friendlier toward me, or I will raise the rent."

Shawn changed to his vampire state and gave a low hiss. He wanted to follow Katherine, but first, he was going to kill this man and take his blood. He followed the lanky, pasty-skinned man with greasy, brown hair combed down across his forehead and a thin, wax-caked mustache that wrapped his thick, puckered, wrinkled lips. He sensed the man's name was Tweed.

Shawn followed him for a couple of blocks, traveling toward the docks. The thin man entered a dimly lit area, took a pouch of tobacco, rolled some, and lit a cigarette. A horn sounded out in the bay. Shawn checked for humans, stepped off the roof, and landed on top of the man. He dragged him into the alley, sank his teeth into his neck, and drained the blood from him. Savoring the last mouthful, he threw the man onto a trash pile.

He again followed Katherine, traveling by rooftop, and watching her walk home at a good pace. She stopped when she met her brother outside a bar, took the bottle of beer from him, emptied it, and handed the bottle back to him.

The brother told her, "You shouldn't be paying that man money for our spot near the docks."

She told him, "I do what needs to be done to keep our livelihood. If we don't pay, we have no business." She gave him a little shove and then continued to her home.

She lived in a city house with her brother and sister and two other couples. Shawn watched her go into the house, stayed for a while, and sensed her movements. He floated to the window looked in, and Katherine was taking a bath, a beautiful sight, naked with warm, wet skin. He smiled, drifted away from the window, and headed home to Washington.

A week later, he was in line to buy Katherine's meat pies. It was early evening. The port was still bustling with people coming from the shipyard. It was the time of day when humans ate their second meal. Humans only ate two meals a day, one mid-morning and one in the early evening. There were few obese people in this age. Meat pies, with their potatoes, carrots, peas, crust, and meat, were popular. They filled people's stomachs just enough to keep hunger away until their next meal. Civilization was recovering, but still had further to go; it had been a long road, slower than Shawn had hoped. Humans lit their cities with energy coming from power stations. A monetary system had taken shape, and people bought limited amounts of food in food stores. People listened to the radio. There was no television. For entertainment, they went to local taverns, plays at the theaters, or attended neighborhood socials. Not many police walked the streets in this age, and some cities were still lawless.

Newly built anti-gravity cars and trucks were traveling the roads. Only the very rich could afford a car. Shawn saw aircraft again in the skies. Typical for humans, technology started to progress. It had been four centuries since the Great War. The population of the planet was still a third of what it was before the war.

Katherine was talking to a young man who was asking her for a date. She politely turned him down. Finally, it was Shawn's turn. "How are you this evening, Katherine. I'll have two pies and a large ale."

"There you are handsome. I haven't seen you in months. I thought you had traveled on. A large ale—funny you are. Do you like the meat pies, the paprika about them?"

"Yes, I like the pies, especially the taste of the paprika. Tell me, are there police around here, patrolling?"

Katherine curiously looked at Shawn. "Yes, there are—police."

"So, how's your clothes-making coming?" he asked, trying to change the subject quickly.

"Fine, when I have time to work on them, but I have to work here 'til eight in the evening. Everything is so expensive. I made this shirt I have on now, actually."

"It's beautiful," he said.

"Beg your pardon, hungry we are, too," the man behind Shawn said.

"I'll come back again...when you aren't so busy. I like the shirt."

Katherine gave Shawn the two meat pies, smiled, and again gave him an odd look as he handed her the money.

"You talk so strangely sometimes," Katherine said. "Come see me again."

Shawn walked a couple of blocks to where the street children were. He gave the pies to a couple of the orphans and watched them scurry away into an alley when he sensed Katherine coming his way.

She was half a block away and continued walking toward him. "I didn't think you ate the pies. There is no paprika about them, by the way, and you always buy two. Spices are expensive and scarce. I haven't seen paprika in a year."

"You caught me. I like to feed the children."

"Yes, you certainly must—meat pies are expensive...Come on, walk me back to the stand."

"What are you doing in this part of the city?" Shawn asked.

"Meeting some people, but they showed not. You're not from around here, are you?"

"No, I'm not. Why does it show?"

"Nobody says 'police' anymore—that is an old term. We call them 'poles.' And there aren't many poles around—you should know that."

"I see. Well, I'm from the East," he said.

They walked together for a while in silence as Shawn took in Katherine's full scent. She smelled sexual, and he knew she found him desirable. He looked at the luscious spot on her neck, where he wanted to place his mouth. The smell of her sweet blood made him want her and long to taste her.

Katherine gave a little laugh and said, "You're very well dressed and must be a man of money. There are few of those around these days, and you also lack the everyday desperation of this life. What do you do for a living?"

"Travel and buy fish for food stores. My family has money. Is life hard here?"

"Sometimes. I guess I can't complain. It used to be much harder, I'm told. Life is better, but it is tedious."

"Yes, it was very hard."

"How do you know? You look to be the same age as me—maybe a little older."

"Right—I mean—I heard, too," he said defensively. "Do you feel safe at your stand?"

"Somewhat, but I have to pay for my stand's location. I make more money there, but a lot, I have to give back. I am going to move the stand. I will have to tell these men, though, I don't like dealing with them, the way they look at me... Here we are. To work, I have to go. Date, do you?"

"Sure, I do. We will have to go on one. You'll see me soon. I travel a lot in this part of the country."

Shawn stayed longer and followed Katherine home. She had stopped to buy a bottle of wine; he could sense she was still in a sexual mood. She arrived home, took a bath, went to a room in the house, and knocked on the door. One of the married women answered and invited her in.

This was not a surprise to him. He had seen this in Katherine's mind—the thrill she had going to this woman's room after her husband left and having sex with her. Shawn knew this was the only woman she had sex with. She liked the pleasure this woman gave her, and Katherine was an adventurous soul. Shawn also knew that Katherine had not admitted to herself that she also desired women.

The street was dark, so he floated across and went to the second floor, side window. A dim light was coming from the window when he approached and looked in. They were sitting on the bed, drinking wine, giggling, and taking each other's clothes off. The woman kissed Katherine passionately. They kissed each other's breasts, tasted each other's tongues, and the woman put her head between Katherine's legs, and her head went back.

Shawn floated away from the window to give them privacy. He sensed the excitement in Katherine, and it excited him in turn. Shawn floated into the sky slowly, thinking of the sensuous sight he had seen, feeling the lust she had felt. Why was he doing this! He realized, then, floating in the night sky, he was going to turn her. He had developed strong feelings for her. Victoria was right—he had fallen in love with her. He was going to make her a vampire, and he hoped to spend the remainder of his existence with her. Shawn went horizontal, stretched out, increased his speed, and flew home, leaving the lights of Tacoma a blur behind him.

Anne was in Amsterdam with Renee, attending one council meeting after another. Juliette and Peter were traveling with Marilyn and Eric. Shawn went to visit Victoria, and they made love in her couch and talked.

"I've decided I'm going to turn Katherine, but I'm not sure when," he told Victoria.

"Are you sure? It can be risky. It was rough with Peter in the beginning."

"I have seen her a lot lately. I have to be careful. She thinks I talk funny—and she uses new terms and figures of speech I'm not sure of. She likes me, though."

"If she's a woman, and you've been with her, I'm sure she likes you," Victoria laughed, pinching Shawn on his side.

"I'm going to wait and talk to Anne when she comes back from Amsterdam. Let her know what I'm going to do. See what she says."

Two weeks later, Shawn was back at his perch, looking down on Katherine's food stand. She wasn't there; her brother and sister were busy selling the remainder of the meat pies and closing the stand. It was a warm, humid night, and the smell of various foods and human blood was strong.

He heard a ruckus up the street, seamen fighting over a card game. He scanned the minds of the brother and sister to see where Katherine had gone. She was paying their extortion money to the criminal gang that controlled this area of the port and had gone to the docks this time. Shawn looked west, sensed her location, and ran the rooftops toward her. He wished she would take her brother with her, but he probably would be of no use. Where Katherine was a leader, capable, and courageous, he was not.

Shawn stopped and scanned the area. There she is. Something is wrong, he realized and took to the air. Upon reaching the narrow, dimly lit street, he looked down and saw Katherine with two men.

He heard one of the men shout, "You had Tweed killed, you little bitch!"

He saw the man pull from his sleeve a long, thin knife with a razor-sharp point. It disappeared quietly and effortlessly into Katherine's stomach and reappeared coated with blood. A frightened, shocked look appeared on Katherine's face, followed by a loud gasp. This happened in an instant as he arrived.

Shawn screamed and immediately changed to his vampire state and flew at the men. He broke their necks as quickly as Katherine could blink and threw them to the roof above. Katherine was sitting against the side of the building, holding her stomach with blood-saturated hands. The blade had pierced her all the way through. The smell of her precious, sweet blood pulled him to her. He changed back to his human form and gave her his best, "you caught me" smile.

She sat looking at Shawn with eyes wide. "You're a vampire. Now it all makes sense."

Shawn sat next to her, put his arm around her, and pulled her close to him.

"You smell of sweet jasmine," Katherine whispered with a frightened voice. "My mother loved the smell of jasmine... Am I'm going to die?" she asked suddenly.

"No, my precious, I won't let you die." Shawn could feel her heart starting to race. He looked into her green eyes and calmed her. He bit his finger, squeezed blood out, and then inserted it into her stomach wound to stop the bleeding and begin the healing.

Katherine gasped. "Now, I know what you are—I see the strangeness about you." She tried to push away, but Shawn held her with his arm.

"You are not going to let me go, are you?" Katherine whispered weakly.

"No, I'm not—I want you," Shawn said. "I always have."

Katherine squirmed in Shawn's arms. "Your eyes, they draw me in, as if they call me to you and your life. They make my head swim. You have always beguiled me. You make me want you."

"No, I haven't," Shawn insisted. "I want to be with you. I want to protect you. I need companionship for the ocean of time I must cross. Vampires need love almost as much as we need blood. The angels have made it so. I am going to make you a vampire, and give you a great gift. You know what I am now, and you would avoid me. You would never let me be near you. Just like the feelings you are having now—to get away. The revulsion, I see on your face."

"Please, let me go—I have to take care of my brother and sister."

"They can take care of themselves. I have sensed this. They want to handle their own lives now—they just haven't told you."

"Please, Shawn, don't make me a vampire. What gives you the right to do this to me?" Katherine declared, again trying desperately to push him away. "Let me go! Stop charming me!" She pleaded as she tried to free herself.

"I have never charmed you," Shawn whispered in her ear as he held her firmly but gently. "What you feel comes from you. Heaven gives me the right. The Archangel Michael demands it of me. The angels in Heaven gave me the ability. Humans know little of the forces that occupy your world, what it takes to keep evil from taking over your world. I will make you a vampire tonight because it is what the angels want and what I want. I am a guardian, and it's my nature, a Heaven's Killer. Humans must pay the cost for this. We protect you yet spend our long lives in the shadows."

Shawn's eyes dialed into the microscopic; he could see the veins in Katherine's neck, the pores of her skin starting to moisten from anxiety. He smelled her fear and felt the quickening start in himself for the change. "Calm yourself, a great life awaits you." He changed to his vampire form, and his mouth went to her neck to have what he craved—her soft neck and blood.

He could hear her whisper, "Will I like being a vampire?"

"Yes, eventually, you will."

He gently inserted his teeth into Katherine's neck, piercing her artery, his mouth filling with her blood, the sensuous sweetness of it distracting to him, his mind filling with images of Katherine's past. He shook these off; he must remain aware. Remember, he said to himself, drink until her heart almost stops. He brought his mental focus to the finite; he entered and traveled her bloodstream to her heart. His powerful senses were at their height. He sensed every cell in her heart, became part of them, and waited for the right moment to return. He was the strong beats of her young heart, straining to pump the ever-decreasing supply of blood. He then felt it slowing, barely beating, quivering, and at the precise moment, when her heart was giving up the fight, he returned to himself.

Katherine had turned pale, and death was overtaking her. Barely a breath came from her, and he felt fear for her. Shawn quickly tore his wrist open with his blood-teeth and poured his blood into her mouth. "Please, Michael—make her live!"

More and more, until her mouth started to move and she drank the blood on her own. Shawn fed her until her color returned, and her beautiful face changed to show briefly the face of a new vampire. Her blood-teeth formed and were as white as polished ivory against her ruby lips. Her eyes turned the vivid blue of the Herit bloodline.

He had done the angels' work and changed her to a vampire. He scooped her gently into his arms and rose into the air, taking his precious changeling to the Bryce family home. He laid her on the bed in his room, next to the couch she would sleep in, and then called Victoria to tell her what had happened. She wished him luck and told Shawn she would come after Katherine had adjusted and had her strength. He then called Anne and broke the news to her. There had been a few times in six hundred years when he had made Anne speechless. She congratulated him and babbled that she would inform Marilyn and Juliette. She would bring them home as soon as Katherine was ready to receive them.

Katherine had gone through the change very well, though she complained terribly about the pain in her stomach. He told her it was her blood sac forming, and she would not be eating any more meat pies. Unfortunately, getting her to feed for the first time was a different story.

Three weeks had passed when he woke to Katherine staring at him. It was around noon, and she still slept on the other side of the couch. It was common for him to wake and see her looking at him. They would talk, and he would explain vampire etiquette or tell her a little about the other family members. He explained to her why vampires were on Earth, and all the reasons blood was so crucial to vampires. He did not tell her about the Esmanaa.

He had tried to get her to feed, but she told him she was not ready; the thought of it made her sick. She was now pale and sickly looking, her eyes sunken and dark.

"My stomach is hot. I don't feel well," Katherine whispered.

"You need to feed, Katherine. There is not much time left to complete the change. Please, don't make me sorry I turned you. Survive, Katherine! You are rejecting the angels. They will burn you from the inside out. It will be a horrible death."

"The angels from the old Christian religion? Turns out, they're real after all?" Katherine smiled a dreamy smile and sighed. "You know, I was attracted to you before I found out you were a vampire."

"You're not attracted to me now? How could you not be?"

Katherine laughed. "Well, at least I don't feel like getting away from you anymore. I guess you won't lock me in the cellar and drain my blood nightly."

"I love you Katherine, I would never let anything happen to you, but this I have no control over. You must feed. I will find a murderer for you, somebody that doesn't deserve to live."

"You will take me to a bad person. When I do this, I will like blood. The thought won't make me want to vomit."

"Yes, love," Shawn assured. "And you will like blood after—I promise. Please!"

"Yes, take me, if that will make the burning go away! I feel terrible. I am so weak. I can see now I have no choice anymore. I want to live with you. I love you. I have loved you since the first time I saw you."

Shawn held out his hand. "Drink my blood. You will feel better. We will leave for Spokane this evening. Feed, my love, and live!"

Katherine moved to him, took his hand, and half lay on top of him. She smelled his neck and then turned. He felt her touch his neck, picking her spot, then her blood-teeth entered his throat and the potent nectar-filled her mouth. When she finished, she didn't move away from him. She laid her head on his chest, and he stroked her soft hair.

"I feel better, thank you," Katherine whispered. "My whole being quickens from your blood."

"You must drink from me whenever you can. Take my blood. Use it to make yourself strong, so we can be together and travel through time together. Human blood is for nourishment. What the bible does not tell us is that some angels can be hard, taskmasters. Angels are not white creatures with wings. They have many ways, from saints to warriors. They have declared that humans owe us their blood for the protection we give them."

Katherine stayed close to Shawn, and, as she fell to sleep, she murmured, "Why couldn't you have been just a wealthy, handsome young man?"

Shawn flew Katherine to Spokane the next evening. Spokane was not the little city it was six centuries ago when Anne had taken him for his first feeding. It was mostly in ruin, rundown, and dilapidated, home to an abundant criminal element. Spokane had come to the attention of the Bryces recently because of slave trading that involved homeless children. The lack of medical care and disease had produced many orphans.

It was early autumn, with a refreshing breeze, Shawn went to an area that had working lights and landed on one of the roofs. Spokane had not enjoyed the progress of other towns. A rundown saloon had drawn his attention, and he could hear a piano playing off in the distance. He turned to see the terrible look of Katherine; she had not fed in three weeks.

"How are you feeling?" Shawn asked.

"Feeling weak this night. Strength, I have not to do this."

"I will be with you—I will help you," he told her.

He bit his wrist and offered it to Katherine, and she drank. He allowed her to take as much as she wanted. Shawn wiped the excess from her lips with his finger. He loved the feel of her lips. He could see the blood had made Katherine feel better, but it would not last.

"Let's go! You need to feed," Shawn urged her. "When you drink human blood for the first time, a new life force will be yours. You will then realize what you are."

"What you made me. Let's find some blood and get this over with," Katherine whispered. "I don't want you to hurt this way, and I can sense your desperation."

They stepped off the roof, floated to the ground, and walked down the street. A fight in the saloon had spilled out onto the street and turned into a giant brawl. There was a flash of a knife, and a man fell to the ground.

Shawn and Katherine traveled on, and soon, he felt the signal he was looking for and headed toward it. They had arrived at a narrow, dimly lit street, across from a bakery. Two men were coming down the street with two, poorly dressed children, and Shawn could feel the fear coming from the children. He took hold of Katherine and floated to the roof directly above them.

"Can you sense the fear from the children?" Shawn asked her.

"Yes, I can. This is terrible," Katherine answered.

"Look into my mind, Katherine. Let me take your senses to these men. Can you see their evil? This is why we are here. This is what we feed on."

"I feel it. How horrible."

The men went down a small alley and knocked on the back door of the bakery. A slightly overweight man wearing a filthy white t-shirt and old dungarees answered and stepped outside. A stringy, grey-haired, skinny hag of a woman followed him. The baker was upset with the men. They brought two children instead of three. He had contracted slavers to pick the six children up the next evening. The one-child asked for something to eat and promptly received a loud slap across the face. The woman grabbed the children and dragged them through the door and down the cellar stairs. Shawn could hear the children's screams and the clunking of their shoes, hitting the wooden steps. The three men continued to talk about when the next delivery of children would come. Soon, the other two men continued down the street, while the baker rolled, and lit a cigarette and stood by the back door for a smoke.

Shawn searched the area for other humans, but there were none. "This will be your target. Project your senses outward. Do you feel other humans?"

"No, only that man, and what is in the house," Katherine answered.

"Do you think this man should live?"

"No, he doesn't deserve to live," Katherine said. "But I'm not sure if I should be his executioner."

"The angels give you the right. It's time to be strong. Propel yourself at him. Remember to slow yourself when you get near. Knock him unconscious with the force of your body. As soon as your mouth closes on his neck, you will know what to do. Everything will become natural after the blood starts to flow into you."

Shawn saw her lick her lips in anticipation and stand at the edge of the roof. He saw her change into a vampire, ready to feed. Her eyes turned, and her blood-teeth grew. She gave him a weak smile. Then, with no prompting, she launched herself at the man, flew straight and true toward him, hit him, and knocked him back into the building with a loud bang that shook the wall of the building. Shawn followed, but she needed no further encouragement from him. Her mouth came down on the man; blood flowed down her throat and out the sides of her mouth. She was the lion, and he, the prey.

Shawn spoke to her. "Remember to spit the last mouthful on the neck wound."

She released her bite, and blood spilled down her chin and neck. Katherine looked toward the sky, shook her head, and then clamped her mouth back to the man's neck. Shawn watched her drain the man, then her head fell back, and she let out a loud cry. She was experiencing the quickening—a high power was coming over her. Translucent wings appeared and then disappeared.

The attack was loud and made the woman come to the back door. Shawn made quick work of her. Relief filled him, and Katherine reached over and wiped below his eye. He saw blood tears on her fingers.

They went to the basement, released the children, and herded them upstairs to the outside, then watched them run away as fast as their little legs would take them.

Shawn would take Katherine feeding every three days over the next two weeks. He would take her to Spokane and teach her how to feed using the children slave traders as their prey. They would wash in the lake when they returned, she enjoyed the lake, and Katherine loved being with him. Like all vampires, she took to the water right away. Her beauty had returned, and she was adjusting well as a vampire.

Katherine had been a vampire for six weeks the evening Shawn woke to feel the lust she had in her. She slid on top of him, kissed him passionately, and tore at his pajamas, ripped the top off and pulled his bottoms down. She continued to kiss him with passion building in her, biting him on the chest and licking at the blood. Katherine was a woman full of desire. She slid back up and put him inside her as her mouth came down on his neck. Her hips rocked against him as she suckled and drank from him. Then, surprisingly, Shawn saw her go into a trance. *She is traveling back in my life,* he thought. When they finished their lovemaking, they lay in each other's arms.

"You went into a trance. What did you see?" Shawn asked.

"I was you when you were human, and there was a girl always with you."

Shawn could see Katherine had become serious. Something was bothering her.

"When I sleep, it's not like it used to be when I was mortal. I feel like I'm floating. I don't sleep as deeply as I used to. Something is watching me—I know they mean no harm…I feel love. I ask who they are, but they never answer."

"They are your angels," Shawn replied. "You will not sleep like you did as a human. Your soul will not stay with your body when you sleep now. It is unusual for them to come to someone at such a young age. They must want something from you. They always want something from me. Someday you will meet Herit, a powerful angel that started our bloodline. She will teach you about our choir of angels, and guide you through your life as a vampire and guardian."

Chapter Twenty

K atherine woke at five in the afternoon and sat straight up on the couch. Three vampires pulled into the garage in a large, anti-gravity car. One of the Crimmian servants ran out to meet them and help the driver with the luggage. She looked at Shawn, the creature that had made her a vampire. Earlier she had felt such desire for him. She had desired him her last days as a human, daydreamed about him, and that desire had returned. The blood made her feel much more alive, far more than when she was a human, creating a far stronger love for him.

Sleep still had him in its grasp. He was not quite awake, and she leaned over and kissed him. Now her concern was with the arrival of the new vampires, and for sure, she would be dealing with them. Katherine had quickly grown to rely on Shawn, a feeling she was not used to having in this world. She had always been the leader. He showed her patience and kindness, and she needed him to survive—it was a responsibility she knew he loved to do.

She felt love for him, but she did not trust it yet. After all, he was a vampire. She was sure Shawn knew how she thought. He knew everything else.

"The vampires are Anne, Marilyn, and Juliette," Shawn told her sleepily. "Anne has informed me she wants to meet you alone. Anne is head of the family, and she has this right."

"No, Shawn. Alone, without you?"

"Yes, Katherine, and you shouldn't say no to me—especially in front of other vampires. It's Anne's way, and she wants to meet you alone. You can talk freely with her. You will be fine. You'll like them—you'll see."

"All right, if it's expected of me. Come along shortly, you will?"

"Yes, I won't leave you alone for long," Shawn promised. "Now go get yourself ready and go meet your family members."

Katherine went to the shower, washed, and dressed in fine clothes left for her on the big bed. These were Juliette's clothes, much nicer than she had worn or made when she was human. Shawn always made sure she had the best. Butterflies were swarming inside her middle when she started down the hall to the stairs. Steady, she said to herself. She was used to walking into the unknown—she had done it all her life—but the task now at hand was harder. They were vampires.

The house was large, with plenty of furniture from a time of indulgence when people had plenty of room in their homes. Ten families would live in a house like this in her time. Life had changed so abruptly—the unusual man that attracted her was a vampire, and he had given her a strange life. Two of the vampires were in the sitting room drinking tea while the matriarch, Anne, was outside on the other side of the lake.

Katherine walked across a large room with chairs, couches, and a fireplace. Large portraits hung on the wall, and she easily picked out Shawn's. She heard them call this room a gathering room. Katherine decided as she walked toward the entrance to the sitting room that she would introduce herself first and then see what happened. "Hello, Katherine, I am." Oops, wrong dialect, her brain screamed at her.

Two beautiful young women were sitting on the sofa drinking tea and talking. They turned, gave her a warm smile, one stood, and held her hands out to Katherine.

"Come, let us look at you. You are beautiful," Marilyn said softly. "I'm Marilyn, and this is Juliette, and we hope you are feeling better."

"Hello, Katherine," Juliette added. "You're looking well, I know it's been rough getting past that first hurdle of feeding…Shawn must be taking you to feed often."

"Yes, he does. Shawn is very good to me. It amazes me how my thoughts on blood have changed so quickly." Katherine gave a nervous laugh and added, "But I am a vampire now."

"When I was a changeling, Shawn would take me on trips with him," Juliette said. "He also took me on one of my first feedings. I loved going with him. Shawn was fun and exciting. He will take good care of you."

Suddenly, Katherine realized that Marilyn was the girl she had seen in her dream. "Marilyn, you knew Shawn when he was human."

"Yes, we went to school together and were sweethearts. I have known and loved Shawn for a long time, all of my six-hundred-year life. Now, Katherine, Anne waits for you. It is time for you to go meet her."

"Sure I will," Katherine said. "I mean—I will go meet her."

Marilyn gave Katherine a friendly smile. "You will learn to speak English here. Such a funny dialect the humans have now, don't you think, Juliette?"

"Our language has taken a turn," Juliette answered.

Katherine went out the side door and down to the lake. It was a warm summer eve. The stars stretched across a clear sky, and a large, full moon kept them company. The hoot of an owl traveled the lake. She used her vampire eyes to look across the water. Anne was under a small waterfall, the moonlight reflecting off the falling water, washing soap from her hair.

Her appearance startled Katherine at first; Anne was a young, beautiful woman. Not what she thought a two-thousand-year-old vampire would look like. Katherine saw Anne turn and look directly at her. She stripped her clothes off, laid them on a wooden lawn chair, and dove into the lake. She swam toward Anne with a feeling of nervousness.

Then in an instant, Anne was in her head, and she could hear her voice.

You are beautiful. I knew Shawn would pick someone like you.

This brought a smile to Katherine's face and took away her nerves. As she approached Anne, she felt this ancient vampire open herself to her. She was old—Katherine could see that by the depth of her eyes. The way the moonlight shimmered off her skin.

"I'm delighted you think I'm beautiful. I am old, unfortunately. I am Anne, as you know, and I am amazed to meet a changeling of Shawn's."

"You're very kind, and I'm happy to meet you," Katherine said. She felt Anne in her head, more forceful than before, learning about her, quickly going through her head, and then her probing stopped.

265

"My apologies. It's much more efficient."

Anne swam in a circle around Katherine, saying, "You're a charming, young vampire. I hope you find our family pleasing to you. You must make yourself at home—we are your vampire family now. We are not a human family, which you will find out."

Katherine watched this vampire glide effortlessly through the water, her hair wetted back, the flash of her ancient eyes, making her feel welcome.

"I know a secret about you," Anne teased, "I wonder if that was one of the reasons Shawn selected you. I wouldn't put it past him."

"What is it—this secret, you know?" a concerned Katherine replied.

Anne swam toward Katherine spoke into the water, "You've been with a woman."

Katherine could feel the soft kiss of Anne's lips on her neck as she took in her scent. She could feel her naked legs wrapping around her, like steel bands that made escape impossible.

"I'm going to take some of your blood. You can have some of mine in return," Anne told her seductively. "I will be gentle."

Katherine could feel the sharp points of Anne's teeth on her neck. Then the slide of the fangs as they slowly, deeply, found their mark, and the blood leave her. She wasn't afraid of this vampire—on the contrary— she felt safe and wondered what she would do next. Anne released her and swam back, licking the blood from her lips.

"You have a beautiful home—it's so big—and I love the lake and the water," Katherine stammered.

Anne gave her a mischievous smile. "Of course, you like water—you're a vampire. Come swim with me. We can talk."

As they swam, Anne asked Katherine about her life as a mortal, about her brother and sister, the death of her parents. What attracted her to Shawn? She told Katherine that the new dialect was charming, but she would teach her the King's English. They swam until they came to a large, smooth rock. The surface of the stone was just below the water, and Anne showed her the perfect place to sit.

"Take some of my blood, Katherine. This will allow us to bond."

Anne guided Katherine's mouth to her neck. The smell of her blood and the taste of her were intoxicating. The sweet, powerful taste of her—again a quickening. The strength of Anne's blood pushed her back through the centuries, and she found herself looking across a wooden table at men playing cards. This was an ancient saloon, a time she had read of in an old book, and they called it the old west. She was Anne and knew what she knew. Her blood travels had happened again.

There was a tall, skinny man with a thin mustache that had too much wax on the tips, and the professional gambler, dressed in his black suit, with a narrow black tie contrasted by his freshly laundered white shirt. The gambler wore a large-brimmed, black hat, which he placed on the table next to him, and kept a small revolver secretly hidden in his black coat. Then there was the city council member, with his darting eyes and a smile that was not sincere.

The gambler looked up and smiled at them. "You're looking as beautiful as ever."

"Yes, she certainly is," mumbled the thin man. "Your mother must have been a sight to see."

"Thank you, gentlemen, but that's not going to help you. I will still take your money." Katherine heard Anne say.

"I'm sure you will," said the councilman. "Where did you learn to play cards so well? I sometimes wonder if you're a psychic, beautiful lady."

"I can assure you, gentlemen, I'm not a psychic. My daddy taught me how to play cards, and he was one of the best. A little luck is also helpful, something you men don't have tonight." Anne laughed and searched the saloon with her senses. Something isn't right; Katherine could feel it, and Anne was searching the humans for the cause. Suddenly, a man stepped away from the bar. There were beads of sweat on his forehead. He had drunk his courage and now took his Colt revolver from under his jacket and pointed it at the head of the gambler.

"You bastard, you cheated me! I lost my store and family!" the distraught man screamed.

A loud bang, with a puff of grey smoke, and the invisible bullet entered the back of the gambler's head. His blood and bone splashed over Anne's face. The slug left the gambler's head and struck Anne's chest just above her left breast. Katherine, felt the burn of the metal, heard screams and shouting as the gunman was subdued. Then the gambler fell from his chair, wet, red blood swiftly claiming his clean white shirt.

Katherine heard the panic and commotion, and she saw where the bullet had struck Anne's chest. The shot worked its way out of her and fell onto the table. The wound healed immediately, leaving only a small, round, red spot on her smooth, white skin. The humans backed away with their mouths wide open and shock on their faces. They stared at each other, expecting someone to give a logical explanation, but none came.

Then as if a hand had grabbed hold of her, she was yanked back through time and found Anne staring at her as she came back to reality. "You can see into our lives like Shawn. You are a rider of vampire blood. How interesting."

Katherine looked into Anne's deep, blue eyes. She could feel the pull, and her eyes were as Shawn's—she fell into them and lost her sense of herself. She felt love coming from Anne, and that surprised her. She sensed a profound power, saw it in her eyes—it was there, and no vampire could miss it.

"Come, let's go inside, sweet Katherine. We will have plenty of time together. You'll get used to me."

When they arrived back at the house, Shawn was in the sitting room with Marilyn and Juliette. They joined them, and Katherine answered many questions and told her new family all about herself.

Katherine was thirteen years a vampire when she found herself sitting in the Black Water Lounge in Big Hope, Louisiana. Big Hope had grown into a small city on the edge of what the humans now called the Great Iberian Bayou. Shawn had brought her to his home in the bayou two years earlier. He told her he wanted a change from the house in Washington. Shawn explained to her that they were there to finish his search for the remaining bayou gold and to continue his research on the lost treasures of Egypt.

Katherine had grown comfortable with Shawn, and it had not taken her long to embrace her life as a vampire. She loved Shawn. It amazed her that she fell so deeply in love with a vampire. She asked Shawn if he had manipulated her feelings. He told her no, it was her emotions, and the intensity was due to her vampire blood. What alterations he could do for her love, she would soon notice, as she grew older.

Shawn would teach her about her life as a vampire, and he was quick to tell her more serious lessons would becoming. The idea of immortality had occupied her thoughts of late. Shawn would say to her their lives were long, and there was plenty of time for lessons. He did teach her how to control riding vampire blood.

The idea of immortality scared her sometimes. Imagining living forever frightened her. She asked Shawn about immortality. He told her when he was younger that it had scared him, too. As she grew older, she would get used to the idea and accept that a time would come when she wouldn't remember her beginnings. She would develop patience for time and the solitude that would come with a long life.

Katherine knew Shawn loved coming to this bar on Saturday nights to play the piano, sing, and drink wine. He made friends with most of the patrons. He made friends with everybody. She would ever so slightly practice looking into their minds and was aware that some of the people were suspicious of them but said nothing. Humans thought differently about vampires now. Much of their folklore was about the Guardians, vampires that had helped them through bad times. However, nobody really wanted to meet one.

They would take the longboat out into the swamp, to search for the scattered gold bars hidden in the muddy bottom of the swamp. Shawn would stay in the boat, project his maps into the dark swamp night, do his research, and write on his maps. She would swim through the brackish waters, and, every so often, find a gold bar. Sometimes she would come face to face with a crocodile, would give it a wrestle, and hold on to its back, skimming above the sandy bottom, through the swirling sand and tall bottom grass. Shawn would call her his great crocodile fighter. Sometimes they would just spend the night lying in the bottom of the boat looking at the stars, making love, and talking.

Shawn had taken her from a life of hardship and given her this life. She loved Shawn for many reasons—mostly for the kindness and love Shawn showed her. Katherine would listen for hours to the strange stories he would tell her about his life as a vampire: his experiences with the dark wolves and the horrible demons. He would tell her about the age of high technology before the war. And he told her about the witch that had seduced him in this very swamp.

This was when she first became aware of the quest he was on and the existence of the Esmanaa. He would become earnest when he talked of the Esmanaa, and this was when Katherine's fear of losing her maker started.

She knew she inherited Shawn's unique gifts, and her vampire skills were growing faster than normal. She had great strength, moved so quickly that no human could see her, and could fly for hours alongside Shawn and walk undetected amongst the humans. Her psychic abilities were also progressing rapidly.

These same psychic abilities detected a vampire flying toward the lounge. Katherine looked at Shawn, and he, too, had sensed the woman. Shawn continued to play the piano with a big smile on his face. The vampire landed outside and came through the door. It was a stunning, blond-haired woman with black, tight leather pants, black leather boots, a green silk blouse, and a black leather jacket. Every man in the place stopped what they were doing and looked at her. Some couldn't take their eyes off her, which annoyed her and the rest of the women.

Katherine had met Victoria briefly a few times after Shawn turned her. She also remembered Peter, an absolute hunk of a man. Unfortunately, he was not with her. Katherine knew Victoria was Shawn's lover for centuries and was very aware that Shawn loved her deeply. It amazed her how vampires had long love affairs with more than one. Shawn told her it was because they were eternal and had the blood of the angels. This gave them immense abilities to love.

Victoria looked at Shawn with a smile, and her eyes lit up. She then made eye contact with Katherine and gave her a smile.

The Chinese barkeep went wide-eyed as she walked toward the bar and asked, "Do you have whiskey here?"

"Yes," stammered the man. "We just got a shipment in."

"Then give me a bottle and three glasses," Victoria said as she slapped money on the bar. Victoria brought the bottle and three glasses to the table and took a seat. "You're looking well, Katherine. Vampire life must suit you. Do you remember me? I'm Victoria."

"Thank you. I do remember you and Peter. He didn't come with you?"

Victoria filled two of the glasses with whiskey and shoved one toward Katherine. "No, he didn't. He is on his own now. He went to South America with Juliette, Marilyn, and Eric Nicholas. I worry about him, but he is with good vampires."

Katherine drank half the glass and giggled. "Yes, he is quite the vampire."

Victoria laughed. "Well, you feel like all the other Bryce women. I see you have found out about one of Shawn's favorite pastimes."

"I have. He loves coming here, and I don't mind."

"I see that about you, pretty Katherine. I'm sure we are going to be good friends."

"You have known Shawn all of his vampire life?" Katherine inquired.

"When I first saw Shawn, he was on a balcony, and he had been a vampire for two months. I have known him for six hundred years since. Spent many of those years with him—not all—sometimes we need a break from each other. And there are changelings."

"I see," Katherine said.

Victoria downed her whiskey and refilled both of their glasses. She asked, "You spent time with Shawn before he turned you?"

"In a way, yes. He would come around, and I thought he was attractive. I liked talking to him. He was different and talked with an old dialect. He was strange to me sometimes, and his eyes floored me. And he didn't eat the meat pies I sold—he gave them to the street children. The one time I needed help desperately, he was there. He saved my life, but he was a vampire, and he made me one."

Victoria finished her glass of whiskey. "Well, I see why Shawn was drawn to you. So, you are here in Louisiana, scavenging the last of Shawn's gold bars. You know, he really comes to this swamp for privacy."

"There's nothing wrong with a little privacy," Shawn laughed as he approached the table.

Katherine watched as Victoria and Shawn embraced and kissed passionately. She could see the strong bond they had for each other and that they loved each other deeply.

They sat back down, and Victoria filled the glasses with whiskey.

"So, Peter is traveling?" Shawn asked.

"He left with Juliette—no surprise there. They are with Marilyn and Eric. They have gone to South America, so I have come to visit you and Katherine."

"You have something to tell me," Shawn said.

"Yes, I'm sorry to say, the Esmanaa are starting to become active again. They have awakened. Erdin came to me and told about the new technology they were developing. A machine that will hide them from us."

Shawn turned to Katherine and told her, "Esmanaa sleep for decades, and we hear nothing from them. Then they wake up and start their trouble."

"Herit says the Esmanaa want to kill our family," Katherine said. "They hate our family."

"They hate Herit blood," Shawn clarified.

Victoria stayed for a month, and through that time, she had been banished from Shawn's couch. A detail she didn't appreciate. One night, she decided to try to join them. She listened to them from the doorway heard their moans of ecstasy. A desire grew in her to taste Victoria's vampire's blood. She could smell her blood and knew it held tremendous power. The taste of an older vampire's blood aroused her-- Anne's did. She wondered if Victoria's blood would, too. Victoria was strictly for men, but she wondered what it would be like with her. Closed and guarded, that was what Victoria was to Katherine. Shawn left himself open for her to see—Victoria certainly did not.

Anne also left herself open to her and made her aware of her desires for women. Anne loved her, treated her special, and introduced her to others as if she were the most important vampire in her life. Katherine learned that Anne held high esteem in the vampire world and learned why her bloodline was powerful.

Thinking of their lovemaking always brought a smile to Katherine's face, the energy and pleasure she got from her. When she was with Anne, she knew she desired women. Shawn had told her he always knew this about her. She had made love to Marilyn in her couch. That was the way her vampire family was, and sometimes it seemed Shawn was the odd one out.

Victoria was kind to her, touched her, and talked at length about interesting ideas, but her mind and her past were shut off to Katherine. If she could take some of Victoria's blood, she knew, she could more easily learn about her past. Victoria always talked about the Esmanaa to Shawn. This also annoyed Katherine.

Katherine had asked her angels and Herit about Victoria. The angels hid the future and Victoria from her. There was a vague fear she had that came with Victoria, and the angels were of no help. The way Victoria talked about the Esmanaa—how to attack them and fight them—made Katherine afraid Victoria would get her maker killed.

Herit had been with her a lot in the last few years. Herit took Katherine to Heaven and asked her not to tell Shawn, but he knew. Herit was preparing her, and for what, she didn't know. Herit would not talk of the future with her.

Well, here goes, Katherine thought.

"Can I join you?" she asked with a shaky voice from the doorway.

There was silence, and then Victoria answered, "Yes, Katherine, join us." Naked, Katherine floated into the couch.

Victoria sat up and embraced her, took her hand, and placed it between her legs. "Is this what you desire? Does it feel to your liking? I can see in your head, young one. I know what you think about me." Victoria kissed Katherine passionately. "Is my taste what you expected? Victoria turned to Shawn and said. "I'm going to take her blood, and she will take mine."

Shawn nodded his acceptance and took her hand. Katherine felt a strong, deep bite, more forceful than she had ever felt. Victoria drank her blood, finished, and licked her neck and ear. "The blood of Herit is strong in you. Now it is your turn. Drink from me, sweet Katherine."

Katherine embraced Victoria, kissed her, and took in her overpowering scent. She could sense the blood below her skin—she penetrated her neck—and drank. This is what she wanted, and she traveled Victoria's blood, farther and farther back in time. Suddenly, she was a young woman, dressed in ancient clothes, in a stable putting ointment on a horse's foot. An old man was standing behind her, dressed like a king she had seen once in an old book.

Annoyed and angry, he said, "You will, Daughter, marry this O'Dea, and I will hear no more of your complaining or I will take that crop to you." Katherine could feel the fear Victoria had for this man.

"Yes, Father, I will do as you say." Katherine woke to see Victoria and Shawn staring at her. Victoria looked at Shawn. "She's just like you!"

Shawn and Katherine would leave the swamp and travel to other places in the world. Katherine would spend time with Victoria as she came and went. The one constant in her new life was Shawn's love and his preparations for her to survive as a vampire. He made sure her skills with a slayer were superb, and he always gave his blood freely to her. He brought her to the wolves and gave her an adventure she would never forget and showed her how to survive in the sun. But the feeling of foreboding for Shawn and Victoria would return often. She traveled the world with Shawn and still saw great destruction from a long-ago war. Shawn would introduce her to other vampires—all had respect and fondness for Shawn, except the Vampire Council, which had respect for Anne, but was unsure of Shawn.

Chapter Twenty-One

K atherine was ninety years as a vampire, and her time with Shawn was coming to an end. They had been traveling and were now returning from Amsterdam after attending a ball for the Vampire Council. She wanted to stay with him and couldn't imagine being without him. He always opened himself to her, and she knew he would let her stay as long as she wanted. Katherine had developed a strong bond, a love that only a vampire and a changeling could experience.

She talked him into taking a slow, hovering, ocean liner back across the Atlantic. They spent evenings together walking the decks and looking out over the ocean and at the bright moon that hung above it casting its long reflection over the water. Together, they danced in the lounges to modern music and spent time making love in their suite.

She took his blood often and would travel back to his early life as a human. Shawn's beginnings fascinated her. It amazed her how humans lived such a comfortable life. A life of plenty, it held such contrast to the life she was born into. Unlike Shawn, she liked traveling on vampires' blood. Katherine convinced Shawn to stop in Dalton on the way home. She wanted to see the location of his birthplace. The place she had seen in his long-ago life. They had stayed in a mountain camp for a month and now were preparing to leave in a few days.

She found, next to a clear river, old foundations overgrown with vegetation and filled-in basements where the buildings once stood. Over the centuries, the American East had cleansed itself of the effects of the Great War.

Humans were rebuilding their cities, and comfortable living had returned for them. Significant advancements in science and technology had begun again and in part to the safeguard of human technology by Guardians. The population remained low. Only two in five babies survived their births—a situation that concerned the scientists of the day. Humans now built environmental waste stations to burn off the toxic waste, to rid the world of the poisons brought about by their violent past.

Dalton was no longer located in the State of New York. The District of New England was the location's name now and bordered the District of Penn to the south. Twelve districts made up the old United States. These zones were part of the United Americas, which encompassed North America.

Katherine had rented a summer camp next to a lake. Wealthy people from the cities now had summer homes on the many ponds and lakes in this area. Katherine was making her way uphill, following the depression of an old, overgrown road Shawn told her he once lived.

"My house was at the top of the hill!" Shawn yelled ahead to Katherine.

"Shawn, look! The black tar from those old black roads. There's nothing left—only the big oak trees."

"It's been almost seven centuries," Shawn said, exasperated.

"Come on, let's go back to Mason Lake."

Katherine now was comfortable being a vampire—it was who she was. She loved her maker for the gift he had given her, a life with far more layers, far more possibilities than her human life. As a vampire, she did not have the worry of survival or the constant struggle for the needs of human life. She had developed a strong bond with her maker and now laid in his arms, this was their last night in Dalton. They did not need to talk. Each could easily form their words in each other's minds if they wished.

"The angels final started talking to me about Victoria," Katherine whispered.

"Why do you talk about Victoria with the angels?"

"I feel a danger with her, and it has to do with you," Katherine said, stroking Shawn's face and kissing him. "Don't be mad with me."

"You are starting again?" Shawn whispered. "What did they say?"

"They sidestep a lot of my questions, but in our choir of angels, they sing her praise. They feel she is a loyal warrior angel and will bring the downfall of the demons. Some call her queen of the vampires. How peculiar! They told me her maker was one of the first vampires to fight the Esmanaa and the first to kill one. They said he died a terrible death. There's something else, Shawn. Herit wants to know why you don't come to Heaven anymore."

"I know what the angels expect of me. They hide the future from me now, so I don't go. Always remember this, Katherine—the angels guide Victoria in this quest. She had no choice in this, and she could not refuse them, and neither could I. I love her very much. No matter what happens to me, Victoria is not the reason."

The sun came over the trees, and the vampires sat up to watch it rise. Katherine watched the sun strike Shawn in the face. How beautiful he looks in the light, Katherine thought. His face shimmers and sparkles as if he is not entirely of this world.

Katherine pulled Shawn close to her. "I love to watch the sunrise. I always think how beautiful, how lucky we are, the angels allow us to see it." She sat and watched the sunrise above the trees. She listened to the insects awaken and heard the songs of the birds that began the day. She sat for a good hour with her maker and enjoyed the start of the day.

"Let's go inside. We will travel tomorrow eve," Shawn said.

The next evening as they were leaving, suddenly Shawn stopped and look south. She felt an unease come from him. "What is it, love?"

"An unusual energy coming from that direction. Can you feel it?" A perplexed Shawn said.

"No! What do you think it is?" Katherine asked.

"It's not the Esmanaa. Maybe some type of witch. Most unusual, though. Let us see what this is. A quick look, and then we'll head home. Follow me."

Katherine rose in the air, gave a couple of stretches, and turned south to follow Shawn. They followed the sense to an old mineshaft, fifty miles north of the abandoned city of Pittsburgh. Pittsburgh lay in ruins. The humans gave little attention to rebuilding this once-industrial stronghold. Vegetation had overgrown the city, and the smokestacks had long ago fallen to the ground. Old steel smelting furnaces were still rusting in their final stage of decay. The end of a long-past industrial age…Skeletons of old high-rise buildings in their last death throes…It was becoming common to hear the roar and see a massive cloud of dust and debris when a skyscraper finally fell and came to the end of its long, slow death.

Katherine and Shawn landed in a clearing with knee-high, green field grass. The grass traveled up a steep hill to join with a birch-and-poplar-forested hill. At the start of the rise was an opening to an abandoned coal mine.

"It's in there—I've never sensed this before," Shawn said. "Let's go, I'll bring Victoria back to investigate."

"We can go in there now," Katherine said, trying to reassure him. "It's a weak sensation, probably some residue of a past event. Some horror of long ago—likely the Great War. Besides, you have your slayer."

They floated across the field slowly. Katherine knew Shawn was nervous and worried about going into this cave with her. She knew if Victoria were here, he probably wouldn't feel so anxious. *He is always so protective of me,* she thought.

"Stay behind me," Shawn said. "You're probably right. The feeling is from a long-ago event that happened in the cave."

The vampires entered the dark cave, and the smell of moist, moldy air hung heavy. She heard the slow drip of water coming from a crack in the stones above. They went slowly into the cave and soon came to a large vein of coal. Scattered about were centuries-old, rusted cooking pots, utensils, picks, and shovels with their wooden handles gone, rotted over the ages.

"These are tools leftover from the early years of the Dark Ages," Shawn explained as he reached down, picked one up, and watched it crumble in his hand.

"They were desperate—life had lost all meaning—all they had was survival. In this part of the country, their lives didn't last long. They would come to the caves to escape the radiation. Here they found shelter from the nuclear storm, scraped the coal from the walls to cook what little they had, and to keep warm during the nuclear winter."

They continued walking and passed side shafts that branched off from the main shaft and traveled to a destination unknown.

"The sensation is getting stronger," Katherine said.

"It's just ahead. We're almost there," Shawn answered.

They came to a large cavern. In the center was a pool of red liquid twenty feet across, and as thick as syrup. Katherine could sense a dark evil coming from the pool. It made her sick.

"The earth and coal have masked the strength of this evil from us. Stay here, Katherine. I'll take a look, and then we will leave here quickly."

Katherine watched Shawn cautiously approach the pool. She saw a distortion, then a large, blue circle made of swirling dark energy form behind him, the center much blacker than the inside of the cave. It formed and then quivered as a figure stepped through. Katherine sensed Esmanaa and recognized the apparition as the demon Shenti. He had come through a dimensional portal, and Shawn didn't know he was there. Terror swept through her. *Thank the angels he couldn't form into a physical presence,* she thought. In his hand was a brown rod as long as he was tall, with yellow markings that swirled around the shaft and ended at a yellow tip. The point was sharp and much thinner than the rod.

"Behind you!" Katherine screamed.

Shawn turned, and Shenti drove the tip into his chest. Twisting the rod, the demon broke the tip off, and then withdrew the spear. Shawn's eyes rolled back into his head, he collapsed to his knees, and then to the cave floor. Shawn lay motionless. Shenti turned with a wicked smile and pointed the rod at Katherine.

"Red death and legs of lead you will have." A loud, harsh noise rose in her head, vibrating her very being, then subsiding. The demon gave an evil laugh and stepped back through the portal.

Katherine immediately was at Shawn's side, yelling, "Wake up! Please, wake up!" Katherine felt a heaviness steal over her and then a quick rise of evil energy coming from the pool. The pool started to swirl and bubble. She shook Shawn and yelled, "Wake up, wake up!" Katherine knew he was alive, but he was unconscious and turning white.

A creature crawled out of the pool, two-feet tall and covered in a thick, red liquid. The head was small with long, pointed ears, yellow eyes, and a long, thin mouth with rows of sharp teeth. The ghoul was mostly belly, little chest, with long arms and legs, and fingers that ended with razor-sharp nails. The same with the feet.

Another ghoul crawled out of the pool, and then another, and soon there were ten and increasing. Shenti had cast a spell on her to slow her speed, and now she felt heavy and lethargic; her legs were as heavy as stone and were hard to move. Katherine grabbed Shawn and pulled him effortlessly to her chest with one arm. She still had her strength. With the other, she took Shawn's sword from the scabbard on his back. Terror went through her. Now, she was glad Shawn had taught her how to use a slayer.

Katherine shook Shawn. "What is the matter with you? I need you to wake up!" No response came. His lifeless body lay limp in her arms. She knew she had to get him out of this cave. She slowly got her legs working and started to back out of the cavern. A ghoul attacked her, and then another. She swung the sword and caught the first, which shattered into small, black shards of glass and then disappeared. Glass pierced her, burning her skin. The next ghoul landed on her, biting her shoulder and raking her with his razor nails. Katherine grabbed the ghoul and threw him against the cave wall; again, the creature shattered like glass.

Katherine changed to her vampire state. "Bastards, you are!" She crouched and hissed at the ever-increasing number of ghouls. She held Shawn and fought her way back down the mineshaft. Surrounded, she fought desperately and then realized no vampire would detect their distress. They were too far under the earth, and her mental energy would never reach Anne or Victoria.

More ghouls rushed her. She killed most, but some got through her defenses. They tore at her flesh, bit her until she peeled them off, and threw them against the stone walls. Touching the creatures burned her hands. She continued to back her way down the cave, fighting off the ghouls. She swung the slayer repeatedly, but they kept coming. At times, she dragged Shawn by his shirt collar while fighting off the ghouls.

The evil creatures would continuously try to surround her. The spell still affected her legs, but she continued to fight her way down the mineshaft, wiping the blood from her eyes so she could see, her clothes soaked in blood, and her maker still motionless. She swung the sword and struck down the ghouls, but she was losing; there were too many. At times, she would have to stop, stand over Shawn, and fight off waves of these evil creatures. Then she would continue on fighting her way down the mineshaft, talking to the angels in a loud voice.

"I need your help to save him! I came to you to talk as you wanted, and now I need your help! I'm hurt—you must help us, or Shawn will never kill another Esmanaa!"

Katherine was becoming desperate; she was weakening and losing too much blood. As she fought her way, she noticed a light in one of the side shafts, and then Herit's voice in her head: *Lucifer has tricked us. Follow me, and I will show you a faster way out.*

Katherine wiped the blood from her eyes and face, and she saw Herit inside the light. Down the side shaft, she went, following the light and fighting off the ghouls. The voice spoke to her again: Anne and Victoria know of your plight. Stay strong, they are coming. See the opening? You are almost there.

Katherine looked down the shaft and saw an escape from this horrible place. She continued to fight off the ghouls, but the loss of blood made her thoughts come slowly. The light from the angel disappeared, terror and loneliness swept through her.

She continued to fight her way toward the opening in the side shaft, the cuts and puncture wounds taking their toll. The ghouls tore her skin from her, and her clothes hung from her in shreds.

She had done her best to keep these horrible creatures from her maker, but her own blood now covered him. The ghouls followed her out onto the hill with no let-up. She carried Shawn over her shoulder and fought her way up the grassy hill next to the opening of the mineshaft and tried to take flight but couldn't. She swung her slayer, repeatedly striking down the ghouls. When she reached the forest, she saw a flash—it was Victoria. Diving into the ghouls, Victoria sliced through them and killed them by the hundreds, but the ghouls still came from the opening in the side of the hill. Katherine wiped more blood from her face and then realized Anne was standing next to her.

Katherine fell to her knees, holding Shawn, and grabbed hold of Anne's thigh. "Thank you, Herit," she whispered.

Katherine looked into Anne's eyes and knew she looked a sight— desperate fear on her face and soaked in blood. She was losing consciousness, so she shook her head, knowing she could not pass out—not now.

"Katherine, try to stay awake. We will be leaving very soon," Anne told her.

Anne shouted to Victoria, "Get Shawn out of here. I will cover you!"

Victoria flew to Shawn and took him from Katherine. "I'm taking him to my home. It's closer. Don't stay long!"

"I'll follow you with Katherine," Anne shouted. "Katherine, you will have to let go of my thigh. Michael wants to send a message to Lucifer for his deceit."

She raised Deceida above her head, and a beam of light came from the darkness above and traveled true to the slayer. An intense narrow beam that pierced the night and was absorbed by the sword from heaven. She watched Anne lower the Deceida and point it at the ghouls. A crack and then a wave of brilliant light came from the slayer, lit the night, and washed over the creatures burning them where they stood. Thousands of beings shattered and fell to the ground. Anne gathered Katherine into her arms and start the flight to Victoria's home. The wind rushed over her face and helped her stay awake.

"Shenti came out of nowhere," Katherine gasped. "He had a long rod with a yellow tip. Stuck Shawn, he did and left the tip in him. That is when he collapsed."

Darkness crept over her again, the light calling her—the angels, with their songs and praise. Katherine fought to keep herself awake. She felt the wind still; she looked down and watched the lights pass quickly by. She drifted back to the light and the angels' praise. She had saved her maker. They told her the knowledge to wake Shawn was coming.

Katherine was aware they had placed her on a hard table and were washing her with warm water. She was next to Shawn's lifeless body and heard Anne, Victoria, and then Peter and Juliette, discussing what to do for Shawn.

Anne was always at her head, stroking her, holding her hand. "Can you hear me? You are at Victoria's, and we are going to bury you. You will heal in time."

"How is he?" Katherine asked with a weak voice.

"We can't wake him," Anne whispered in her ear. "Do you know how to wake him?"

"No, but the angels told me the answer will come."

The vampires looked at each other, and Victoria said, "We better find out soon."

*****

Anne knew she could save Katherine; they would bury her, and she would survive. Katherine had hundreds of cuts and bite marks on her body. They gave her blood and prepared her for burial. Shawn was her worry—he was completely white, and veins in his flesh started to show. She did not understand why his vampire body was not clearing the poison. Why it did not clear the tip of the spear from his body like it would a bullet?

The wound in his chest had completely healed over. He lay there, motionless. Anne knew she must do something, and also knew there was not much time left. The demons had their hold on Shawn and were pulling him to their dark world.

Anne sensed the witch coming over the trees. It wasn't Pandora, but it was a powerful witch, and she was landing on the front lawn.

"The witch knows the answer," Anne whispered.

Anne floated up the stairs, out the front door, and onto the lawn. A young girl stood barefoot on the dew-covered grass. She wore a light blue linen tunic with a rope around her waist. A dagger hung from the line. She looked young, maybe eighteen, with white hair that flowed down past her shoulders, and had white skin to match. Her face was pixie-like, with small features, light, pink lips, and vivid, blue eyes.

"Greetings, vampire, I am Jessamine, the daughter of Pandora."

"How is Pandora?"

"My mother died this past year and went to join Eos."

"I am sorry for that news," Anne said as she looked at the young girl. "How old are you child?"

"I have no age. My mother was a thousand years old when she died. I do the work of Eos to ease the suffering in this post-war world.

"Your mother was a dear friend and a good witch."

"She talked of you and Shawn," replied Jessamine. "She told me how she fought and killed a demon with you."

"She saved Shawn's life that night, and I will never forget what she did. Why are you here? Have you come to help Shawn?"

"I know how to save Shawn. Will you take me to him?"

"Follow me, witch," Anne said. "How did you know of Shawn's plight?"

"My psychic abilities are vast, and I travel and live freely between this world and the spiritual. The dark angel Lucifer tricked the warrior angels of Heaven, but he did not count on the strength of Katherine. Lucifer was not aware of Katherine, but he knows her now. The Archangel favors Katherine. Vampire, you must trust me when I go inside."

Anne led the witch to the side door and started to enter, when Jessamine hesitated and stared briefly outward, her eyes searching. "What is it Jessamine? What do you see?" Anne asked as she watched the witch draw a symbol with her hand.

"I see great power is in this house—and heartache."

They proceeded down the stairs, and Jessamine went to Shawn's side, touching and caressing his face. "We meet at last, Father. Mother told me about you." Jessamine turned and said, "There's not much time left. The spell is progressing, and soon he will be Lucifer's."

Anne and Victoria looked at each other; the reaction and what Jessamine spoke was very unusual. *Is this one really a witch,* Anne thought. *There's something different about her.*

"Jessamine, where do you come from? You said Pandora was your mother?" Victoria asked as she looked Jessamine up and down.

"I came from the Louisiana Bayou, conceived in the bottom of a swamp boat. My mother was a witch, and my father a vampire."

"That's impossible. Vampires don't conceive—they love and change!" Victoria insisted.

Jessamine looked at Victoria and said, "They can if The Mother wills it."

She placed her hand on Katherine's forehead, and her eyes glowed white as she stared at Katherine. The vampires saw her lips move, but they could not understand the strange words she spoke, and Victoria started to move toward her.

Anne stopped her. "Wait!"

They then heard Jessamine say, "Now I see what you are up to Michael. All the signs are here."

Jessamine would not elaborate; what she saw was for The Mother. The witch asked the vampires to leave, except for Anne. She told them what she had to say was for Anne's ears.

She took the knife from her side and placed it over the spot the spear had entered. Jessamine worked the knife into him and soon found the spear tip. She worked the tip out of Shawn's chest and held it with the knife, never touching the tip with her hands.

It was a brownish-yellow, oozed, and was not solid. The smell became terrible. She dropped the tip to the floor where it fizzled, popped, and then burned with a dark blue flame and disappeared.

Jessamine turned with a sad look on her face. "It will take time for all the poison to leave his body. Watch him closely during this time. He will be susceptible to evil. I am sorry tragedy is coming. Some angels require a payment for the removal of the demons from this world. The payment is Bryce's blood."

"Why would the angels want Bryce blood?" Anne asked.

"The demons came from these casts, and they, too, felt humiliated," Jessamine answered, and then pointed a finger at Katherine. "Know this—that one is the queen. She walks the earth. The Age of the Queens has arrived."

Jessamine floated up the stairs, turned, and nodded toward Shawn. "Remember, Anne, when the end comes, get him to ground." Jessamine floated out the door and into the night.

The veins disappeared, and Shawn's color improved. His eyes fluttered and then opened. "Where is this? What happened?"

Anne leaned over Shawn, relief on her face. "The demons tricked you, and they almost killed you. Katherine got you out of the cave and now lies next to you. Pandora's daughter came, took the spear tip from you, and saved you."

"The daughter of Pandora!" Shawn turned and touched Katherine's face. "Katherine, can you hear me?" She opened her eyes and smiled, then closed them.

"We are going to bury her," Anne told him.

"Then bury me with her," Shawn insisted.

Anne leaned over Katherine and whispered in her ear, "You saved your maker, and you saved Shawn for me. Thank you."

They buried Shawn and Katherine in the basement of Victoria's house. Shawn held Katherine as the dirt fell over them. Anne never told anyone about the conversation she had with Jessamine.

Chapter Twenty-Two

T he first years after the attack at the cave, Shawn would feel the poison of the spear tip. He felt the evil elixir take over him, clouding his thoughts, whispering lies in his head, and making him lose track of time. The voice was always female and told him she was Lucifer's witch, Malin. Sometimes, the voice led him to northern Canada, tricking him, leading him to the dark wolves so they could kill each other. The evil witch told him the dark wolves would kill him if he didn't kill them first.

He lived in the woods like an animal and killed hundreds of wolves. He would take shelter in caves, wash in the brooks, and feed on the deer. He never wore clothes—he was always naked hunting the wolves, avoiding all contact with vampires. Always, the voice whispering in his head, calling him to Lucifer's dark world.

Shawn woke in a dark cave covered by a large bearskin. He knew what cave this one was—it was the one under the mammoth northern pine. There were many small caves in this frozen land. He would wake in one and find himself with no recollection of how he got there or how to go home. He would have these moments of lucidity before Malin returned to his head. Wrapped in the bear hide, naked underneath, he stumbled outside. It was late afternoon, and the bear hide shielded him from the weak sunlight. He remembered killing the bear and the witch telling him to leave the head on the hide: Hollow the head out, pathetic vampire. Wear it on your head like a mask so the wolves can see how ferocious you are.

Malin's mocking cackle would laugh and ring in his head. The forest he found himself in had huge pine trees spaced five to ten feet apart, with a snow-covered canopy high above him. Snow and pine needles covered the ground. He could sense wolves, and then it would come to him. He must kill all the wolves. The witch would come to him: *Vampire, we must go kill the wolves. Don't you remember? We must kill. Now get your slayer, stupid vampire. Get your slayer, or I will send the demons.*

He went to get his slayer; he always did what Malin ordered. Shawn made his way through the forest, where he sensed the wolves. He came to a clearing and heard the crunch of snow under his bare feet. Everything here was frozen except the wolves and him. Off in the distance, he saw five dark wolves traveling across the field. The late sunlight sparkled off the snow.

There they are. Go and kill mighty vampire. Use the great power those filthy angels gave you. Feel the hate toward the wolves. Their evil…Isn't it beautiful?

Shawn shook his head with confusion on his face. He knew this wasn't what he wanted, but the voice spoke, and he did what the witch said.

"I don't know what to do. Why won't you leave me alone?" He pleaded.

Lucifer wants you. Don't you remember, pitiful vampire? I told you this. You cannot fathom the chaos and darkness Lucifer will bring to you for killing his demons. Now attack the wolves! Or I will make the blood come from your ears again.

A terrible, high-pitched shrill started in his head. What little will he had left… He shot across the field with his slayer in hand. He maneuvered around the wolves to approach them from behind, running at a blinding speed, leaving a cloud of frozen snow behind him. His speed far higher than theirs, turning his head and bringing into focus the small frighten, snow mice scurrying into their white holes. He fell upon the wolves, took their heads, and mutilated them with a terrible hatred that burned through him.

Feel the evil. Isn't it delicious? Come with me. Go to the cave and jump in the pool. Lucifer awaits you. It's your fate. Didn't those whore angels tell you that?

Blood now stained the virgin snow. Malin had made him crazed. He slashed at the dead wolves changing back to human form and screamed his hatred while the voice in his head laughed at him.

Shawn woke the next night crouched next to a large red oak tree, his bearskin next to him stained with blood. It was pitch black in the woods, yet he saw. He heard the howl of the cold north wind and the rustling of night creatures back in the forest. Ice caked his bare feet. He put snow in his mouth to help him wake up and try to clear his head. He slithered up the ancient, red oak tree and searched the night with his senses.

He could sense no dark wolves, but he did sense two vampires. His mind was clearing—this was starting to happen more often.

"Vampires," he whispered to himself. He had sensed these vampires before. *They are looking for me. Why are they important,* he thought? Then the voice and the cloud descended on him again.

Kill the vampires. They are horrible creatures: nothing but filthy beasts. Kill them—you have the power. Do what I tell you— Lucifer wants them dead.

"No... I am a vampire. I may know these vampires," Shawn pleaded. He now could feel the poison lessen.

Listen to me, vampire! Lucifer will have you in the end, and the bastard angels should have told you that. The whore Eos knows this. Now kill these vampires! Do as I say—kill these vampires now, so when you come to Hell, Lucifer might take pity on you.

The shrill started in his head again, and he took to the air. He flew toward the two vampires, landing on an access trail next to an old fire observation tower. The old decaying sentry rose toward the sky, past the treetops. The red paint long ago flaked off its rusted steel frame. Down the trail, two women stood. He knew they were vampires, and he quickly entered their heads. *They know me,* he thought, *and I should know them.*

"Shawn, its Marilyn, and Anne! Don't you recognize us?" Marilyn yelled.

"No—you are here to kill me!" he screamed back as he paced back and forth across the trail holding his head. "Malin says you are filthy vampires."

"We are here to help you. Look at us, and try to remember who we are," Anne pleaded.

He crouched, hissed at the vampires, and changed for the attack.

"No, Shawn, don't do this," Marilyn begged.

He charged the vampires; they turned and ran from him. He caught the one that spoke to him first, drove her to the ground and had his hands around her neck. The other vampire was quickly on him and forced him off with her superior strength. Then they both were on him, trying to hold him down, rolling through the snow. As he quickly threw them off, the stronger one delivered a powerful blow to his jaw, and it startled him awake.

"Shawn, stop this—somebody will be killed!" Anne yelled. "Please, stop!"

He stopped fighting, looked at the women, and then remembered who they were. His memories flooded his head. He then heard the voice as it finally left him.

We will meet again, vampire. Lucifer has not finished with you, and neither have I!

His head started to clear, and Anne and Marilyn's faces came into focus. He was himself again.

"Shawn, it's me—Marilyn!"

"Yes, it is," Shawn answered as he lay on the ground. "Where am I."

"You are in the forest again," Marilyn said, trying to reassure him.

Anne then took him, held him, and brushed the frozen hair from his eyes. "That's right, you are in the woods. We will stay with you until you are better."   Anne and Marilyn stayed with him until his body finally cleared the demon's poison, and then they brought him home.

Shawn had been separated from Katherine for two years while he wandered with the dark poison in him. Finally, they were reunited in Katherines last year as a changeling. They came to Egypt and rented a small house from the Crimmian Society on the outskirts of Old Cairo in the area known as Giza and had made it their home.   Shawn spent this time in Egypt searching for antiquities filling the room on top of the pyramid with gold and jewels. He would find the tombs, take the gold, leave the antiquities behind, and send the location to the right authorities, it was what he liked to do, and it helped fill his time.

They lived in Giza for ten years, and Katherine had stayed with Shawn through this time. It was a hot night, and they had gone to downtown Giza to a large showing of Egypt's antiquities at the newly opened Giza Museum. Shawn wanted to see the relics he had found and turned over to the museum.

"Shawn, there's the scepter we found," Katherine said and gave a wink and a laugh. "The big, red rubies embedded in it. Do you remember the night we found it?"

"Yes, I do. How could I forget?" Shawn laughed.

"Look, there's the chair with all the rubies that were with the scepter. We put that to good use."

"I believe they call it a throne," Shawn laughed. "And it certainly was very noble that night."

They continued to enjoy the exhibits. Every so often, they would come across something they recognized.

Katherine pointed her finger at the hanging, ancient, pre-apocalyptic aircraft. "Do you remember any of those?"

"I remember some," Shawn answered.

"You were in a war as human?"

"How did you know about that?" Shawn asked.

"I have my ways—your blood, and Herit," she answered.

The feeling came on suddenly. It started the same as last time, rapid detection of an Esmanaa coming at a fast speed, traveling in his direction. Shawn cloaked himself. A chill went through him; somehow, the demon knew where he was. When an Esmanaa showed himself this way, he knew where his target was.

Shawn grabbed Katherine's hand and said quickly, "Cloud your mind—do it now! Follow me!"

"What is the matter?" Katherine said, hurrying behind him.

"Esmanaa!" Shawn shouted over his shoulder. "Follow me!"

They quickly crossed a large common area where ancient aircraft hung from wires and darted in and out of the people, then down a hall toward the main stairs.

They hurried down the stairs, then a corridor, and arrived at one of the display rooms. Shawn looked at the weapons and decided on the short, broad sword that had belonged to a long-dead Roman legionnaire. The sign read, "Gladius" and said that the diggers had found the sword at Alexandria, in a lost, buried Roman barracks. He broke the glass case and took possession of the sword. Alarms started to sound, so they hurried to a side door and forced it open, to find themselves in an alley. The demon had slowed, probably deciding on the best way to attack them. The Esmanaa locked onto something, most likely Katherine.

"Katherine, clear your head, and block your thoughts like I taught you."

"I'm trying, Shawn, but my head hurts," Katherine said. "It's like the cave, sad and nauseating. That horrible smell!"

"It's a demon, and he knows where we are. Come on, this way."

They ran down the alley until they reached a dead end, and Shawn yelled to Katherine, "Jump to the roof, Katherine!"

They jumped four stories, ran, and leaped to the next roof. Police were arriving at the museum, so they continued to run for three more rooftops. The demon was near and would catch up to them anytime now. Shawn stopped at a rooftop fire escape door and took Katherine by the hand.

"Listen to me carefully," Shawn told her. Shawn was afraid, but it was not for him—it was for her. She was too young and weak to be near an Esmanaa. "He's coming, and we can't escape him. When he lands, he will try to torment us, and then he will charge."

"Shawn, you're afraid. I've never felt you so afraid."

"Listen, there isn't much time. When I tell you, take to the air as fast as you can. Fly as fast as you can north. Do not fly in a straight path. Change your course often—fly to Crete. Remember the olive orchard? Go there! Bury yourself for two days, and when you come out, sense your surroundings, if you detect the demon, go back to the ground. The Esmanaa can't detect you when you are in the ground."

"No, I don't want to leave you! Let me stay and help you! We can fight the demon together!" Katherine pleaded.

"The demon would kill you right away. I cannot protect you. I will be busy fighting for my life. Do as I tell you—I will tell you when to leave!"

Katherine's voice was shaky as she said, "Yes, I will do as you say. You will come for me, won't you?"

"I will come if I can. If I am not there, make your way to the house in Amsterdam, stay by yourself, and use what I taught you to survive. Renee will protect you until Anne comes. Now stand behind me—he's coming!"

Shawn allowed himself to change. He grew his body by a third; his fangs became long, polished white; his fingers extended and developed sharp, pointed nails; his eyes turned a deep blue with transparent slits in the middle.

A terrible sound pierced his head. The demon was announcing his arrival. He landed a short distance in front of them, already changed into his demonic form. The building shook from his weight. Katherine held Shawn's arm, and he could feel her shaking. This was Shenti, the short, stocky, ugly one.

He cocked his head back and forth as he took them in. Bulging round knobs protruded from his thick skull, and large, black eyes, blinking rapidly. "I have been looking for you, Bryce, and now I've found you. Thanks to my spies and this young vampire."

"You found me, but this will be the night you join Charun," Shawn growled.

"How lucky you are Shawn to survive the poison. Horsa told me to watch out for you, but he's weak of will and only likes pleasure. Charun is in Hell serving our father, Lucifer, and I am sure I can kill you. I told Horsa that I would take care of you, and then I will gain favor with Zepar. I cannot read your mind, but I can see into the young ones somewhat. She is trying her best to hide, to hide her fear, but she feels like pissing herself. We meet again young vampire. I am impressed you escaped the cave. This time I will eat you before this night is over."

Shenti squatted and started to move back and forth on his short, stocky legs. Shawn drew his sword over his head, holding the handle with both hands, turned slightly, knees bent, ready to strike. "Katherine, go now!"

"To Hell is where you will go, demon!" Katherine said as she shot into the sky. "If you live, someday you will see me again." Katherine turned north and flew toward Crete.

"I'll let the young Bryce escape for now," Shenti spat at Shawn. "She's too weak to bother with, but you will leave this world tonight."

"Do your best, demon. Tonight, you will be with Lucifer."

Shenti bent his head forward and charged. Shawn tracked the demon as it came for him and, at the precise moment, shot into the air, bringing the sword down and slicing a deep gash across the demon's back. He could feel the vibrations from the blade travel into his arm from the dense flesh of the beast. He saw the sharp edge of the blade curl over and wished he had his slayer.

The demon spun and charged again, tackling Shawn around his waist, propelling them to the next building, then down through the roof, to the top floor. The building shook and groaned. Shawn caught Shenti with a punch to the jaw, driving him through the wall and into the next room. He flew through the hole in the wall with the sword extended in front of him. Shawn forced the slayer through Shenti's stomach, and the blade immediately broke at the hilt.

Shawn knew the museum was two buildings away, and he was desperate to make it back to the weapons room. He flew up, exploding through the roof, and turned toward the museum when Shenti caught him. Shenti held him from behind, raked his fingers across Shawn's back, ripping his shirt and flesh from him. The monster drove him through another roof, crashing down two floors before being stopping.

Shawn plunged his pointed fingers into the side of the demon. Shenti flipped him off his back. Quickly, he charged back, tore at the demon's flesh, and repeatedly smashed his face with his fist. Shenti was dense, and Shawn's blows only penetrated so deep. The terrible fighting went on—room to room. They flew at each other and clashed with great force. They held each other in their deadly grasps, wrestling, trying to gain an advantage. The monster was bleeding his brown, sickening blood. The blood was spraying from his mouth with each breath he took. Again, Shawn hit him in his face with his fist. The demon spun, knocking Shawn's feet from under him. Shenti then grabbed Shawn and threw him through the outside wall, partially collapsing the roof above. Shawn allowed himself to fly through the next wall and into the museum. Landing on the floor, he quickly rolled to his feet.

He found himself in a large storage room and was moving toward the door when Shenti crashed through the wall. The Esmanaa was on Shawn's back and drove his fingers into Shawn's side, he screamed and dropped to the floor, flipping Shenti over his shoulder. Then Shawn landed on top of him and again pummeled his face with his fist. He looked into the demon's black eyes. "I have you, and you will die tonight, demon!"

Across the room, Shawn saw an ancient chariot with a spear in the side rail. He stood, holding the demon by the throat, and threw him through the wall, then flew toward the chariot, grabbed the spear, and turned. Shenti was racing toward him; he brought his arm back and hurled the spear into the neck of the evil creature. The demon staggered, snorted, and stopped, broke the spear, and pulled it from his neck.

Shawn saw a long, medieval sword resting on a finishing worktable with a four-foot blade and a long hilt. Shawn seized the sword, turned, and saw the demon standing there with his many bleeding wounds. The monster had a look of puzzlement on his face as if he could not believe he was losing the fight.

"What are you? How can you be a vampire?" Shenti said as blood sprayed from his mouth. "That pig Michael has given you great power. I must warn Zepar." Shenti turned, dazed, and staggered, trying to make an escape.

Shawn flew at the demon with the long sword and struck him across his stomach, giving him a deep gash, spilling his organs. He spun and slashed his neck with the long blade. Shenti fell to his knees. "Are you ready to join Charun?" Shawn asked. He struck Shenti in the neck repeatedly, as if he was chopping down a tree. Finally, his head fell to the floor, and the demon's body followed. A terrible smell filled the room, the demon's body starting to sizzle and pop. Dark blue flames consumed its form.

Shawn became aware of the sirens and the humans coming to investigate the destruction. People gathered outside, talking excitedly of Guardians or vampires fighting. He raised his head to the heavens, decreeing, "This is for you, Herit! I send this demon to Hell in your name!"

He staggered and leaned on a pillar for a brief time. The demon had hurt him, but he had to go to Katherine. He didn't want to leave her unprotected, and it was time to leave the museum, and fast. He followed the openings back into the alley, flew straight up, and turned toward Crete, leaving the lights of Giza behind him.

When he arrived, he used the sea and The Mothers's power to soothe his wounds. The bleeding had stopped, and his injuries were healing. Shawn could not sense Katherine. She had followed his orders and buried herself. He made his way to the orchard and buried himself to wait for Katherine to show herself. Shawn came out the second evening to a cool, ocean breeze. Through the foggy night he saw Katherine's hand poked through the dirt, and then a vampire rose from the ground with a cloud of windblown dust behind her, Katherine saw him and fell to her knees in relief. "You survived! Thank you, Michael!"

She ran to him and threw her arms around him and cried, "I didn't know if I would ever see you again. There were so many angels with me. The angels prayed for strength and courage for you, and they sang of a mighty battle between a demon and a Guardian. How terrible the fight was! Some of the songs were happy, and some were full of despair. I didn't know if you survived."

"Shenti is dead," Shawn whispered to her. "I have sent him to Lucifer in Herit's name."

"The demon frightened me. Never could I imagine the evil coming from that monster!"

Shawn wiped some of the dirt from her face and kissed her lips softly. "They are the demons we fight. Charun and Shenti were the weaker, and the two stronger still live. There once were five, and now there are two."

"What are we going to do now?" Katherine asked.

"First, we'll wash in the ocean. We will go north to Athens and feed. And then go home to Washington. We cannot go back to Giza for some time."

They washed in the ocean and floated in the surf, holding each other. Shawn held Katherine, soothed her, and offered her blood. "No, I can wait for your blood. You need to feed first."

They left the water and lay on the sand. Katherine used her blood on his wounds until they were healed.

"When I was buried, I asked the angels why they talk to me so much," Katherine whispered.

"What did they tell you?" Shawn whispered back.

"They told me someday I would have your abilities, and they wanted to prepare me. They said someday they would use me to rule our world. They said living creatures in this world have limited contact with Heaven. Creatures from this world could not handle the energy of Heaven. They must prepare me so I can come to Heaven. And, I told them if the demon killed you, I would find the demon and kill him."

Shawn kissed Katherine and stroked her hair. "My protector. I'm so glad I have you."

Shawn's killing of Shenti had sent shock waves through the vampire community. Vampires wanted to know who this "Shawn" was and why he started an all-out war with the Esmanaa. The vampire council ordered Shawn to appear before them and explain what took place in Giza. They also wanted to know the details of how he killed Shenti.

Chapter Twenty-Three

S hawn and Katherine had traveled extensively during Katherine's changeling years. Now Katherine lived at the house in Washington and would go on short trips by herself or at times travel with Anne and Marilyn while Shawn took this time to resume his relationship with Victoria. The world was a dangerous place for a young Herit and a Bryce vampire.

It had been forty years since Shawn killed Shenti in Egypt. The remaining Esmanaa had gone into seclusion at their fortress in Norway and only came out at carefully selected times to kill and take revenge on the vampires. The killing of a large number of vampires was becoming a concern for the council. Most vampires did not have the strength to face an Esmanaa.

Another disturbing development had occurred over the past five years. Vampires had learned through their spies in the human governments that some of the best scientists and minds in this world had turned up missing. They were the lead scientist in the research and development of flux divergence and interdimensional portals. Flux divergence was a key principle of a cloaking device and a weapon that could instantly kill a vampire. This had finally given the Vampire Council the push to take the fight to the Esmanaa.

Shawn and Victoria now traveled everywhere together. They were staying in the fortified city of Lanzhou, in the Gansu Territory. Vampires had tracked the missing scientist to this area, and they were here to meet Anne. China was no longer a country; long ago, the United States of America's nuclear arsenal had destroyed it. Most of China was still in ruins. The state had splintered into small provinces, all run by independent rulers. The population was extremely low in this part of the world, which made it a perfect hiding spot. The Great War and the plague had almost wiped out the Chinese. This land was now composed of many small areas populated by xenophobic humans that had become isolated in their region of the country.

Anne had just arrived and supplied Shawn with the latest information on the location of the missing scientist and where they were being held. The Esmanaa had built a development and production facility. They were using human physical science to make up for their abilities stolen by the Archangel. Anne told him the council had located the facility and had learned about an electronic cloaking device the Esmanaa had developed at the facility located in the Datong valley by the Yellow River.

The devices were a small, black, extremely radioactive medallion the demons wore around their necks. The radiation powered the flux divergence given off by the device, and this is what gave it the cloaking ability. The council had also learned that they were still working on a new weapon—a vampire killer—at this facility. Anne told him the Vampire Council wanted the buildings, equipment, and weapons destroyed.

The following evening, they traveled up the Yellow River into the Himalayas, highly cloaked. The vampires followed the map given by the council and came to the facility located in a lush, green valley, one of many in this area. They immediately sensed an Esmanaa as they approached the facility. The new cloaking device was at work, or they would have detected the demon much sooner. They took shelter and realized that the Esmanaa was Zepar himself. This could change their plans—they were not sure they could handle Zepar.

"The Vampire Council wants this place destroyed," Anne said, "but with Zepar here, I don't know..."

"We can handle him," Victoria said in a hurried voice. "We can realize a great victory if we kill him here."

"He is mighty, Victoria. I have felt his strength," Anne reminded. "He is a very dangerous demon."

Shawn allowed his powerful, supernatural sense to spread over the compound. The compound held close to a hundred slaves guarded by many paramilitary guards with automatic weapons. The facility was made up of three sections of barracks. One for the guards, one for the workers or slaves, and a better area for the scientist.

The vampires concealed themselves in the high, wet grass and slowly approached the chain-link fence that surrounded the compound. There was a large, corrugated, metal manufacturing building located in the middle with dirt streets running from the building toward a reddish, dirt road that ran the perimeter. For some reason, maybe they felt they well hidden the buildings and stockade fence had no security cameras.

Let's get closer," Shawn said. "We need to find out more information and pray to Michael our cloaking ability is enough."

They separated, and each took a different side of the compound. Shawn slithered through the high grass, levitating a couple of inches above the ground. He made his way to the electrified fence and then started to sense the mental energies of the humans. He first learned that the cloaking device the Esmanaa used gave off a large amount of radiation, which the human scientist feared. Most of the humans were prisoners and slaves, very much afraid of their jailers. They lived in terrible conditions under the constant threat of torture, rape, or worse, being killed and eaten by Zepar. Shawn also became aware that they were working on a prototype of the new weapon. The weapon could penetrate vampires and pull them apart at the molecular level.

Suddenly, lights came on at the end of the compound. There was a concrete landing pad with rotating red lights at the corners. A long, silver, anti-gravity transporter appeared and landed. The carrier was a sleek, silver rectangle with a tapered front and rounded anti-gravity pontoons on the sides. A large door opened in the back to allow access to the cargo bay.

The humans attached hoses to the craft and started to purge a white vapor from the aircraft vents. A ramp extended out the back, and they unloaded various boxes of parts for their weapons. One of the boxes was marked "Radioactive Cesium." For the cloaking devices, Shawn thought.

Shawn continued his trip down the fence, concealing himself in the high grass, wetting his face and clothes in the night dew. He stopped his movement as an old-time flatbed truck burst out of the lush forest, bouncing on a narrow, wet, dirt road, approaching a gate that was rolling open. The truck entered and went to an area by the landing pad.

Shawn saw dead bodies, their shirts pulled up over their faces, lying in the tall grass. Humans again hurried to the spot, always under watch, where they loaded the bodies onto the truck, and then the truck left the same way it came. The human families had sold these wretches into this life, and he could feel their despair.

Shawn continued to work his way down the fence until he came to a small side street. The street connected to the road that circled the perimeter of the compound. The way traveled a short distance and ended at a different structure—it was far more elaborate than the rest. An acidic stench filled his nostrils, maggots covered the ground, he shut his eyes and told himself they were not real. Shawn knew Zepar was inside this house, and he could sense the radiation coming from the dwelling.

There were two guards at the entrance with automatic weapons. Shawn saw large, double oak doors with symbols carved into them. The symbols represented the various demonic powers. He had learned these symbols long ago, from the angels, and the crooked human stick figure represented the demonic forces in this world.

The doors swung open, and Zepar came out onto the porch, fully changed to his demonic form, and in each hand, he held spikes, vampire slayers. A spike could do terrible damage to a vampire if it pierced the heart.

He looked at both of the guards and bellowed, "You don't know when a vampire is right in front of you?"

Zepar swung his giant fists and knocked both guards into the street. Shawn could sense the life leave each of the humans, and Zepar stood there, a huge hulking body, snorting and staring, with his bulging, black eyes. A harsh grinding sound filled his ears, maggots covering the ground before him. He was the most powerful demon in this world. "Vampire Shawn Bryce, we finally meet. Show yourself to me if you dare. You will find me far more formidable than Shenti."

Shawn stood up, floated over the fence, and began his change. He grew as large as he could, hoping to put on his most fierce face and eyes, and the longest fangs and nails. He reached back, drew his slayer, and took a defensive stance, legs spread, ready for the attack. Waves of melancholy and despair washed over him. He tried to muster his defenses, but the demon was trying to weaken him. Then for the first time, he felt The Mother in his head, only a small part and heard, *I will help you*, and the sensations stop.

Zepar charged, and Shawn parried, step to the side, swung around, and cut the demon across his arm. Shawn took to the air, and Zepar followed. Shawn arced around the manufacturing building, trying to maneuver, to attack from behind, but the demon was too fast. Zepar closed the distance, caught Shawn around the waist, and held on with a vise-like grip. Sirens went off in the compound, along with many searchlights. Zepar tried to penetrate Shawn's side with his fingers, but Shawn caught his hand and held on. Zepar's deadly embrace pinned his other hand to his side.

They continued straight up into the sky while Shawn tried to free himself. If they left the bounds of earth, Shawn would quickly die. Zepar was stronger than he was. Finally, Anne flashed by and sliced the demon across the back with Deceida. Shawn twisted, brought his knee up, and caught Zepar under the chin, knocking himself free. They fell back to Earth to land a small distance apart on the perimeter road. Automatic weapon fire rang out. Shawn felt one of the bullets penetrate his side.

The vampires continued to press the attack. Victoria flew by the demon, cutting him again across the back. An enraged Zepar swung at her and missed. Anne landed on one side of the beast, Victoria, to the other, and Shawn, in front. The vampires flew forward at the same time. Victoria cut the demon's neck and flew off. Shawn drove his slayer into Zepar's chest while the monster swung wildly and caught Anne with a blow to the face, forcing her into the ground and rolling her against the fence.

Shawn swung his slayer, again and again, driving Zepar back, away from Anne. Suddenly, the demon charged forward, grabbing Shawn around the throat, and then the monster brought a spike around in an attempt to end Shawn's life. Shawn caught the spike hand and used his slayer to cut the beast across the arm, weakening Zepar's grip. Then Shawn struck him in the face with the hilt of his sword and flew back into the air. Zepar started after him, continuing his attack.

Anne flew by and drove her sword into his back; he cursed, twirled, and swung at Anne with his spikes and missed. Zepar flew back to the road and landed, shrugging his shoulders, feeling his wounds, and cocking his head back and forth. The demon stood solid, but now he was snorting his putrid brown blood.

Zepar wiped blood from his eyes and roared, "Your angels think they are clever, hiding this Shawn, this son of Herit, from us! I will kill you, Shawn Bryce, just like I killed Herit! And I know about you Anne and the angles tricks. Horsa and I will kill all of you. The others were weak, but Horsa and I are strong. I will send you back to your angels in good time."

Again, automatic weapon fire ripped through the vampires. Guards came down a side street and went out onto the road, in force, behind Zepar and charged at them firing their weapons. The vampires harden themselves to absorb the bullets. Zepar then charged swinging his spikes. Shawn, Anne, and Victoria again met Zepar with their slayers. Back and forth, they fought, the vampires striking the demon and drawing his rancid blood. More bullets hit the vampires, and finally Victoria flew at the guards, taking a heavy toll on the humans.

Zepar was a powerful beast and kept Shawn and Anne at bay with his vampire killers. One would move in and try to strike at the demon while the others drew his attention. Anne slips in the dirt, Zepar saw his opportunity and swung his spike, catching her in the side. Anne fell back into Shawn's arms, holding her wound, blood spilling from the gash. Shawn screamed his indignation at the demon and took Anne back away from the fighting while Victoria did her best to draw the demon's wrath.

He sat Anne against the side of a building, looked to see Zepar pushing Victoria back towards them. Shawn threw his slayer aside, took Deceida from Anne. The slayer from heaven form to his hand, its metal rang, and he felt high energy shoot up his arm and into his body. Shawn flew at Zepar and swung the sword catching the demon repeatedly with its blows.

Finally, Zepar had enough and withdrew from the fight shooting straight into the sky, turning east, and flying out of sight. Anne was pale and sat slumped against the building, holding her bloody side.

Shawn immediately went to Anne and flew her to the river. He washed her side with the water and opened his wrist to drip blood into her wound. He brushed the bloodstained hair from the gash on her face, wiped the blood from Anne's face and hair.

Anne stood and touched his cheek and said weakly, "I'm all right. I will heal."

"We must do better when we fight the Esmanaa," Shawn said, exasperated. "Zepar is powerful and is going to be hard to kill."

"If we don't do better—someday—they will kill one of us," Victoria added.

When the vampires arrived back at the facility, there were no guards. The humans were leaving as fast as they could gather their meager belongings and as quickly as their legs would take them. The vampires found explosives in the guards' weapon room, set the bombs, and ignited a massive ball of fire, consuming the manufacturing building along with all the parts and weapons. They destroyed the plans to the vampire weapon and dropped the radioactive materials into a deep ravine in the Himalayas. The vampires caught up with the scientist, making their escape, and warned them not to speak about the weapons or they would answer to the Guardians.

The vampires returned to their homes and continued their lives. The remaining two Esmanaa took refuge in their mountain fortress. The Vampire Council proposed a plan to enter the fort and kill the two Esmanaa. Shawn quickly rejected the idea. Someone would lose their life trying to enter the fortress to kill the likes of Zepar and Horsa. Shawn had learned the best way to fight the demons was in the open.

Chapter Twenty-Four

T he hunts had intensified for the demons, to catch them in the open. Shawn knew the Esmanaa now used modern technology to hide from the vampires. They would leave their fortress in Norway to kill vampires and then return to the safety of its walls. The Esmanaa had killed over a thousand vampires and posted a large bounty for the death of any Vampire Council member, especially Anne. They placed a bounty worth a fortune on the heads of Shawn and Victoria. The council bickered on how to handle the war with the elusive Esmanaa.

Shawn stayed with Victoria, hunting the Esmanaa, trying to trap them when they came out to kill vampires. Anne, Marilyn, or Renee also traveled together for the same purpose. Shawn made sure Katherine always had either Renee or Marilyn with her in these times of open hostilities with the Esmanaa.

Shawn and Victoria had arrived at a large house the Crimmians had rented under the direction of the council. The home was located outside Haarstad, Norway. Now, the best course of action was to come as close to the demons as possible: to always sense them and know where they were. The vampires, at a close distance, could cloak themselves and still see through their enemies' new technology.

They were getting comfortable at the house, waiting for Anne to arrive with the latest plan of action from the Vampire Council.

"The council is going to attack the fortress," Shawn said. "I know they are—it is a desperate plan. If that is their plan, they are going first, and we will follow."

"I'm sure they know that," Victoria said. "You made that quite clear to them last year. The only reason they tolerate you talking to them that way is Anne. You worry so much these days."

"They are weak and ineffective."

"Do not let the council hear you say that! Right now, we have the council, and you need to think of Anne, and be careful." Victoria wrapped her powerful arms around him and held him tight. She looked directly into his eyes. "They are attacking the Esmanaa because they are desperate! Do you understand?"

"Yes, I understand. These are dangerous times, and the angels do not talk to me anymore. I can still feel their presence, but they keep their distance. They talk to Katherine now. There is a darkness coming. I have an uneasy feeling about the future, and the angels don't want me near. They don't want me to find out what's going to happen."

"I sometimes wish I could walk away from this fight," Victoria said. "Let the council handle it. I'm tired of this. I am almost fifteen hundred years old. This war with the Esmanaa has become such a burden for me. Now I am so afraid of what it will bring!"

Shawn watched Victoria go to bed and slip between the covers. "Come to bed and look under the covers."

Shawn walked to the bed and pulled the covers back. Victoria was naked. She looked the same as the first time he had seen, centuries ago, when he had few responsibilities. She was beautiful, with young, smooth skin that felt like velvet to his touch. Shawn lay on top of her, pulled the covers over his head and shut out the world. He kissed her passionately—he kissed her body, between her legs, until he heard her special moans of pleasure, slid back up her body and penetrated her neck with his blood-teeth. He made love to her and sipped at her sweet blood until he felt the ecstasy only a vampire could feel.

"The end is coming. I can feel it. That's why the angels don't talk to me."

Victoria held him, soothing him, drank his blood, and then suckled the excess from his neck. "I love you, Shawn! I hope, in the end, we will still love each other." They fell asleep in each other's arms.

Anne arrived with Marilyn the following evening with the council's decision. They had decided to storm the fortress and end the Esmanaa's reign of terror. The Vampire Council was becoming unpopular and losing support with the covenants. Vampires believed their leadership caused many needless deaths among their kind.

Shawn had never agreed with the idea of entering their stronghold. His experience with the Esmanaa was to fight them in the open, not where they were the strongest. Unfortunately, they had not been successful catching the demons away from the fortress.

"Anne, this is a dangerous plan to enter the place where they are the strongest!" He pleaded and then asked, "Who's coming from the council for this attack?"

"Stephen, Hector, Hegamar, and Constantine will arrive over the next couple of days," Anne replied. "We will enter the stronghold through the vents. Once inside, the plan is to go directly to the demons' location and kill them. We only stop to remove the guards. A spy informed the council there is a vampire killer in their possession."

"I thought they were all destroyed," Shawn said.

Anne shook her head. "No, there is one left, a well-placed spy told the council. We must be careful of this and locate the weapon as fast as possible."

Shawn shook his head in disagreement. Anne had brought Marilyn, and now he was afraid for her. He took Marilyn aside to talk. "How is Katherine?"

"She is well, but she worries about you. She wants you to come home. She is with Renee, Caitlyn, Juliette, and Peter. Anne told her not to leave Washington, to stay home—to stay with Renee."

"Good, she should not be traveling now. Marilyn, when we enter the fortress, I want you to stay with me. Stay close to me, do you understand? I think the council has become desperate to save their honor. Their judgment has become clouded to the dangers of this attack."

"I'll be with you or Anne—I will be all right," Marilyn replied. "Remember, I drank Bricius's blood, too. I'm no pushover. I have the slayer you gave me, and I know how to use it."

"I know you will be fine. I couldn't bear to lose you. I see Renee is staying back now?"

"She is with the others. Anne told her she is next in line to lead the family if anything happened to her. She wants her to stay away from the fighting and be with the younger family members, out of danger. That's why she finally decided to bring me. It's almost morning, and I'm tired. Come on, let's get some rest.

The following night, the council members arrived one at a time. When all were present, Stephen projected layouts of the Esmanaa fortress. The front and entrance to the fort were old sketches by Victoria, and there were newer elevation drawings. Over the years, vampires had gathered more information on the layout of the stronghold. Still, they knew little of the inside.

"The Bryces and the Kenmare will go into this auxiliary vent," Stephen told the group. "The rest of the council will go into the main vent. We will leave tomorrow night at ten o'clock, fly directly to the vents, remove the screens, and enter the fortress. We should have no problems getting through the vents—they are big enough and will lead us directly inside. Probably, at first, we will meet humans with weapons. When any of us contact the Esmanaa, the rest of us will converge on that area. With the angels' blessing, we will rid this world of them for good. Make sure your slayers are sharp—we are going to need them."

Constantine stepped forward and set a black briefcase on the table. "I brought the bomb. It's simple—open the briefcase, set the timer, and flip the switch. It is made with R486 and will blast a large hole in the side of the mountain."

"I don't like the way you have split us into two groups," Hector complained to Stephen. "The two Esmanaa slayers should be on separated teams."

"My family and Victoria will be with me," Shawn shot back. "It's time for the council to lead the way."

"Again, you do not know your place with me. You are not the leader here—the council is the leader."

Shawn looked directly at Hector. "Then lead, but the teams will stay as Stephen has described. My leader is the angels, and they have led me all my vampire life."

"Enough of this," Hegamar bellowed.

"We will follow the plan that I laid out," Stephen commanded, staring hard at Shawn. "When this is over, you, Shawn, will appear before the council to answer to charges of insubordination. The Vampire Council rules vampires in this world. Not you! Again, I tell you, Anne, get your fledgling under control!"

The following night, they left the house at ten and started their flight to the fortress. They flew low and hugged the terrain, curving around the mountains and up the valleys, hoping to keep their attack a secret. Dressed in black, they flew like dark, guided missiles toward their target. Shawn felt a nagging foreboding that he could not shake. The weather was foul; snow and ice pelted his face as he flew. The wind was strong and had formed a headwind that made their flight more difficult. Shawn wondered if this was the night angels saw thousands of years ago.

The vampires curved around the last mountain, and the fortress came into view. They separated and flew to their entrance vents. As Shawn neared the vent, the searchlights came on, and sirens sounded. He landed on a ledge in front of the vent and quickly pulled the cover grating from the opening. All four entered the circular vent, traveled a short distance, and removed the vent cover that led into the complex. They peered out and found themselves looking down a hallway at a large group of guards. Soon, small flashes erupted from their automatic weapons. The roar of the guns was deafening.

From the cover of the tunnel, Anne told them, "We will harden ourselves and move fast to kill the humans."

They left the safety of the vent, feeling bullets hit them; they attacked the humans with blinding speed, using their slayers and killing them. Shawn looked around the corner of the hallway, saw another group of guards coming toward them, and they immediately started shooting. Again, the vampires accelerated themselves down the hall, absorbing the gunfire, attacking the humans with no mercy. The vampires fought their way toward the area where they sensed the two Esmanaa. Stephen's group was also struggling to reach this spot.

Shawn wondered why the Esmanaa were not moving toward Stephen and his group. They came to a large dining area. The humans had piled chairs and tables to form a firing line for their final stand against the intruders.

The room erupted in a massive volley of gunfire. The vampires moved with blinding speed to avoid as many of the bullets as possible. Still, Shawn could feel bullets hit him. The fighting was fierce and bloody as the vampires used their slayers to kill the humans. Shawn sensed a sharp rise in radiation coming from the Esmanaa location as Stephens's group contacted the demons. Shawn looked at Anne and yelled, "It's their weapon—the vampire killer!"

Accelerating as fast as his vampire abilities would allow, he came to the area were the Esmanaa were fighting Stephen and his group. As he moved toward the demons, he sensed Hegamar losing his three-thousand-year life. On arriving, he saw Hector fall to the floor in a pile of dirt. Horsa was standing with Zepar, who was handling the weapon. Stephen and Constantine had taken shelter behind a thick concrete wall.

On arriving, Shaw had surprised the demons and now flew at Zepar, tackling him, grabbing the weapon, and holding on for his life. He drove Zepar out of the room and down the hall. Eventually, he was able to wrestle the gun from the demon's hand. Zepar threw Shawn off and flew down the hall and through a hidden exit. Horsa slammed into him from behind, driving him further down the hall, trying to take control of the weapon. Shawn fought with him, but like Zepar, he gave up the fight and left through a hidden exit.

Shawn destroyed the weapon by repeatedly slamming it on the concrete floor and breaking it into pieces. He returned to the area where the vampires were standing over two piles of fine, grey dirt.

He knew the other vampires were in shock and disbelief that they had suffered such a loss, and again the demons had escaped. Escape was becoming a common tactic of the Esmanaa.

"The Esmanaa are heading west!" Stephen yelled. "Has the council done enough for you now--Shawn?"

"I have destroyed the weapon," Shawn said. "I believe that was the only one. I grieve for these two, Stephen—you can sense my sorrow— but I did tell you that this would be dangerous."

Stephen stood, looking at the piles. "We will find two urns for their remains so we can return them to their families. Constantine set the timer. We will leave the bomb in their armory. I want this place to be a hole in the side of this mountain."

Constantine had blood tears in his eyes. "Yes, Stephen, I will be happy to blow this place back to Hell." Then a harsh, angry look from Constantine directed toward Shawn. "Why didn't you arrive sooner, Shawn? You might have saved them."

"Anne, take your group and follow the Esmanaa west," Stephen ordered. "We have them on the run. We've forced them out of their lair, and this time you must finish the job."

Anne also had blood tears in her eyes—she had known these vampires for thousands of years. "As you wish. We will follow the Esmanaa to the Americas, but Shawn answers to no one on the council. Shawn was fighting the guards, Remember that-- Constantine!"

"Bryce's always have an excuse!" Constantine growled.

Stephen nodded his head. "Go and avenge these vampires."

They left the fortress and headed west, a massive explosion shook the mountain, and a fireball rose high into the night sky, tearing the demons' stronghold from the side of the mountain and raining the debris down on the frozen valley below.

They flew to Newfoundland and took shelter in an empty hunting lodge near the old city of St. John's. With the loss of their technology, the Esmanaa were now vulnerable to the vampires' senses. The vampires again could detect their whereabouts from a much greater distance.

The Esmanaa traveled to northern Canada and took shelter in the small, rebuilt city of Caribou. Exhaustion had overtaken the vampires; their spirits were low, and they needed rest. They laid their bedrolls near the fireplace of the lodge. Anne told them they would feed before they resumed the chase. They would need the strength of the blood.

"Shawn, you must stop your little war with the council," Anne scolded. "We have lost two council members, and the other members will not stand for any more of your insults."

"If I survive. Who's to say I will live—or Marilyn or Victoria...or you? When we finally corner these demons, they will give us a terrible fight. It will not be easy killing these two. This I know. Why aren't there more council members with us?"

"Politics! They want to get rid of you," Anne sighed.

"Shawn is right," Victoria said. "We all should think about the chance of losing our lives. Decide if we want to go further or go home, and let the council handle the demons. Sometimes I want to leave, but I would shame my maker, so I go forward. Maybe I will be with Erdin again."

"Shawn, what will you do?" Marilyn asked.

"I will continue the hunt. I have to. The angels have always known I would be at this fight. The angels require Victoria, Anne, and me to be there, but Marilyn, you don't have to be. The angels were never sure about you being here."

"I will stay with you. I go where my family goes," Marilyn said. "It is Shawn's fate, and now mine to be here. My angels have always told me time might come when I must stay with Shawn and help in his fight with the Esmanaa."

"We should get some sleep," Anne sighed.

Shawn laid his head down, allowing himself to sleep, he drifted and entered the warm, rejuvenating light. Many angels were with him. He could feel their love; he heard their songs of concern, but they would not talk to him. Shawn sent his mental thoughts to them. I know you will not speak to me, and I know the end is coming. Give me the strength for this, the courage. Shawn then heard Herit's soft voice.

You always had the courage to fight the Esmanaa. Know this—the time of the Esmanaa is ending, it will be because of your sacrifice and others. Now listen to me. The demons are going to the portal—Hell's Hole! The cave where the evil creatures attacked you and Katherine. Do not let them get inside the cave! You are going to have to be strong now, and you will have to sacrifice. Michael has seen the end. Dark times are coming—prepare yourself.

Her voice drifted off, and Shawn allowed himself to drift in the light. He listened to the angels sing their litany of songs of past battles, of great warrior angels, and of his struggles with the Esmanaa. They were giving him courage for a terrible fight. The following evening, he woke and told the others, "We have to go to the cave where Shenti attacked Katherine and me."

"You're sure of this?" Victoria asked.

"Yes, that's where they're going. Herit told me, and we can't let them enter the cave."

"We'll feed and then fly to the cave," Anne told them. "I'm sure we will need all our strength soon. You are to stay with me, Marilyn."

"I'll be your shadow," Marilyn assured.

The vampires gathered their belongings in silence, strapped their slayers on their backs, and left for St. John's. The Esmanaa hadn't moved from Caribou, so they took advantage of the time to feed before their trip back to the cave. They entered St. Johns; it was a cold night with a cloudy sky and a light snowfall. They quickly located their victims and fed. The vampires took to the cold air and started their trip to the cave in The District of Penn.

Shawn sensed from the others that they also knew the end of a long quest was near. Shawn had lived his whole vampire existence for the events that were about to unfold. He felt a sense of foreboding; in a naïve way, he hoped it would be just Victoria and him facing the Esmanaa. They all would have to fight as they never fought before. He remembered the angels did say he would need the help of his family.

"They're moving. Can you sense it?" Shawn yelled to the others. They all nodded their heads. The Esmanaa were heading south toward the cave. The vampires increased their speed and arrived at the cave before the Esmanaa. As they landed, Shawn thought how the place looked the same. He remembered coming the first time, but he had no memory of leaving and hoped he didn't repeat that night.

"We will block the entrance to the cave," Anne yelled. "When the fight starts, Shawn, you take Horsa, while the rest of us attack Zepar. Michael, be with us this night," Anne whispered, "or we will be with you."

It was almost midnight when Shawn sensed the Esmanaa coming fast from the north. The monsters landed already changed to their demon form. A strong sense of dark energy came with them; it hung heavy all around them. It brought sadness, and then maggots and flies appeared all around them. The demons had long daggers shaped like spikes, sharp and thick. Shawn started his change, and so did the others. They drew their slayers and made eye contact with each other, reassuring themselves.

"Your end has come!" Shawn yelled to Horsa and Zepar.

"The Herit's and Kenmare's have taxed us for centuries," Zepar spat back. "Tonight, we will rid this world of you. And then we will hunt your family and kill them. We will deliver you to your precious angels, just like we did your two council members. Do you hear me, Michael? We will make a fool of you tonight, as you did us!"

"We will end this tonight, Zepar," Shawn promised as he raised his head to the sky, "Michael, we do your work tonight!"

Victoria advanced and spoke, "Erdin Kenmare will be avenged!"

Horsa snorted and said, "No, another Kenmare will die tonight."

Anne lowered Deceida—the blade hummed and burned brightly for the fight.

"Attack!" She yelled.

Anne, Marilyn, and Victoria flew at Zepar; they flew around him, in and out, keeping their distance trying to avoid the sting of the spike. They would fly in, stab at him, cutting him, trying to wear him down. Shawn allowed Horsa to charge him. He sidestepped the demon, swung his sword, and gave Horsa a deep gash across his neck. He would repeatedly dodge him and strike him with his slayer. The fight went on this way, and eventually, the demons connected with some of their blows. Shawn moved in and then out, changed directions and moved in again, slicing the hand that held the spike. Horsa roared his displeasure.

The three vampires started to drive their swords deeper into Zepar. The vampires were always aware of the location of the demons' spikes. They dodged and parried the thrusts of the weapon. Shawn was wearing Horsa down—he could stand in front of him, exchange blow for blow with Horsa, and avoid most of his punches. The demon's blows did not let up, though; they were mounting on the vampires. Sometimes, the spike would find its mark, and blood now stained the vampires' clothes.

The fighting continued, Shawn now thrust his slayer through Horsa and delivered cuts to the demon's neck. Both beasts were bleeding their brown, putrid blood. Shawn heard a scream; Zepar had spiked Anne in her thigh. Marilyn took advantage, flew in, and drove her sword into Zepar. Victoria tried to come from behind, but Zepar turned and thrust his spike into her side, flinging her to the ground. Victoria screamed, clutched her wound, and rolled to her feet.

Shawn quickened the pace of his attacks. Horsa was fading quickly. More and more, Shawn drove his slayer deep into Horsa's body and finally brought his slayer down on Horsa's arm, severing it. A look of horror came over the demon's face. Shawn knew he would try to make his escape. He was ready. Horsa leaped into the air, and Shawn was on him, driving the monster into the ground with his sword across his neck.

"Not this time!" Shawn spat. "Lucifer awaits you!"

He slid the blade across the demon's neck and cut deep. The beast spits brown blood from his mouth, and the putrid blood spurted from his neck. Shawn sawed with his sharp blade, and the demon's head came off. Horsa in death burned with a dark blue flame, giving off a foul, dark blue smoke, and then melted away.

Zepar snarled as he swung at the vampires with his fist and spike. Blood was now coming from his mouth and from the many cuts and puncture wounds. A large gash cut across his stomach. Shawn yelled to the others, "He's going to try to escape!"

Zepar stood, snorting, looking at Shawn, an evil, cruel smile across his face. "It's time for you to pay the devil, vampire."

The demon flew up, but quickly changed his direction and flew toward Marilyn. A chill struck Shawn as Zepar grabbed her in a bear hug and flew her through the entrance of the cave.

Shawn, full of panic, yelled, "Follow him!"

Shawn flew at the entrance, terror searing his brain. Suddenly, a dark blue, shimmering light covered the entrance to the cave sealing the monster and Marilyn in. Shawn flew with all his strength into the dark energy, but the field threw him back with a massive electrical shock to his body. Victoria and Anne also tried to penetrate the force field, and they were thrown back. He again tried to penetrate the evil energy field and received the same results.

Shawn was panic-stricken, and then he remembered what Katherine had told him. He yelled to the others. "Up the hill. There's another entrance!" Shawn flew up the hill and found the side opening that Katherine had pulled him through years ago. The energy field was weaker at this entrance, and they eventually forced themselves through.

Shawn ran down the side tunnel, toward where it connected with the main shaft. To the right, he could sense a severely wounded Zepar escaping through another side tunnel, his escape pool closed off by the vampires. And to the left, a dissipated life force of an eight-hundred-year-old vampire, Marilyn Bryce.

He raced down the main shaft, crying, "No! No! No!" As he arrived, he saw Marilyn collapse into a fine, grey pile of dirt, and her bent sword lying nearby. He fell next to the pile and screamed so loud the earth fell from the ceiling of the cave and filled the air. Anne fell to the ground next to Marilyn, crying and wailing. Shawn had never heard such sounds come from her. Victoria fell against the cave wall, holding her badly wounded side, blood tears running down her face.

Shawn raised his head and cried, "You bastard, Zepar! You will pay for this!"

He then screamed to the angels, "Bastards, is this what you hid from me? I curse you! Are you satisfied now? Do not worry! Zepar will not live long!" Shawn and Anne sat and held each other. Shawn whispered in her ear, "How are we going to live without Marilyn? What are we going to do, Anne? We will never be able to kiss her again, feel her flesh, or taste her blood. What will we do?"

"I don't know how we go on, but we will kill Zepar—that, I know," Anne whispered back. "What we do after that, I don't know." Again, they held each other and cried.

The morning had come. Shawn and Anne held each other most of the day, going from thoughts of utter despair to hatred and revenge.

Victoria lay curled against the cave wall, holding her deep side wound. Shawn forced himself to his feet and staggered down the mineshaft to the entrance.

It was a rainy day, mixed with sleet, with a deep chill in the air. He could hear the rumble of thunder off in the distance as he watched the fog roll down the valley. He walked out into the rain and let it wash over him, wash the blood still coming from his eyes. He looked up at the sky, but all he saw were grey, thick clouds to match his sorrow and soul. He thought he might lose his mind.

He heard Victoria sob behind him. "Come back. You are going to need all your strength. I'm so sorry!"

"Tell me after I kill Zepar, how do I live the rest of my vampire life? How will I go on in this world without Marilyn? She has been a part of me all my human and vampire life."

"You will have to find your own way," Victoria replied. "When Erdin was taken, it took me many years to want to go on."

Shawn looked north and sent a strong mental message to the demon. I can feel you, Zepar—I know where you are. I am coming for you! I will follow you to Hell if I have to! He raised his head again and washed his face with the rainwater. He rinsed the blood from his eyes and wiped them with the back of his hand. "I knew when the angels stopped talking to me that this would end badly, but I always did as they asked. I have lived for centuries and done their bidding. Now they allow this to happen. They could have warned me! No, they stopped talking to me! That is what they did."

"They couldn't tell you, Shawn," Victoria sobbed. "These events had to unfold the way they saw them. The angels said they weren't sure who the third Bryce was, but I think they did know and were aware of the outcome. I knew it was Marilyn, it had to be, it couldn't have been Renee. You always knew your family would be with you at this fight. The angels told you. You didn't want to admit it to yourself."

Shawn looked at Victoria. She was pale from her many wounds and had a bad stomach wound from the spike. "Let me give you some blood."

"No, you will need all your blood for what's coming," Victoria said.

"He is north. Can you feel him? I feel you, Zepar. I know where you are."

Victoria weakly replied. "Yes, I feel him. He's trying to get away, but he can't, and he knows it."

"No, he won't. He is hurt and won't travel far enough to escape me." Shawn raised his head and yelled to the angels. "You will get what you want—no demons in this world. Are you pleased?"

"Shawn, don't be mad at the angels. Don't disrespect them," Victoria murmured weakly.

Shawn turned, walked back into the cave, and sat next to Anne. They held each other for the remainder of the day and cried. Evening came, and Anne stood up, found a cloth sack in her pack, and scooped Marilyn's dirt into it.

"Shawn, gather her sword," Anne said. "We will take it home. Tonight, we will find Zepar and kill him. If it takes my life, he will die. I will avenge you, my love, my dearest Marilyn. I can't imagine what life will be like without you." She again bent and sobbed, then rose and leaned against the cave wall. Finally, she gathered herself and flew toward the opening of the cave and into the night. The vampires flew north with one thought in their heads—the death of Zepar.

Chapter Twenty-Five

W hen night arrived, the vampires left the cave and flew north. Zepar had not traveled far, a couple hundred miles. Shawn knew the demon's wounds were severe, but he still was a very dangerous foe. Shawn channeled his many emotions into one goal, and that was revenge. Marilyn's loss weighed heavily on him, and he knew he had to keep his head when he met Zepar again. Later, the crushing sorrow would return and stay for a long time. He could sense the same in Anne, and he sensed guilt in Victoria. They all were determined that Zepar would die tonight—or they would.

As he flew north, Shawn thought it strange that they were now so near to his and Marilyn's ancestral home. They flew with great purpose toward the area where they felt Zepar. The vampires cloaked themselves, so Zepar would have no warning and no chance to escape. The demon was east of the large, modern city of Corning.

Zepar had taken refuge inside a small, abandoned steel foundry. The humans built the factory at the end of the Great Dark Age after the radiation levels had dropped to a safe level. The building, with its large foundries, was much longer than it was wide, and was made from corrugated sheet metal and iron beams.

The humans scavenged the materials in those days, now brown rust covered most of the building, and vegetation protruded through its walls and roof. They landed on the west side of the building, where they felt the strongest sense of the demon. All three drew their slayers and stood shoulder to shoulder in a small field with rotted, wooden picnic tables used by the workers long ago to eat their lunch.

"Come out, demon!" Shawn yelled. "It is time to finish our business."

"Zepar, it is Anne Bryce. I am the maker of the vampire you killed, and I will send you to Hell tonight for what you did. You will not leave here tonight. It is not the angels that want your life now—it's the Bryces—and we will have it." Anne held Deceida high, and the sword's metal rang.

Zepar exploded through the foundry wall and landed in front of the vampires. His head moved clumsily as he spun it back and forth to take them in, his breathing loud and raspy. He still bore the many wounds of the evening before and had new ones. Two fingers were missing on his left hand, and a large gash that started at his jaw traveled down and across his neck. Marilyn had made him pay for her life.

The monster held a deadly spike in his right hand and started his lateral, back and forth movement, preparing to strike at the vampires. His cocky smirk gone, he now had a deadly serious look on his face. The demon was going to make his last stand.

"You think I'm weak now, but I'm not. Lucifer is with me," Zepar spat. "I have lured you here to show your angels what happens to vampires that challenge me. I have given you pain, and now I will take your lives and send you back to the pig, Michael."

"We know better, Zepar—it will be you who will burn in Hell this night," Anne answered. "You are the weaker now, and I will have your life. Your time in this world is over."

The demon charged, and the vampires avoided his first attack, adding to the cuts he already had. The vampires flew around him. The first vampire in was a decoy. As the demon swung at his tormentor, the rest flew in and delivered their blows.

The battle began to weaken Zepar and bring about his end. The monster would swing his spike back and forth to keep the vampires back, snorting and bleeding his brown blood from his nostrils and mouth. Shawn would strike and push him with both his feet, knocking him to the ground. The rest would deliver blows until he could rise back to his feet. The vampires also received blows and wounds, and they, too, were tiring.

An exhausted Victoria lingered too long; Zepar pivoted and again caught her in the stomach with his spike, driving her hard into the ground. She tried to stand, but her many wounds, and the two wounds to the abdomen, would not let her. She collapsed and lost consciousness. Shawn cursed, and Anne intensified her attack. The fight went on, and slowly, they beat the demon down. They attacked from opposite sides, delivering wounds upon wound to the beast. Finally, Zepar had fallen to his knees and lowered his head. Shawn thought they had finished the demon and moved in to deliver deathblows to the Zepar's neck. He should have been more careful, but he wanted the demon dead. He had become tired and emotionally drained. As Anne and Shawn raised their swords to strike Zepar's neck, the beast sprang to his feet and pivoted around, driving the spike into Shawn's chest, piercing his heart.

Shawn fell backward, feeling his heart quiver, his slayer falling from his hand. He landed in a sitting position on the ground with a sense of disbelief, looked at his chest, and then turned his head to look at Victoria. She raised her head slightly, looked at Shawn with bloody tears, and then her head fell back to the ground, eyes shut.

He heard Anne scream, "You filthy bastard!" She struck Zepar with Deceida like a madwoman.

Shawn fell back onto the ground—he saw the stars and the night clouds move across the sky and felt the cold wind blow on his face. He heard the screams of Anne and the death screams of the demon. Then everything faded. His vision slowly went dark, and his hearing lessened, sounds dialed down, and the world became silent.

Shawn was floating in darkness. He felt peaceful and saw with his mind's eye light in the distance, but he was unable to move toward the light. He felt no panic and sensed no angels. Then he felt Herit and heard her voice in his spirit.

Michael and The Mother are deciding your fate. Rest for now.

He floated in a tranquil dream state. Another light moved toward him and grew in intensity, a light so big, so bright, it burned like none he'd ever seen, and that scared him. How could he stand such a light? The light engulfed him and held him in its strength—a beautiful peace went through him. A powerful voice sounded in his spirit.

I am The Mother Eos, and I have you now. I will protect you and heal you. Rest, for a long sleep, awaits you.

Anne felt terror watching another changeling fall because of this monster. She was on Zepar, wrapping her legs around his waist, holding the demon's head with one hand, and sliding her slayer across his neck with the other. The blood made the dark one slippery, but she held on.

Anne had to kill the weakened Zepar swiftly so she could get to Shawn. She knew Victoria lay unconscious on the ground and would be of no help. With a final burst of great strength, Anne twisted the demon's neck, heard a snap, and drove the beast into the ground. She used Deceida, its metal glowing and ringing, to saw off his head.

Anne held Zepar's head in the air. "I curse you, Zepar! May Lucifer look unfavorably on you! Hear me, Lucifer—he has disgraced you! Vampires no longer fear you!" She threw the demon's head to the side as it burst into blue flames and went to Shawn.

"Shawn!" Anne yelled.

She saw how pale he was. "Michael, no!" She screamed. Veins started to rise on his face. "Please, Michael, no, not him, too!" She wailed. "Not another one!" She frantically pushed her finger into Shawn's chest. The spike had penetrated through his heart, but she could feel the arteries and veins still attached. The heart had stopped beating. Biting her wrist, she poured blood into the opening.

Anne remembered what Jessamine had told her the night they had buried Katherine: "Get him to ground." She would take him where she had first found him so long ago. The place was near, and she would bury him there.

She went to Victoria and shook her. "Can you hear me, Victoria?" She was unconscious. Anne brought her inside the building and hid her; she would take care of her later. With blinding speed, she gathered the slayers and packs, left them next to Victoria, and rushed back to Shawn.

Anne gathered Shawn in her arms and flew him as fast as she could to where the Unadilla River flowed into the Susquehanna. On the far side was a flat, forested area. She took him there, back in the woods, and dug a deep grave so no one could find him.

She held him, wiped the blood from his face, and dried blood from his lips. He had become ashen, and the veins protruded even more on his face. Anne cried, her bloody tears falling on his face. "I love you, Shawn! What a kind soul you were—what a mighty vampire you became." Anne bit her wrist again and poured her blood into Shawn's mouth. She gave as much as she could; she still had to bring Victoria home. She kissed him long on the mouth and whispered in his ear. "I will come back to you when you have healed enough, and I can move you. You will be all right, I will then take you home, my love and we will be together. The angels won't take you from me."

Anne placed Shawn in the grave. She tore bloody fabric from the front of her shirt and put it over his eyes. She watched him lying in the grave and cried. She still could remember the first time she saw him in that ancient, wrecked car. How he looked! She shook her head, raised it to the sky, and screamed. "Please, Michael, don't take him, too!" She pushed the damp, fresh earth into the grave and sobbed. She told herself she must get the strength to leave and return to Victoria, but she did not want to leave him. She lay on the ground next to the grave and cried.

Anne saw the many, small points of light form and then start to swirl and dance. They went faster until they formed a light that grew bigger. Inside the light, she saw the figure of a woman.

"Herit," she whispered.

Michael has sent me.

"No, please don't take him!" Anne cried. "Please, Michael— we rid this world of the demons. Please, give me this!"

I have not come for Shawn. Michael has sent me for you! The slayer of Zepar, a great warrior vampire—and that is you. It is you that the angels look on most favorably. You have brought so many honors to our family, and you were always the vampire to fight the demons. You were Michael's hope to destroy the Esmanaa.

"Then why did they give Shawn the great strength?" Anne cried out.

You always had the strength. He was at the battle, but more important, he was the one that changed Katherine and would pass on this strength to the Queen of the Vampires. Shawn will survive. The angels even now sing his name, but he will stay here in this world. A champion for the human race—and now The Mother has a purpose for him. The great Archangel Michael wants you to sit at his council, to exist as a great warrior angel in Heaven. He has sent me for you.

"My life is over on this world?" Anne asked. "After all these years, it is over?"

Yes, your time here in this world has ended. Lucifer will never allow you to live in this world, and Shawn is under the protection of The Mother. Already Lucifer is preparing to send his most powerful witch Malin. There is no choice for you—prepare yourself.

"These past years have tired me. Will I see Marilyn?"

You will—she is waiting for you. Then you both will rest and regain your spirit.

An arm and a hand extended, wrapped in the same intense light. It came to Anne's chest; a heart appeared in the palm of the hand. It sparkled in the warm light, gave a couple beats, stopped, and then disappeared. Anne turned grey, and veins protruded through her skin as she and her beauty crumbled into a pile of beautiful, grey dirt. Powerful energy rose and surrounded the grave; the air filled with an electrical charge. The sky came alive with thunder and lightning. A strong wind came and blew Anne's dirt into the leaves of the forest to remove any signs of where Anne buried Shawn. Two bright lights floated and hovered near and received the message from The Mother.

Angels, hear me. Shawn is under my protection. I will release the vampire when he is ready to live in this world again. When he has a purpose again!

The two bright lights rose higher into the night sky, only to dim slowly and disappear. Twenty-five hundred years of life in this world ended for Anne.

*****

Victoria became aware that she was floating in the light. Where are my angels? What has happened? The demon had hurt Shawn, that she knew. Her thoughts were cloudy; she wasn't sure what happened to him. She would rest for a while. She knew she would find a terrible horror when she woke. Then she heard Erdin's voice speak to her.

I am proud of you! My beautiful love, the angels sing of your greatness. You rid the humans of the demons. You helped destroy the demons and fought as a brave warrior. You have avenged me and done all the angels have asked of you.

What about the Bryces?

The Bryces have paid dearly…

What do you mean? She sensed nothing coming from the angels. What has happened to the Bryces? Tell me! She listened, but nothing came back to her. She felt herself start to waken and slowly left the light. The world began to come into focus. She felt the pain in her stomach and the pain in her soul. She sat up and found herself in a small room inside the foundry. She thanked the angels that she had stopped bleeding. Victoria pulled a shirt from her pack and wrapped her stomach to cover the two deep puncture wounds.

She saw the three packs and swords, and it all came back to her. Zepar had spiked Shawn in the heart. She stood up, staggered forward, and pushed the door from its hinges. Staggering, she crossed a wide hallway and knocked the outside door out into the field where they fought the night before. She stumbled out and froze—something was different.

For eight hundred years, she had sensed Shawn, and now there was nothing. She could not feel him. She fell to her knees, her body turned to ice, and the weight of her grief drove her back down to the ground. Victoria's eyes filled with bloody tears; she could not sense Anne either. How could she be the only survivor? She knew they wouldn't leave her. Where were they?

Erdin had told her the Bryces had paid dearly. There was no sense of them. Had the fight moved elsewhere? She raised her head and sensed four vampires coming at a breakneck speed. It was Renee, Katherine, Juliette, and her Peter. She sent her thoughts to Peter. Help me, Peter. I'm hurt and confused. I don't think I can make it home.

Katherine was the first to land; the others were close behind her. Victoria pulled herself to a sitting position, sat against an old tree stump, and held the cloth against her open stomach wounds. She saw the panic in Katherine's eyes.

"Where are they, Victoria?" shouted Katherine. "Where is my maker? I can't sense him. What has happened to my family?"

"I don't know! I lost consciousness during the fight. Marilyn's remains are in the building with their swords and their packs. I think they're gone, Katherine. Where is Renee?"

Katherine fell to her knees and screamed. "Esmanaa shit, it is! I always knew you would get Shawn killed!"

Renee, Juliette, and Peter landed next, and Juliette immediately fell to her knees, crying. "What has happened to our family, Victoria? Where is Anne? I have sensed her for four hundred years, and now I can't."

Katherine and Juliette held each other and cried. Victoria thought she would go mad from their sounds of anguish. She fought off the feeling that she was going to lose consciousness again. Now she realized the Bryces that fought with her had perished, and the grief was unbearable. There was no sense of them in this world, they were not here.

The horrible day has come," Renee said as she fell to her knees, crying. Peter went to Victoria immediately. "The demons hurt you, Vick. I have to get you home."

Katherine was now standing over Peter and Victoria. "All this death, Victoria. Was it worth it? Why are you still alive when Shawn, Anne, and Marilyn are not?"

"Stand back!" Peter warned. "This is not Victoria's fault. This has been a long time coming, and we all know that. Those damn demons killed them. Our lives have always been about those demons, and you should know that—your angels told you that. Get back, I warn you!"

Victoria raised her head, tried to focus her eyes. "I'm sorry, Katherine. I wish I wasn't alive. We all knew what we were getting into, and we knew we could lose our lives. Marilyn died the second night, and last night I saw Shawn spiked in the heart and watched him fall. I don't know what happened to Anne. The last I knew, she was still alive." Victoria collapsed against Peter and cried.

"This serves no purpose," Renee cried out. "Let's gather their belongings and go back to Washington. We can decide what to do from there. Peter needs to take Victoria home. I wish you well, Victoria. I hope this is worth the price my family paid."

"We need to search for them!" Katherine yelled in a desperate voice.

"Listen to me—there's no sense of them. They are not in this world!" Renee cried. "Can't you feel it? Why don't you talk to your angels? I'm going home. I can't stand this place!"

Victoria knew the Bryces had rejected her. They would not follow Peter to her house.

"Peter, take me home," she whispered weakly.

Peter gathered Victoria, cradled her in his arms, and flew her home. Victoria could feel the wind, and it woke her, which only made the emotional pain worse. She strained as hard as she could, and there was nothing. There was no sense of the three Bryces. Victoria buried her face in Peter's chest and gave long sobs of despair. She cried as hard as she had ever in her long life. Her biggest fear had come true—the Esmanaa had killed Shawn. She remembered what Shawn said to her two nights before. Now, she would live and bear a terrible loss. She continued to cry, turning Peter's shirt red.

"Try to calm yourself," a concerned Peter whispered to her. "Abigail is coming. I can sense it. I am going to bury you, and hopefully, she will be there to help me. Katherine and Juliette will change their minds—they won't blame you forever. They know better."

She still remembered the first time she saw Shawn on the balcony. When he left Anne's guidance, standing on her lawn in Ireland. She had always been afraid of him dying, but she really thought he would survive.

"Oh, Michael, he did not survive! Why didn't you let him live?" Victoria cried out.

She pushed her face into Peter's chest again and cried. Sleep finally overtook her. She welcomed it. Peter took her home, and with Abigail's help, they buried her. Victoria would remain in the ground for a year before coming out and starting her life without Shawn.

Chapter Twenty-Six

Time passed slowly after the battle with the Esmanaa. Victoria still had an overwhelming sorrow, an emptiness to her life. Life served no purpose for her, a burden she bore every day. She had remained buried until Erdin came to her and forced her to come out, to leave the peace that was the light. She asked about the Bryces, but he said nothing. The angels did not talk to her now—only sang songs of her. Victoria sat for months and did nothing, replaying the events of that night in her head.

She wandered the mountains and woods around her home. She did this to take her mind off her loss of Shawn and the others. She had the wall around her house torn down and replaced by high shrubs. She had no desire to live in a fortress anymore. Shawn had always teased her about that wall. He would say how medieval it was of her.

Toward the end of the first year, after that horrible night, the Vampire Council called her to Amsterdam. Peter went with her; he was with her almost constantly those early days after she came out. She gave what information she knew of the three-day fight and the deaths of the three Bryces to an indifferent council. Renee had taken Anne's place on the council and treated her cordially in questioning her about the loss of her family members.

Victoria sensed Renee's thoughts were elsewhere, and grief was still a part of her life. Victoria took this opportunity to ask Renee about the other members of her family. Renee told her that Juliette was doing better than Katherine, but they showed little interest in everyday life. She and Caitlyn also had a sadness that lingered and never went away. Renee talked to her about Shawn, told her how she never expected Shawn to live to be an old vampire. A deep sadness had taken over her family, Renee told her, and she did not know when it would leave.

Five years passed. Now Victoria spent much of her time in the wilds of northern America. She would live as she had in her early years as a vampire when she grieved for Erdin. When he sent her to the Green Isles to hide her from the Esmanaa. She would live for months unkempt, living on deer and bear's blood, which she let dry on her face and hands. She had to live as she felt. A few times, she would return to Colorado to try to lead a civilized life, but always gave up and returned to her woods.

It was there she had the dream of Shawn lying in a grave. A couple of weeks later, she had another dream while sleeping under a large rock that jutted out of the side of a forested hill. She would push leaves in the opening to block out the light. She was waiting out the day, and she dreamt of Shawn as a young human boy in an old town.

Victoria lay on the dirt floor of her little cave, sifting dirt through her fingers, allowing the moldy smells of the cave and soil to fill her nose. The mother's earth helped her feel better. Small bugs would crawl on her dirty legs, but she didn't care. She lay through the following night and the next day, sleeping for numbness, thinking about the dreams.

Maybe Anne had taken Shawn to his birthplace. It was near where they fought Zepar, but what happened to Anne? She sat up, hitting her head on the rock above.

Victoria whispered, "Maybe he's there. Katherine knows where his town is, but we aren't on the best of terms." She shook her head. Sometimes she wondered if she was thinking straight. "Shawn, Anne, and Marilyn are gone," she sighed to herself. The sound of her voice speaking the words brought tears to her eyes. She pushed the leaves aside and looked outside. Twilight had crept over her woods. It was summer, but still, there was a chill to the air. She would go to the river and look for the deer. That night, she sat and watched the clear water flow by, listening to the sounds of the river, calling her to its soothing waters.

Most of her time she spent sitting, not moving, staring off at all the sights her vampire eyes showed her, and listening to the sounds of the forest, picking out the subtle tones of the animals living their lives. She numbed herself to the passage of time—something which, unfortunately, she had plenty of. Sometimes she thought the river was speaking to her, telling her to go home and live her life again.

She would walk the bank of the river and count the many fish that swam against the current this time of year. Humans in this age were aware of their environment and had come a long way in cleaning the earth.

Victoria stared at the flowing river water and whispered, "I miss you, my love, and there is still no sense of you. I think I'll go home next eve."

That night her sorrow hung heavy on her, so she would walk the riverbank. It always made her feel better. Deep in thought, she saw four deer come out of the woods to drink from the river. Victoria yelled at the deer, "You came to me tonight! Isn't that kind of you?"

She went at the deer with her vampire speed. The deer shot down the riverbank and Victoria stayed behind them. When the deer bounded and leaped over rocks and fallen tree trunks, she matched them. The deer were in a panic, they knew something unnatural was after them.

Victoria picked one large buck and stayed with him, running behind him; it was exhilarating for her. It drove the sadness from her head briefly. Eventually, she leaped on the deer's back and pulled his head back by his antlers, riding the deer as they crashed to the ground.

She would roll with the deer, crashing through the underbrush, and end the struggle with her teeth sunk into the animal. The buck would kick and let out high pitch screams as she drained the animal of its blood. Deer's blood was lighter than humans and didn't quite have the nourishment of human blood, but it would do. When she was done, she would raise her head and scream a blood-curdling scream to release her built-up tension and sorrow.

She went back to the river. She thought of Peter—thank the angels, she had him. She had not made love to him since that night, or to any vampire. She had thought of taking her life, but she could not do that to Peter. She loved him and did not want him to have these feelings too.

Peter started to spend time with Juliette again. She would even come by the house and stay for short periods until grief would overtake her, and they tired of looking at each other. They made each other think of that horrible time. Juliette would apologize to Peter and then go home.

Sometimes, Juliette would talk to Victoria and tell her Katherine was another story; she grieved, brooded, and stayed by herself. Juliette also said to her that the angels had stopped talking to Katherine. Victoria remembered Shawn telling her how fickle the angels were. How they never told the whole truth.

Victoria was aware the angels had left all of them. Victoria knew Katherine was a powerful vampire for her age, and she had inherited Shawn's abilities. However, she was still young and might not survive the sorrow of facing eternity without her maker.

Victoria went home, and time passed. She was wiping paint from her hand with a white rag. She had been painting and watching a news report on one of the many video projectors making up a wall in her studio. The humans had colonized Mars, and the news was about food riots. Peter loved modern human electronics and had them everywhere. Holograms would walk through their home now. Peter made them tell her jokes, trying to bring a smile to her face.

A few years ago, she had started to paint again. Painting allowed her to escape her feelings and focus her attention on her work. She would paint most evenings, using her art to push her sadness to the back of her mind. Victoria rarely traveled and spent a lot of the time in the woods around her home. Once a month, she would go to Denver to feed.

This night Victoria raised her head; she could sense Katherine coming. Was she coming for her? No, she had something to tell her. Victoria set her brush down on the easel and rubbed and clasped her hands. She had not seen Katherine for twenty years since that horrible night.

"Damn!" she whispered as she turned and stared out the window. "It all keeps coming back." All those feelings came rushing back as she rubbed her hands again, licked her lips, and stood up. "Steady," she whispered to herself.

Katherine landed on the front lawn and waited for Victoria to come to greet her. Victoria smiled; Shawn would always wait on the front yard on first arrival. She floated down the hall, across the foyer, and out the front door and onto the porch. Katherine stood on the front lawn, wearing her traveling clothes—all black, with black boots and a black leather jacket. Katherine was a beautiful woman, and tonight she was trying to wear a smile.

"How have you been?" Katherine gushed. "Well, I hope… I pray your grief has lessened. I am sorry that I hated you."

Victoria could feel the sadness in her and saw her eyes fill with blood tears. She knew Katherine could feel the same in her. Victoria floated to Katherine, embraced her, and they both cried.

"I'm sorry, Katherine, but I didn't choose Shawn. I don't think anybody did," Victoria sighed. "I fell in love with him for the same reasons you did. I prayed that they would find somebody else. You see, it was never a choice—it was always about who would be there at that moment in time."

"I was so angry," Katherine cried. "My feelings went from anger to sadness and loss. I have forgotten how to live. My despair consumes me, I decided to end my life and could see no other way. Living for eternity the way I felt was impossible, so I got drunk that night, but I fell asleep. The Archangel Michael spoke to me. He wants me on Earth—he has a purpose for me, and he told me what happened to Anne and Shawn to try to heal my sorrow."

"He told you about Shawn and Anne?" Victoria asked hurriedly. "What did he say?"

"The Mother heals and protects Shawn. The angels wait as we do until the earth releases him. That is why they do not speak of him. Eos forbids it. Shawn had suffered a terrible wound to his heart from the demon and could have lived or died, but Michael did not take him. The Mother wanted Shawn. She has a purpose for him, and Michael thought Shawn lost faith in the end. Michael always knew Anne would lead the destruction of the Esmanaa. That was why he had Bricius change her and give her his power. Anne took Shawn and buried him where he was born. She buried him in Dalton, and that is why we cannot sense him. Michael knew Lucifer would not let Anne live in this world because she was the slayer of Zepar. She was alive, but Herit took her heart, and The Mother scattered her dirt to leave no trace."

Victoria's voice became shaky. "He's alive? Are you sure?"

"Yes, I'm sure he lives. I'm going to Dalton—come with me. We can find him together."

"Let me get my things. I don't see how we will find him if he is buried, but I will certainly go with you."

Katherine located the town of Dalton close to morning. They took refuge in an old, thick-walled, concrete passageway built into the side of a steep hill. The tunnel only went back a short way and entered into a fallout shelter from a time when humans had first developed their atomic technologies. The folly of this shelter was not lost on Victoria after living through the Great War. She knew no human would want to live after such devastation.

They made their home in the shelter for the next couple of weeks. The humans occupied the summer camps and hunting lodges. Dalton had little left from its days as a small, American town, only old foundations and sections of old roads, rusted guardrails grown over with vegetation, and remnants of an old cemetery. Katherine showed Victoria where Shawn lived when he was a human boy. They located the foundation of his house and found an overgrown cemetery nearby, which they searched extensively.

The vampires searched the woods and the surrounding areas for any clues or a sense of Shawn. They huddled together during the day in the fallout shelter, slept, and talked of Shawn, Anne, and Marilyn. Katherine explained to Victoria how much love she also had for Anne and how she and Marilyn had been lovers. Victoria told her how she had handled the loss of her maker, Erdin.

They spent two weeks searching the woods and old Dalton for some signs of Shawn. They found nothing, and now spent their time at the river. Right from the first, the river attracted them. It was there they felt some comfort or a vague sense of him.

It was early morning, and the sun was rising. They were following the riverbank, returning to their day shelter. Victoria walked along the riverbank while Katherine waded in the water, following alongside. Swallows swept through the air, landing by their nest on top of a crumbling, concrete bridge column. Both vampires knew there were two humans nearby. They rounded a bend and found them fishing on the riverbank.

"Are you catching anything?" Katherine shouted.

"Nothing yet! We just started," one of the men yelled back.

Suddenly the men's expression changed, and they backed away from the water, away from them, fear taking over their legs. They had seen the vampires' shimmer, and it had startled them. They now knew what they were, and it gave them an unnatural feeling.

"Easy mortals, we mean you know harm," Katherine said as they walked by.

Katherine laughed and told Victoria, "They know we are in this world, but still, they are so shocked when they see us."

"They never really look at us to see us for what we are," Victoria told her. "On the rare occasion they do see us, they are too frightened to truly look at us." Bryces have always loved to fool with humans, Victoria thought. Her spirits had lifted these past couple weeks staying with Katherine. They were going to leave soon but first would search the river. They had gone east on the river and were now traveling west on the other side.

Katherine stopped suddenly and looked off into the distance, straining to sense something. "It's Shawn! It's a slight sense of him. The earth hides him from us, but I know he is alive now. Suddenly Katherine's expression changed. "Can you feel that? It is very faint. It's coming from up the river."

"No, I don't feel anything," Victoria answered. "We have been in the sunlight for an hour. We should go back to the shelter, or we will have to feed. We can come back this eve."

"You're right, we can come back. I know he is there. We are going to find Shawn," Katherine promised. They went back to the shelter and talked of the day's events before sleep took them.

The next eve they woke and immediately heard the soothing music in their heads—a powerful force had concentrated by the river. The energy was from The Mother. Victoria knew because she had felt it coming from Pandora that desperate night, fighting for her and Shawn's lives.

"Do you feel that energy?" Katherine asked.

"The energy is from Eos... The Mother and also there is a witch down by the river. This has to be about Shawn. There were always witches around him. It is probably Jessamine."

"Let's go and see," Katherine said excitedly. "Maybe she's here to help us."

The vampires immediately flew to the energy of the witch. They came to the river they had walked the night before.

"Look, Katherine, that's Jessamine." The witch was on the other side of the river and rose to travel toward them. She floated across the river and landed in front of them.

"Greetings, vampires. I am glad to see you looking well, Victoria. It is an honor to be with a great vampire warrior. The warrior angels sing your glory, the destroyer of the Esmanaa."

"I don't feel like a warrior these days. I believe my fighting days are done. Why have you come?"

"The Mother heals and protects my father. She will give him back to the angels when she decides it is time. When he can survive again in this world. When the pain will not be too much for him. I regret to tell you Eos will not let you approach his grave." Jessamine pointed her finger to a wooded area. "He is there, healing!"

Victoria could feel the energy build. She had felt this electrically charged air before. The source was the woods that Jessamine pointed to. She could sense it was far more powerful there. They did not have the strength to enter the woods.

Katherine started to float forward, and she stopped her.

"Careful, Katherine. As vampires, we cannot confront The Mother. We know he is alive now. We will see him again. I believe that now. That must be enough for now." Red tears spilled down her cheeks.

"Queen, you will see your maker again, but not tonight," Jessamine said. "The Mother will not let you enter the woods. You must leave this place."

"We should go..." Victoria cried. Victoria told the witch, "Thank you, Jessamine, for showing me he is alive. I have been sad for so long."

Victoria and Katherine returned to their homes. They had grown close once again. Victoria kept in touch with Katherine and Juliette for the next five years after the visit to Dalton. They would reassure each other about Shawn. Juliette would often visit to see Peter, and Katherine would occasionally come for short stays.

Victoria had just woken and was lying in her couch. She was being lazy and planning her trip east to show paintings she was working on. She had started to travel somewhat and was now making love again with Peter. He was lying next to her and beginning to wake from his day's sleep. Their eyes met, and she smiled at him.

"Good eve, sleepy," Victoria said in her soft, seductive voice. She gave him a kiss, sat up, and stretched. "Are you ready to help me pack for my trip?"

"If you want me to. You know I'm a terrible packer. Juliette is coming to stay with me while you're gone."

Peter pulled Victoria next to him and rolled on top of her. "You're better these days, Vick. Life has come back to you. What is the matter? I didn't mean to shock you!"

Victoria flew up, pushing the top of the couch so hard that it slammed against the ceiling and broke. Peter landed on the floor with a frown on his face. "What is the matter with you?" Peter asked, sitting on his rear and looking up at her, wide-eyed. "You have plenty of time before you have to leave."

"Thank you, Mother!" Victoria cried out. "It's Shawn! I can feel him—he's north of here—it's him! I can sense him now as I can sense you!"

"Calm down. Shawn's alive—we knew that, right? Call Katherine!"

"No, she's with him—I can sense it. She has him! She's taking him west, probably home! I'll call Juliette!"

As soon as Victoria went to the video phone, it activated, and Juliette's hologram appeared in front of her, leaving a message. "Shawn is in New Chicago," the recording announced, "Katherine has gone to him. Come quick, Victoria—Shawn is alive!" Victoria got herself ready and packed a small bag as fast as she could, then went to Peter.

"I will call you as soon as I can. He is alive, Peter. He has come back to us."

"I will follow next eve, Vick. Try to relax."

Victoria was in the air, flying toward the Bryce home in Washington as fast as her vampire abilities would allow. The closer she came, the stronger her sense was of Shawn. His life force was strong, which gave her even more hope.

Later, she arrived at the Bryces family home. Their red flag, the one with the family crest, was waving in a slight breeze above the high steeple.

Victoria had not been there for more than twenty-five years. Katherine, Juliette, and Caitlyn now lived in the house. Renee lived in the house in Amsterdam to take care of the council business. The world was free of demons for the first time in thousands of years, but the Vampire Council had severely damaged its reputation with its handling of the Esmanaa over the millennia. The Bryce family had gained much respect, and vampires now saw them as the first family of the vampires. Victoria could sense the excitement inside. She also could sense Shawn!

She landed on the front lawn by two stone monuments that read "Anne" and "Marilyn." She could see the foundation of a third and saw where they had removed a stone.

"Hello, Victoria, it's good to see you," greeted Caitlyn, standing behind her. "Katherine had Shawn's removed five years ago. It was no longer needed, she told us. Shawn was alive, and we all would know that soon. Katherine and Juliette are in the basement with Shawn. It's a joyous night for our family, and I'm sure it is much the same for you. Come, let me take you to him."

Victoria walked with Caitlyn toward the house. It was a clear, warm night with a sky full of stars. She could see the mist rise off the small lake. She felt the excitement in her rise to an unbelievable level. *Heavens,* she thought, and felt giddy, like she was going to cry any minute.

Caitlyn was looking at her, smiling. "We all feel that way."

They walked up the steps, across the porch, and into a large foyer. Victoria saw paintings of Anne, Marilyn, and Shawn on the walls. She gasped—two swords hung by the pictures. The blows Shawn and Marilyn had given the demons had twisted and bent their slayers. Deceida had stayed straight and true, the same as the day the angels forged the blade and removed it from their light. Victoria had lost her sword and had not gone back to retrieve it, nor ever had it replaced.

Victoria followed Caitlyn down a hall and across a large art studio. She saw many of Anne's paintings. What an artist she was…She always thought it funny they both were artist. They came to a large, bronze door. Caitlyn opened the door, and they went down curved stone stairs. She saw a figure lying on a marble table, two large burgundy candles burning at the head. Candlelight danced on the red brick walls and warmed the blue tile floor. Jasmine, the scent of Herit, was heavy in the air. Katherine and Juliette rushed to her, and they embraced. Katherine took her by her hand and brought her to the table.

"He has come back to us. The Mother has released him from his long sleep."

Victoria's eyes filled with blood tears—Shawn's skin was coarse and white and clung to his bones. They had cleaned him, applied oils to his skin, and started two blood infusions—one in the arm and the other in his leg. Victoria bent over him and kissed him, her bloody tears falling on his face.

She whispered in his ear, "You have come back to me. The darkness that left this world long ago has finally left me as well."

Juliette and Katherine also started to cry again. "At least we have one of them back," Juliette cried.

"Yes, we do," Katherine wept. "He was conscious when I found him, but he has gone back into a deep sleep. He knows you are here, Victoria."

An emotional Victoria stood by Shawn for hours and watched him, afraid he might disappear. Then she felt a hand take hold of her and looked down to see Shawn looking at her.

"Hello," a weak voice said. "How have you been?"

"Terrible," Victoria cried and laughed at the same time. "I thought I had lost you."

She looked into his eyes and sensed another power in him, the power of The Mother. She felt him enter her mind, find what he was looking for, and then leave as quickly as he came.

"You look tired, go rest," he sighed. "I will be with you soon, my love." She watched as he closed his eyes and fell back to sleep. She saw the blood tear leave the corner of his eye and travel down his cheek. Victoria went upstairs, and Katherine took her to Shawn's room.

"You can stay here," Katherine said. "That is what he would want."

Victoria entered the room. The Crimmian servants hadn't touched his belongings since the last time he was there. They tried to clean around the clutter, but the room was still the same, junk and maps piled on his desk, and the furniture was old and faded. She looked into his couch, and there was no bedding and knew Katherine had not been staying here.

She walked to the double doors and threw them open. Joy replaced exhaustion. She walked out onto the balcony and looked at the stars in the sky and the clear lake, a slight mist clung to the water. She could see the pink hue of the new day brighten the night sky, making the stars sparkle like crystals in a chandelier. Yes, she truly felt happy for the first time in a long time.

A vampire flew over the trees and floated to the lawn, it was Renee, and now she was head of the Bryce vampire family. She looked at Victoria and yelled, "A glorious night, is it not? Have you seen him?"

"Yes, a beautiful night—and I have seen him! He will be with us soon!"

Renee bounded up the stairs and through the doors—the crying started again. Victoria's thoughts came quickly as she looked across the lake at a deer standing at the shore, drinking the clear lake water. She watched a loon sweep across the water, separating the mist to land close to shore, looking for an early morning meal.

She had spent fifteen hundred years in one way, living for the destruction of the Esmanaa. What would she do with her life now? She had not thought about this because of her grief, but she would try to make it a life of peace. She would no longer be the harsh vampire she once was.

She looked up and watched the stars disappear one by one, as the early morning light slowly moved across the sky. She looked at the two small monuments to Anne and Marilyn and watched the morning light cast its warm glow over the dew-covered stones.

How much sadness would Shawn have, she did not know? She sensed it was still there. She would be with Shawn—that she knew—and she would grow strong again. She would stay with him and help him find his way through his grief.

The Bryces still had to face the loss of Anne and Marilyn, and that would take time to heal, but at least they had Shawn back. Victoria prayed they would grow strong again, to live on as the great vampire family they were and had always been—Shadow Angels that came long ago to this world, to rule the night and serve humankind.

The End

SHADOW A: pg1

www.ingramcontent.com/pod-product-compliance
Lightning Source LLC
Chambersburg PA
CBHW061927170626
46813CB00006B/2331